Life / Afterlife

LIFE / AFTERLIFE

Revolution and Reflection in the Ancient Greek Underworld from Homer to Lucian

SUZANNE LYE

OXFORD
UNIVERSITY PRESS

Oxford University Press is a department of the University of Oxford.
It furthers the University's objective of excellence in research, scholarship,
and education by publishing worldwide. Oxford is a registered trade mark of
Oxford University Press in the UK and in certain other countries.

Published in the United States of America by Oxford University Press
198 Madison Avenue, New York, NY 10016, United States of America.

© Oxford University Press 2024

All rights reserved. No part of this publication may be reproduced, stored in a retrieval system,
or transmitted, in any form or by any means, without the prior permission in writing of Oxford
University Press, or as expressly permitted by law, by license or under terms agreed with the
appropriate reprographics rights organization. Inquiries concerning reproduction outside the scope
of the above should be sent to the Rights Department, Oxford University Press, at the address above.

You must not circulate this work in any other form and
you must impose this same condition on any acquirer

Library of Congress Cataloging-in-Publication Data
Names: Lye, Suzanne, author.
Title: Life / afterlife : revolution and reflection in the ancient Greek
underworld from Homer to Lucian / Suzanne Lye.
Description: New York, NY : Oxford University Press, 2024. |
Includes bibliographical references and index.
Identifiers: LCCN 2024007790 (print) | LCCN 2024007791 (ebook) |
ISBN 9780197690208 (hardback) | ISBN 9780197690215 (epub)
Subjects: LCSH: Greek literature—History and criticism. |
Voyages to the otherworld in literature. | Future life in literature. |
LCGFT: Literary criticism.
Classification: LCC PA3015.R5 V6759 2024 (print) | LCC PA3015.R5 (ebook) |
DDC 880.9/382033—dc23/eng/20240414
LC record available at https://lccn.loc.gov/2024007790
LC ebook record available at https://lccn.loc.gov/2024007791

DOI: 10.1093/9780197690239.001.0001

Printed by Integrated Books International, United States of America

for my family and ancestors
in this world and beyond

Contents

Acknowledgments	ix
Texts and Abbreviations	xiii
Introduction	1
1. The Synoptic Underworld: Overview of a Narrative Construct	14
2. Afterlife Poetics and Homer's Heroic Underworlds	41
3. Becoming Blessed and Underworlds of Judgment	78
4. Crafting Heroic Blessedness through Underworld Scenes	114
5. World and Underworld: Democratizing the Afterlife through Underworld Scenes	155
6. Plato's Underworlds: Revising the Afterlife	205
7. Epilogue: The Afterlife of the Afterlife	251
Bibliography	263
Index Locorum	279
Subject Index	287

Acknowledgments

THE ROAD TO the Underworld is neither simple nor single, as Socrates says in the *Phaedo* (107e4–108a2). This has proven true for my investigation into Underworld scenes. Since I first had the idea for this project over a decade ago, the road to this book took many detours and zigzags with occasional rest stops and stalls along the way. To help me bring light to Underworld scenes and guide me through the darkness and obstacles of the writing process, I have had many guides and companions. I will list a few here who, along with the many whom I leave unnamed in these pages, continue to be the voices in my head and close to my heart. They all continue to fuel me with their encouragement to explore different worlds and peoples from the distant past so I can tell their stories.

I am grateful to be a part of multiple communities of care who have supported me through many rough patches and also celebrated milestones with me along the way. I would like to start by acknowledging Jan Bremmer and Gregory Nagy, who first nurtured my interest in Greek religion and epic and gave me faith that I belonged here in the field of Classics. They continue to inspire me with their scholarship and generosity in supporting me. I would also like to thank the faculty of the UCLA Classics Department for taking a chance on me as a nontraditional candidate, allowing me to pursue my dream of being in academia. In particular, Kathryn Morgan, Sarah Morris, and Alex Purves have urged me to follow curiosity with rigorous analysis and guided me through the many stages of this project. Additionally, I would like to thank my UCLA graduate cohort (Michael Brumbaugh, Robert Groves, Charlie Stein, and Brian Walters) for helping me to hone my thinking and skills as an academic during many intense seminar discussions, reading group meetings, and late-night conversations debating obscure linguistic phenomena.

My colleagues in the UNC-Chapel Hill Classics Department—faculty, staff, and students—also have my gratitude for their ongoing support. Sharon

James, James Rives, and Patricia Rosenmeyer have been incredible mentors who have been models of how to combine kindness with intellectual rigor. Olivia DuCharme has been a wonderful research assistant and partner in proofreading and chasing down sources. My chair Donald Haggis and the UNC Classics office staff have bolstered me with their encouragement and administrative support at each stage. On an institutional level, UNC's Center for Faculty Excellence, Institute for the Arts and Humanities, and Office of the Provost have each awarded me research grants and sponsored writing groups that have helped me through the final revisions process.

I am grateful for fellowships from Harvard's Center for Hellenic Studies and the Loeb Classical Library Foundation in 2021–2022 to complete my book as well as summer scholarships earlier in the writing process from the American School of Classical Studies in Athens and American Academy in Rome to explore material culture. A special thank you to Dartmouth College and Paul Christesen for their support through a postdoctoral fellowship. Many thanks as well to Stefan Vranka at Oxford University Press, the anonymous referees, Theodore Reiner, and the entire production team for their guidance, advice, and professionalism throughout the production process.

The number of colleagues who deserve my thanks could fill a whole chapter of this book. It took more than a village to get me to this point. The following colleagues have provided generous feedback on individual chapters and at colloquia: Ra'anan Boustan, Joel Christensen, Stamatia Dova, Radcliffe Edmonds III, Andromache Karanika, Eunice Kim, Olga Levaniouk, Sheila Murnaghan, and Ruth Scodel. Additionally, I owe special thanks to my "squad," the supporters who have been there with encouragement, advice, and insights as I have navigated my way through life as a scholar. Of particular note are the following people: Justin Arft, Tolly Boatwright, Helen Cullyer, Al Duncan, David Elmer, Lauren Donovan Ginsberg, Devin Grammon, Rebecca Futo Kennedy, Donald Mastronarde, Lisa Marie Mignone, Jackie Murray, Victoria Pagán, Nandini Pandey, Amy Pistone, Tim Shea, Amit Shilo, Erika Weiberg, my Dartmouth WriteBuddies group (Cindy Cogswell, Marcela Di Blasi, Tatiana Reinoza, and our leader Michelle Dionne Thompson), and the 2020–2023 leadership team of the Women's Classical Caucus. I also send a shout-out to anyone who is in an individual or group chat with me—you know who you are! You have kept me connected to the world and been valuable interlocutors over time sharing ideas and offering advice almost daily to keep me focused and in balance.

Finally, I offer the deepest thanks and acknowledgment to those who have cultivated my interests over time and seen me transform from scientist to

Acknowledgments xi

humanist: my family. My father George Lye first introduced me to the ancient world, while my mother Lola Lye modeled how to pursue my studies with diligence, positivity, and energy. My sister Michelle Lye Watson has been a calm, supportive presence along the way, reminding me to go outside sometimes and live in the world as well as the Underworld. My large extended family has shown me how to dream big, work hard, serve others, and build joyful, diverse communities in unfamiliar and sometimes unwelcome spaces. I send eternal gratitude to my maternal grandmother Pearl Chuck (*in memoriam*), the matriarch of my family, who started from humble beginnings in the Caribbean, inculcated the value of education in her children and grandchildren, and is hopefully now enjoying the rewards of a blessed afterlife. To end, I give special thanks to Luke Moland, my love, anchor, cheerleader, and favorite companion on this journey through life, and to my children Anika and Max, old souls in young bodies whose curiosity, joyfulness, and wisdom are a daily blessing in this world.

Texts and Abbreviations

THE GREEK TEXTS used in this book are from the *Thesaurus Linguae Graecae* (*TLG*). Unless otherwise indicated, all translations are by the author. Latinate names for heroes and transliterations of original Greek words are used throughout. Abbreviations of ancient authors and works follow the conventions of the *Oxford Classical Dictionary* (*OCD*).

Introduction

What we call the beginning is often the end
And to make an end is to make a beginning.
The end is where we start from.
—T. S. ELIOT, "Little Gidding," *Four Quartets*

LIFE / AFTERLIFE: *Revolution and Reflection in the Ancient Greek Underworld from Homer to Lucian* explores the mechanics, function, and impact of ancient Greek Underworld scenes. As a space for the ancient imaginary, the Underworld is a place of revolution for authors to foment ideas that can challenge the status quo and an audience's perceptions of their lived reality. The Underworld is also a realm of multiple temporalities in which souls often revolve through cycles of reward, punishment, and rebirth. A unique and ancient form of embedded storytelling and commentary, Underworld scenes appear within narratives across time and in different genres. Because of their nonlinear *chronotope* and placement within a narrative, an Underworld scene acts as both a mirror of the real world and a space where characters and the audience can reflect on their lives and events in the past, present, and future. By tracing the development, evolution, and application of Underworld scenes through the works of such authors as Homer, Hesiod, Pindar, Aeschylus, Aristophanes, Plato, Vergil, and Lucian, this book shows how authors have used afterlife depictions as internal commentaries to communicate a specific call to action for their audiences in response to cultural, religious, and political changes in their worlds. The premise of this study is that the literary Underworld is a highly dynamic metaliterary space in which authors both require the active engagement of each new audience in the interpretive process and universalize key narrative themes by referencing different time periods, spaces, authors, and genres. Underworld scenes present the long-term effects of actions in life on an individual's postdeath experience. They are, therefore, a

Life / Afterlife. Suzanne Lye, Oxford University Press. © Oxford University Press 2024.
DOI: 10.1093/9780197690239.003.0001

space for authors to scrutinize and challenge traditional religious and cultural beliefs and practices. Because life is so short in comparison with the afterlife, Underworld scenes depicting the society of the dead can have a particularly strong impact on how audience members perceive the protagonists or events of a story—as well as their own society.

For this study, the "Underworld" is defined as the place where the dead live and congregate as a society, whether under the ground or on islands at the edge of the world. Underworld scenes portray both the society of the dead and contact with their realm, which can appear in narratives as an encounter with chthonic figures and landscapes, such as occurs in a heroic *katabasis* (descent to the Underworld) or a *nekuia* (conversation with the dead). A basic and widely accepted definition for *katabasis* is a "Journey of the Dead made by a living person in the flesh who returns to our world to tell the tale" (Clark 1979, 32).[1] The terms *katabasis* and *nekuia* are often interchangeable, but the latter emphasizes conversations with souls and chthonic deities to consult for information and future-casting (*nekuomanteia*).[2]

In their construction, Underworld scenes connect to each other by relying on the audience's knowledge and memory of other similar scenes from myth, such as Odysseus' Underworld encounter in the *Nekuia* (*Od.*11) or Hesiod's description of Tartarus (*Theog.* 721–819). Furthermore, they activate and engage each other persistently, a function which is present in our earliest Homeric examples and beyond. Although Odysseus' *Nekuia* is assumed to be the earliest appearance of an extended Underworld scene and the primary referent for later Underworld scenes, I argue that such scenes are more widespread and influential in Greek literature than previously thought. The first fully conceived Underworld episode appears much earlier with a ghostly visitation in the *Iliad* (23.69–107) when the hero Achilles, during a grief-wracked dream, speaks with his dead companion Patroclus. In this scene, the ghost describes the Underworld and postdeath experience, providing an account

---

[1] Clark (1979, 32) differentiates visions or dreams of the afterlife from *katabaseis*, saying that "such Journeys in the flesh are to be distinguished from mere 'Visions of the Otherworld.'" In this study, I show that *katabaseis* and visions of the afterlife are inexorably linked to each other and must be read as types of Underworld scenes.

[2] When capitalized, the term *Nekuia* refers to Book 11 of the *Odyssey*. A *nekuia* is not to be confused with a *nekuomanteion*, a technical term, which refers to a consultation with an oracle of the dead who calls forth a ghost to provide information that it brought with it to the grave. For more about ancient necromancy, see Clark (1979, 61) and Ogden (2001).

Introduction

that places the heroic deeds and specific events of the epic in a larger existential context.

Such stories of the realm of the dead put cause and effect into stark, incontrovertible terms before the viewers' eyes. Often offering cautionary tales and using frightening images, Underworld scenes give a broader context for the meaning of actions in life—whether for fictional or historical characters—and they invite audiences to participate in defining essential qualities of a "good life" for different types of people, whether heroes, citizens, leaders, or philosophers, by showing how those qualities translate into a blessed afterlife, the most desirable outcome after death.

By analyzing Underworld scenes from different authors and genres across time, it is possible to detect revolutions in thought for Greek communities in different time periods and contexts. Although Underworld scenes need to have enough elements that reflect the audience's society to be relatable, they represent an alternative, often surreal reality that an author can manipulate to idealize, reaffirm, or challenge existing beliefs. Because Underworld scenes create a network of references to other narratives by recalling other Underworld scenes, they invite the audience to compare different viewpoints on the relationship between life and the afterlife. Additionally, these scenes prompt the audience to contemplate the long-term implications for those views because the questions they raise are literally ones of life and death. In the earliest Underworld scenes, for example, we see competing ideas of whether the afterlife and the dead are readily accessible to the living and whether souls have any memory or self-awareness. These preconceptions shape the identity and actions of a hero within a story as well as how the audience might characterize that hero in light of additional information, such as his ability to survive an Underworld encounter and his relationships with any dead comrades, parents, or friends he meets along the way.

In later Underworld scenes, there is a shift toward a more inclusive afterlife society that is more integrated into civic life and more open to contact for a greater variety of people across socioeconomic classes. Athenians from all backgrounds who died in the Peloponnesian War were analogized in various media to the great heroes of the past and celebrated with public honors. Funeral orations and grave *stelai* integrated the memory of these warriors into occasions and monuments within the city, narrowing the perceived distance between the living and the dead. The portrayal of accessibility and permeability across the life–afterlife barrier changed over time in Underworld scenes, reflecting shifts in cultural practices and religious beliefs. Underworld scenes recall and link to each other, activating different networks of stories with new additions or unexpected omissions. These background stories then become *para-narratives* pointing both to the themes and ideas which an author wants to promote and also to the political and social pressures of the author's time period.[3] For example, an epinician poet celebrating an athletic victory might prefer to highlight an Underworld similar to Homer's *Nekuia*, which is filled with famous heroes, in order to elevate his patron's *kleos* and standing in his local community to the status usually reserved for mythic heroes. Thus, an Underworld scene, through its ability to collapse multiple stories within a brief space, creates connections in at least two timeframes, the historical and the literary, responding to stressors from both.

Underworld scenes appear in diverse sources such as epic, drama, philosophy, political speeches, religious texts, and vase paintings, a ubiquity that scholars have long tried to explain and interpret. Individual scenes often seem superfluous to the plot of their frame story. This, however, is one of the main reasons for their use. By removing the protagonist and audience from the "real world" and pausing the forward motion of the main story, the author has room to introduce other themes and ideas for the audience to consider when interpreting the larger narrative. In most analyses to date, Underworld scenes are viewed in isolation or with only a single antecedent (usually Homer) rather than as part of a larger tradition, in which authors engage with the narrative past and communicate directly with audiences. By seeing post-Homeric Underworld scenes as primarily engaged with the *Odyssey*'s famous Underworld scene in Book 11 (i.e., the *Nekuia*), most scholars have overlooked resonances with other afterlife depictions in Homer and elsewhere. In contrast, I approach Underworld scenes as interconnected pieces on a continuum, which act as literary vehicles for an ongoing conversation among authors, their predecessors, and their audiences. I argue that they use *hypertextual poetics*, a type of intertextuality, which activates multiple narratives simultaneously to influence how audiences interpret a given scene and its context. With this premise, even the *Nekuia* can be seen to engage hypertextually with other Underworld scenes in the Homeric corpus and possibly also in katabatic poems that are no longer extant.

---

[3] *Para-narratives* are stories that are referenced in a narrative, which, having been called to mind, then exist alongside the central story. *Para-narratives* shadow a story and fill in supporting details that the author may or may not have provided elsewhere. By giving context and background information, they can influence the audience's interpretation of protagonists and events in the story. For a discussion on the concept and uses of *para-narratives* in Homeric epic, see Alden (2017, 2000).

Introduction 5

Hypertextual linking explains how any given Underworld scene can recall other Underworld scenes with the latter's stories shadowing the main scene and communicating additional context, ideas, and values from the author to the audience. With hypertextual poetics, an author can insert names or places, often in the form of lists, whose items become *hyperlinks* (or "links") referring to specific, well-known narratives. These links engage the audience in comparing stories and considering certain themes and ideas that the author wants to highlight about his hero and overall story. Because of this, Underworld scenes can be viewed as a unique register of narrative communication, one that serves the metaliterary purpose of connecting authors and audiences across time and space. As a phenomenon in Greek literature, Underworld scenes act as nodes in a network of texts that link to each other *hypertextually* through their shared use of Underworld scenes. Thus, Achilles' necromantic encounter with Patroclus in the *Iliad* can draw from multiple Archaic Greek visions of the afterlife that are activated in the course of the scene. These "shadow scenes" then hover closely in the background to inform the audience how the author sees both the hero Achilles and his circumstances in the larger context of epic heroism. An Underworld scene such as this, therefore, is not only entertaining but also crucial as a way for the poet to provide more context about the fundamental values and motivations of epic heroes such as Achilles and his peers, who strive on the battlefield during life to achieve the type of glory (*kleos*) that would elevate them to be immortalized in song.

Underworld scenes defy simple characterization. Whether in Homer's Underworld depictions in the *Odyssey*, Aristophanes' comic portrayal of afterlife society in the *Frogs*, the Orphic Gold Tablets' instructions for salvation, or Plato's differing versions of afterlife judgment and geography across multiple dialogues, Underworld scenes resonate with and recall each other across time and genre, often to revolutionize the way people think about the world. Viewing Underworld scenes in isolation or with only a single antecedent (usually Homer), as most previous studies have done, obscures their critical importance and long history as a tool for promoting fundamental changes to how ancient Greeks at different points in time conceived of themselves, their place in the cosmos, and their relationships to both the gods and their own past.

Life / Afterlife treats Underworld scenes as embedded, connective literary units, which are used rhetorically by authors to capture changes in thought, communicate new possibilities about the afterlife, and encourage audiences to take certain actions during life. To do this, Underworld scenes contain a unique spatial and temporal reality, or chronotope, and certain recurring features.[4] The scenes themselves fall into two major categories, heroic and judgment-based, with most scenes having some elements of both and the latter type becoming more prominent over time. Built on such premises, Underworld scenes are inherently instructive with authors using different configurations of the afterlife to promote calls to action for the living. For example, an egalitarian Underworld where souls are not self-aware, as in Homer's *Nekuia,* highlights the importance of heroic actions during one's lifetime and of *kleos* through song as a form of immortality, since one cannot expect rewards after death. By contrast, Plato adapts his predecessors' Underworld scenes to reframe the soul's afterlife period as only one stage in the cycle of existence, thus encouraging his audiences to take certain actions while alive, such as practicing philosophy, to improve their Underworld experiences over the course of many iterations of life and death. Within each work, therefore, Underworld scenes act as an internal escape from the pressures of time, location, and plot, allowing authors to present to the audience what they view as the critical issues of the main narrative and of their time periods. An author, using certain chthonic characters and katabatic heroes, makes abstract concepts and ideas more visceral, forcing protagonists and the audience to think about and react to the presence of death and their own mortality against a backdrop whose chronotope operates outside of everyday reality. This jolt from the real world occurs in journeys that strip away life to its essentials and involve moving through treacherous landscapes, facing physical trials against supernatural figures, and conversing with ghosts.

In their construction, Underworld scenes are catalogic, often containing names of famous chthonic figures and places with little or no explanation of their role, larger significance, or actual location. Because of this, an Underworld scene removes the pressures of descriptive exposition, which allows authors to appeal to audiences to "fill in" the stories evoked as they move through a set of carefully curated references in the course of a scene. These audiences, which come from both the author's contemporary context and also later, bring different cultural frames and insights into their interpretations of the Underworld scene. Although these contexts may be unknown to the author, he or she can still influence audience interpretation by configuring chthonic landmarks and denizens in an Underworld scene to

---

[4] The word "chronotope" or "literary artistic chronotope" is a term coined by Mikhail Bakhtin and refers to the specific space-time continuum in which a story occurs. For more general discussions on the definitions of chronotopes developed by Bakhtin (1981), see Morson and Emerson (1989) and Nightingale (2002).

Introduction 7

reflect his or her values. Additionally, the author can signal an expected response to an Underworld scene by depicting the reactions of protagonists or an internal audience within the story itself. In the *Nekuia*, for example, the Phaeacians' wonder at hearing about Odysseus' journey to the Underworld and subsequent treatment of him as a noble man worthy of glory (*kleos*) and gifts (*timai*) indicate his heroic status to external audiences.

When creating encounters with the dead, ancient authors could choose from a distinct set of narrative types and images related to the Underworld, which were broadly circulating among their audiences through traditional myth and religious practices. These include stories about heroic quests by mortals into the Underworld (*katabaseis*), ghostly visitations by souls to the living, necromantic conversations with the dead to gain information (*nekuomanteia*), and descriptions of afterlife society with distinct topographic and sociopolitical structures. Within this set of Underworld representations are certain persistent images and attributes that give clues for interpretation. Although each scene may lead to different conclusions about the values presented in a specific text, they operate together to force the audience to weigh the aspects presented in the current Underworld portrayal against those known from other versions. In this way, a particular vision of the Underworld connects an individual work to a network of texts, influencing the interpretation of the given account. For instance, when Socrates imagines himself conversing with Homer, Orpheus, and Ajax in the afterlife (Pl. *Ap.* 41a–c), he evokes a rich tradition related to afterlife blessedness, judgment, and reward that can be traced to Homer's *Odyssey*, Hesiod's *Works and Days*, Pindar's *Olympian 2*, and Aristophanes' *Frogs*.

Because they are anchored in traditional belief, Underworld scenes are often explanatory, didactic, and protreptic. They use their inherent religious authority to direct the actions of characters and instruct audiences through *exempla* about individual and community actions that lead to the best future outcomes. Moreover, by relying on ingrained cultural knowledge and lived religious experience, the author of Underworld scenes invites the audience to collaborate as an active partner and agent in interpreting meaning. Thus, an Underworld scene on an Orphic Gold Tablet, such as the one from Thurii that mentions the "grove of Persephone" (no. 3 / A4/ *OF* 487), relies on the audience to recall the same phrase in a verse from the *Odyssey*'s Circe episode (*Od.* 10.509) and also the context of Odysseus' heroic Underworld encounter. The poet assumes the audience knows who Persephone is, her role in the *Nekuia*, and other myths about her identity as the queen of the Underworld, such as the one told in the *Homeric Hymn to Demeter*.

8   LIFE / AFTERLIFE

An Underworld scene, therefore, is not only the place where characters face mortality but also where new stories and background information enter the consciousness of the audience. This enriches the narrative experience and illuminates important themes to consider in relation to the frame narrative by both introducing new strains of thought to consider about the nature of the cosmos and reaffirming shared beliefs held by the author and his audience. As conduits to different texts and contexts, Underworld scenes can thus be described as *intertexts* or "text[s] *between* other texts," in which both the author and the reader share the role to "make the intertext visible and communicable" (Plett 1991, 5). In such a scene, the author steps out of his role as narrator and looks at his story as a reader and interpreter remarking on his own creation by connecting it to similar afterlife narratives. In turn, different audiences interject their own experiences and knowledge to give meaning to the signs and references that the author uses. By allowing this exchange, the Underworld makes itself into a site of embedded authorial commentary that engages in a conversation directly with the audience about traditional values, beliefs, and reality itself. The imaginary space of an Underworld scene offers authors an opportunity to reaffirm and challenge deeply held beliefs while also redefining the stakes of a story for its characters and for the audience. Through their relatively stable structure across literature from different time periods, Underworld scenes provide authors with a shared, well-established, imaginary landscape where they can communicate and reflect on social, religious, and political ideas directly with their audiences.

To demonstrate the ways that authors build and activate networks of Underworld scenes, I have divided this book into seven chapters which correspond roughly to time periods that reflect changes and trends in afterlife representation across genres. Each chapter is subdivided into shorter sections that focus on a particular work or group of works (mostly literary but also artistic) as case studies of Underworld scenes that respond to tensions particular to their immediate contexts, such as reconceptualizations of heroism or the desire to reframe how afterlife judgment determines an individual's status among the dead. In each section, I present Underworld scenes in dialogue with each other and with period-specific ideas about the nature of heroism, afterlife judgment, human-divine relations, and poetic authority. Such comparisons highlight how shared features in different Underworlds anchor scenes and their authors together to create spaces for dialogue, reflection, and revolution.

In Chapter 1, "The Synoptic Underworld: Overview of a Narrative Construct," I start by presenting specific analytical tools and a new methodology for approaching Underworld scenes. I give an overview of the different types of Underworld scenes, the different ways they appear in our extant texts, and the different strategies scholars have used over time to explain them. I describe the common, somewhat limited set of motifs that formulate the basic "toolbox" for authors to construct Underworld scenes and bring them into dialogue with their corresponding narratives. For example, references to familiar figures such as Persephone, Tantalus, Heracles, or Minos and features such as the rivers and halls of Hades frequently appear in Underworld descriptions but in different configurations, which suggest a variety of authorial stances. To close out this chapter, I discuss what is at stake in the use of Underworld scenes, delineate their general mechanics, and show how my approach, unlike previous interpretative approaches, is cross-applicable in analyzing Underworld scenes regardless of genre.

In Chapters 2 and 3, I more closely analyze the types of Underworld scenes in our earliest Archaic examples, showing how my approach reveals new interconnections between their afterlife narratives as well as new insights into how authors engage with their contexts. The afterlife scenes of these periods give the earliest indication of how literary Underworlds build intertextual networks with traditional myths and engage in a larger discourse with each other. In Chapter 2, "Afterlife Poetics and Homer's Heroic Underworlds," I analyze Underworld scenes in Homer as representing the category of "heroic Underworld scenes" because they feature heroes and their afterlives. In general, a heroic Underworld is one that emphasizes epic heroes and the *kleos* they have won through epic song and myth. The *arete*, or excellence, of traditional mythic heroes, which is celebrated in Archaic epic, is tied to their actions and prowess in war. Heroic Underworld scenes, therefore, have formal features that characterize heroes as exceptional and separate from regular mortals. By exploring the inner workings of heroic Underworld scenes, my approach reveals interconnections between the many Homeric afterlife narratives and offers new insights into how epic poetry engages with their audiences and immediate contexts. The afterlife scenes in the Homeric epics give the earliest indication of how literary Underworlds build intertextual networks with traditional myths. They also show how Archaic authors situate their stories in a larger discourse across works in order to define the value of heroes and heroism in epic poetry and early Greek culture more broadly. The first set of case studies in this chapter includes the Homeric Underworld scenes in the *Iliad* and the *Odyssey*, with special attention to their variety and how each episode works within its immediate context to frame crucial moments in the action. For example, in the *Iliad*, Achilles does not go to the Underworld to experience a necromantic encounter. Patroclus' ghost, however, brings him and the audience into the Underworld space through its extended description of Hades and the fate of souls. The ghost's "insider information" about the afterlife then influences Achilles' interactions with other characters and, most importantly, his future course of action in the main narrative. Such sophistication in this early afterlife representation reflects a deep, ongoing discourse about the changing nature of the relationship between the living and the dead. The Homeric poet's concerns with Achilles' mortality in the *Iliad* and with his afterlife in the *Odyssey* are presented to the audience through the two epics' Underworld scenes, which become a crucial space for reflecting on the heroic code and the meaning of *kleos*. Additionally, this chapter discusses the famous *Nekuia* and its relationship to other Underworld scenes in the *Odyssey*, including those in Books 4, 10, and 24. Book 24's *nekuia* portrays a conversation about heroism between the souls of Agamemnon, Achilles, and Ajax, a grouping that revisits a similar conversation in Book 11. The later scene is able to both address the issues raised in the earlier scene and give a final assessment of the themes as the epic draws to a close. Using these two Underworld scenes and these particular characters, the poet is able to portray his hero Odysseus as exceeding the greatness of Achilles.

In Chapter 3, "Becoming Blessed and Underworlds of Judgment," I focus on the second major type of Underworld scene in the ancient world: Underworlds of Judgment. I show how authors build out literary Underworlds as a moral space. Underworlds of judgment feature the segregation of the dead into different geographic regions of the Underworld space based on their actions in life. Such scenes imply a moment of judgment or sorting based on morality right after death to determine a soul's afterlife experience. These scenes also often include a reference to formal afterlife judgment by chthonic figures, whether designated judges of the dead or deities. Case studies in this chapter include Underworld depictions in Hesiod's *Theogony* and *Works and Days*, as well as in the *Homeric Hymn to Demeter*. Although these Underworld narratives function similarly to the Homeric Underworld scenes as embedded narratives that incorporate information and figures outside the main narrative's time frame, they are more prescriptive in their commentary about how the living should conduct their lives in the upper world and what they might expect in the afterlife based on their actions. These case studies underscore that Archaic authors understood Underworld scenes to be communicative and often didactic commentaries, not only about myth but also about their own contexts in the real world. Throughout this chapter, I demonstrate how Underworld scenes of judgment reinforce Archaic Greek

Introduction

cultural norms, such as a society based on hierarchal patriarchy, and reflect an ongoing debate about the relationship between an individual's actions in life and their afterlife experience.

In Chapter 4, "Crafting Heroic Blessedness through Underworld Scenes," I turn to Underworld scenes of the Classical period, starting with a discussion about the increasing dominance of a tripartite Underworld, which features an afterlife hierarchy based on the idea of a hierarchy of "blessedness" (as expressed by the adjectives *olbios* and *makar*). These Underworld scenes combine aspects of heroic and judgment-based Underworlds, with an emphasis on the latter, and they mostly reject the equalizing Underworld envisioned in Homer's *Nekuia*. Instead, they move toward an afterlife society that mirrors the society of the living with individuals being able to maintain their status across the life–death barrier. To illustrate this expansion and its subsequent effect, I examine how the early fifth-century BCE epinician poets Pindar and Bacchylides combine aspects of the heroic and judgment-based Underworld scenes inherited from the Archaic period to transform how their audiences would conceive of the barrier between life and death. Additionally, I discuss how these poets heroized living, aristocratic individuals through Underworld scenes by setting up analogies between their patrons and famous heroes. In the final section, I focus on the Orphic Gold Tablets as an example of how mystery cults heroized individuals by combining Underworld scenes with initiatory rituals, thereby expanding what qualified as a deed worthy of *kleos* and opening access to the blessed afterlife of heroes to a broader range of people.[5] By using initiation rather than birth or excellence at aristocratic competition as the criteria for access to a blessed afterlife, these Underworld scenes make heroic *kleos* available to everyday individuals, even if those rewards would mostly come for individuals after their death.

In Chapter 5, "World and Underworld: Democratizing the Afterlife through Underworld Scenes," I focus on how some of the strategies used by the epinician poets and mystery cults later become systematized in Underworld scenes appearing in civic and political spaces, particularly in Classical Athens and its spheres of influence. I argue that the frequency of Underworld scenes across media, such as on stage and in funerary rituals, leads to a "democratization" of the Underworld that revolutionizes who can be included within

---

[5] The Orphic Gold Tablets are protective amulets found on the dead whose placement in the tombs of certain individuals suggests that their texts were paired with rituals from mystery cults which guaranteed the deceased a blessed afterlife (Edmonds 2004; Graf and Johnston 2007; Bernabé Pajares and Jiménez San Cristóbal 2008; Torjussen 2014).

the cohort of blessed heroes and how the dead are perceived as continuing members of the community. From having ghosts on stage in Aristophanes' *Frogs* to erecting grave *stelai* in frequented places with accompanying public funeral orations for the war dead, authors and artists use Underworld scenes of this period to create more points of contact between the living and the dead and to weaken the existential divide between them. In the specific context of Athenian democracy, I examine the ways in which authors, artists, and other practitioners use Underworld scenes to incorporate the world of the dead into both "official" religious practice and mundane, everyday spaces in an effort to reinforce a political narrative defining Athenian identity. I argue that Underworld scenes in these contexts not only question the finality of death, but they also make the barrier between the living and the dead more permeable and the blessed, Golden-Age type afterlife more accessible to all individuals. Using Underworld scenes to incorporate the dead into regular civic life was an important form of political propaganda to generate popular support for Athens' self-image and ongoing military conflicts, particularly during times of strife.

Chapter 6, "Plato's Underworlds: Revising the Afterlife," focuses on Plato's adverse response to the democratizing trends in afterlife construction and Underworld scenes. In this chapter, I argue that Plato divorces Underworld scenes as much as possible from lived religious practice by presenting multiple, often conflicting versions of the traditional Underworld across his dialogues. Instead, he uses Underworld scenes of judgment borrowed from his predecessors and contemporaries to undermine and reject traditional beliefs about the afterlife by presenting such scenes as rhetorical tools approximating reality for the purpose of argument rather than absolute truth. Additionally, he employs Underworld scenes to redefine the types of actions and beliefs that could bring a person *arete*, *kleos*, and a blessed afterlife. In the case studies of this chapter, I examine Underworld scenes from the *Apology*, *Gorgias*, *Phaedo*, and *Republic* to show how Plato co-opts and overwrites traditional elements to promote his own idiosyncratic vision of the afterlife. I further suggest that his detailed descriptions of the Underworld landscape in the *Phaedo* and the "Myth of Er" in the *Republic* wrest autonomy from his audience in engaging with the mythic material by guiding them to his singular insight about the correct path to blessedness. In his Underworld scene formulations, Plato leaves less room for audience interpretation, and his Underworld scenes are as guided and tightly constructed as the dialectic arguments in which they are embedded. In this way, Plato's Underworlds remove both the permeability and accessibility of the afterlife that the fifth-century BCE Athenian context

Introduction 13

was promoting in other media. Plato uses Underworld scenes to establish a new social hierarchy based on philosophical rather than religious or political affiliations. While keeping the same general structures of a judgment-based Underworld and sometimes even saying that he borrows his Underworld myths from authoritative sources such as Homer, Plato nevertheless fundamentally alters the moral geography of the Underworld chronotope and changes how the hierarchy of blessedness works. In his scheme, the practice of philosophy, more than any other action, leads to the best afterlife outcomes, and this is the one consistent feature of his many Underworld scenes. Despite his preference for dialectic argumentation, Plato, like authors before him, treats Underworld scenes as an appropriate venue to engage in important existential debates and influence his audiences' worldviews.

In the final chapter, Chapter 7, "Epilogue: The Afterlife of the Afterlife," I speak briefly about the reception of Underworld scenes by authors in later periods. I discuss the use of Underworld scenes not only in new cultural contexts but also in newly created genres, such as satire. I include a brief discussion about the persistence and stability of Underworld scenes and show how the methodology presented in this book can be successfully applied across Underworld scenes in various genres and time periods as well as in new cultural contexts. I give brief examples from satirical works such as Lucian's *True History, Dialogues of the Dead,* and the *Downward Journey* as well as from Vergil's *Aeneid* in order to show how the configurations and underlying structural language of Greek Underworld scenes transcend their original religious, poetic, and cultural contexts while maintaining their authoritative weight and communicative purpose. Post-Platonic authors demonstrate the continued recognition by authors and audiences of Underworld scenes as spaces for communication where it is possible to reflect on inherited traditions and to promote revolutionary ideas that challenge the status quo. These authors, like their predecessors, use the particular poetics of Underworld scenes to speak truth to power, couching criticism and propaganda in mythological and literary terms. I close the book with final thoughts on the Underworld scene as a unique, metaliterary space, which offers a stable, interconnected, and impactful platform for authorial commentary. In viewing Underworld scenes as a space for authors to embed critical commentary, *Life / Afterlife* offers scholars a powerful tool for thinking about how ancient authors and audiences negotiated power, conceived of revolutions of thought, and influenced the reception of their cultures' ideologies and artistic products.

I

The Synoptic Underworld

OVERVIEW OF A NARRATIVE CONSTRUCT

I. Achilles' Dream

In the dark depths of grief and the middle of a fever dream, Achilles receives a visit in his tent from the ghost of his dearest friend Patroclus, who describes the Underworld from a first-person perspective. Until Patroclus' ghost appears to discuss the fate of souls, Achilles is so mired in his own pain, groaning heavily (βαρὺ στενάχων, *Il.* 23.60), that nothing his companions or fellow Greek leaders do can break him from his overwhelming, limb-weakening grief over losing his friend. Despite having avenged Patroclus' death by killing Hector, Achilles delays the burial of his friend, performing multiple rituals of grief that hold up the war—and the epic—from concluding. Even as he orders both the Myrmidons and other Greeks to go through the steps of performing funerary honors that should bring closure, Achilles cannot himself seem to move forward from his grief, indicated by his physical and emotional separation from his men. First, after performing military honors and hosting a funeral feast for the Myrmidons (*Il.* 23.12–34), Achilles allows his men to remove their armor and relax but does not do so himself. Next, because other Greek leaders persuade him vigorously, the grief-ridden Achilles trudges over to Agamemnon's tent (*Il.* 23.35–37). After he arrives, Achilles firmly (στερεῶς, *Il.* 23.42) refuses to bathe and wash off the gore from recent battle and further swears an oath (ὅρκον ὄμοσσεν, *Il.* 23.42) that he will not do so until after the other Greeks had set up an elaborate funeral for Patroclus (*Il.* 23.43–53). Finally, after leaving instructions for Agamemnon and the other Greek leaders, he sits alone on the shore consumed with exhaustion and grief until he falls asleep (*Il.* 23.59-61).

Life / Afterlife. Suzanne Lye, Oxford University Press. © Oxford University Press 2024.
DOI: 10.1093/9780197690239.003.0002

The Synoptic Underworld

As a result, the Greeks are again without their best fighter. Moreover, they are all compelled to prepare a hero's funeral more elaborate than any of the ones described for any warrior who is not a Greek leader, again delaying the Greeks' pursuit of war against Troy.[1] Through this turn of events, the plot of the *Iliad*, tied to the fate of Achilles, essentially stops. It is in this pause of the action that Achilles receives his ghostly visitation, which provides a unique view of the Underworld and serves a twofold purpose: to reintroduce the major themes of the epic to the audience and restart the narrative by giving Achilles a goal with a clear path for moving beyond his grief and returning to the war.

Patroclus' ghost, easily recognizable because of his demeanor, looks, and clothes, appears in a dream to Achilles, and the reaction of each is different. Whereas Achilles wants to focus on their close connection, Patroclus' ghost is more concerned with getting Achilles to let him go. The ghost's first words to Achilles are a rebuke and a demand for burial. Because Achilles, out of a desire for vengeance against Hector, delayed performing Patroclus' funerary rites, his ghost has been unable to join the host of the dead in Hades. The ghost says, "Bury me so I might pass through the gates of Hades as swiftly as possible" (θάπτέ με ὅττι τάχιστα πύλας Ἀΐδαο περήσω, *Il.* 23.71). Instead of ending there, however, the ghost goes on to describe its outcast existence in the afterlife, where the other souls of mortal men keep him far away and do not allow him to mingle with them on the opposite bank of one of the Underworld rivers (τῆλέ με εἴργουσι ψυχαὶ εἴδωλα καμόντων / οὐδέ μέ πω μίσγεσθαι ὑπὲρ ποταμοῖο ἐῶσιν, "the spirits, images of men who have toiled, shut me out, and up to now they do not allow me to mingle with them across the river," *Il.* 23.72–73). The ghost blames this painful exclusion on Achilles' attachment to the earthly body it used to inhabit, that of Patroclus, and commands Achilles to give a parting handshake (καί μοι δὸς τὴν χεῖρ᾽ · ὀλοφύρομαι, "and give me your hand, I beg with tears," *Il.* 23.75).[2] Although our modern understanding of a handshake is one of closeness and proximity, in the ancient

---

[1] Patroclus' burial takes up almost the entirety of Book 23. The other major funerals mentioned are those of Hector at the end of *Il.* 24 and the mass burial of unnamed Greek and Trojan dead warriors in *Il.* 7. Apollo himself performs the burial rites for Sarpedon, king of the Lycians, at Zeus' command in *Il.* 16.

[2] The handshake gesture is common in funerary settings. The most famous Archaic representations of funerary handshakes occur between heroes and deities, representing the stature of the former; later, depictions of a final handshake between living and dead were common on tombstones and white-ground *lekythoi* (Davies 1985, 627–630).

16 LIFE / AFTERLIFE

Greek funerary context, the handshake is a gesture of farewell and of letting go of a dead loved one.

After this command, the ghost further frames Achilles' attachment to its now lifeless, physical body as unusual and at odds with the companions' closeness in life, which can be traced back to when they were boys. Achilles appears to be causing harm, however unintentional, because of his attachment to Patroclus' body. In addition to urging Achilles to bury its body and say a final farewell to it, Patroclus' ghost leans on its relationship with Achilles to request a more glorious burial than might have been planned or appropriate for Patroclus' rank among the Myrmidons or Greek religious custom. Although Achilles questions his friend's demands, he still promises to fulfill them ('τίπτέ μοι ἠθείη κεφαλὴ δεῦρ᾽ εἰλήλουθας / καί μοι ταῦτα ἕκαστ᾽ ἐπιτέλλεαι; "Why have you come to me here, dear one, only to prescribe each of these things?" *Il.* 23.94–95). The ghost then immediately vanishes without responding to Achilles' attempted embrace, at which point the latter leaps up, awake and with purpose.[3]

From this vision of the Underworld, Achilles himself summarizes the following major takeaway as something that gives him a sense of wonder and solace:

ὢ πόποι ἦ ῥά τίς ἐστι καὶ εἰν Ἀΐδαο δόμοισι
ψυχὴ καὶ εἴδωλον, ἀτὰρ φρένες οὐκ ἔνι πάμπαν:
παννυχίη γάρ μοι Πατροκλῆος δειλοῖο
ψυχὴ ἐφεστήκει γοόωσά τε μυρομένη τε,
καί μοι ἕκαστ᾽ ἐπέτελλεν, ἔϊκτο δὲ θέσκελον αὐτῷ. (*Il.* 23.103–107)

"Wow, will you look at that! There is in the halls of Hades indeed some
spirit and image, but one not altogether there in its wits;
for all night the spirit of wretched Patroclus
stood near me, wailing and weeping,
and gave me each order to complete, and it was wonderfully similar to
    him."

---

[3] Although the handshake seems a part of funerary custom and imagery, this attempted embrace is neither what the ghost commanded nor would allow, and it is a moment where the author reminds the audience that the former companions are now existentially different.

Moreover, Achilles expresses a sense of awe that the ghost could project into his tent momentarily from the Underworld. While Achilles does not travel directly into the Underworld, the ghost's detailed description of the landscape with the river, Hades' gates, and a gathering of souls, brings the audience into an Underworld scene.

In an epic celebrating battle and potential death as the best path for a warrior to achieve highly coveted *kleos*, Achilles' moment of insight about something to look forward to after death (i.e., a potential reunion with Patroclus) removes any remaining reluctance to bury his friend and meet his fate when he inevitably returns to the war. This scene, the earliest extant Underworld scene in ancient Greek literature, gives purpose and context to Achilles' next set of actions, including completing Patroclus' funeral and returning Hector's body to Priam. These, in turn, pull the story out of its quasi-stasis. Although there are no further military engagements in the *Iliad*, the scene spurs the plot of the Trojan War story forward toward its conclusion and establishes the motivation for Achilles to reenter the fight and finish his heroic journey. When he returns fully to the war, he does so knowing that he is fated to die at Troy, that his bones will be buried with Patroclus', and that their souls will reunite in eternity. Here and elsewhere in Greek literature, the Underworld scene communicates vital information about Achilles and acts as a literary device and authorial strategy, one that scholars have had difficulty classifying or interpreting because of the scene's complex nature.

In the remainder of this chapter, I discuss the nature of Underworld scenes such as this one in Greek literature as well as various approaches and methodologies that have been used to try to define them. I then present issues and controversies related to their status as a special register in literature that are woven into a narrative but act as "texts between texts" that create complex, relational structures.[4] I offer basic definitions of terms (such as text, intertext, hypertext, frame narrative, and *chronotope*), which I borrow from studies in narratology, intertextuality, and structuralism, since these movements in literary criticism have developed useful language to articulate the connections that Underworlds create with each other. The idea of "intertextuality" is particularly helpful for this discussion because it contains within its definition the idea of communication between texts across temporal and spatial discontinuities. Similarly, a sense of time-space dislocation, which is emblematic of the Underworld chronotope, is a key feature of Underworld scenes that

---

[4] Other special registers of language include such things as ekphrasis and similes.

18 LIFE / AFTERLIFE

allows them to incorporate characters from different time periods without disrupting the timeline of the main plot.

II. Approaches to Underworld Scenes

Representations of Hades, the Underworld, and the afterlife in Greek and Roman literature have traditionally, and until very recently, been studied primarily from a religious, literary, or cultural perspective. Scholars have often tried to extrapolate historical practices and eschatological beliefs about life after death from accounts of rituals and myths surrounding funerary practices, cult beliefs, necromantic encounters, and *katabaseis*. Jan Bremmer (2002, 6) notes a growing interest in the fate and composition of the soul and its final abode from the Archaic to Classical Greek periods, indicating diachronic changes in how Greeks viewed the dead and the afterlife. Bremmer (2015) particularly points to the addition of more specific details about the Underworld journey and its physical environment to the *katabasis* myths of Heracles and Theseus, which had earlier focused primarily on bravery. Additionally, starting in the fifth-century BCE, Greeks seemed to take a more individualized approach to death, which influenced their conception of the relationship between the living and the dead (Mirto 2012, 8). Indeed, the prevalence of representations of the afterlife across genres and media as we move diachronically supports the conclusion that early Greeks continued to negotiate the boundaries between the societies of the living and the dead over time. As we shall see throughout this inquiry, representations of the afterlife in Underworld scenes through katabatic journeys or conversations with ghosts are a crucial part of that negotiation.

Having come down to us in extant literature, for the most part, as embedded narratives, Underworld scenes often appear to be a digression from the "main story," which I will refer to in this book as the "frame narrative." Homeric scholars have long grappled with the sense that Underworld scenes are not strictly necessary for the plot of their primary texts. In the Homeric scholia, we find that the Hellenistic grammarian Aristarchus athetized large sections of Odysseus' *Nekuia*.[5] Well into the mid-twentieth century, famous Classicists Erwin Rohde (1925, 33) and Denys Page (1955, 32) agreed that the Underworld scenes were problematic, with the former arguing that the *Nekuia* has no place in the poem because it is unnecessary for the plot and

---

[5] See Tsagarakis (2000, 11).

the latter concluding that the *Nekuia* is "artificially inserted" and originally independent of the *Odyssey*.[6] Such plot-focused readings tend to be teleological in their outlook, prioritizing the specific event of Odysseus' homecoming and interpreting prior events as building toward that moment. The premise of the *Nekuia* is that Odysseus needs to go to the Underworld realm to get directions home from Tiresias, but this does not happen explicitly, and the hero returns to Circe's island, where she gives him the specific directions he sought. The mismatch between expectation and reality, coupled with the length of the *Nekuia*, has raised questions about this scene's legitimacy, purpose, and placement. Since the *Nekuia* is one of the earliest and most elaborate Underworld scenes we have, undermining its value has had repercussions for other such scenes that model or reference it.

The persistence and similarity of Underworld scenes to each other, both across time and genres, have, however, forced modern scholars to continually reassess the value and function of such scenes. One current trend has been to assume that Underworld episodes serve *some* purpose, although even those who try to find connections among them look at the scenes in piecemeal fashion. Viewing Underworld scenes in isolation while noticing the complexity of their allusions, scholars have tended to approach them in three major ways: as evidence of poetic competition, as reflections of actual religious rituals and beliefs, and as poetic allegory.

The first approach focuses on literary genealogy and attempts to make connections between a specific work and other reported traditions of poetry from the ancient world. Glenn Most (1992, 1019–1020), for example, describes the *Nekuia* as "a catalogue of the varieties of Archaic Greek epos" and divides it into symmetrical parts, suggesting several types of Archaic epos as points of comparison for each section.[7] Additionally, he argues that sections within the *Nekuia* juxtapose Homeric and Hesiodic forms of poetry, with nods to both oral tradition and didactic poetry. Other scholars have similarly pointed out connections in Underworld scenes to other traditions of Archaic poetry,

---

[6] Gee (2020, 23–26) summarizes the back and forth between different scholars of whether and why to remove the Underworld scene. See also Clark (1979, 42).

[7] For a full discussion on how the sections of the *Nekuia* recall different forms of epos, see Most (1989, 1992). Rutherford and Doherty also parse the *Nekuia* and focus on the catalog of women. Rutherford (2000, 93–94), for example, ties it to a possible tradition of *Ehoie* poetry, while Doherty (1995, 112–113) interprets it as a competitive gesture. She argues that it is further proof of Odysseus' cleverness as a poet in reading his Phaeacian hosts' interests and the narrator's sophistication in projecting how audiences in general should receive a bard's performance.

such as the epic cycle (Burgess 2004, 167–168) and lyric poetry (Gazis 2018, 14) because of their focus on deeply personal topics such as grief and individual loss rather than heroic glory. Underworld scenes, therefore, have been used by scholars of Archaic epic, linguistics, and religion to show a poet's or, more generally, the epic genre's awareness of competing poetic forms and eschatologies in the absence of other proofs, whether in the literary or archaeological record.

In a second interpretive approach, Underworld scenes have been tied to a ritual (and often initiatory) framework. Because the action of these episodes follows certain patterns and exists outside of the plot, the overall scenes have been analogized to actual religious practices, which also take place outside of the flow of everyday life, often in a sacred space. In this schema, a hero undergoes a form of death and rebirth at a critical point in his life. The movement to the edges of the world, in the margins of civilization, offers the hero a chance to confront the people and events which led him to his present state so that he can transform his understanding of his motivations and desires, which, in turn, empowers him to reintegrate into the world of the living. This approach has been especially appealing to those who study mystery cult ritual objects such as the Orphic Gold Tablets or ghost-summoning rituals, like Odysseus' in the *Nekuia*, which have roots in known shamanistic rituals. This approach privileges historical contexts for the given Underworld scene to show how the content of the text uses symbolic gestures to connect with the real-world interests and concerns of the audience. Structuralists and New Historicists have found this approach appealing because it connects literary sources to archaeological discoveries and cross-cultural, anthropological theories of humanity.

A third approach that scholars have used to address the peculiarity of Underworld scenes treats them as allegories. In this view, the Underworld scene loosely represents utopian or dystopian aspects of the author's society. Resting strongly on a historicist approach, allegorical readings have been done on a text-by-text basis, tying each to its immediate context rather than to each other. A.M. Bowie (1993, 244), for example, argues that the Eleusinian initiates in the Underworld of Aristophanes' *Frogs* reflect "a way of thinking about participation in and ordering of the state." Along the same lines, David Sedley (2009, 58) points out that the Underworld in Plato's *Gorgias* and its myth of judgment under Zeus' regime "symbolizes a method of examining and improving souls which we are being asked to recognize as superior to the current Athenian political system." Similarly, A. Georgiadou and D. H. J. Larmour (1998, 313) argue that Lucian's account of the afterlife and fate of the soul in the *True History* is a philosophical parody of the journey for knowledge, which makes fun of the sophists and philosophical schools of his day. In the allegorical approach, each Underworld borrows from a store of common myth but is locally applied to a specific historical context and audience. For proponents of this approach, the Underworld journey motif is primarily a convenient tool for expressing ideology, which is tied more to immediate context than to a larger literary gesture.[8]

These approaches have produced rich and varied scholarship on the literary, historical, and religious concerns of ancient Greeks. Each approach, however, has some shortcomings, and none fully address the question of why Underworld scenes appear with such regularity in ancient Greek literature and art over the course of a millennium. By instead approaching Greek Underworld scenes collectively as a metaliterary genre with its own attributes and rhythms, we can better see that they form their own distinct tradition, which encourages interaction between author and audience through metanarrative communication to produce meaning.[9]

III. Defining the Underworld

Identifying the Underworld

The primary feature that defines an epic Underworld is a chronotopic break from the main narrative, in which the audience is taken outside of the main plot and real-world chronology and introduced to stories and ideas that are generally external to the plot but thematically relevant to the narrative. This diversion often occurs alongside a character from the story who has an Underworld encounter, but not exclusively so, as can be seen in ethnographic Underworld scenes, such as those appearing in Hesiod and Plato. Although

---

[8] Edmonds (2004, 30) argues, for example, that the Orphic Gold Tablets "use the traditional pattern of the journey to the underworld to express a protest against the mainstream of polis society." He also suggests that those who were buried with the Tablets were somehow trying to distinguish themselves and may even have been marginalized members of society (Edmonds 2004, 66–69). Gee (2020, 1–2), using a psychological approach, argues that the Underworld is a fictive space that is representative of the unconscious and allegorizes a unifying vision of the cosmos through its landscape and figures such as Heracles.

[9] Edmonds (2004) comes the closest to my approach as does Tsagarakis (2000), who argues that the Odyssey's *Nekuia* is integral as well as informative to the epic because it gives insights into the hero's character and connects him to a glorious tradition.

not all Underworlds have every element, there are certain key features that the epic Underworld contains which repeat to some degree in every Underworld scene and recall many other elements.

An Underworld scene can generally be divided into three parts: entry, encounters, and exit. While the entry and encounters have variable length, the exit is usually short without the level of detailed description as the entry, representing an abrupt return to the frame narrative. The entry typically happens in stages with special attention given to the senses (e.g., light, landmarks, and geographic features). Once the new Underworld chronotope is established, which can be defined as dark, dank, disorienting, and noisy, visitors arrive at their destination, the world of the dead and kingdom of Hades, where they encounter a variety of supernatural elements. These include some combination of souls, supernatural beings, and impossible landscapes, whose presence and placement activate streams of narrative that signal to the audience how the author would like his work to be interpreted.

The audience is led into the Underworld by a narrator, hero, or character, often at hinge points in the story when the protagonist is at a turning point in their life or "stuck" in a situation from which they need to escape. Additionally, such a digression usually occurs at the direction of some external force (human or divine): Circe advises Odysseus to talk to the ghost of the seer Tiresias; Eurystheus orders Heracles to retrieve Cerberus from Hades as one of his labors; Theseus accompanies Pirithous on the mission to kidnap Persephone to pay back a debt because the latter had helped him capture Helen; and Er is told to bring back information of the afterlife to the living.

The stages of an Underworld scene can be seen to loosely align with Arnold van Gennep's (1981) three stages of initiation (separation, marginalization, and reintegration) but are not initiatory in the sense of removing the character from a community and then reintegrating them. The hero is separated from the human world, chronological reality, and mappable space. There is no grand send-off as there might be for a quest or war. Instead, a divine mandate, communicated through signs or a trusted figure, propels the journey into the Underworld space. The time spent in the land of the dead is literally on the margins of the known world, either horizontal (beyond Ocean) or vertical (underground), and contains a society of supernatural beings, including the dead. Finally, full reintegration never occurs, even after the hero, whose story the audience is following, returns to his world because his experience of *katabasis* forever separates him from being "ordinary."

When the author transports the protagonist and the audience to an alien place, the "givens" of everyday life can be temporarily set aside or stripped away completely. Because the Greek Underworld is conceived of as a physical place, authors frequently start Underworld scenes with a description of the landscape and some landmarks. In other types of narration (e.g., ekphrasis and similes), descriptions of place and the introduction of related stories or background information appear organically, adding complication to the main plot without impeding its forward progress or threatening to trap the main character indefinitely. Protagonists, for example, may stumble upon a piece of art that the narrator then describes (as in ekphrasis); a new obstacle may appear, which causes a delay in achieving the protagonist's goals; an analogous situation may be introduced (as in simile); or a character may tell a story at another's request. In these instances, action is put on hold for a brief time but there is still often a sense of forward, goal-oriented progress.[10] In an Underworld scene, however, the plot of the frame narrative is paused while the protagonists enter the alternate reality of the Underworld chronotope. Moreover, a return is not guaranteed, since encounters in the Underworld and the crowding of multilayered, overlapping narratives threaten to distract the protagonists and derail the plot completely. Theseus and Pirithous, for example, were trapped when they tried to kidnap Persephone, and Odysseus lingers well beyond Circe's mandate in order to talk to the ghosts of friends and family, only leaving when threatened by the Gorgon's appearance (Karanika 2011).

Under the guise of giving information to a character, the Underworld signals important themes and relationships for the audience to keep in mind, thus creating a channel of "insider knowledge" between author and audience. Through this pathway, the Underworld scene becomes a special narrative register used to communicate themes and information to the audience by relating the current situation to a larger world of myth. Epic Underworlds differ from other types of special poetic registers because of the sustained nature of their engagement with multiple narratives. These *para-narratives* are continually engaged in order to shape the audience's view of the hero and the plot or themes of the frame narrative in real time as a story progresses.

Entry to the Underworld

Entries into an Underworld scene typically happen in stages, often through a journey motif that distances the hero from his primary destination through

---

[10] For more on time in Greek narrative, see de Jong and Nünlist (2007) and Purves (2010).

a divinely mandated digression. The gradual entry into the Underworld gives a sense of narrative movement, yet everything in the Underworld is standing still in its own time bubble, and the plot of the frame narrative is put on pause while the protagonist spends time in the realm of the dead. While this moment of pause stops a character's progress toward his goal, the motivations and implications of his actions are thrown into greater relief. Each encounter in the Underworld highlights themes and lessons that are important for understanding the frame narrative, adding depth and relevant background information.

The audience learns that to succeed in his goals, the hero must go through an ultimate test, often with divine sanction. The most convenient way to signal this break from the frame narrative is through a journey motif, in which the hero must travel to a place that is perpetually far away, foreign, and unknowable. Despite this, the hero or narrator often points out familiar objects or features in a descriptive transition between known and unknown space, as a traveler might when encountering a new country. At a certain point, however, he realizes that he is completely separated from the world of the living. In the *Odyssey,* this moment occurs when Odysseus unexpectedly encounters the soul of his crewmate Elpenor, whom he expected to be among the living but who confirms that they are all now in the land of the dead. This is the first and perhaps most shocking encounter for Odysseus that lays the groundwork for what he is going to experience next, a series of shocks that reminds him of his motivations and injects a renewed sense of purpose, even urgency, into the frame narrative.

Despite the persistent threat of getting trapped in the Underworld, the hero or narrator describes the Underworld with the curiosity of a traveler and also with a sense of resignation that the only way to continue forward on the larger quest is through the Underworld, a space filled with hidden knowledge, information, and insights about the immediate or distant future. When opening the narrative to the Underworld chronotope, the author forces his protagonist to retrace actual and possible paths to the present moment. The assumption, whether explicitly stated or not, is that the hero cannot move forward into the future without first encountering the past and acknowledging where he (or she) is now. The Underworld scene, therefore, becomes an individual's chance for closure—to resolve outstanding issues from the past, putting both people and fears to rest, so he can move forward to his future and the completion of the story. The hero who exits the Underworld, therefore, is not the same person who entered, at least from the point of view of the audience, who now knows more about him than it did before. After his values, deeds, and relationships with the figures in the Underworld have been put on display for the audience, he is reborn into the plot, which is then rebooted not only as a continuation of the frame narrative but also with the feeling of a "fresh start."

As many scholars have pointed out, Odysseus is a model for this pattern, and the *Nekuia* occurs at a pivotal place in the narrative, in the heart of symmetrical narrative rings (Most 1989, 1992; de Jong 2001). The people and objects encountered in this Underworld scene give a clue to the standard image set of Underworld scenes, which most likely existed before the Homeric epics, and, through the *Nekuia*'s influence, indicate things that Archaic and later audiences have come to expect. These elements include: chthonic deities, guides, landscape features, examples of souls undergoing eternal punishment or reward, allusions to other mortal visitors, and conversations with souls about events relevant to the main narrative.

The deployment of these individual pieces depends on the author's goals, but the existence of an overarching, partially predictable framework is what makes Underworld scenes useful as a literary device and rhetorical tool, while also malleable to serve multiple purposes. By activating a collective mythic consciousness, an author taps into audience expectation while retaining the flexibility to expand or contract each part of the frame to suit narrative needs. In this way, Underworld narratives loosely fit de Jong's definition of a *type-scene* as "a recurrent block of narrative with an identifiable structure and often in identical language, describing recurrent actions of everyday life" (de Jong 2001, xix). Activation of the Underworld framework includes the introduction of certain narrative patterns, such as entry rituals or the acquisition of special knowledge, reminders of the permeability between the worlds of the living and dead, and a shrinking of narrative perspective to a single, voyeuristic viewpoint (that of the hero/narrator) so that the reader and hero/narrator share a sense of disorientation. The difference between Underworld scenes and *type-scenes*, as defined by de Jong and others before her, lies in the former's complexity of narrative sequences and level of intertextual and intratextual connectivity. Underworld scenes go beyond *type-scenes* because they are not formulaic nor do they simply borrow mythical motifs from other similar scenes, as arming, sailing, or fighting *type-scenes* might. Rather than trying to form narrative echoes or turning the audience's attention away to other similar scenes, Underworld scenes bring many stories actively into their singular, dense narrative space so they can be viewed at the same time.

As narrative units, Underworld scenes are relatively complete, with a fairly definitive structure, which includes a formal journey into or description of an

26   LIFE / AFTERLIFE

alternative, imagined geographical space. Indeed, Underworld scenes conjure an alternate reality in which the souls of almost all mortals are imagined eventually to go as a final, often eternal destination with particular landscapes designated for special individuals, such as heroes or sinners. The reliance on the audience to fill in so much of this world differentiates such scenes from other types of narrative episodes and digressions. Moreover, because Underworld scenes often contain a travel element, related attributes such as directions, landmarks, and guides become important signposts. The time it takes to complete the journey to the Underworld disconnects the hero from his reality, layer by layer, such that he loses his sense of the passage of time and exists in an eternal moment, which occurs in multiple time frames (e.g., repetitive, circular, mythic, etc.). Because of this relaxation of the parameters related to time and space, the Underworld becomes "narratologically convenient as a stage for various types of shades to quickly appear and disappear," leading to "narrative freedom" and "poetical brilliance" (Burgess 2009, 109). As a result, the Underworld scene functions as a literary meeting point where protagonists are compared to their mythic peers—and authors to their predecessors—in a long tradition of intertextual communication that can be traced to Homer.

The goal of the entry portion of an Underworld scene, therefore, is to create separation from the reality presented by the frame narrative and then to assert its own chronotope, a space outside of regular time and place which is both synchronic and syntopic. The Greek epic Underworld is a discursive landscape with landmarks (e.g., groves, paths) and obstacles, (e.g., rivers, rocks, or brambles) as well as nonhuman gatekeepers and guardians, challenging the hero on both entry and exit. Although the space itself is emphatically disconnected from any specific mortal realm by being at the extreme ends of the world or deep underground, the identities of the dead are still connected to their place of origin and the soul of any dead person from any time period can appear and engage with the katabatic hero. When souls appear in an Underworld scene, the first glimpse is often of a vast, undifferentiated space with certain figures slowly coming into relief to orient and anchor the Underworld scene.

Encounters with Supernatural Beings

After the initial sense of movement and idea of progression into the Underworld, the main part of an Underworld scene is largely static, as the hero looks around and describes actions that are occurring around him. This includes encounters with familiar figures, often surprising but sometimes

The Synoptic Underworld 27

expected, as when the hero sees judges such as Minos or the narrator refers to "eternal sinners" such as Tantalus or Sisyphus. Encounters with dead heroes, chthonic gods, and specific landmarks appear, for the most part, in catalogic fashion because the author crowds a bunch of references into a short space and assumes the audience knows the stories behind the lists of names. Each reference activates a narrative thread that gives context to the frame narrative, adjusting to how the audience is meant to understand events that happen outside of the Underworld. While each figure and its story challenge the attention of the Underworld visitor and may even distract him from his progress, the catalogic juxtaposition of famous names creates metatextual associations that signal to the audience how to "read" the frame story of his larger journey.

Epic Underworlds are segregated into sections by landmarks and fates of the souls. Where the hero or narrator chooses to spend time talking to souls or various figures tells the audience whether an Underworld scene is primarily heroic or judgment-based. As a rhetorical device, Underworld scenes give authors access to a wide range of historical figures and supernatural entities. The supernatural beings that typically appear in Underworld scenes include souls of the dead, chthonic gods, eternal sinners, and judges, with each figure pointing to the purpose and hidden messages of the particular Underworld scene. Whereas frame stories and their plots must be generally anchored in linear time and space, Underworld episodes diverge from this model by allowing the juxtaposition of characters who come from multiple locations and time periods, both past and future, into a single, more expansive space. Thus, Homer could imagine Odysseus talking to dead companions like Achilles and Agamemnon in the *Odyssey*, and Plato could imagine Socrates anticipating afterlife conversations about justice with Homer, Ajax, and Orpheus in the *Apology*. References to previous katabatic heroes, particularly Heracles, signal to the audience that the author is constructing a heroic Underworld scene and wants his hero to be viewed through a heroic lens. In contrast, an Underworld scene that focuses on the judges of the Underworld and segregation of souls based on deeds or status signals an Underworld of judgment that will hold the hero's actions in the frame narrative to account, often along some moral standard.

The goal of the encounters portion of an Underworld visit is to pass along information to the audience to help them classify the hero and how to interpret the frame narrative against a larger cosmic, religious, or literary backdrop. This becomes possible because of the nature of the Underworld chronotope as *outside* time, thus enabling it to connect to other Underworld scenes in other works which operate in the same chronotopic setting. Thus, the "Golden Age" afterlife presented in the Underworld in Hesiod's *Works and Days* (109–126) can be seen by different audiences to be in direct dialogue with Menelaus' afterlife description in the *Odyssey* (4.561–569), and an author can use Underworld scenes to bring works like these into contact, enhancing the messaging in each.

Exiting the Underworld

The exit from an Underworld is typically abrupt without any retracing of steps or mention of time passing. Often, the protagonist returns to his present or the place where he had embarked upon his journey, no further along than when he left. To an outside observer or peer, he does not physically appear or act any differently. Due to the experience and new knowledge of which he and the audience are aware, however, the hero exists in a new frame of reference. It is as if a filter has been changed: the hero and his motivations come into clearer focus and he is pushed into a class of "special heroes," which includes figures like Heracles, Theseus, and Orpheus.

The abruptness of the ending and lack of reintegration with the main plot gives the hero's Underworld journey a sense of unreality, as if it never happened, yet the audience and those to whom he tells the tale look at the hero in a new light as a person who has a cosmic view and will forever be somewhat removed from the shared human experiences of regular mortals. The intervention that an Underworld scene makes into the flow of the frame narrative sets up a platform for the author to make connections beyond his text in a sustained way through a combination of poetic techniques.

IV. Purpose, Function, and Persistence of Underworld Scenes

In the Underworld scenes of ancient Greek and Roman literature, scholars have identified many levels of connection in individual works between texts and their contexts, both narrative and historical. These connections between texts were historically referred to as "parallels," "allusions," and, more recently, "intertexts," which are all terms borrowed from semiotics and structuralism (Fowler 2000, 115–117). The idea of intertextuality as a defined theoretical approach has pervaded studies of the ancient world to varying degrees over time but was only fairly recently introduced as terminology useful in discussing Underworld scenes. Those who have studied ancient texts had already been reading them intertextually for millennia, and many features of intertextuality as a theory had been applied to ancient texts under different names. Structuralism, however, provided distinct terminology and a key insight into these long-observed connections by arguing that texts are created within a system, meaning that "to read a text thus involves a two-step process: a reconstruction of the matrix which gives it meaning, and the production of that meaning by the act of relating source- and target-texts" (Fowler 2000, 117).

The implications of the fundamental terms of the process that Fowler describes—"text," "intertext," and "allusion"—have varied widely over time. In this section, I begin by defining the most basic terms for analyzing a text and its relationships before demonstrating how Underworld scenes fit into these categories as a specialized type of intertext with a unique purpose and function.

Text, Intertext, Hypertext, and Allusion

Underworld scenes allow multiple texts to be copresent for the audience in a sustained way that affects the reception and interpretation of protagonists and their worlds. In the case of ancient Greek literature, the word "text" must be carefully applied because many of the earliest sources were not written at all but came out of a rich oral tradition. For this study, "text" refers to a structured narrative, an autonomous, coherent unit conveyed orally (through song) or visually (through writing or images).[11] An "intertext" exceeds the normal beginning-middle-end boundaries that are required for texts by incorporating constituents from elsewhere to create relationships between texts (Plett 1991, 5). An intertext, therefore, is a common point of reference between different narratives that highlights a relationship between two texts and anchors them to each other.

Although scholars have tried to categorize Underworld scenes into two general categories (*katabasis* and *nekuia*), the reality is that none of the earliest Underworld scenes fit neatly into either group. Underworld narratives tend to recall both types *as well as* other nonkatabatic afterlife narratives, such as travelers' tales, which is why a different categorization schema, such as heroic versus judgmental, is more productive. Bringing the reader in as a participant in composition through the placement of scant references to multiple afterlife narratives and journey motifs reinforces trust and connection between

---

[11] See Pucci (1987, 27) for a discussion of the overlap between oral and written texts in signifying meaning.

author and audience by reasserting shared stories and values. It also brings more scope for interpretation than can be envisioned by the author because he or she cannot predict what different audiences might see in the material. In the case of *katabaseis*, brief catalogues of famous Underworld locations and figures (such as Tartarus, the River Styx, Hades, and Tantalus) are all that is needed for the audience to conjure a fully developed Underworld ruled by a system of justice that punishes wrong-doers. The collaboration between author and audience in the meaning of these seemingly unrelated items occurs because of the archival and referential nature of the Underworld space, which suggests a particular interpretative path to the audience. As each element in an Underworld scene is unveiled, the audience constantly compares new details to an array of known Underworld narratives, a state that the author uses to lead the audience to an interpretation of the Underworld scene at hand. Of course, this happens to a certain extent in all literature, but Underworld scenes bring an added sense of authority because they use references based in traditional religious systems and also require *sustained* links to multiple points of reference for the duration of the episode.

Underworld scenes have never been defined as a genre per se, but they have generic qualities that audiences recognize for purposes of comparison with different traditional tales of *katabasis*, necromancy, and the afterlife in general. Further, since they are such a specific formulation of narrative, they create links across works that are different from other types of scenes in their ability to be both generalizable as type-scenes but localized in a text through nuanced structures to create relations between their immediate narrative context (i.e., their "frame narrative") and more global themes like heroism. They do more than just connect works with similar scenes together, as might happen with arming scenes, catalogues, and battle scenes. Rather, Underworld scenes give audiences a unique, sustained view of how authors themselves situate their own work against multiple referents, both past and future. The presence of an Underworld scene, therefore, is a powerful, marked tool of communication between an author and his or her audience, since "generic perception is known to guide and determine to a considerable degree the readers' expectations, and thus their reception of the work" (Genette 1997, 5).

This generic perception results in the audience's active participation in the construction of Underworld scenes during the listening, reading, or viewing process, since they tend to be described only sketchily. Even when specific figures and landmarks are named (e.g., Sisyphus, Minos, the house of Hades, the White Rock), these elements are not usually accompanied by detailed descriptions. The audience must "fill in the blanks" of the stories behind them by tapping into the collective memory of their cultures and their knowledge

The Synoptic Underworld

of similar, related myths. The creation of these mental links in the minds of audience members adds to the interpretive experience by recalling additional narratives that are imagined in parallel with the one under consideration. In this way, the links in Underworld scenes do more than just build one-to-one connections that provide a round-trip mental diversion to the audience. Instead, these links build multiple, robust, and sustained connections that constantly nudge the audience's perception of a scene in certain directions.

As a narrative form that relies on reading beyond the immediate text, Underworld scenes connect vertically, or intratextually, with the "frame narrative" (i.e., the text in which they are embedded) and horizontally to other narratives. In the Underworld scene in Achilles' dream, for example, Patroclus' ghost aids the audience's interpretation of Achilles' abuse of Hector's body, his actions surrounding Patroclus' burial, and his reconciliation with his destiny, which includes subsequent events such as his truce with Priam and return to the fighting. Although much later, Vergil's Underworld in Book 6 of the *Aeneid* similarly serves to project the successful end to Aeneas' journey in the frame narrative and his descendants' glorious future to Roman audiences by linking intertextually to Homer's Underworld scene in Book 11 of the *Odyssey* (Clark 1979, 147–183). Thus, these Underworld scenes both connect vertically and horizontally to different narratives in order to display the past and the future at the same time for the audience to digest and assess.

Related to intertextuality is the term "allusion." At its simplest level, an allusion is a link between two texts that is generated by the author, often by a direct quotation taken from one text and embedded within a later text. Ancient commentators more narrowly defined it "as a homage, a borrowing, or a theft" (Hinds 1997, 120). More recently, Classics scholars have distinguished allusion from intertextuality by saying that the former is activated by the author, while the latter is dependent on the reader's interpretative abilities (Fowler 2000, 117; J.R. Morgan and Harrison 2008). Many, however, use these terms interchangeably, only making slight distinctions based on how forcefully they think an author is trying to make a connection between texts (Pucci 1987, 29). Fowler's categories of allusion and intertextuality as based on the connections made by author or audience, respectively, cannot be applied strictly to Underworld scenes, nor is Pucci's equivalency between these two terms completely satisfying to explain how Underworld scenes connect texts.[12] Underworld episodes require continuous participation from both

---

[12] In Fowler's (2000, 117) structuralist reading, the term "allusion" suggests that the power to point the audience to a specific source sits with the author, while the term "intertextuality"

author and audience in a relationship that is not captured by a distinction between allusions as author-driven and intertexts as reader-driven references. Instead, Underworld scenes require a partnership and exchange of roles between author and audience in a separate space from the frame narrative's reality, a distinct chronotope in which to negotiate meaning and insert commentary. While an author may insert a reference to an afterlife judge like Minos, it is the reader or listener who must conjure and apply the myth about that judge based on what he or she knows from many sources and then make the interpretative connection to the protagonist and the frame narrative. In this way, Underworld scenes can be thought of as a space specifically created for such author-audience exchange.

Intertext, Hypertext, and the Roles of Author and Audience

Analyzing Underworld scenes requires an approach to reading that involves the simultaneous consideration of multiple, overlapping relationships between texts, traditional stories, authors, and audiences. A few concepts and terms that are useful for describing these many relationships are *intertextuality*, *hypertextuality*, and *para-narrative*. The first two are closely related in that they describe how narratives create connections to each other, while the third describes how those narratives interact after they are connected.

Intertextuality, in its broadest sense, describes explicit and implicit relationships between texts. The idea of intertextuality received much attention in twentieth-century literary criticism, particularly from scholars who embraced the structural analyses of texts and applied such interpretations to literature, art, and music. Julia Kristeva (1974, 388–389), who coined the term *intertextuality*, started from the premise that "every text is from the outset under the jurisdiction of other discourses which impose a universe upon it."[13] Her approach views every text, therefore, as responding to multiple pressures and operating on two axes—a horizontal axis, connecting author to audience and a vertical axis, connecting a text to other texts (Kristeva 1980c, 66). Intertextuality requires, therefore, "a relationship of copresence between two texts or among several texts," which is within a range of implicit (e.g., allusion)

---

suggests an approach which highlights the audience's power to make connections beyond the author's power.

[13] This translation is from Culler (2001, 116), who has a general discussion of Kristeva's creation and formulation of the term "intertextuality."

and explicit (e.g., quoting, plagiarism) reference (Genette 1997, 1). The idea of texts embedded within a text, which are also communicating outward from the author to the audience, is apparent throughout literature but rarely ever in so sustained a fashion as in Underworld scenes.

Kristeva's (1980c, 66) vertical axis of intertextuality, as a chronological phenomenon, considers the older text to be in a privileged position as a point of comparison against which the more recent text is compared since "the word in the text is oriented towards an anterior or synchronic literary corpus." Along her horizontal axis, she argues for the "progressive creation" of metaphors and signs (Kristeva 1980a, 40). The relationship between texts as they are encountered by readers is often, however, less linear than an author might hope or the term intertextuality might suggest. To better represent the reality of how people encounter the "copresence" of texts in a given work, Genette expands on Kristeva to develop a type of intertextuality, which he called *hypertextuality*. Unlike allusion or intertext, which generally describes a one-to-one relationship between a text and its referent, the term *hypertextuality* suggests that more than one text can be present under the surface of a given text in a more sustained, hierarchical relationship, like in a palimpsest where the underlying text(s) might be obscured but is nonetheless present and discoverable. Genette's *hypertextuality* maintains Kristeva's basic premise of intertextuality that underlying texts were older than the text at hand (Genette 1997, 5–7). This study loosens this chronological dependency, expanding the notion of how *hypertextuality* works by taking the audience's perspective into consideration.

Approaching Underworld scenes as hypertextual obviates the need for strict chronology or the exact dating of Underworld scenes because the final activation of any links occurs at the point of audience consumption. An emphasis on chronology by scholars thus far, particularly of Underworld scenes in the Homeric epics, has often limited how such scenes have been interpreted because this focus on precedent does not give enough value to the knowledge and experiences of the audience. With hypertextual poetics, identifying certain sections of an Underworld scene as "later interpolations" or "original," therefore, is less important for understanding the meaning of a scene than figuring out the narratives being activated. In the case of such scenes, therefore, I build on Kristeva's and Genette's theories of intertextual relationships to include references that *postdate* the text under consideration because interpretation depends not only on the author's intention when including an allusion or reference but also on the audience's application of their experiences with other Underworld scenes to the text. Thus, a person who had read Vergil's or Dante's Underworld scenes first would view the Underworld scenes in the *Iliad* or *Odyssey* as overlapping and resonant with but not necessarily predictive or influential on the former. Although readers or listeners might know that Dante's *Inferno* could not influence Homer's *Odyssey*, they might still expect certain things from the latter based on having encountered Dante first and therefore might interpret aspects of the *Nekuia* through a Christian lens. An author who is aware of this might mitigate such unpredictable drift in interpretation by creating more detailed and robust linking to his or her referents so that there is no doubt he or she is connecting to a particular other Underworld scene. Scholars of Underworld scenes have had a difficult time describing this back-and-forth negotiation over meaning between author and audience, partly because of the limitation in thinking that they must give precedence to one or the other text based on chronology or influence and partly because they often assume that interpretation occurs as a singular event or process, such as might happen in the case of an allusion. Instead, I argue that Underworld scenes promote active, sustained negotiation between the creator of a narrative and audiences throughout the course of the scene and even beyond, which subtly shifts how the latter views the protagonists and story.

The current digital age offers another model that can be useful for understanding how to read and understand Underworld scenes as atemporal *hypertextual* narratives. In web design theory, for example, the visual architecture of web pages relies on connecting content to each other through hyperlinks, that is, highlighted words that refer to additional content that readers can access by choosing to click on them. Web designers determine the value of information on a web page by how they organize their hyperlinks. In the internet age, the term "hypertext" evokes the image of brightly colored words or phrases on a page that, if selected, will lead to further background or related information but which can also be ignored. Websites use hypertextuality in its most straightforward form, with webmasters and communications teams curating information that the user must choose to unlock with a click. Underworld scenes work in a similar way to such websites and operate from the same basic premise of the multidimensional, nonlinear interconnectedness of narratives that invites and expects but does not compel the audience to click or explore. Audiences have the opportunity to bring in a reference based on their knowledge and not access the additional information suggested by the link, but the author does not force the audience to share the same understanding by giving a detailed or fixed description of the reference. For example, an author might name-drop Tantalus in an Underworld scene

The Synoptic Underworld   35

to imply a judgment-based Underworld without telling this character's whole back story, thus inviting but not compelling the audience to incorporate his story into their interpretation of the main content.

In a *hypertextual* narrative, the author takes primary responsibility for creating the links within his or her text at the point of composition into a new creation such that both this new text and its sources are understood together as part of a network of texts. Once the story is made public, however, the interpretation of the text is a joint endeavor between author and audience because the latter must see the connection the author wants to elicit but may also see *more* than the author intends or imagines. The author can, therefore, be thought of as creating a platform or environment in which multiple, multilayered connections between texts (as represented by quotations and allusions) can thrive. This is more akin to how computer scientists might describe hypertexts, which are not single objects with one-to-one connections but "a computer environment which, among other things, allows fast nonsequential access to large amounts of loosely structured texts" (Mai 1991, 49). Narratives can be seen as a type of textual database that "embeds links within the original text to other physically unrelated texts," allowing the user to jump immediately and rapidly from one text to the next (Mai 1991, 49). When envisioned in terms of a web page, the Underworld scene can be imagined as a central page with a series of links that act as an index ready to offer relevant information by activating other pages. Although users click on these links to open new content, their return to the original page does not close the newly opened window. The alternate page, containing its own narrative and information, continues to be "live" in the background along with pages opened by other links from the main page. This creates a cascade of windows operating in the shadows, which share a connection to each other through the original page. This additional background content may or may not also be connected to each other in their own right. The lines between these pages quickly become a tangled web or "network" of content. In the same way that these open windows become simultaneously suspended on a screen, so too do linked narratives become copresent in the reader's mind as "shadow narratives." Operating in the background of an Underworld scene, these situate the primary narrative against a vast array of data that influences its reception. The connected narratives inform and challenge the main narrative for the audience's attention through the presentation of alternative, sometimes competing stories, which ultimately shift the orientation of both text and reader through a transformative experience before returning the latter to the main plot.

Thinking of Underworld scenes as a nexus for overlapping shadow narratives can elucidate their purpose, function, and use better than any single approach by scholars thus far by giving clues to the interactions and expectations of authors and audiences and by suggesting a more involved integration of two or more texts from different time periods and genres with deeper connections than the previously theorized terms allusion or intertext can capture. Thinking about Underworld scenes in this more expansive way also opens up new readings that can directly and fruitfully engage with how the scenes themselves play with ideas of time and space, as they weave together stories from a vast archive of myth, religion, literature, and cultural traditions.

Chronotopic Storytelling

Because of how and where an Underworld scene is situated within a greater narrative, it demands an analysis that takes into account author, audience, and multiple literary contexts. Instead of relying solely on their readers to interpret their works, authors insert an Underworld scene as a key to unlock their work's meaning and rely heavily on the reader to decipher the puzzle. Such a scene, therefore, gives an "insider" view of a narrative and acts as a mode of direct communication from author to audience. An Underworld scene also offers a brief respite from the narrative's flow to contemplate deeper themes that are subtly interwoven into the primary narrative in which the Underworld scene is embedded.

At the point of reader interpretation, the intended chronological relationship between the link and its "hidden windows" of narrative may become destabilized because the reader brings his or her own experiences and knowledge to the author's reference and may incorporate *other* narratives than the author intends, which are both anterior and posterior to the given work. A reader may thus read Homer through the lens of later ancient works and even modern stories, such as those of Harry Potter and Percy Jackson—and vice versa. Ancient Greek Underworld scenes take this into account and are able to link seamlessly between texts from different time periods because of their inherent temporal-spatial flexibility, which allows authors to embed a vast amount of information and commentary within them. The negotiation between author and audience is a more equal partnership accepted by authors who engage with such scenes and recognize that their power to "control the narrative" depends on their ability to activate interlocking background narratives through a particular configuration of details within their

Underworld scenes. These scenes occupy a middle ground between the two approaches of author-centric "allusion" and audience-centered "intertextuality" because the scenes require authors and audiences to engage in more active, continuous negotiation over the interpretation of the text by juxtaposing the frame narrative against an alternative, copresent reality, which in turn has access to other time periods, realities, and narratives. Whether in only a few lines or a fully elaborated description, Underworld scenes perform many complementary and competing functions from the perspectives of the narrative, author, and audience.

Besides defining a relationship between texts, the term *hypertextuality* implies temporal and spatial leaps that are particularly suited to understanding how Underworld scenes operate as embedded commentary. Although the links, which represent other narratives, are not meant to take control of the frame narrative's plot, they nevertheless influence how the events of the plot and actions of different characters will be perceived by subtly introducing additional information for the audience to consider or seek out. For example, when a hero in an Underworld scene mentions seeing the afterlife judge Minos, the process of knowledge-recall primes the audience to envision an Underworld that is based on justice and the segregation of souls into separate areas determined by appointed judges. The addition of such a detail, like the judge of the dead, not only colors how the Underworld scene is interpreted but also prompts the audience to consider the scene's relationship to the frame narrative.

Because they are built using overlapping narratives, Underworld scenes allow the inclusion of multiple, simultaneous, and loosely related storylines alongside the primary narrative. Moreover, as self-contained narratives, Underworld scenes can exist in a more flexible time-space continuum, or chronotope, than the reality of the frame narrative might require. In the Underworld chronotope, time and space can be made specific or universal by activating different mythic paradigms that operate in alternate times and locations. In an Underworld scene, a reference to Theseus, for example, specifically calls to mind other heroic *katabaseis* as complementary and suggests a comparison between the heroes of those stories and the author's protagonist. They also "evoke in the audience a recollection of the other stories that have been told about the hero, and the associations connected with these other tales enhance the meaning of the individual tale" (Edmonds 2004, 10). Similarly, a reference to Tantalus brings to mind other eternally punished figures as well as the more general ideas of punishment after death and segregation of the dead in the Underworld.

The Underworld chronotope is both *synchronic* and *syntopic*, bringing characters from different places and time periods (both past and future) together so that they can be viewed all at once by the audience.[14] Underworld scenes allow multiple intertextual connections since they contain an archive of the entire past as well as imagined futures against which an author can reflect the issues and themes of his or her frame narrative. Because an Underworld scene follows certain, recognizable sequences, or what Kristeva would call "suprasegmental utterances," it can be considered a "bounded text" operating within a somewhat closed system of reference and therefore open to intertextual analysis.[15] Furthermore, the idea of progress, as would be assumed in historical and chronological reality, is put into the background while the visitor to the Underworld observes or is told about features of the Stygian space. Although the Underworld contains knowledge of the future, the information appears simultaneously with that of the past, and the visitor to the Underworld does not encounter it in a linear or urgently teleological fashion.

In such a diachronic collapse, multiple types of time exist simultaneously: the linear time of the protagonist visiting the Underworld, the eternal time of the power structure and landmarks (e.g., the halls of Hades), the repetitive time of the sinners who must endlessly perform their allotted punishments, and, in some cases, the circular time of souls who experience metempsychosis. Further, this multitude of time frames often becomes visible without perturbing the flow of the main plot of the frame narrative. After gaining the necessary information or wider historical perspective from the Underworld, the protagonist/narrator generally ends where he began. Thus, Odysseus returns from the *Nekuia* at his point of embarkation, Circe's island, where he only then receives explicit instructions on the next steps for his journey home, although he was supposed to receive this information in the Underworld from Tiresias. Similarly, in Hesiod's *Theogony*, the story of the generational struggles of the gods continues after the *Tartarographia*, with no direct effect on the plot of Zeus' rise to power, as if the Underworld episode never happened. These are just two examples of how Underworld scenes seem to exist in their own temporal bubbles that do not stretch the plot's time

---

[14] Gee (2020, 3–5) similarly highlights the importance of the audience's viewpoint, arguing that Underworlds by nature follow a "journey-vision" paradigm that contains linear and circular space, with the former referring to movement through terrain and the latter creating a space that gives a wider vision of the universe.

[15] A "bounded text" is a text which operates within a specific historical and social context (Kristeva 1980b, 38). For Kristeva, the "text" is by nature intertextual because it is always referential, whether to verbal utterance or recognizable situations.

linearly. The point of entry is chronologically the point of exit, so almost no time may seem to pass in the primary narrative's plot during the course of the digression into an Underworld scene.

From a narrative perspective, an Underworld scene's time distortion provides an opportunity to juxtapose the present storyline against related or even competing narratives using a technique called "side-shadowing," which allows the "actual" and the "possible" to be simultaneously present (Morson 1994, 117–119). Therefore, not only does an Underworld scene like a *katabasis* call to mind multiple Underworld stories with which to compare itself, but the characters within the Underworld also offer different potential realities against which to assess the protagonist. Seeing time and space all at once creates a constant tension between synchronic and diachronic narratives fighting for primacy. For example, the stories of Odysseus' peers as copresent narratives suggest several outcomes that were possible for Odysseus, ranging from no return (Achilles, Ajax) to disastrous return (Agamemnon). Such shadow narratives display a "simultaneity not *in* time but *of* times: we do not see contradictory actualities, but one possibility that was actualized and, at the same moment, another that could have been but was not" (Morson 1994, 118). By including an Underworld journey in a narrative, a single text can activate a network of texts, which all look to each other for meaning and also tap into the audience's expectations and conceptions of the afterlife. In this way, the author can direct the reading of his or her own work by suggesting specific narrative connections for the audience to consider. Underworld scenes become the author's tool within a narrative for literary and social criticism and an opportune moment of pause in the story for self-reflection because they are "synoptic" for the audience, giving a perfect vantage point for viewing the stories, issues, and traditions that are relevant for situating the author's work.

To use Underworld scenes as embedded commentary, authors must make their case for each scene's purpose in the details of how they construct them and take on the combined role of narrator, reader, and critic of their own work. By aligning themselves with their audience in this way, authors become partners in interpretation, nudging the audience to view their creations against whatever narratives they evoked while also accepting some loss of control over their work's reception. By operating under the premise that the purpose of Underworld scenes is to provide connectivity to other narratives for authorial commentary, scholars can more easily identify the mechanics of how such scenes are built and how they function as oases for contact between author and audience as well as between texts. As we shall see, ancient Greek Underworld scenes have a recurring set of story patterns and figures, and the inclusion or exclusion of expected elements brings different messages from the author into focus.

V. Conclusions: The Implications and Influence of Underworld Scenes

The consistency between descriptions and the pervasiveness of certain myth types within Underworld narratives suggest that Underworld scenes are a stable and unique genre of storytelling, whose purpose is to step outside of a work's main plot and connect the frame narrative to other stories. Such scenes are not limited to a particular genre, such as epic, although later Underworld scenes are often traceable to early Archaic epic through similarities in their Underworld depictions, which indicates that ancient authors and audiences had specific expectations in creating connections between their and others' Underworlds.[16]

As embedded narratives, Underworld scenes condense the actions and themes of the main story into an abbreviated space while also situating their primary narratives within a dynamic historical and literary tradition. By activating a network of texts with such scenes through allusions and narrative patterning, authors and artists can employ similar stories of ghostly encounter (*nekuia*), underworld journey (*katabasis*), eternal punishment, and reward for the blessed. The narratives connected through these linked features influence the interpretation of the frame narrative by opening up a dialogue between texts across time and genre. Furthermore, the crucial function of individual Underworld scenes can be gleaned from their locations within their frame narrative and from the relationships they establish with the narratives they evoke. The following chapters give analyses of individual Underworld scenes within their immediate narrative and temporal contexts, showing how each's embedded authorial commentary connects to audiences and promotes both reflection and revolutions of thought.

---

[16] This has led to such statements as "a mortal visiting the Underworld is an epic theme" (de Jong 2001, 271), although the Homeric epics do not contain any actual *katabaseis*, only scenes that have elements or figures that seem "katabatic" because they bring to mind the *katabasis* story pattern.

2

Afterlife Poetics and Homer's Heroic Underworlds

I. Introduction: The Heroic Underworld

As discussed in the previous chapter, scholars have had a difficult time defining Underworld scenes, since their variety and appearance across genres and time periods present challenges both of categorization and interpretation. Homer's epics, our earliest extant source of Underworld scenes, were highly influential and seem to have provided certain templates that were borrowed and developed by later authors. The Homeric poems present the audience with an Underworld suited to the world of heroes, whose lives and deeds are the central concern. The most famous epic Underworld scene is the *Nekuia*, which takes up the entirety of Book 11 of the *Odyssey*. Because of its length and placement in the *Odyssey*, it has often overshadowed the other Underworld scenes that are spread across the *Iliad* and *Odyssey*. As a result, the importance and impact of these other Underworld scenes have received less attention. In this chapter, I examine Homer's Underworlds as a group, bringing the lesser-known ones to the forefront to show how they interact with each other and the *Nekuia*. I argue that they are all networked to each other and perform a similar function of providing commentary on heroes and the nature of heroism by using the hypertextual poetics unique to Underworld scenes. I further argue that, as they are formulated, these Underworld scenes are examples of the "heroic Underworld scene" and offer a template for such

Life / Afterlife. Suzanne Lye, Oxford University Press. © Oxford University Press 2024.
DOI: 10.1093/9780197690239.003.0003

LIFE / AFTERLIFE

scenes, which were used and expanded on by later authors to explore key themes and ideas in their works.[1]

Heroic Underworld scenes tend to focus on a single hero's encounter with the world of the dead, usually on a quest mandated by a supernatural being to retrieve some necessary item or information that can only be obtained in the Underworld or in contact with ghosts.[2] The audience experiences the journey and its obstacles along with the hero from the first-person perspective of a mortal viewer, whose fear of the world of the dead, wonder at encountering the supernatural, and knowledge of Greek myth and religious beliefs are meant to resonate and activate connections. According to most scholars, the two primary forms of heroic Underworld scenes are *katabasis* and *necromancy*. Raymond Clark defines *katabasis* as a "Journey of the Dead made by a living person in the flesh who returns to our world to tell the tale," which he differentiates from "mere 'Visions of the Otherworld'" that might include descriptions of the Underworld or ghostly visitations (Clark 1979, 32). A *katabasis*, as the term implies, focuses on the descent into the Underworld by an individual who is almost always identified as a hero either by birth or deeds. Underworld scenes, particularly heroic *katabaseis*, have frequently been cast as a feature of epic poetry, with some scholars going so far as to call them "the most distinctive of epic conventions" (Gregory, Newman, and Meyers 2012, 441(iv)) and even a "characteristic trait of heroic biography" (Calvo Martínez 2000, 67). This association between epic poetry and Underworld stories is rooted in the fact that many Underworld journeys in myth are completed by heroes, whose stories are similarly central to the Homeric epics.

In the *Nekuia*'s extensive Underworld scene, Odysseus' description of his journey is similar to familiar mythic narratives of heroic *katabaseis*, such as those of Heracles, Theseus, and Orpheus (Calvo Martínez 2000). Such narratives were used by early philosophers, shamans, and wisdom practitioners to claim authority by associating themselves with extraordinary access to hidden knowledge (Benzi 2021, 89).[3] Odysseus' brush with the Underworld, while often identified as a *katabasis* because of the journey element of his

---

[1] The other major type is a "judgment-based" Underworld scene, which is the subject of the next chapter.

[2] For a discussion about this retrieval from the Underworld of specific items or hidden knowledge and the roots of the latter in the Archaic wisdom tradition, see Benzi (2021, 90–91).

[3] For a discussion of the shamanistic role Odysseus adopts in the *Nekuia*, particularly during the blood sacrifice to call the dead, see Bowra (1952, 78–79).

story, is not technically a *katabasis*, since he does not enter the Underworld itself. Instead, as the name of the episode implies, the *Nekuia*—a conversation with the dead—falls more firmly into the category of *necromancy*, the other major type of Underworld scene, which Daniel Ogden (2001, xix–xx) defines as "a communication with the dead in order to receive prophecy from them" that often involves interaction with ghosts and access to hidden information. Such conversations with the dead may be incited by a ritual, as in a religious context, or may happen unbidden, as in dreams. Most heroic Underworld scenes contain the underlying assumption that the hero will encounter ghosts and gain information from them or from their surroundings. Odysseus' goal in the *Nekuia* is necromancy, as he seeks out Tiresias to receive prophecy at Circe's command, yet his journey shares features with and, therefore, links to narratives of *katabasis* that were probably circulating during the composition of the poem.[4]

Despite the persistent association made by scholars between *katabasis* and epic, there are no true *katabaseis* in either of Homer's epics, according to the term's strict definition. There are, however, many scenes throughout the *Iliad* and the *Odyssey* that are reminiscent of famous myths of *katabasis* (and *nekuiai*), which the poet seems to expect the audience to know. The categorization of Underworld scenes as inherently "epic" or Homeric is a by-product not only of their popularity but also of textual survival. The confusion between *katabaseis* and *nekuiai* seems intentional by ancient authors.[5] Accepting Underworld scenes as simply a part of epic convention has obscured the possible reasons for *why* they have this association and *how* they create the impression of being "epic" and, therefore, authoritative. Important points that modern scholars have either missed or disregarded are that (1) there are multiple, somewhat conflicting Underworld scenes in the Homeric epics; (2) at least three Homeric Underworld scenes seem to be following predefined narrative conventions, perhaps copying an older rhetorical use of such scenes; and (3) other Archaic poems, particularly those by Hesiod and the *Homeric Hymn to Demeter* (which I will discuss in the next chapter) also use Underworld scenes in a similar fashion but for different purposes.

---

[4] For more on the tradition of *katabasis* narratives in ancient Greece, see Clark (1979), von der Mühll (1984), Edmonds (2004, 2021), Calvo Martínez (2000), and Benzi (2021).

[5] For an overview of this debate concerning the categorization of the *Nekuia*, see Nannini (2010, 267–277).

The overlap and inherent intertextuality between different types of afterlife depictions make the distinction between *katabasis* and necromancy difficult to sustain, and such separation does not seem to have been observed by ancient authors, who regularly treated these two broad types of Underworld encounters interchangeably. Homer's Underworld scenes are so complex and so integral to their protagonists' characterizations that they became natural models for later Greek writers who wanted to achieve the same popularity or claim the authority of these revered epics. What emerges by analyzing Underworld scenes in Homer and early Archaic poetry is a set of common features that make up the "poetics" of heroic Underworld scenes. These features allowed them to be recognizable and accessible as templates by later authors, who, in turn, expanded and adapted the scenes to highlight the heroes of their works and create hierarchies for mortals in the afterlife through judgment. Individual features that are common to both types of scenes persistently create connections rather than distinctions, suggesting that ancient authors almost always viewed *nekuiai* and *katabaseis* as being in conversation with each other. Thus, in examining early Underworld scenes, it would be more useful to adjust perspective and view the different types of scenes as inextricably connected and engaged in active dialogue with each other at all times. In the following sections, I examine key features and patterns from the heroic Underworld scenes in the *Iliad* and the *Odyssey* to show how such scenes perform intertextually and create conduits for communication between author and audience.

II. Homer's Interlocking Underworlds

The Homeric epics contain multiple heroic encounters with many Underworlds that are in active dialogue with each other, the *Nekuia* being the most famous of them. In the *Odyssey* alone, there are at least four Underworld scenes that give a detailed vision of possible afterlives, including in Books 4, 10, 11, and 24. They portray visions of afterlife society and conversations with ghosts or other supernatural beings. Interspersed throughout the epic, these Underworld scenes slow down the epic and give information that actively supports the poet's overall argument for an Odyssean type of heroism and *kleos*, which challenges those in the *Iliad*.

The *Odyssey*'s *Nekuia* occurs because Circe tells Odysseus to seek Tiresias' ghost for information about the future so he can continue his journey to Ithaca. Odysseus does this, but he also has many more interactions before and after this designated plot point. The extended conversations and visitations

Odysseus has in the Underworld with Elpenor, Anticlea, mythic female heroines, Heracles, and leaders from the Trojan War amount to extra scenes in the *Odyssey*, which do not have a clear purpose from the perspective of the main plot (Odysseus' return to Ithaca). Odysseus' encounter with his mother and the souls of heroines during the *Nekuia* does not directly pertain to his mission of traveling to the Underworld, but it does appeal to his Phaeacian hostess Queen Arete, who offers to increase his guest-gifts (*Od.* 11.335–341).[6] The poet has Odysseus spend a significant portion of the *Nekuia* naming heroines and describing their stories. From the perspective of Odysseus' journey home, nothing is overtly gained by this catalog. Immediately after Queen Arete's intervention, King Alcinous, her husband, steps in to shift attention away from the heroines and asks Odysseus to tell of his dead comrades from the Trojan War, which extends narrative time in the Underworld scenes further (*Od.* 11.362–376). Such seemingly tangential encounters, however, make up the greater part of the *Nekuia* and thus cannot be treated as subordinate to the main heroic action or easily discarded for not advancing the plot. In the *Nekuia*, for example, Elpenor's ghost firmly establishes and verifies the Underworld *chronotope* to both Odysseus and the audience and highlights the extraordinary journey that Odysseus is taking to the land of the dead. Similarly, the Underworld scenes in *Iliad* 23 (Patroclus' ghost), *Odyssey* 4 (Menelaus' afterlife in Elysium), and *Odyssey* 24 (the suitors' descent) occur at crucial points in their poems' narratives but often have not been categorized as actively interacting with the *Nekuia*.

The conundrum of how to treat the seemingly nonessential encounters within and outside of the famous *Nekuia* can be resolved by analyzing how they function and what they add to the characterization of Odysseus and his journey. To do this, one must look at the connectivity of these mini-episodes as well as how the author sets up links and anchor points to create a heroic Underworld scene that communicates his vision for his particular hero and

---

[6] Doherty (1995, 65–86) argues that Odysseus uses the catalog of heroines to appeal directly to Arete, who acts as a narrative double for Penelope, recalling scenes elsewhere when she is rebuked by Telemachus (*Od.* 1.258–259) and when she faces the disguised Odysseus upon his return to Ithaca. Doherty says the immediate interruption of Arete's speech by Echeneus and Alcinous indicates that she spoke out of turn, since the latter as king was the person who had authority to grant guest gifts. The exchange between these characters creates the opportunity to extend the Underworld scene through the direct request of the internal audience. More recently, Arft (2022, 110–116) discusses Arete as an underworld queen figure whose interrogation helps frame Odysseus' heroism and afterlife fame. Arft (2022, 234–239) concludes that her role in the epic is to frame Odysseus as a *nostos* hero whose *kleos* comes more from his return than from his deeds at Troy.

poem. The following discussion of the *Nekuia* looks at how the narratives evoked by distinct encounters—especially with the ghosts of Elpenor, Anticlea, mythic heroines, and Heracles—expand the audience's view of Odysseus' character and promote a vision of Odysseus as an exceptional hero.

The Homeric epics present many afterlife possibilities: they assign a mindless existence to most ghosts (*Od.* 10.495), a special afterlife in the Elysian plain to Menelaus (*Od.* 4.561–569), a companionable society to the Greek heroes of the Trojan War (*Od.* 24.1–204), and an existence of isolated despair to the unburied (*Od.* 11.57–78, Elpenor's ghost; *Il.* 23.69–74, Patroclus' ghost). [7] The difference between these afterlife depictions in Homer and those of later poets was primarily one of emphasis. Before looking at these later ones, however, it is important first to create a baseline of understanding, which we can do by analyzing how the Homeric Underworld scenes operate.

As discussed in the previous chapter, Underworld scenes overtly signal their beginnings and ends, while their middle sections show the most variability. Entry into the Underworld, for both long and short Underworld scenes, involves disorientation and the distortion of reality so that different expectations of time and space temporarily supersede those of everyday life. In the Underworld, chronological time pauses and the linear movement through space cannot easily be tracked, as the protagonist and audience reorient themselves into a new frame of normality. By transporting the protagonist and the audience to this alien, but not necessarily unfamiliar place,[8] the author strips away the "givens" of everyday life and reality and allows a new space-time continuum, or chronotope, to emerge.[9] The Underworld chronotope allows for diachronic collapse and collocating people, in the form of ghosts, from different time periods. The presence of these ghosts and the stories they share in this syntopic and synchronic environment give the audience a synoptic view of the hero's journey, which would not otherwise be accessible. The changed chronotope is apparent in the Homeric Underworld scenes, and its strong presence helps to underscore the motivations and character of the hero.

---

[7] For more on the contradictions in Homeric Underworlds, see Burkert (1985), Sourvinou-Inwood (1981, 1983, 1995), Bremmer (2002), and Edmonds (2021, 2011a).

[8] The scholarship on the Underworld and eschatology in Greek religion is extensive, and its conceptualization by scholars can be traced through works by Rohde (1925), Sourvinou-Inwood (1981, 1995), Bremmer (1983, 2002), Burkert (1985), and Edmonds (2004, 2011a, 2011b).

[9] For more on the term *chronotope* and how it is used in literature, see Branham (2002), Bemong (2010), Dunn (2002), Nightingale (2002), Morson (1994), and Bakhtin (1981).

In the *Odyssey*, there are several episodes referring to the Underworld and afterlife journey that use similar time and space markers to disorient the reader and establish the unique chronotope that is an essential part of the poetics of the Underworld. Thus, the idea of "Homer's Underworld" as simply being the *Nekuia* episode needs to be reconsidered and replaced with the idea of "Homer's Underworlds." The two most famous epic scenes that illustrate a multiplicity of Underworlds in the Homeric poems are the *Nekuia* in Book 11 and the descent of the suitors into Hades in Book 24, with the latter often treated as secondary and supplementary rather than a distinct Underworld scene. To these examples, however, I would also add Circe's instructions to Odysseus at the end of Book 10 and the prediction of Menelaus' transportation to the Elysian Field in Book 4. From the *Iliad*, I would include the visitation of Patroclus' ghost in Book 23 and Hades' alarm at Poseidon's earthquake in Book 20. Each of these Underworld scenes locally reinforce the events immediately surrounding them in the narrative; together, however, they also support the poet's larger argument for each epic, particularly in relation to the status of their primary heroes. Through them, we can see how heroic Underworld scenes can characterize heroes and mark them as special in ways that complement and highlight their actions in the frame narrative. The echo of their greatness in an Underworld scene reinforces any deeds portrayed elsewhere, adding extra layers of proof to the poet's argument for the worthiness of their subjects.

III. Building the Heroic Underworld: Circe's Nekuia and the Nekuia

To illustrate the poetic construction and networking of Homer's heroic Underworld scenes, I center Odysseus' *Nekuia* as a reference point in the discussion of each scene, since it is the most extensive Underworld scene in Homer. Moreover, it has the most complete set of elements for a heroic Underworld scene, including a clear transition from the "real world" chronotope into that of the Underworld, which makes it a good benchmark. Odysseus' (and the audience's) first introduction to the Underworld chronotope, however, does not occur in Book 11 when Odysseus sets sail from Circe's island, but rather in Book 10 when Circe forecasts Odysseus' journey to see the shades. Already, we can see that Homer's most emblematic Underworld scene enters the audience's view as an intertext with another Underworld scene, which

48   LIFE / AFTERLIFE

becomes its main and most immediate (but not only) referent (Clark 1979, 53–54; von der Mühll 1938).

Listening to Circe in Book 10, Odysseus envisions what his journey will be like ahead of time, and we as the audience are simultaneously taken along for this "narrative within the narrative" as witnesses to their exchange. Although Circe's story seems fairly straightforward, it is important to remember that her Underworld account is still *reported speech* told by the narrator Odysseus in the voice of Circe to an audience of Phaeacians (*Od.* 10.503). The *Nekuia*, which describes the same Underworld journey that the audience heard in Book 10, is also narrated by Odysseus, but this time in his own voice as his personal recollection of the journey based on first-hand experience (ἡμεῖς δ᾽ ὅπλα ἕκαστα πονησάμενοι κατὰ νῆα ἥμεθα, "and we sat down in the ship, after arranging each piece of equipment," *Od.* 11.9–10). Although the two accounts occur in different books, they are presented as the same story, that is, Odysseus' journey to the edge of the Underworld. They are, however, two *versions* of the same story, meant to be considered together like variations of a theme in music. Side by side, they illustrate the malleability of the Underworld scene in different contexts as well as the interplay between author and audience as they negotiate their expectations of each other.

By presenting his Underworld encounter as a quest mandated and facilitated by the gods, Odysseus projects a persona to the Phaeacians that is at odds with the reality of his appearance as a shipwrecked wanderer, whose status is under question when he arrives. The Underworld scene, more than the other episodes from the *Odyssey's Apologos* (Books 9–12), underscores his status as a hero, leader, and favorite of the gods, subtly making the argument for why it is in the interest of the Phaeacians to help him when he has very little to offer them. As a clever narrator, Odysseus manipulates how he and other characters in his story are seen by his Phaeacian audience and uses his double narration of the Underworld scene—first through Circe's voice and then his own—to build credibility. A closer reading and comparison show how the differences between the two scenes further contribute to a sense of disorientation and otherness during the second scene's beginning because the landmarks in Odysseus' and Circe's versions do not correspond.

Odysseus' report of Circe's vision of the Underworld draws the Phaeacian audience in on an intellectual level while his subsequent, first-person account attempts to affect them on a more visceral, personal level. Additionally, Odysseus presents himself as someone who has wisdom that is pertinent to his listeners and can give them valuable insights into the hidden space of the Underworld. When he speaks to Elpenor's ghost, a transitional character hovering between his former life and the afterlife, Odysseus establishes a new

Afterlife Poetics and Homer's Heroic Underworlds 49

baseline for reality, which includes the ability by him, a living man, to talk and interact with ghosts and the supernatural. In his storytelling, Odysseus presents himself as someone with whom his audience can sympathize but also as someone who has special access to supernatural powers and may, in fact, be superior to them, regardless of appearance.

After Circe's initial directive to go to Hades in Book 10, the narrative turns the audience's attention to the concrete aspects of the journey: the ship, the details verifying the crew's arrival at the prescribed destination, and the rituals needed to evoke the souls of the dead. Circe tells Odysseus to keep his attention on the handling of the ship and to trust the divinely sent wind, a non-human force, to take him to the right place, so he only needs to take action when he sees certain landmarks. She says:

"διογενὲς Λαερτιάδη, πολυμήχαν᾿ Ὀδυσσεῦ,
μή τί τοι ἡγεμόνος γε ποθὴ παρὰ νηῒ μελέσθω·
ἱστὸν δὲ στήσας ἀνά θ᾿ ἱστία λευκὰ πετάσσας
ἧσθαι· τὴν δέ κέ τοι πνοιὴ βορέαο φέρῃσιν." (*Od.* 10.504–507)

"Godly son of Laertes, many-wiled Odysseus,
don't let the lack of a pilot for your ship concern you at all;
but after setting up your mast and unfurling your white sails, sit down,
and let the gust of the North Wind (Boreas) carry [the ship] along for you."

In this passage, Circe tells Odysseus to focus first on the mundane human aspects of setting up his ship for sailing but then to rely on forces outside his direct control to carry him to his destination. The hidden forces directing the journey themselves create a feeling of uncertainty and removal from reality. Odysseus is then told vaguely that he would "pass through Ocean" (*Od.* 10.508) and that he must look out for a specific set of landmarks to gauge his position. [10]

Circe does not tell him how long the journey will take him, either in time or distance, but she does introduce a series of geographical features with the word ἔνθα that will indicate he has arrived. The deictic adverb ἔνθα typically provides spatial and temporal information; it can mean either "there" (in place) or "then" (in time). Since it directs the audience's gaze in specific directions, ἔνθα should provide clarity. In Underworld scenes, however, it most often means *both* "there and then," which paradoxically disorients even

---

[10] In this instance, "Ocean" not only signifies the body of water but also the very boundary of the world.

as it intends to specify. The word ἔνθα, common to many early Underworld scenes, allows a poet to pile on information catalogically, such that names and objects are set next to each other with little context or explanation from the author. The deictic ἔνθα itself signals a different, more vivid mode of storytelling, one from the traveler's first-person viewpoint, which takes in and reveals information to the audience in a paratactic stream of information without much explanation. In Underworld poetics, this "ἔνθα-mode" of storytelling is not meant to visualize a map of the space that others may follow but to draw attention to concepts and themes that are relevant to the narrative. In the Underworld, this form of storytelling turns the audience's attention away from the action at hand toward deeper thematic considerations by steeping the audience in seemingly random local details.[11] The arrangement of the ἔνθα signifier and the pieces of information it flags demonstrate how important it is as a tool for constructing Underworld scenes. As seen in the following passage, the word ἔνθα creates nodes in the description, signaling a change in direction, either of the viewer's perspective or of an agent's activity. Here, Circe's instructions give a distinct list of markers as well as spatial dimensions intended to orient Odysseus upon his arrival at Persephone's grove so that he can visualize it and perform his ritual correctly:

> ἀλλ' ὁπότ' ἂν δὴ νηΐ δι' Ὠκεανοῖο περήσῃς,
> ἔνθ' ἀκτή τε λάχεια καὶ ἄλσεα Περσεφονείης
> μακραί τ' αἴγειροι καὶ ἰτέαι ὠλεσίκαρποι, (510)
> νῆα μὲν αὐτοῦ κέλσαι ἐπ' Ὠκεανῷ βαθυδίνῃ,
> αὐτὸς δ' εἰς Ἀΐδεω ἰέναι δόμον εὐρώεντα.
> ἔνθα μὲν εἰς Ἀχέροντα Πυριφλεγέθων τε ῥέουσι
> Κώκυτός θ', ὃς δὴ Στυγὸς ὕδατός ἐστιν ἀπορρώξ,
> πέτρη τε ξύνεσίς τε δύω ποταμῶν ἐριδούπων· (515)
> ἔνθα δ' ἔπειθ', ἥρως, χριμφθεὶς πέλας, ὥς σε κελεύω,
> βόθρον ὀρύξαι ὅσον τε πυγούσιον ἔνθα καὶ ἔνθα,
> ἀμφ' αὐτῷ δὲ χοὴν χεῖσθαι πᾶσιν νεκύεσσι,
> πρῶτα μελικρήτῳ, μετέπειτα δὲ ἡδέϊ οἴνῳ,
> τὸ τρίτον αὖθ' ὕδατι· ἐπὶ δ' ἄλφιτα λευκὰ παλύνειν. (520)
> (*Od.* 10.508–520)

---

[11] Felson (2004, 253–255) would classify the deictic use of ἔνθα in this passage as "deixis *am Phantasma*: fictional deixis" in which objects are imaginatively brought into existence by the act of pretending to designate them. Of course, there are also elements of "ocular deixis" as well since Odysseus points out some objects that one might see in the real world.

Afterlife Poetics and Homer's Heroic Underworlds

But when you should indeed make passage through Ocean with your ship,
there is an overgrown promontory and also the sacred groves of Persephone
as well as tall poplars and the willows that shed their fruit
 early, (510)
on the one hand, beach your ship **there** upon [the shore of] deep-eddying
Ocean, **but** you yourself go to the dank house of Hades.
There Pyriphlegethon and Cocytus, which is a branch of the River Styx,
flow into Acheron, and there is also a rock and the meeting of two loudly
 resounding rivers; (515)
and there, hero, **when** you have approached nearby [this location], as I
command you, dig a pit of about a cubit in each direction **there** and **there**,
and around it pour a libation for all the dead, first with honey mixed with
milk, and **then after** with sweet wine, and third, **in turn**, with water; and
over that, sprinkle white barley.

The repetition of deictic markers such as ἔνθα builds an internal framework
that cues the audience to consider different aspects about the Underworld
space: the space, the chronology, the people, and the hero. The passage is held
together additionally by the stacked μέν . . . δέ . . . μέν . . . δέ construction,
creating the sense of consecutive yet contrasting actions. The "μέν . . . δέ" back-
and-forth pattern alternates between describing the landscape as a whole and
Odysseus' specific actions. The first μέν (*Od.* 11.511) and first δέ (*Od.* 11.512) separate the verification of the location and Odysseus' personal actions in finding
the ritual site. The αὐτοῦ after the first μέν (*Od.* 11.511) correlates with the first
ἔνθα (*Od.* 11.509), bringing the description of the landscape into the μέν clause
where he needs to beach his ship. The second μέν (*Od.* 11.513) introduces general identifying features in Hades. These not only mark the right location
for Odysseus but also situate the scene in a familiar mythic setting: the traditional stories of *katabasis* and necromancy predating or coexisting alongside
the Homeric epics.[12] The second δέ (*Od.* 11.516) narrows the vantage point of

---

[12] As stated earlier, it seems clear that the Homeric poems inherited certain features of an
Underworld narrative type from a specific set of images familiar to the audience and whose
sources may include shamanistic literature (Bowra 1952, 78–79). Ekroth (2018, 51) argues
that Odysseus' pit ritual may have been borrowed from the Hittite-Hurrian sphere in
the Eastern Mediterranean rather than being originally part of Greek religious practices.
Norden (1926, 5) and von der Mühl (1938) convincingly argue that an early epic on the subject of Heracles' *katabasis* to Hades existed and may have been known to several early poets,
including Homer. That is not to say that Homer's Underworld was purely derivative since
the poet may indeed have been the first to use the Underworld narrative type in the way
that we see his successors do, as an embedded scene and literary digression. Nevertheless,

52   LIFE / AFTERLIFE

the hero's actions to his immediate vicinity, away from the larger, sweeping
view of the scene presented by μέν.

The inclusion of ἔπειθ' (*Od.* 11.516) seems redundant but, in fact, performs
two functions. First, it reinforces ἔνθα in a connective rather than solely ad-
verbial function. It is what Anna Bonifazi (2008, 35–36) calls a "discourse
marker" with a pragmatic, procedural meaning that cues the audience to a
context outside of the word's meaning.[13] Second, it emphasizes the spatial aspect of ἔνθα in this passage as separate from its temporal meaning. The word
ἔνθα is almost synonymous with ἔπειτα because they both contain temporal
scope. In combination, they are not just synonymous but can also take on
procedural meanings, especially in relation to other words, thus acting as discourse markers that set up a noncausal sequence of items (as opposed to propositional discourse markers). When placed together, the two adverbs bring
the ideas of space and time to the forefront, again highlighting entrance into
the Underworld chronotope with the author creating a metaliterary moment
to guide the audience through the set of directions and images. Besides the
ἔπειθ', another key indicator that this discourse marker is being employed in
this passage is the αὖθ' (*Od.* 10.520), which is succeeded a few lines later by
αὐτὰρ ἐπὴν (*Od.* 10.526). The occurrence of these two words in proximity
makes the temporal gap "verbally explicit," as Bonifazi describes it, because
the αὐτὰρ ἔπειτα acts as a "performative break that coincides with the suggestion of a visual shift—the mind's eye, of course—that is at that moment
needed by the receivers" (Bonifazi 2008, 49). Considering the context of
Odysseus walking his listeners through his steps into the Underworld, the
deictic sequence of ἔνθα coupled with the occurrences of αὐτὰρ and αὐτὰρ
ἔπειτα all function beyond their individual definitional meanings to build
the Underworld chronotope by guiding the audience through the exercise
of verifying the location as indeed the ancient Greek underworld they were
expecting (with some additional twists relevant to the narrator's goals).

The last two instances of ἔνθα with the relative pronoun ὅσον ("as much
as"), indicating quantity, along with the unit πυγούσιον ("cubit") delineate
a measurable distance in distinctly human terms as opposed to the larger
landscapes introduced by the previous ἔνθα-markers. As a group, therefore,

---

Homer's vision of the Underworld seems intended to activate multiple Underworld
narratives for his audiences ranging from the necromantic to the katabatic.

[13] Bonifazi (2008, 36) defines "discourse markers" as the group of words in a sentence that do
not contribute to the meaning of an utterance (propositional meaning) but rather refer to
how the utterance should be received (pragmatic, procedural meaning).

Afterlife Poetics and Homer's Heroic Underworlds

the ἔνθα-markers have a funneling effect, taking the audience from the sight of the promontory at the edge of Ocean to a concrete piece of earth, which is where the central ritual of the episode will occur. The area above the pit is designated by ἐπί ("over"), orienting the audience into a three-dimensional view by adding a sense of vertical space to the horizontal space created by the ἔνθα-markers.

When ἔνθα appears again, its meaning shifts from spatial to temporal, correlating with the ἐπὴν in 526, but it still introduces a directional message:

αὐτὰρ ἐπὴν εὐχῇσι λίσῃ κλυτὰ ἔθνεα νεκρῶν,
ἔνθ᾽ ὄϊν ἀρνειὸν ῥέζειν θῆλύν τε μέλαιναν
εἰς Ἔρεβος στρέψας, αὐτὸς δ᾽ ἀπονόσφι τραπέσθαι
ἱέμενος ποταμοῖο ῥοάων· (*Od.* 10.526–529)

But when you have supplicated the glorious race of the dead with prayers,
then sacrifice a full-grown ram and a black ewe, turning
them towards Erebus, but you yourself turn away from them
making your way towards the streams of the river.

This high level of local detail related to direction and location is a crucial aspect of setting up the Underworld chronotope because it gives a sense of familiarity and tangibility to the space in what is otherwise a strange, unreal, and intangible place, imagined to be distant from everyday reality. The specificity of Circe's directions also proclaims that these small, somewhat obscure cues have important meanings.[14]

Besides giving hidden signals to the audience, Circe's directions also generate a sense of anticipation so that the audience looks out for the particular landmarks and rituals she describes in the second account, Odysseus' "real" Underworld voyage, the *Nekuia*. Interestingly, Odysseus does not confirm the landmarks that Circe names but lists a new set of spatial and temporal markers. This leaves a gap between the author's actual narrative and the

---

[14] The *Odyssey* has several ἔνθα narrative sequences, which generally occur when a character is recounting an adventure in the past. Some examples in the *Odyssey* include Nestor's description of the heroes dying in Troy (3.109–111) and the encounters with the Cicones (9.39–75), the Lotus-Eaters (9.82–104), and the Cyclops (9.105–236). The ἔνθα mode of description is sometimes used in *ekphrasis*, although it only appears once in the famous "Shield of Achilles" passage to point out a particular scene on the shield (*Il.* 18.497). No other scenes outside of the Underworld, however, have such densely packed usages of ἔνθα to describe an environment or temporal sequence of encountering objects.

audience's expectations, a dissonant space breaking the contract of story-telling and therefore creating a pause in the proceedings that the audience must reckon with.

Odysseus tells the journey to Hades as experienced from his perspective, although he often keeps the same words that Circe used, thereby linking the two passages intertextually so that they are "heard" together through the course of the narration.[15] This Underworld scene, which can be called "Circe's *nekuia*," shadows the *Nekuia* as an active *para-narrative* that is linked hypertextually and meant to be read in conjunction with it.[16] The shift of the verbs from infinitives with imperative force (κέλσαι, ἰέναι, ὀρύξαι, χεῖσθαι) in Circe's *nekuia* to first or third person (ἐκέλσαμεν, ἤομεν, ὄρυξα, χεόμην) in the *Nekuia*, where actors in the ritual are named or indicated, personalizes the account while also creating a strong connection between the two passages. The repetition of these verbs, with similar shifts in each of person and mood, anchors the scenes to one other, creating a two-way link that strengthens the relationship between the scenes at the word level.

Book 11 of the *Odyssey* begins with Odysseus and his crew following Circe's instructions to the letter, actively setting up the mast and sail before taking their seats (ἐν δ' ἱστὸν τιθέμεσθα καὶ ἱστία νηΐ μελαίνῃ, / ἐν δὲ τὰ μῆλα λαβόντες ἐβήσαμεν, "and we set up the mast and the sails in the black ship, and in it we embarked taking the sheep, *Od.* 11.3–4). The hero, as narrator, re-iterates that his voyage is specially marked by the gods when he makes Circe an active agent, who provides the wind in his sails (ἡμῖν δ' αὖ κατόπισθε νεὸς κυανοπρῴροιο / ἴκμενον οὖρον ἵει πλησίστιον, ἐσθλὸν ἑταῖρον, / Κίρκη ἐϋπλόκαμος, δεινὴ θεὸς αὐδήεσσα, "Fair-tressed Circe, fierce goddess who speaks in a human voice, sent for us, in turn, a favorable sail-filling breeze, as a goodly companion, blowing behind the ship with the dark prow," *Od.* 11.6–8). This interplay between what the gods provide and what humans do continues into the next line, in which Odysseus' crew looks after their rigging while the wind continues to drive them to their destination (ἡμεῖς δ' ὅπλα ἕκαστα πονησάμενοι κατὰ νῆα / ἥμεθα· τὴν δ' ἄνεμός τε κυβερνήτης τ' ἴθυνε, "and after we took pains to arrange each piece of equipment, we sat down in the ship; and both the wind and pilot drove it on a straight course," *Od.* 11.9–10). Already in this passage, however, Odysseus the narrator has begun to alter the

---

[15] For more on repeated and intratextually referenced passages in Homer, see Burgess (2010), Marks (2010), and Tsagalis (2010).

[16] For more on how *para-narratives* sit alongside the main narrative, see Alden (2000, 2017).

story by the addition of a pilot (κυβερνήτης). Earlier, Circe had said a guide was unnecessary and all the crew needed to do was sit back and let the North Wind carry them to their destination (*Od.* 10.505–507). He then inserts further details, such as information about the environment and the Cimmerians' land, that expand on Circe's description of the journey to Hades while also refocusing it through *chronotopic* markers and other figures that reference information and myths outside of the immediate version of the story. The result is a multilayered, intertextual, and interactive narrative experience that prompts the audience to recall and reflect on other versions of Underworld scenes both within the *Odyssey* and elsewhere.

IV. Building the Chronotope in the Nekuia

There is no doubt that the *Odyssey*'s central Underworld scene is the *Nekuia*, comprising all of Book 11. In it, the poet accomplishes several important things in addition to creating a major hinge point in the epic from which the narrative drives toward Odysseus' inevitable *nostos*. The Underworld scene here serves to underscore the aspects that make Odysseus, as a hero, unique from other heroes, particularly his peers on the battlefield at Troy and the ones who also completed a *nostos*. The *Nekuia* is a purpose-driven narrative, therefore, which frames Odysseus' character and fixes his status as a hero.

The *Nekuia* starts with a sharp focus on how Odysseus reacts to his environment, including how disoriented he feels while transitioning into the Underworld chronotope. The narrative accomplishes this through details about light and location and then, during the central portions of the narrative, through Odysseus' conversations with ghosts. At the beginning of Book 11, the narrative emphasizes physical disorientation through the removal of those features—light, the sun, sky, and stars—that signify location and the passage of time.[17] On top of this, another disorienting feature is that Circe's major landmarks are missing from Odysseus' account—either he sees something different from what Circe described or he, as a storyteller, is building on her description by adding observations most relevant to him and his audience. Despite the omissions and additions, Circe's *nekuia* is constantly

---

[17] Plato notes in *Timaeus* 38c6 that, for the Greeks, these particular heavenly bodies define and preserve time. Ustinova (2009, 13–52) discusses the role of sensory deprivation in narratives, particularly caves and underground caverns like those leading into the Underworld.

present in Odysseus' as a shadow narrative that informs and adds layers to his account while also flagging his bravery by continually highlighting the strangeness and disorienting nature of his journey. The disconnect and disorientation between the accounts make Odysseus appear very human, even as he undertakes a superhuman journey. Judging by their strong reactions to the news, the crew sees the upcoming journey as nearly impossible:

ὣς ἐφάμην, τοῖσιν δὲ κατεκλάσθη φίλον ἦτορ,
ἑζόμενοι δὲ κατ' αὖθι γόων τίλλοντό τε χαίτας:
ἀλλ' οὐ γάρ τις πρῆξις ἐγίγνετο μυρομένοισιν.
(*Od.* 10.566–568)

Thus I spoke, and the spirit inside my crew was broken,
And sitting down there, they groaned and tore their hair in grief,
But no good result came to those weeping.

The crew here vividly recalls the emotion of the hero himself, who had a similar reaction when Circe informed him of his impending journey:

ὣς ἔφατ', αὐτὰρ ἐμοί γε κατεκλάσθη φίλον ἦτορ:
κλαῖον δ' ἐν λεχέεσσι καθήμενος, οὐδέ νύ μοι κῆρ
ἤθελ' ἔτι ζώειν καὶ ὁρᾶν φάος ἠελίοιο. (*Od.* 10.496–498)

Thus she spoke, and truly my spirit was broken;
And I sat, crying on the bed, nor did my heart even now
Still want to live and see the light of the sun.

By describing dying as the inability to see the sun, Odysseus foreshadows the first-person account he tells of the journey in Book 11. Odysseus and his crew reluctantly follow Circe's orders, crying all the time, as they embarked (ἐπὶ νῆα θοὴν καὶ θῖνα θαλάσσης / ἤομεν ἀχνύμενοι θαλερὸν κατὰ δάκρυ χέοντες, "we went to the swift ship and the seashore, grieving and shedding big tears," *Od.* 10.569–570).

Whereas Circe's account foretelling the route was more focused on spatial landmarks, Odysseus frames his narrative with time, particularly noting the setting of the sun after a full day's travel as the advent of a shadowy darkness that continues to be a topic of conversation throughout the *Nekuia* (τῆς δὲ πανημερίης τέταθ' ἱστία ποντοπορούσης. / δύσετό τ' ἠέλιος σκιόωντό τε πᾶσαι ἀγυιαί, "and the sails of the ship were stretched full all day long; and the sun

Afterlife Poetics and Homer's Heroic Underworlds

set, and all the paths fell dark," *Od.* 11.11–12). [18] He follows this with a description of the Cimmerians, a group whose presence signals that Odysseus is still in the human realm near civilization. He emphasizes, however, the temporal and spatial strangeness of their environment, which has the sense of being otherworldly:

> ἡ δ' ἐς πείραθ' ἵκανε βαθυρρόου Ὠκεανοῖο.
> ἔνθα δὲ Κιμμερίων ἀνδρῶν δῆμός τε πόλις τε,
> ἠέρι καὶ νεφέλῃ κεκαλυμμένοι· οὐδέ ποτ' αὐτοὺς (15)
> Ἠέλιος φαέθων καταδέρκεται ἀκτίνεσσιν,
> οὔθ' ὁπότ' ἂν στείχῃσι πρὸς οὐρανὸν ἀστερόεντα,
> οὔθ' ὅτ' ἂν ἂψ ἐπὶ γαῖαν ἀπ' οὐρανόθεν προτράπηται,
> ἀλλ' ἐπὶ νὺξ ὀλοὴ τέταται δειλοῖσι βροτοῖσι. (*Od.* 11.13–19)

> And [the ship] reached the end of deep-flowing Ocean.
> And **there** are the people and city of Cimmerian men,
> who have been concealed in a misty cloud; nor **ever** does **Helios**,
> shining with his rays, look down upon them,
> neither **when he** proceeds toward the starry sky,
> nor **when** he turns to go back to the earth from the sky,
> but **night** in its entirety is spread over wretched mortals.

Odysseus clearly defines the Cimmerians as mortal men (Κιμμερίων ἀνδρῶν, 11.14), but they are presented as a borderland people living in a transitional space between the norms of reality and that of the Underworld chronotope. [19] This concern with elements of light and darkness as well as with time sequencing recurs at several other points in the middle of the narrative as well, highlighting Odysseus' separation from the living world and

---

[18] The topic of light and darkness recurs in Odysseus' conversations with the ghosts of Elpenor (11.57), Tiresias (11.93–94), and Anticlea (11.155–156) as well as in his encounter with the eidolon of Heracles (11.619).

[19] Scholars from antiquity associated these people with the historical Cimmerians, who were thought to be located in the far north because of their long nights and were described by Herodotus as occupying the region north of the Black Sea and Caucasus during the eighth century BCE (Herodotus, *Histories*, 4.11–12). Heubeck and Hoekstra (1990, 77–78) argue that the Cimmerians' historical reality has little bearing on their presence in the *Odyssey*, since what is being described in the *Nekuia* is a mythical geography. Their presence in the narrative functions on multiple levels, both to give another landmark of the "beyond" and further underscore Odysseus as exceptional beyond other humans in what he witnessed and did.

also signaling his presence in a type of scene that would have been familiar to the poet's audience from their traditional myths and religious beliefs—a katabatic visit to the Underworld.

Upon arrival, Odysseus meets the ghost of his shipmate Elpenor and again highlights the darkness of the region (Ἐλπῆνορ, πῶς ἦλθες ὑπὸ ζόφον ἠερόεντα; "Elpenor, how did you come under the dank gloom?" *Od.* 11.57) before expressing his disorientation at having his shipmate arrive earlier than he did (ἔφθης πεζὸς ἰὼν ἢ ἐγὼ σὺν νηῒ μελαίνῃ, "going by foot, you arrived faster than I with my dark ship," *Od.* 11.58). The question not only represents Odysseus' natural curiosity but also calls on the audience to make note of the environment, as it is the first explicit acknowledgment of the spatial and temporal distortions that pervade the Underworld chronotope.

Elpenor's ghost acts as a bridge between the two chronotopes and makes the audience feel comfortable with the discrepancies. Of course, Odysseus is still in an imaginary landscape talking to a ghost, but the figure of Elpenor normalizes the interaction. When Elpenor's ghost explains that he died the night before by falling from Circe's roof, it seems to make sense that he, so recently dead, would be the closest ghost to the shore where Odysseus lands. It also seems logical that new arrivals to the Underworld would be in the same physical location. Elpenor acknowledges the different chronotopes and helps both Odysseus and the audience make the transition into the Underworld. Elpenor's first job as a character, therefore, is to indicate the differences between the Underworld and reality by shocking Odysseus into remarking on the strangeness of his comrade's presence. Elpenor's position in space and in the text also emphasizes the location and movement of Odysseus into the Underworld, suggesting that the linear time and space of the real world intersects the eternal time of the Underworld at specific points.[20] By intertwining these strands of time, the author repositions the character in his own story and resolves the disorientation by allowing him to move between different strings of time. This temporary overlap and movement between chronotopes give the author a way for his hero to navigate back to his own place in the story but with new knowledge and perspectives gained from encounters with the other strands of time. This happens because alternate,

---

[20] Purves' (2006, 181–195) conclusions of "falling to one's death" as a temporal marker in the *Iliad* can also be applied in the *Odyssey*. She argues for two basic time frames, mortal and immortal, which are experienced by humans and gods, respectively. I suggest a third time frame which occurs in the Underworld, which has elements of both of these other times and which produces multiple levels of narrative time operating simultaneously.

viable outcomes for the protagonist come to light as real possibilities for the narrative direction. Odysseus' grief over the Underworld journey and statement about not still seeing the light of day come to fruition (*Od.* 10.497–498). The poet here also suggests that Odysseus could end his journey in the Underworld (i.e., never return), meeting a fate similar to those of various souls he encounters in the episode, such as Elpenor, Agamemnon, Achilles, Ajax, and Heracles.

Elpenor took the "quick" route to the Underworld by accident the day before, but he ends up at the same entry point as Odysseus in the present moment. Since Elpenor is the last person to die in the main narrative, he is still hovering at the threshold of Hades and can act as a link between Odysseus' diachronic world and the synchronic Underworld. The poet signals the importance of the Underworld chronotope through his placement of this encounter with Elpenor first.[21] The conversation about how and when individuals arrive in the Stygian space prepares the audience for the fact that characters from multiple time periods are about to appear.

This same strategy is employed elsewhere and can most clearly be seen in the shorter Underworld scene in Book 24 of the *Odyssey*, the "little *nekuia*," which also starts with chronotopic marking. While Odysseus' transition into the Underworld chronotope emphasizes disruptions in the temporal field, the suitors' entry focuses more on spatial anomalies. The ghosts of the suitors traverse rough, dark terrain. The scene starts with the god Hermes in his role as psychopomp with special emphasis on his influence over men's consciousness and perception (Ἑρμῆς δὲ ψυχὰς Κυλλήνιος ἐξεκαλεῖτο / ἀνδρῶν μνηστήρων· ἔχε δὲ ῥάβδον μετὰ χερσὶ / καλὴν χρυσείην, τῇ τ' ἀνδρῶν ὄμματα θέλγει, / ὧν ἐθέλει, τοὺς δ' αὖτε καὶ ὑπνώοντας ἐγείρει, "Cyllenian Hermes called forth the souls of the suitors; and he held a beautiful golden wand in his hands, with which he charms the eyes of any men he wants, and in turn also awakens those that are sleeping," *Od.* 24.1–4). His presence as a representative of the divine and his control over slippery transitions such as those of sleep and wakefulness indicate that the narrative is entering an important, marked moment that is "between" the lines of the story, the chronotope where Underworld narratives generally exist. As with the *Nekuia*, the poet takes the audience out of the narrative of Odysseus' return to convey, by a third-person narrator, something important that cannot fit into the frame narrative's linear timeline.

---

[21] This has some logic because Elpenor is unburied and so recently dead, but it cannot be assumed that his ghost would be the first Odysseus would talk to or see since time works differently in the Underworld.

60   LIFE / AFTERLIFE

This movement into an abstracted "in-between" place within the narrative is mimicked and made visible by the image of the souls walking in line to the netherworld. They do not appear suddenly in Hades by a short route as Elpenor seemed to do in Book 11.[22] Instead, they float along behind their guide Hermes, a fact emphasized by the description and naming of milestones along the way and the use of verbs of motion in the scene:

τῇ ῥ᾽ ἄγε **κινήσας**, ταὶ δὲ τρίζουσαι **ἕποντο**. *(5)*
ὡς δ᾽ ὅτε νυκτερίδες μυχῷ ἄντρου θεσπεσίοιο
τρίζουσαι ποτέονται, ἐπεί κέ τις ἀποπέσῃσιν
ὁρμαθοῦ ἐκ πέτρης, ἀνά τ᾽ ἀλλήλῃσιν ἔχονται,
ὡς αἱ τετριγυῖαι ἄμ᾽ **ἤϊσαν**· **ἦρχε** δ᾽ ἄρα σφιν
Ἑρμείας ἀκάκητα κατ᾽ **εὐρώεντα κέλευθα**. *(10)*
πὰρ δ᾽ ἴσαν Ὠκεανοῦ τε **ῥοὰς** καὶ **Λευκάδα πέτρην**,
ἠδὲ **παρ᾽ Ἡελίοιο πύλας** καὶ **δῆμον Ὀνείρων**
ἤϊσαν· αἶψα δ᾽ **ἵκοντο** κατ᾽ **ἀσφοδελὸν λειμῶνα**,
ἔνθα τε ναίουσι ψυχαί, εἴδωλα καμόντων. *(Od.* 24.5–14)

Having set [the suitors' souls] **in motion** with this [wand], he led them along and they **followed**, shrieking. Just as when bats flutter around shrieking in the recess of an awful cave, when one from his place in the chain in which they hold themselves together has fallen off of the rock, so too the shrieking souls **went**; And the kindly healer Hermes **led** them down **dank paths**, and they **went past the streams of Ocean** and **the White Rock (Leuke)**, and then passed **by the gates of Helios** and **the realm of Dreams**. And straightaway, they **reached** the **asphodel meadows**; and **there** the souls dwell, images of the dead.

The physicality of their progression "thickens" space in the same way that the loss of light thickens time in the earlier Underworld passage of Book 11 to make it "artistically visible" (Bakhtin 1981, 84).

Based on the three Underworld scenes of Books 10, 11, and 24, we can infer certain elements which meet audience expectation, including the appearance of supernatural entities (souls or chthonic gods), obstacles for a

---

[22] Elpenor makes no mention of Hermes leading him into the Underworld, even though he has the same unburied status as the suitors. Instead, after Elpenor describes breaking his neck, he says, "my soul went down to Hades" (ψυχὴ δ᾽ Ἀϊδόσδε κατῆλθε, *Od.* 11.65).

hero to overcome, conversations with the dead, and predictions about the future. A large part of the poetics of the Underworld is an emphasis on how unnatural it is for the dead and living to mingle together. After the initial shock of entry into an Underworld scene, the narrative continues along a different track from the frame narrative as a new normal for reality is established. Within its alternative chronotope, the Underworld scene seems aware of itself as a narrative digression. Characters, living and dead, almost always remark on how unlikely their interactions are, and the narrator keeps the chronotopic markers visible to the audience. This incongruity is broadcast to highlight how remarkable the heroes are who do cross this barrier. Although this poetics of the Underworld builds a pattern of familiarity that welcomes the visitor to treat its space and denizens as if it were the real world, the environment is constantly offering reminders that it is a constructed space and not a proxy for the mortal world, which means that certain rules of engagement do not apply. This is particularly apparent in the *Nekuia*.

As if worried that the initial entry and early conversation with Elpenor's ghost were not enough of a signal to the audience of the Underworld chronotope, the poet features two other characters who refer to the lack of light in the Underworld. The opening of Anticlea's speech mimics the conversation with Elpenor's ghost through its references to the darkness and lack of sunlight. Odysseus' mother asks how he could cross into the gloom, where it is difficult for living eyes to see (πῶς ἦλθες ὑπὸ ζόφον ἠερόεντα ζωὸς ἐών; χαλεπὸν δὲ τάδε ζωοῖσιν ὁρᾶσθαι, "How did you come under the dank gloom, while you are alive? Difficult indeed is it for living men to see these things," *Od.* 11.155–156); and she later asserts that he will soon be eager for the light, commanding him to make haste in going toward it (ἀλλὰ φόωσδε τάχιστα λιλαίεο, "but struggle towards the light very swiftly," *Od.* 11.223). Later, Tiresias also begins his conversation by creating two categories of people: those that live in light and those that live in darkness. He asks why Odysseus would leave the sun to visit the gloomy land of the dead (τίπτ' αὖτ', ὦ δύστηνε, λιπὼν φάος ἠελίοιο ἤλυθες, ὄφρα ἴδῃ νέκυας καὶ ἀτερπέα χῶρον, "why ever, unlucky one, did you leave the light and come here to see corpses and a joyless land?" *Od.* 11.93–94).[23]

Repeated mention of the sun and its light informs the audience that Odysseus has entered a dark, unknowable place. As a living man, Odysseus' life can be measured in human time and can be mapped through the

---

[23] For a discussion of light and vision in the *Iliad*, see Dué and Ebbott (2010) and Gazis (2012; 2018, 10–13).

coordinates of heavenly bodies. The focus on spatial and temporal disorientation throughout the Underworld scenes helps the audience recognize Odysseus' preeminence as a hero, as evidenced by his success in entering the Underworld chronotope and in arriving at the correct location for the consultation with the dead. It also reminds the audience that the scene is linking to multiple narrative frames, which operate simultaneously. Each conversation represents a new beginning in which multiple narratives are engaged and layered as *para-narratives*. Presenting the same conversation about light three times enhances the audience's sense of déjà-vu and temporal repetition, another subtle indicator of nonlinear time and considerations to keep in mind.

In addition to these brief but consistent reminders of the Underworld chronotope, the central sections of Underworld scenes themselves have consistent patterns that make up the poetics of the Underworld. Although there is too much variety in Underworld scenes to create a full list of similarities, the audience can rely on certain common features within the framework of an afterlife encounter that act as intertextual links between almost all Underworld scenes. These include conversations with souls and visions of chthonic figures that would otherwise be inaccessible. These characters usually have a personal connection to the visiting hero or some defined interest in the frame narrative's outcome. Besides containing souls of the friends or family members of the protagonist, Underworld scenes almost always have references to famous katabatic heroes, such as Heracles, Theseus, or Orpheus, as well as to famous sinners, such as Tantalus, Sisyphus, and Ixion. Cerberus is also frequently mentioned in Underworld scenes as are Persephone, Hermes, Hades, Minos, and (later) Charon. Each case in the next part of this chapter explores how the poetics of the Underworld translates into a language of commentary and communication between author and audience, with each figure legitimizing the poet's authority. Before proceeding, however, it is important to note the lack of detail in the endings of Underworld scenes. They usually end abruptly without much transition back to the real world, as happens in both Circe's *nekuia* and the *Nekuia*. When the Underworld scene ends, the plot almost always proceeds in both space and time from where it left off before the start of the scene, as if the digression had never happened. After the *Nekuia*, it is still night when Odysseus returns to Aeaea, and the Underworld scene in Book 24 is inserted while Odysseus is moving between two locations. The time spent in the Underworld does not seem to correspond to a similar passage of time in the frame narrative, and there is a feeling that events in the real world are put on pause while the hero (or narrator) visits the Underworld. Nevertheless, after the close of an Underworld scene, the audience and often the characters are in a very different mental space because of the revelations in the Underworld.

V. Building Narrative Networks through the Underworld

While the previous section looks at the general poetics that form the framework and chronotope of Underworld scenes, this section examines how these poetics create conduits between narratives through necromantic encounters that allow Underworld scenes in Archaic literature to act as self-contained commentaries within their frame narratives. The author's reliance on the audience to recognize the connections necessitates various forms of subtle communication between author and audience that constitute a hidden language, whose meaning is determined by each individual in the audience. In the *Nekuia*, it quickly becomes clear that the order of the ghosts' appearance is not chronological or even genealogical, but rather thematic. The ghosts appear in groups that correspond to the themes interweaving the epic as a whole, questioning assumptions about social bonds, history, heroism, and *nostos*.[24] Each set of ghosts reinforces aspects of Odysseus' identity. They are each stuck contemplating and talking about their lives and deaths, through which they offer specific points of comparison to the epic protagonist and his journey. Here and in other Underworld scenes, the audience is given a view "behind the scenes" of the narrative, as the author displays his influences and presents his own interpretation of his characters and his work within his tradition.

Such authorial commentary can be easily identified in the parts of the *Nekuia* that are clearly extraneous to the plot of Odysseus' mission. These encounters in the Underworld are the most obvious attempt by authors to embed internal commentaries that could reliably survive with their works by being intractably interwoven into these critical episodes. Their number and protracted nature point to their perceived dependability as a literary conceit. The Underworld framework can set the stage for an intimate and familiar mode of communication between author and audience, which results in a collaborative contemplation of the frame narrative's themes through a web of links connecting to other stories. Different parts of the *Nekuia* open several

---

[24] For a discussion on the relationship between the *Nekuia* and the rest of the poem, see Tsagarakis (2000).

possible storylines in rapid succession to communicate specific messages and values to the audience.

Despite his fear and initial dread, Odysseus lingers with the ghosts coming out of Hades beyond his reported purpose and mandate. As the scene extends, figures representing different historical points in time crowd the landscape, and these transmit messages, directly and indirectly, both to Odysseus' internal audience, the Phaeacians, and to external audiences of the *Odyssey* as a whole. Persephone is said to have sent Odysseus a host of women, who, from his perspective, represent historical figures and events. The poet presents them and their stories in the format of an epic catalog (11.234–327), with each ghost saying her name and story in order (προμνηστῖναι, 11.233). As the catalog progresses, a subtle pattern emerges: each woman is not only famous in her own right but also famous for her son or sons. Placing them so closely after Odysseus' encounter with his own mother, the author seems to suggest that Anticlea should be seen as part of this catalog of heroines, or at least as its prelude, which would lend further glory to *her* son Odysseus. Moreover, the specific inclusion in the catalog of Alcmene and Leda, whose sons (Heracles and the twins Polydeuces and Castor, respectively) found ways to defy death and escape the Underworld, strengthens an association between Odysseus and *katabatic* heroes. This catalog, therefore, in addition to the intertextual connections it makes to other types of poetry and myth, interacts with Odysseus' Anticlea encounter as a *para-narrative*, predicting Anticlea's future place among the heroines because of her famous son Odysseus.

In addition to promoting a narrative tradition of women and their famous sons, inclusive of Odysseus, the extensive treatment of these "ghostly" women represents the perils of becoming too lost in the past and in history, as well as losing one's place in the main narrative.[25] The ghosts are distractions for Odysseus that endanger his *nostos* no less than the monsters, storms, and gods he has already encountered. As Benjamin Sammons (2010, 91–92) argues,

---

[25] Tsagarakis (2000, 71–89) compares the *Odyssey*'s catalog of women to Hesiod's *Ehoiai*; he also argues that Homer chooses to give a catalog of heroines instead of heroes because of Odysseus' close association with powerful women in the poem. Most (1992, 1019) also makes this connection but more broadly to a type of *epos* he calls a Hesiodic-style catalog of women, or *ehoiai*. Hirschberger (2001, 132–133) argues that the catalog of women allows for each heroine's point of view to be stressed, giving them a voice in the space of the dead, while at the same time other, perhaps more well-known versions of their tales become suppressed.

"what emerges from Odysseus' catalogue is rather the enormous variety of persons and events that the past encompasses. In the place of pattern, we discover ramifying narrative possibilities for which the 'wives and daughters of champions' serve as points of departure." The narratives, once activated by these figures, situate Odysseus' story against a certain subsection of myth that plays concurrently with the story at hand. As they enter the audience's mental landscape, they compete with each other for primacy and create a feeling of continuous anxiety, which adds to the audience's sense of suspense and gives metaliterary information pointing to the poet's efforts in the Underworld scene's construction. By pausing the frame narrative to tap into the Underworld's archive, the poet shows ingenuity in adapting and relating traditional, well-known material to express his virtuosity.

Against the backdrop of many competing stories and alternative outcomes for heroes, Tiresias' summary of Odysseus' future in such a short space shows that the *Odyssey* itself is only a brief narrative moment that is brought to life by the poet's craft. The seer's words do not give Odysseus clarity for the immediate task of sailing home but rather general warnings and ritual necessities he must attend to at a distant point in the future (*Od.* 11.99–134). Moreover, instead of engaging with Tiresias, Odysseus seems more interested in the other ghosts and their stories, rather than the implications of the seer's predictions. The drama and stories that appear in the *Nekuia* threaten at this point to become the primary narrative, and the scene creates suspense through its extended narration, which contributes to a natural tension present in almost all heroic Underworld scenes that the hero, as a mortal, may not fulfill his quest or leave the Underworld at all. The narrator points out this anxiety in the text with a well-timed interruption to the catalog of women. When he is about a hundred lines into his catalog of women, Odysseus breaks off and addresses his Phaeacian hosts, briefly removing his audience from the Underworld and inviting it back into the chronological time of the real world. This break is signified by Odysseus' reference to the night's passing away before he could name all the women he saw (*Od.* 11.328–330). The narrator suggests that all the audiences of the Underworld scene (Odysseus, the Phaeacians, and the reader/listener) have become lost in the chronotope of the dead, wrapped in a heavy silence (ἐγένοντο σιωπῇ, *Od.* 11.333).

This interruption within the Underworld scene subtly reasserts the frame narrative's primacy in the consciousness of the audience before returning to the Underworld narrative, where the poet continues his indirect commentary on the *Odyssey's* themes.[26] It also places the *Nekuia* back into its original storytelling context, showing that the Underworld is a pretext for something else and reminding the audience that this part of the epic is in the voice of Odysseus (not an independent or reported narrator like Circe or a Muse-inspired bard).[27] The interruption itself is a regular bardic strategy seen throughout the Homeric poems, like an invocation to the Muse, to recall the attention of a potentially flagging audience and remind them of the singer's performance (Minchin 1995, 27–28; Doherty 1995, 65–66).

In this way, the author demonstrates that he actively makes choices between competing histories: he knows his options and uses the Underworld to show some of the possible narrative alternatives to his audience while stressing his own epic narrative as the dominant one. He reveals his awareness of the *para-narratives* and also cautions the audience not to become trapped in single narratives or timeframes. With so many narratives to consider, the audience is forced to contemplate the relationship between them and Odysseus' story on a microscale to make sense of why the hero has not yet continued his journey to Ithaca. Of course, there is entertainment value in the storytelling, but that alone cannot explain the survival or extent of afterlife stories within the *Nekuia* and the *Odyssey* as a whole. In giving so much space to contemplation of the Underworld, the poet suggests that he and his audiences found such scenes to be relevant and crucial parts of the epic, packed with information that was necessary to understand the hero's journey—and the hero himself.

By exploring the different sections within the *Nekuia*, we can begin to see how each of them interacts together like sentences in a paragraph to send a global message to the audience about how to interpret the Underworld scene and think about Odysseus as a hero. In the *Nekuia*, the first two ghosts who appear are Elpenor and Anticlea. These ghosts introduce two social

---

[26] Other scholars have developed several theories about this interruption, often referred to as the "Intermezzo," and what it may be communicating, including a test of the guest-host relationship (Tsagarakis 2000, 89–94), a turning point in the relationship between Odysseus and the generally hostile Phaeacians (Rose 1969, 404–405), the end of the *performance-time* of Part I of the *Odyssey* (Taplin 1995, 31), or simply a structural divide in the *Nekuia* separating it into symmetrical halves (Most 1992, 1016).

[27] Sammons (2010, 88) points out that the Catalog of Women in the *Nekuia* is unique because catalogs of such extent are generally not given in the voice of mortal characters but are reserved for gods or bards.

structures—friendship and family—which are relevant to Odysseus (and his audience) as the underlying reason for his journey to Troy and his relentless drive to return home. As the scene unfolds, the narrator uses these encounters to develop Odysseus as a character, displaying his society's values and also reminding him of why he must complete his journey to Ithaca. The scenes with the ghosts of Anticlea and the heroines place Odysseus within a tradition of heroic men through association. The conversation with Elpenor's ghost, on the other hand, uses Odysseus' own actions to define the hero's character. Odysseus, the stalwart friend and leader, promises to fulfill a last request and give honor to a comrade who was in his care. The audience is reminded through this ghost that, despite his appearance at this point in the *Odyssey*, Odysseus is not just a castaway adventurer or disreputable vagrant discovered by Nausicaa, reliant on the good will of the Phaeacians, but a brave ruler of men who are willing to follow him to their deaths.

Furthermore, the Elpenor encounter establishes a direct link beyond the *Odyssey* to a larger conversation in epic about heroes and heroism because it recalls a similar scene of ghostly request for burial by Patroclus' ghost in the *Iliad*. By juxtaposing these ghosts, the author gives authority to these encounters and subtly pits Odysseus and Achilles (as well as the epics that feature them) against each other in light of how they treat their dead companions, showing the heroes as both leaders and comrades. This comparison between the two heroes is much more explicit later in the scene when Odysseus converses with the ghost of Achilles, but the audience, familiar with the *Iliad*, might have noticed a similar narrative pattern, especially since the topic of burial occurs again in an other-worldly encounter in Book 24 of the *Odyssey*. This later scene, which describes Achilles' burial, suggests to the *Odyssey*'s audience that they can use the *Iliad*'s funerary descriptions as a point of reference.

Elpenor's request not only connects these Underworld scenes but also has a predictive function, offering a way back into the frame narrative from the Underworld scene. After describing his accidental death, Elpenor's ghost orders the burial of his body, thereby foreshadowing that Odysseus will end his Underworld journey at the location where he started: Aeaea. This shows that, even before he talks to Tiresias, Odysseus' necromantic journey is beginning to reveal his future. The nature of the Elpenor ghost's supplication is half-request and half-threat. It starts with the command to perform burial rights, but in a very specific way to create the type of tomb that might be the object of *kleos* through eventual recognition or even cult honors by sailors passing by in the future:[28]

μή μ᾽ ἄκλαυτον ἄθαπτον ἰὼν ὄπιθεν καταλείπειν
νοσφισθείς, μή τοί τι θεῶν μήνιμα γένωμαι,
ἀλλά με κακκῆαι σὺν τεύχεσιν, ἄσσα μοί ἐστι,
σῆμά τέ μοι χεῦαι πολιῆς ἐπὶ θινὶ θαλάσσης, (75)
ἀνδρὸς δυστήνοιο, καὶ ἐσσομένοισι πυθέσθαι·
ταῦτά τέ μοι τελέσαι πῆξαί τ᾽ ἐπὶ τύμβῳ ἐρετμόν,
τῷ καὶ ζωὸς ἔρεσσον ἐὼν μετ᾽ ἐμοῖσ᾽ ἑτάροισιν.᾽ (*Od.* 11.72–78)

Don't forsake and leave me behind, unwept, unburied, when you go
lest I become some kind of scourge of the gods on you,
but burn me with my armor, whichever belongs to me,
and heap up a burial mound for me on the shore of the gray sea,
the marker of an ill-fated man, and one for men in the future to know;
complete these things for me and fix an oar on the tomb,
the one with which I rowed while alive with my companions.

The focus on pain and supernatural punishment as well as the continued connection between the living and the dead are highlighted in this passage. Patroclus' ghost makes a similar entreaty:

εὕδεις, αὐτὰρ ἐμεῖο λελασμένος ἔπλευ Ἀχιλλεῦ.
οὐ μέν μευ ζώοντος ἀκήδεις, ἀλλὰ θανόντος· (70)
θάπτέ με ὅττι τάχιστα πύλας Ἀΐδαο περήσω.
τῆλέ με εἴργουσι ψυχαὶ εἴδωλα καμόντων,
οὐδέ μέ πω μίσγεσθαι ὑπὲρ ποταμοῖο ἐῶσιν,
ἀλλ᾽ αὕτως ἀλάλημαι ἀν᾽ εὐρυπυλὲς Ἄϊδος δῶ. (*Il.* 23.69–74)

You sleep, and you have forgotten me, Achilles.
You were not uncaring when I was alive, but only now that I am dead;
bury me as swiftly as possible so that I may pass through the gates of
Hades. The souls, images of dead men, hold me at a distance,
and they do not allow me to mix with them at all beyond the river,
but I roam about just so throughout the broad-gated house of Hades.

---

[28] While Circe's island is remote, other sailors found their way to her shores and were turned into beasts before Odysseus and his crew arrived. This suggests that her island is not so remote that it is outside of the reach of regular mortals.

The two passages use similar imagery and language: Elpenor fears being left behind and forgotten (*Od.* 11.72–73), and Patroclus accuses Achilles of doing just that (*Il.* 23.69).[29]

Both ghosts appeal to their commanders' emotions, grief, and sense of loyalty, wanting to maintain their connection and, thereby, be memorialized. In the latter case, Patroclus has become a ghost that haunts Achilles—what Elpenor threatens to become to Odysseus (τι θεῶν μήνιμα, "a kind of scourge of the gods," *Od.* 11.73). The verb νοσφισθείς has a sense of "turning" in its meaning, indicating a shift in position away from the dead comrade.[30] Additionally, both ghosts are essentially asking for burial rites that would lead to cult worship.[31] Elpenor's ghost is explicit in this through his use of the words σῆμα and τύμβῳ along with his statement that "future men would know it," (ἐσσομένοισι πυθέσθαι, *Od.* 11.76). Patroclus' ghost only asks that his ashes be held in the same urn as Achilles', but there is the assumption that this highly elaborate vessel will be celebrated in future worship and rituals directed towards the hero (μὴ ἐμὰ σῶν ἀπάνευθε τιθήμεναι ὀστέ' Ἀχιλλεῦ, ἀλλ' ὁμοῦ ὡς ἐτράφημεν ἐν ὑμετέροισι δόμοισιν . . . ὀστέα νῶϊν ὁμὴ σορὸς ἀμφικαλύπτοι χρύσεος ἀμφιφορεύς, τόν τοι πόρε πότνια μήτηρ, "don't let my bones be placed away from yours, Achilles, but just as we were raised together in your home . . . may the same urn enfold us, the golden amphora, which your mistress mother provided," *Il.* 23.83–84, 91–92). The use of this urn in funerary rites culminating in a tomb worthy of cult is verified in Book 24 of the *Odyssey*:

---

[29] Achilles had been so engrossed in his own grief that he had, to a large degree, forgotten about the needs of Patroclus' burial until receiving instructions from the latter's ghost. Just like Odysseus, Achilles was blinded by his own goals and did not "see" the dead man until he was visited by his ghost.

[30] The idea of turning away from the ghosts is reminiscent of when Circe tells Odysseus to turn his face away from Hades and the dead during the initial sacrifice in the *Nekuia* (*Od.* 10.526–529). The ghosts of Patroclus and Elpenor demand that their leaders neither turn away from them nor continue with their lives until they perform proper funerals for their comrades. See Martin (2014) for more on the demands for funerary honors by these two figures and how it relates to Underworld status.

[31] Bremmer (2006, 20) argues that, in the early Archaic period of the Homeric poems, such noteworthy burials would be associated with tomb cults, ancestor cults, or city-founder cults of important, godlike figures. Early audiences may still have attached some significance to these grave markers, around which hero-cult worship arose later during the last decades of the sixth century BCE. The bibliography on hero cult is extensive, and its treatment by scholars can be traced through works by Rohde (1925), Nagy (1981, 2012), Burkert (1985, 1983), Antonaccio (1994, 1995), Lyons (1997), Boehringer (2001), Ekroth (2002), Pache (2004), Currie (2005), Bremmer (2006), Larson (2007, 1995), and Jones (2010).

70   LIFE / AFTERLIFE

... δῶκε δὲ μήτηρ
χρύσεον ἀμφιφορῆα· Διωνύσοιο δὲ δῶρον
φάσκ' ἔμεναι, ἔργον δὲ περικλυτοῦ Ἡφαίστοιο. (75)
ἐν τῷ τοι κεῖται λεύκ' ὀστέα, φαίδιμ' Ἀχιλλεῦ,
μίγδα δὲ Πατρόκλοιο Μενοιτιάδαο θανόντος,
χωρὶς δ' Ἀντιλόχοιο, τὸν ἔξοχα τίες ἁπάντων
τῶν ἄλλων ἑτάρων μετὰ Πάτροκλόν γε θανόντα.
ἀμφ' αὐτοῖσι δ' ἔπειτα μέγαν καὶ ἀμύμονα τύμβον (80)
χεύαμεν Ἀργείων ἱερὸς στρατὸς αἰχμητάων
ἀκτῇ ἔπι προὐχούσῃ, ἐπὶ πλατεῖ Ἑλλησπόντῳ,
ὥς κεν τηλεφανὴς ἐκ ποντόφιν ἀνδράσιν εἴη
τοῖσ', οἳ νῦν γεγάασι καὶ οἳ μετόπισθεν ἔσονται. (*Od.* 24.73–84)

And **your mother provided a golden amphora**; and she said
it was a gift from Dionysus and the work of the famous Hephaestus.
**In it, your white bones are laid, brilliant Achilles, and mixed
with the bones of the dead Patroclus, son of Menoetius**, and
apart from those of Antilochus, whom you valued beyond all other
companions after Patroclus died. And around them then **we, the
sacred host of spear-wielding Argives, heaped a great and noble
tomb upon a projecting part of the shore by the broad Hellespont,
so that it can be seen from far out at sea by men alive now and by
those born in the future.**

The highlighted sections of this passage indicate imagery and language already seen in *Iliad* 23 and *Odyssey* 11. This passage shows the fulfillment of Achilles' orders for the interment of his and Patroclus' bones (*Il* 23.236–248), establishing another link that reinforces the connection between these passages.

Following Patroclus' ghost's commands, Achilles tells the Greek leaders to preserve Patroclus' bones in a golden vessel until he himself dies and not to build a tomb (τύμβον) until they both are dead and the Greeks are ready to sail away, implying that this tomb will be a significant marker for future (δεύτεροι) generations:

καὶ τὰ μὲν ἐν χρυσέῃ φιάλῃ καὶ δίπλακι δημῷ
θείομεν, εἰς ὅ κεν αὐτὸς ἐγὼν Ἄϊδι κεύθωμαι.
τύμβον δ' οὐ μάλα πολλὸν ἐγὼ πονέεσθαι ἄνωγα,

Afterlife Poetics and Homer's Heroic Underworlds

ἀλλ' ἐπιεικέα τοῖον· ἔπειτα δὲ καὶ τὸν Ἀχαιοὶ
εὐρύν θ' ὑψηλόν τε τιθήμεναι, οἵ κεν ἐμεῖο
δεύτεροι ἐν νήεσσι πολυκλήϊσι λίπησθε. (Il. 23.243–248)

And let us place the bones in a golden urn and in fat applied in two layers,
until I myself should be hidden in Hades.
And not a very great tomb do I command to be built,
but such as is suitable. But at a later time,
set up [a tomb] broad and high, Achaeans, whoever of you,
surviving me, might remain among the many-oared ships.

The *Odyssey*'s repetition of the process of heaping a tomb (σῆμά τέ μοι χεῦαι, *Od.* 11.25; τύμβον χεύαμεν, *Od.* 24.80–81), honoring the dead with the collection and burial of bones after a funeral pyre, and creating a marker for potential hero-cult worship on a shore "for future men" who will see it from afar ties these passages together intertextually and gives a deeper meaning to Elpenor's request than if it were interpreted without knowledge of the Patroclus passage working in the background.[32] Odysseus responds simply that he will fulfill the request of ghostly Elpenor (ταῦτά τοι, ὦ δύστηνε, τελευτήσω τε καὶ ἔρξω, "I will do these things for you, ill-fated one, and see them through to the end," *Od.* 11.80), just as Achilles answers Patroclus' ghost (αὐτὰρ ἐγώ τοι πάντα μάλ' ἐκτελέω καὶ πείσομαι ὡς σὺ κελεύεις, "and surely, I am accomplishing all these things, and I shall do what you command," *Il.* 23.95–96).

Despite Elpenor's lack of proven heroic valor, the nature of his request to Odysseus raises notions of loyalty and heroism closely connected to the *Iliad*, instantly and efficiently linking the two poems through their Underworld scenes. The ghosts of Elpenor and Patroclus are both mournful characters who, full of regret, beseech their leaders with large requests. This makes more sense in the *Iliad* episode because of the close relationship between Patroclus and Achilles. It is somewhat perplexing that Elpenor, a minor character whose only speaking part is as a ghost, could make such demands of his commander. Given this history, the Elpenor encounter seems to be a poetic ruse for creating links to the Iliadic scene with Patroclus' ghost. The Underworld scene thus allows the poet to introduce significant amounts of external information in

---

[32] The heaping up of a tomb can itself be seen as a Homeric type-scene. Pucci (1987, 18–20) has argued that such formulaic repetition creates allusions connecting different sections of the Homeric poems together, although the meaning of each scene must be interpreted by its local context.

72   LIFE / AFTERLIFE

this way through its *para-narrative* links, all of which contribute to the interpretation of Odysseus' current situation and character.

The conversation with Elpenor's ghost and ensuing promise then become palpable as a subtext to Odysseus' actions in Book 12 of the *Odyssey*, when he returns to Circe's island and carries out the funerary ritual for his fallen comrade. This expands the reach of the Underworld scene into the frame narrative, allowing the audience to understand the motivations behind Odysseus' actions. Odysseus is dutiful in fulfilling Elpenor's request, just as Achilles was, although Elpenor is noteworthy only for falling off a roof, not for any heroic action. Elpenor is hardly the equivalent of Patroclus in heroism or affection, but the author, nonetheless, creates the analogy between the two. Elpenor's prominent placement in the *Nekuia*, therefore, might be read as an ironic "inside joke" between author and audience, yet it is this irony and sense of a mismatch that draw attention to the issues the author wants the audience to consider. Moreover, Elpenor's request creates a narrative bridge out of the Underworld chronotope back into the plot by making Odysseus return to Circe's island. Finally, the Elpenor episode characterizes Odysseus in a way that gives additional poignancy to the loss of the rest of his companions, which comes soon after (*Od.* 12.417–419).

The *Odyssey*'s Underworld scenes do not end, however, with presenting Odysseus as a leader and companion; they also bring up the importance of familial succession and spousal relations, both of which are pertinent to Odysseus' upcoming return to Ithaca. Odysseus' profound grief over his mother's presence in the Underworld and the information she gives about home and family remind the audience of Odysseus' motivation for return, despite the many obstacles along the way that would hold him back. Presented as a doting son, Odysseus tearfully mourns his dead mother, reaching out to her for news of home along with a physical embrace (11.84-87, 11.152–224), echoing Achilles' attempt to embrace Patroclus' ghost (Ὡς ἄρα φωνήσας ὠρέξατο χερσὶ φίλῃσιν, οὐδ᾽ ἔλαβε· ψυχὴ δὲ κατὰ χθονὸς ἠΰτε καπνὸς ᾤχετο τετριγυῖα, "Thus having spoken, he reached out with his own arms, but he could not grasp [him]; and the soul went below the earth, just as smoke, emitting a shrill sound," *Il.* 23.99–101).[33] Through Anticlea, Odysseus is thrust back into the concerns of chronological time. With the news he receives from her, he could have chosen to stay away from Ithaca for an easier life, but instead he steels his resolve to complete his journey and defend his home.

---

[33] This is the same sound and word used to describe the suitors' ghosts in *Odyssey* 24 (ὡς αἱ τετριγυῖαι ἅμ᾽ ἤϊσαν, "just so, the ghosts [of the suitors] went, emitting a shrill sound," *Od.* 24.9).

Afterlife Poetics and Homer's Heroic Underworlds

Odysseus' interactions with both Elpenor and Anticlea bring the Underworld chronotope to the audience's attention because time is shown to be stacked on itself. The two characters died at different points in historical time but are simultaneous here in the Underworld, and their ghosts are stuck mentally in the past, continually reliving the pain of their last moments of life even into the present when Odysseus encounters them. At the same time, the narrative also gives glimpses of upcoming episodes in the main narrative: Odysseus will give Elpenor's body a proper burial immediately after leaving the Underworld and will also find his destitute father in Ithaca, just as Anticlea describes. The two encounters drive the post-*Nekuia* plot since they force Odysseus to re-engage with his *nostos* by adding urgency to his journey. Book 11, in many ways, marks the beginning of the final phase of Odysseus' return to Ithaca, since his story is so moving that the Phaeacians eventually ferry him home.

VI. Framing Odysseus as a Special Hero with the Nekuia

The final section in the *Nekuia* situates Odysseus in the tradition of heroes by suggesting that he will gain the stature of Heracles. As reported by Odysseus, the "ghost" of Heracles draws a comparison between them in the following:

διογενὲς Λαερτιάδη, πολυμήχαν' Ὀδυσσεῦ,
ἆ δείλ', ἦ τινὰ καὶ σὺ κακὸν μόρον ἡγηλάζεις,
ὅν περ ἐγὼν ὀχέεσκον ὑπ' αὐγὰς ἠελίοιο.
Ζηνὸς μὲν πάϊς ἦα Κρονίονος, αὐτὰρ ὀϊζὺν (620)
εἶχον ἀπειρεσίην· μάλα γὰρ πολὺ χείρονι φωτὶ
δεδμήμην, ὁ δέ μοι χαλεποὺς ἐπετέλλετ' ἀέθλους.
καί ποτέ μ' ἐνθάδ' ἔπεμψε κύν' ἄξοντ'· οὐ γὰρ ἔτ' ἄλλον
φράζετο τοῦδέ γέ μοι κρατερώτερον εἶναι ἄεθλον. (*Od.* 11.617–624)

Zeus-sprung son of Laertes, many-wiled Odysseus,
oh, wretched one, indeed you too endure some sort of evil fate,
which I also bore while [alive] under the rays of the sun.
On the one hand, I was the child of Zeus, son of Kronos, but I had
boundless woe; for I was subjugated to a man very much worse than I,
and he inflicted on me hard labors. He even sent me to this place here
to lead away the dog [Cerberus]; for he did not think there to be still
another more mighty task for me than this.

74   LIFE / AFTERLIFE

In this passage, Heracles and Odysseus are under similar orders, the latter by Fate (κακὸν μόρον) and the former by a man. Both are associated with Zeus—Heracles identifies himself as the son of Zeus and also addresses Odysseus as διογενὲς ("Zeus-sprung")[34]—and are sent to seek out something that only exists in the Underworld environs. Heracles' assessment of his visit to Hades as being the mightiest labor that his human master could contrive transfers the accolades of his success to Odysseus, since they both, by this point, have completed their mandated Underworld tasks. To the extent that authorial intention can be determined, the appearance of Heracles at the end of Odysseus' visit to the Underworld demonstrates that the author wants the reader to connect the two heroes, thereby elevating Odysseus' heroic status to the audience, both Phaeaecian and otherwise (Karanika 2011). The comparison of Odysseus to a hero like Heracles from an older generation, while common in the *Iliad*, is rare in the *Odyssey*, and so particularly marked (Alden 2017, 173–175). The passing reference to Theseus and Pirithous (*Od.* 11.631) also gives evidence to support the grouping of Odysseus with katabatic heroes.[35]

To further underscore the enormity of Odysseus' task (and success), the final section of the *Nekuia* presents famous denizens of the Underworld, thereby following the familiar mythic model of heroic *katabasis* and preserving its traditions and prestige within Odysseus' journey.[36] Each feature or figure contextualizes Odysseus and reinforces the Underworld chronotope by confirming what the audience "knows" about the chthonic space from collective religion and cultural myths. By saying that Odysseus saw Heracles (in the form of an *eidolon*, at least) and by having Odysseus assert that he would have seen Theseus and Pirithous, the author situates his Underworld against a backdrop of *katabatic* poetry. Additionally, Odysseus also says he sees the figures of Minos, Tityus, Tantalus, and Sisyphus, who all live in different zones of the

---

[34] This focus on a hero's relationship to Zeus is reminiscent of the fact that Menelaus only gets his blessed afterlife because of his relationship to Zeus as his son-in-law.

[35] For later audiences, the *Minyas*, an epic dated to the 6th century BCE (Lloyd-Jones 1967, 216–229), would have supported an interpretation that Odysseus' sighting of Theseus and Pirithous was katabatic by firmly placing these heroes in the depths of the Underworld.

[36] Tsagarakis (2000, 100–103) observes that Odysseus' conversations in the *Nekuia* with friends, relatives, and strangers "have primarily a place in the thematic motif of *catabasis* but they have been transferred to the *nekyomanteia*." Possible traditions influencing this *Odyssey*'s incorporation of *katabasis* into necromancy include a pre-Homeric *Katabasis of Heracles*, the *Epic of Gilgamesh*, and myths about the descent of Theseus and Pirithous, although the evidence of these are fragmentary.

Underworld and are caught in unending cycles of action with no discernable links to linear time or to the real world of the narrative (Johnson 1999, 12–13). Their presence in Odysseus' account underscores the Underworld as a "site of repetition" (Purves 2004, 163) and also legitimizes the hero's visit to Hades by reminding the audience that his Underworld corresponds to that of heroic *katabasis* stories and of ancient Greek legend. No details are provided for these figures: Odysseus knows them by sight and the audience is expected to know them by name. As Odysseus visually surveys the Underworld topography, the audience follows along as "readers" of the mythic heroes, who become "signs that need only to be seen to be recognized, pointing at narratives that are fixed and eternal as the punishments and privileges of the heroes themselves" (Sammons 2010, 98).

Unlike the women in the earlier catalog who are tied temporally to the past, threaten to trap Odysseus in their stories, and represent progress in storytelling but no movement through the plot, the famous male heroes represent an "eternal" status, as they are forever present in the Underworld (not needing to be sent by Persephone) and celebrated simply by name without the need for their stories to be told. They are known. As in the earlier catalog of women, the ghosts of Greek leaders reinforce Odysseus' place in the pantheon of heroes. The poet keeps the audience guessing whether Odysseus will simply be the famous son of a heroine, as suggested in the catalog of heroines, or whether he will end up on the narrative path toward eternal fame through privilege or punishment as represented by the heroes.[37] Ending with Heracles' assertion that Odysseus is similar to him strongly suggests a positive outcome for the latter after his death and also establishes Odysseus as belonging to the "eternal" group of heroes rather than the "temporal-ephemeral" group portrayed by the catalog of women.[38] Heracles' words to Odysseus are not really a conversation as much as a device that establishes Odysseus as a heroic peer, indicating to the reader that Odysseus' necromancy is in the same

---

[37] Even as a hero, at this point in the narrative, Odysseus still could get "stuck" in the Underworld realm as Theseus did as a form of punishment for seeing the chthonic realm. Although Odysseus' *kleos* is already guaranteed to a certain extent by the very existence of the poem, the author is offering suggestions as to the nature of Odysseus' *kleos* and how he compares to other famous heroes.

[38] Odysseus had already been offered (and had rejected) immortality via marriage to Calypso (*Od.* 5.203–220). If he had accepted, his life and afterlife would have been similar to Menelaus', which came by virtue of marriage to Helen. Odysseus chose to be a hero in the model of Heracles, however, who lives out his mortal existence enjoying earthly *kleos* before death.

class as Heracles' *katabasis* and other paradigmatic *katabaseis*. This juxtaposition is the most forceful argument by the author for a particular interpretation of Odysseus as being in the same class as the greatest Greek heroes. After these messages are conveyed, the narrator gives the hero a swift exit from the Underworld. Odysseus tells his audience that he panics when he is confronted with too many narratives and temporalities, and the *Nekuia* ends abruptly.[39] Odysseus seems to realize that he has become stuck in the process of narrative exchange and has fallen into the danger of getting further lost in time and memory as "thousands of dead" (μυρία νεκρῶν, *Od.* 11.632) approach him to tell their stories.[40] Although his Phaeacian audience is captivated and would probably have him continue, Odysseus and the poet cut off the never-ending streams of narratives to draw everybody back to the story at hand: the *Odyssey*.

VII. Conclusions

By surviving an Underworld encounter, an individual such as Odysseus proves his physical, spiritual, and heroic mettle, not only by moving across nearly impossible physical obstacles but also by facing his past through a series of characters, which force him to assess and resolve issues that hinder the completion of his journey. The person he was, is, and will become (in the *Iliad*, in the Underworld of the *Nekuia*, and in the second half of the *Odyssey*, respectively) all meet each other in the Underworld scene, and his evolution between these three states is visualized in his progress through the Underworld and in conversations with and among ghosts. Through their constructions of the Underworld and choices of ghosts, landmarks, and actions, authors communicate themes, values, and information about humanity and the heroic experience, which are specific to the story at hand and universally applicable by audiences across time.

By framing the hero through the poetics of a heroic Underworld, an author lays bare different characters and themes for deeper inspection by the audience. Such evaluation is communicative and, in the heroic Underworld,

---

[39] The abrupt return seems to be a feature of early Underworld poetics, and the assumption seems to be that the path of entry is also the path of exit. This is not the case, however, in later Underworlds such as in Vergil's *Aeneid*, in which Aeneas exits through an ivory gate (*Aen.* 6.893–901).

[40] Karanika (2011) connects the abrupt end to the *Nekuia* with the mythic traditions of Heracles and the Gorgon.

tends to be subtle. Nevertheless, the idea of judging and commenting on individual or community values, whether in relation to the hero or of society more broadly, is picked up by later authors in the Archaic period who use the Underworld scene as the setting for cosmic, incontrovertible judgment and who link afterlife experience to choices made by individuals while alive. The next chapter will show how post-Homeric poets of the Archaic period incorporated, emphasized, and elaborated on ideas already contained within Homer's Underworlds to communicate messages about not only heroic glory and accomplishment but also how the living could achieve the blessed status and afterlives of heroes.

3

Becoming Blessed and Underworlds of Judgment

I. Introduction

The heroic Underworlds in Homeric epics created a structure, template, and poetic framework for myths of Underworld encounter.[1] Within these, later authors were able to find fertile ground to elaborate on ideas about religious, cultural, and social mores that not only affected their literary characters but also had implications for the real world and their audiences. A major trend in thought about the Underworld that can be traced back to Homer but expanded over time was the idea of the Underworld as a place of cosmic judgment. Such judgment, occurring only for mortals after death, would determine their eternal, posthuman existence and could serve as a moment for reconceiving accepted beliefs regarding the relationships between mortals and the gods. Death became a time for a "grand sorting," from which no human could escape, and authors began to flesh out the various factors influencing this crucial moment by inventing Underworld scenes with greater details about both the physical landscape and the society of the souls dwelling there. These Underworld scenes negotiated two problems that had broader implications for the poets' audiences: accessibility to a good afterlife and permeability across the life/death barrier.

---

[1] For a general discussion about the poetics of Homeric underworld scenes, see Dova (2012) and Gazis (2018).

Life / Afterlife. Suzanne Lye, Oxford University Press. © Oxford University Press 2024.
DOI: 10.1093/9780197690239.003.0004

Becoming Blessed and Underworlds of Judgment

In heroic Underworld scenes, such as those discussed in Chapter 2, only special heroes could move back and forth between the worlds of the living and the dead and gain access to the Underworld's resources. Furthermore, the Underworlds they witnessed were not particularly appealing but rather fulfilled most of their expectations and fears of Hades as a dank, dark, gloomy place full of suffering and unhappiness. There were, however, glimpses throughout the Homeric Underworld scenes of gradations of afterlife experience for different souls determined by some combination of their genealogy, relationship to the Olympian gods, and deeds in life. These pointed to an idea that there was a powerful, supernatural entity assigned to weigh and decide who was worthy of afterlife honors.

The realm of the dead, according to our earliest sources, is described as a kingdom and is, therefore, inherently hierarchical. Proximity to the gods, through favors or familial relationship, and the accrual of glory (*kleos*) and honors (*timai*) from deeds in life are increasingly represented as creating status among the dead. The figure Minos is mentioned in passing for the first time in Greek literature near the end of the *Nekuia* as the mythic judge of the dead (*Od.* 11.567–571), followed by a list of famous sinners, including Tityus, Tantalus, and Sisyphus (*Od.* 11.576–600), who are all undergoing eternal punishment for offenses against the gods. While no beneficial afterlife states appear in the Homeric Underworld scenes, there is the assumption that these sinners are worse off than other souls. In this particular section of the *Nekuia*, Odysseus observes their presence but does not engage with any of them or discuss the larger implications of what afterlife judgment might mean for him, a hero, or other mortals. Placed as they are within the Underworld scene landscape, the presence of a judge and mythic sinners undergoing punishment works to reinforce his indirect assertion to his Phaeacian audience that he is in the same class of katabatic heroes who have access to these unseen parts of the Underworld and has returned from "death" to the land of the living to tell the tale.

Such references to judgment and the sorting of shades that Odysseus describes give a glimpse of an afterlife that is not solely gloomy and mindless, as the Homeric poems have generally been interpreted to promote. Rather, competing and often contradictory strains of belief about the Underworld appear throughout the epics. Scholars generally agree that the heroic Underworlds in Homer, particularly the *Iliad*, cast a bleak picture of the afterlife, possibly as justification for a heroic code centered around *kleos*, which emphasizes prowess on the battlefield and the avoidance of ignoble death at all costs.[2] In such a scheme, immortality for the individual is not carried across the life–death barrier but is understood to be achieved through epic song and rituals by the living. The suggestion, therefore, that deeds and choices contribute to an individual's experience in the afterlife would have diluted this message. Christiane Sourvinou-Inwood, who generally agrees with this interpretation, has argued that the Homeric poems show awareness of a differentiated Underworld, and that the groupings of souls in the Underworld are based on the judgment of earthly deeds by the afterlife judge Minos.[3] She concludes that this idea was a part of early Greek religious belief and philosophy and that the poet chooses to downplay this for the purpose of closing off this option, which might have detracted from the Homeric focus on the importance of immortality through the epic remembrance of a hero's glorious deeds in life.

Post-Homeric Underworld scenes push back on the notion that Underworlds could only be gloomy places with "mindless heads" of the dead by envisioning a reward structure for certain categories of the dead based on the attainment of "blessedness" (*olbios* or *makar*). This assumes judgment and gradations of this status, which inform the sorting of the dead. Although they are not explicit about who does the judging or sorting, the new Underworld configurations mimic what we see in the Homeric Underworld scenes and give more information about how the groupings of Underworld souls come to be. In the *Odyssey*, for example, the audience is told that Menelaus will go to a special afterlife in Elysium because he is a son-in-law of Zeus through his marriage to Helen, and the Greek leaders appear together in a group, separate from the other dead, when they talk to Odysseus in Book 11 and encounter the suitors in Book 24. The *Odyssey* presents this information in a way that is somewhat unmarked from the perspective of the story of Odysseus' homecoming, but there are key ideas and metaliterary cues that emerge, particularly the idea of "blessedness" as a state of being with different degrees. These are brought to the forefront of post-Homeric Underworld representations, which begin to focus more on afterlife judgment. The setup for Underworld

---

[2] For an overview on beliefs about the dead and how they have changed over time, see Vermeule (1979), Bremmer (1983, 2002, 2010), Garland (1989, 1985, 1981), Sourvinou-Inwood (1995, 1981, 1983), and Mackin Roberts (2020, 110–125).

[3] Sourvinou-Inwood (1995) has argued that the variability in Homeric afterlife depictions represent an ongoing competition between traditional and emerging beliefs about death in Archaic Greek religion. Edmonds (2011a) has argued similarly, proposing that the *Nekuia* is so detailed because it is an outlier trying to challenge traditional religious views of a more vibrant afterlife.

Becoming Blessed and Underworlds of Judgment

scenes of judgment involves creating separate spaces for the dead, sorting souls based on predetermined criteria, and linking actions in life to the criteria. We can detect this process in Archaic literature starting with Homer, who is the earliest poet to show us the general landscape of the heroic Underworld and to associate types of "blessedness" with special people such as heroes. In the *Theogony*, Hesiod adds details to the Underworld space with promises of justice and judgment built directly into the Underworld structures. Expanding on this idea in the *Works and Days*, Hesiod ties human behavior on earth directly to Underworld outcome by presenting repercussions for different ways of living and showing how the actions of the living might confer *timai* to the dead. Likewise, the *Homeric Hymn to Demeter* presents the idea of death and a return from the Underworld as a negotiation for status that involves prescribed ritual actions. These mortal actions can help individuals accrue certain kinds of *timai* that affect their afterlife experiences by allowing them to achieve the status of being "blessed."

In the next section, I discuss these changes as well as the terms for "blessedness" in Archaic literature. I also demonstrate how the authors of these works, starting with the Homeric epics, use these ideas and how they might inform judgment in the Underworld to embed commentary. Finally, I discuss the implications of tying the malleable, attainable concept of "blessedness" to Underworld representation, which eventually leads to the dominance of judgment-based Underworld scenes over time.

II. Categories of Blessedness in Homer

In relation to Underworld scenes, two particular words for "blessed" come to describe similar ideas: *olbios* and *makar*. They each refer to a way of life marked by special status, which includes not only the environment and trappings of wealth but also moral and religious dimensions. During the Archaic period, *olbios* is primarily associated with mortals and *makar* almost exclusively with gods. Slippage between the two terms by poets trying to assimilate their mortal subjects to certain heroes was a popular way for authors to break down the barriers of immortality and introduce a *makar*-type afterlife as a possibility for mortals.[4] By describing particular people with the title of

---

[4] The terms and their derivatives become more interchangeable by the fourth century BCE, although *makar* is always most closely associated with the uniquely blessed state of the gods (de Heer 1969, 56).

olbios or *makar* and giving more detailed descriptions of the Underworld landscape, poets contributed to the idea that high earthly status could be mirrored beyond death to create a better afterlife and that this system would be based on degrees of "blessedness." The particular terms *olbios* and *makar* are, therefore, marked because they signal the poet's vision to the audience of a mortal's status along a spectrum in comparison with famous heroes and gods.

The concept and lifestyles associated with "blessedness" in the terms *olbios* and *makar* have particular eschatological resonance. Both refer to a supernaturally pleasant existence and a sense of status conferred by a close relationship with the gods. They also imply the intermingling of divine and mortal agents and a unique breakdown of cosmic divisions. The term *makar* is simpler to define because it is more exclusively associated with the gods. As Cornelis de Heer (1969, 6) observes, "to be μάκαρ is to be divine, to have a home secure against adversity, to be untroubled by wind and rain, to enjoy perpetual sunshine, to enjoy oneself all day long." Semantically and emotively, therefore, the "μάκαρ-sense is inseparable from the θεοί-sense" and assumes that "the gods are deathless, lead an easy life, do not eat human food and so do not need to submit to toil and hardship" (de Heer 1969, 4–5). The word "*makar*" describes an aspirational lifestyle and state of being "beyond human hope" and almost always refers to a state of being that is characteristic of gods and their dwellings. In Homer, *makar* is rarely applied to humans and, in such cases, is a marked term containing hidden information directed to the audience, such as when it describes a god disguised in human form (e.g., *Il.* 24.376–377).

Early Archaic poetry is clear in its distinction of *makar* as designating "the status of eternal happiness enjoyed by the gods, set apart from any productive labor" (Calame 2009, 200) and as a title reserved for the gods with reference to their way of life when they are in their native realm. The gods are often called *makares theoi*, or simply *makares*, terms implying that they have no worries related to food or environment and focus on pursuing their own enjoyment and personal pleasures. The gods might sit in council with each other and make requests of Zeus, but not many details are given except that their home is different from earth and does not need cultivation. The *makares* designation contains these meanings and emphasizes their separation from mortals along a specific range of attributes that the more generic term *theoi* does not. The Homeric poems play with this distinction between the terms, with the poet employing them in Underworld scenes to convey important information about the heroic protagonists. *Makar* in the *Odyssey*, for example, is almost always accompanied by the noun *theos* and appears only about thirty

Becoming Blessed and Underworlds of Judgment 83

times in the whole epic.[5] It is the special designation of the gods, particularly when they are conceived of as a group. The term *olbios*, on the other hand, is primarily associated with human beings who have the visible trappings of wealth that mark them as personal favorites of the gods who have intervened directly on their behalf. Being *olbios* means having possessions (gold, land, sons, etc.) "in such a large quantity that they arouse the admiration of others" as, perhaps, a king or aristocrat may have (de Heer 1969, 8). This stark distinction between *makar* and *olbios* holds true throughout Archaic poetry (Foley 1994, 63n486–89).

In Homer, the use of the term *olbios* generally points to the hero's designation as a favorite of the gods rather than to his actual wealth, which is rarely given in detail. A blessed hero's earthly prosperity is understood since he is a leader and warrior who gained the spoils of war. It was assumed that the gods (particularly Zeus) dispensed gifts that led to a person's designation as *olbios* (de Heer 1969, 14). Being described as *olbios*, therefore, implies that an individual's "blessedness" or wealth comes via supernatural forces and not only through his own mortal prowess or means.

Stamatia Dova (2012, 53n68) observes that "*olbios* is attributed only to mortals in Homer," and that Odysseus seems to prefer *makar* as a form of address in new situations. This may be out of an excess of caution because the gods could be in human disguise, but it also can be attributed to Odysseus' craftiness in situating himself politically against his interlocutors. When he encounters Achilles' ghost, Odysseus places the dead hero in the category

---

[5] The rare application of *makar* or its derivatives to mortals is brought to light by the fact that one of the only times in Homer that *makar* is used in the superlative and in the positive to refer to actual mortals (as opposed to gods disguised as mortals) is when Odysseus first addresses Nausicaa on Scheria (an otherworldly place similar to the Underworld), during a time when he is unsure whether she is a god or mortal (*Od.* 6.149–161). In these instances he calls her parents and siblings "thrice blessed" because of her (τρὶς μάκαρες μὲν σοί γε πατὴρ καὶ πότνια μήτηρ, / τρὶς μάκαρες δὲ κασίγνητοι, "while thrice blessed indeed are your father and mistress mother, / thrice blessed too are your siblings, *Od.* 6.154–155) and then later refers to her future husband as "the most blessed of all men by far" (κεῖνος δ' αὖ περὶ κῆρι μακάρτατος ἔξοχον ἄλλων, / ὅς κέ σ' ἐέδνοισι βρίσας οἰκόνδ' ἀγάγηται, "but that man in turn is the most blessed in his heart above all others, / who would prevail with his bride-gifts and lead you to his home in marriage," *Od.* 6.158–159). Odysseus' uncertainty explains the use of *makar* here as does the fact that he has already encountered many goddesses living on islands such as Scheria during his wanderings. The use, however, should not be underestimated since it adds to the supernatural atmosphere in Scheria that evokes a divine existence by recalling the other instances where *makar* appears, both in this poem and elsewhere. In another instance, Telemachus uses the phrase μάκαρός ἀνέρος to refer to a hypothetical father for himself (*Od.* 1.214–220). The phrase μάκαρός ἀνέρος is an oxymoron, since μάκαρός is the native state of the gods. Here, it adds to the fabulousness of the imagined situation.

of the divine by referring to his status in the afterlife as μακάρτατος (σεῖο δ᾽, Ἀχιλλεῦ, / οὔ τις ἀνὴρ προπάροιθε μακάρτατος οὔτ᾽ ἄρ᾽ ὀπίσσω, "but no other man before was more blessed than you, Achilles, nor shall there ever be in the future," *Od.* 11.482–483).[6] When such an unexpected substitution of terms occurs, the poet is underlining his verse with a subtle, yet important message for his audience. The effect of addressing Achilles with the *makar* epithet is to elevate him to a plane of existence equivalent to the divine. It takes him out of the running for the earthly title of *olbios* so that Odysseus, still alive among mortals, can take on that high-status mantle of being "the best" in the sense of being the most *olbios*.[7]

Achilles' immediate rejection of the description μακάρτατος in this passage can be construed as the poet's way of telling his audience that it is not yet time to elevate Achilles to the *makar* level of existence that would remove him from the human sphere. Odysseus' greeting also emphasizes the temporal overlaying of the Underworld *chronotope*—past, present, and future converge for Achilles' ghost (Dova 2012, 24). Odysseus, in the guise of being respectful, attempts to freeze Achilles as μακάρτατος and put him in the same category of honors and level of existence as the gods. The outright rejection of the other-worldly title *makar* reminds the audience of the criteria against which to judge Odysseus as a hero at this point in the primary narrative: Achilles' heroism is still the standard by which other heroes should be defined at this stage in the *Odyssey*, and he should be classified using human categories of blessedness, even though he is a ghost, so he can remain an apt comparandum to Odysseus. Achilles' strong reaction makes the honorific title into a central issue of the interaction, forcefully calling the question of degrees of blessedness to the audience's attention through the use of the superlative of *makar*. Additionally, the use of μακάρτατος might foreshadow the eventual presentation of Achilles in a *non*-gloomy afterlife later in Book 24, where he no longer cares how he is addressed by his comrades and passes over Agamemnon's honorific greeting without comment.

---

[6] The manuscripts and editors waver between using the comparative or superlative, and the line is sometimes written with μακάρτερος instead of μακάρτατος, but the *makar* root remains in this position of the line (Dova 2012, 24–25).

[7] While many men could be considered *olbios* at the same time, the setting and conversation suggest a competition for status between the Greek leaders, which recalls Achilles' claim in the *Iliad* of being the best of the Achaeans. Moreover, when Agamemnon's ghost enters, it does not address the group as *olbioi* but rather singles out the ghost of Achilles and then later shifts this designation to Odysseus.

In Book 24 of the *Odyssey*, the poet uses the term *olbios* to signal status between heroes. The term is used to describe both the dead Achilles and the living Odysseus, allowing them to be compared as peers and heroes of the mortal plain of existence. The Underworld scenes of Book 11 and 24 together show the replacement of Achilles with Odysseus as the quintessential hero by the end of the *Odyssey*'s primary narrative, which is signaled poetically by the transfer of the address *olbie*.[8] The gloomy Underworld of the *Nekuia* fits a war-centered, Iliadic world where heroism is defined by deeds on the battlefield being immortalized in song. The later Underworld is more suitable to the end of the *Odyssey*'s narrative, which shows Odysseus as the hero of a completed *nostos* whose successful return home and survival are as important as his battlefield deeds at Troy.

By using *olbie* as his first greeting to the soul of Achilles in the Underworld (ὄλβιε Πηλέος υἱέ, θεοῖσ' ἐπιείκελ' Ἀχιλλεῦ, / ὃς θάνες ἐν Τροίῃ ἑκὰς Ἄργεος, "**blessed** son of Peleus, god-like Achilles, who died in Troy far from Argos," *Od.* 24.36–37), Agamemnon's ghost assumes that earthly honors have traveled with Achilles into the Underworld and presents the ghosts as interacting with each other as if they were still alive. The *olbie* greeting highlights the latter's material wealth and esteem on earth to the audience, suggesting the importance of a physical body and physical possessions that have no place in the afterlife of the *Nekuia* in Book 11. These, however, are important factors in the Underworld narrative of Book 24, which occurs after Odysseus regains his status in Ithaca.

Achilles' ghost does not reject the honorific title here as in *Odyssey* 11 when Odysseus addresses him as ruling over the dead (*Od.* 11.485). The audience can assume that Achilles accepts the *olbios* designation as the respect due to him. It seems natural that the ghost of Agamemnon would address a former comrade as he knew him from the Trojan War—as the best of the Achaeans. The address also emphasizes Achilles' heroic status as a significant identity marker that carries over beyond the battlefield into the afterlife. Later in the episode, Agamemnon's ghost more properly employs the title *olbios* for the living Odysseus after hearing the dead suitors' tale of events at Ithaca (ὄλβιε Λαέρταο πάι, πολυμήχαν' Ὀδυσσεῦ, "**blessed** son of Laertes, many-wiled Odysseus," *Od.* 24.192). This is the more appropriate Archaic usage of the

---

[8] Dova (2012, 24) argues that this elevation of Odysseus to the level of Achilles might have been a fundamental motivation for the two Underworld scenes. For more about the uses and formulas of a *makarismos* in ancient Greek poetry, see Santamaría (2023).

term *olbios*, which is reinforced by Odysseus' recent change in status from wanderer to king. Having just regained his kingdom and wealth through divine assistance, he is the epitome of an *olbios* mortal. His heroic deeds and successful *nostos* earn him this *makarismos*, which is particularly marked when coming from a supernatural entity (Agamemnon's ghost). Moreover, because it is the term so recently used to designate Achilles, it draws the audience to compare the two Greek heroes. The honorific title *olbios*, repeated in such rapid succession, confers upon Odysseus a status equal to that of the famous hero Achilles. The poet of the *Odyssey* makes sure that his audience sees Odysseus as *olbios* due to divine favor *and* wealth, allowing him to be classified among the greatest Greek heroes.

Such linguistic sleight of hand in the Homeric Underworlds created openings for later authors who use Underworld scenes and "degrees of blessedness" in innovative ways. Through their compositions, poets are able to promote worldviews and perspectives for certain "actions in life" that are motivated by the looming specter of afterlife judgment. For example, Hesiod's epics and the *Homeric Hymn to Demeter*, with their didactic agendas, transform myths of the afterlife in Underworld scenes into a more explicit vehicle for prescriptive communication. These poems show afterlife judgment and outcome in Underworld scenes to audience members both to establish cosmic hierarchies and to influence behavior directly and indirectly. These later Underworld scenes use the basic model of Underworld scene construction seen in the Homeric epics. Their consistency further suggests that ancient authors treat them as culturally understood communicative devices in their poetic toolboxes to convey central messages and themes related to their frame narrative, rather than as novelties, imitations, or extraneous digressions.

An early step to categorizations of blessedness was defining the range the term covered and identifying how different forms of blessedness might appear. This was conveniently mapped through the geography of the Underworld, making it not only a perceivable physical space but also a moral space. For example, "Tartarus" is not only a region in the deepest part of the Underworld but also a manifestation of Zeus' form of justice, representing the ultimate exclusion from society for those opposing him as the ruler who brought stability to the world of the author. While Homeric Underworld scenes give hints of the Underworld's moral geography, other works from the Archaic period more explicitly make this connection. The particular poetics involved in creating and employing an Underworld chronotope, therefore, is not limited to Homer nor to heroic *katabaseis*, and later scenes actively recall ideas and structures from the Homeric Underworld scene. In approaching a wider range of afterlife-related scenes with this in mind, it becomes clear that a similar poetics of the Underworld occurs in a much wider range of Archaic texts than has previously been observed and serves a similar function of presenting an author's commentary and internal interpretation of his or her own work. Later Underworld scenes fall along a spectrum between the two primary types of afterlife scenes (heroic and judgment) and often reference these earlier models as shorthand to communicate global themes or valuations of characters to audiences. In the next section, I turn to a closer examination of how such messages are embedded in the Underworlds of Hesiod's poetry.

III. *The Judgment of Heroes: Making Mortals Blessed in Hesiod's Underworlds*

The Underworld scenes in Hesiod's *Theogony* and *Works and Days* contain a similar structure to the ones in the *Iliad* and the *Odyssey* but offer value judgments tied to the details of Underworld geography to show the hierarchy and relationship between their denizens. Underworlds of judgment emphasize the landscape of the Underworld as a moral geography, which gives additional information to the audience about the characters in that space and the cultural norms the author assumes. This is different from heroic Underworlds, which contain fewer details overall and emphasize the stories of the characters more than the space or morality of their deeds. The *Theogony*, for example, gives a clearer layout of the regions in the Greek Underworld space than other extant contemporary works, assigning locations for individuals receiving rewards or punishment to different places. The judgment that such segregation implies allows post-Homeric authors to characterize different figures through the shorthand of where they are specifically located within the Underworld. While the *Theogony* implies this conflation of space, morality, and justice, Hesiod's *Works and Days* takes the further step of using the Underworld geography to indicate the status of individuals by suggesting afterlife judgments of character as a determinant of where an individual ends up after death. Because such assessment is based on actions shown in the narrative at hand as well as those which are out of the immediate view of the audience, an Underworld of judgment can contribute more globally to the framing of individual characters and the larger narrative themes in a given work.

In this section, I first discuss how Hesiod's Underworld geography in the *Theogony* intersects with the ideas of blessedness (*olbios/makar*), status, and honors (*timai*). I examine how the poem sets up the Underworld landscape and presents the chthonic gods as individuals who embed morality into the fabric of the space through their identities, honors, and actions. Through gods such as Styx, Tartarus, and Hades, the Underworld's layout reflects figures who are both individual beings and parts of the geography. Their rewards or punishments are place-based, and they infuse their positive or negative relationship with Zeus' justice and system of rule into the makeup of the Underworld. Their presence in various locations thus divides the space into sections that communicate the values an author wants to emphasize. Through this moral geography, the audience learns how to judge particular individuals based on which section of the Underworld they inhabit because their proximity to different chthonic landmarks speaks to cosmic status and honors from Zeus.

Expanding the discussion from there to the *Works and Days,* a didactic poem, I show how this connection between the ideas behind place-based blessedness (*olbios/makar*) and afterlife assignment become the basis for Underworld scenes of judgment. Hesiod's poems illustrate how the Underworld from early Greek beliefs was used as a space to mirror the poet's values and to emphasize the importance of the more direct instructions given in the other parts of the poem. Descriptions of the Underworld suggest a moment of formal judgment and sorting for various denizens of the space and also reinforce the reasons behind taking any recommended actions. As with the Homeric Underworlds, each Hesiodic Underworld is uniquely suited to the poet's message through careful curation and cannot be readily interpreted as a statement about universally held contemporary beliefs or popular views of the afterlife. Each Underworld scene does, however, leverage ideas already present in the larger contemporary context, including in other extant epic sources we can trace, and thus allows us to infer the cultural language and expectations of authors and their audiences based on the details given in individual Underworld scenes. In the following, I first examine how the idea of blessedness and divinely bestowed honors are built into the Underworld *chronotope* and then proceed to discuss how such a temporal and topographic foundation creates the platform on which Underworld scenes of judgment are built.

Cosmic Chronotopes in the *Theogony*

Hesiod's many landscapes of the afterlife expand on the ideas of blessedness (*olbios/makar*) by tying levels of blessedness to different figures' closeness to the Olympian gods and adherence to justice through their actions.

Becoming Blessed and Underworlds of Judgment 89

The *Theogony* presents one of the earliest descriptions of the layout for the Underworld and gives the underlying reasons for its structure through its Underworld scenes. The embedded morality in its geography gives tangible meaning and visible results to afterlife judgment. In this poem, the divisions between mortals and nonmortals are laid out spatially through cosmic mapping, such that Zeus' justice and the values inherent to his reign can be tracked using the landscape in which different beings dwell. In the *Theogony*, the Underworld is a distinct kingdom ruled by gods and located in a physical space connected to both earth and sky. Its sections are determined by the stable universe set up under Zeus and its unique brand of justice, which he unleashes upon attaining his kingship: Tartarus is the prison of Zeus' enemies; Hades and Persephone rule as monarchs over a vast, dark kingdom; Styx, as a river, is a physical boundary of the Underworld and also the overseer of divine oaths; and time itself, as humans perceive it, is created cyclically through the exchange of residence between the gods Night and Day (*Theog.* 717–815). Hesiod focuses the *Theogony* on the gods and their politics, and his vision seems to confirm the Homeric *Nekuia's* conclusion of the afterlife as a place of dread and punishment, although it does not actually show any mortal souls undergoing judgment or punishment. [9] The *Theogony's* description of the landscape and chthonic deities establishes the idea of justice early on as a fundamental, stabilizing building block of the existing cosmic and Underworld structure. [10] Punishment for those who sinned against Zeus (the Titans), reward for those who were his allies (Styx), and dwellings with distinct locations for the deities Hades, Persephone, Night, and Day form a geographic division of Underworld space into regions and neighborhoods.

In the *Tartarographia* (*Theog.* 775–816), Hesiod creates an Underworld scene and establishes an Underworld *chronotope* that is linear, genealogical, teleological, cosmic, and separate from the one in the poem's narrative of the gods' wars of succession. Earlier in the poem, the narrator projects the distinctiveness of the Underworld *chronotope* by conflating geographical and temporal attributes:

---

[9] For more on Hesiod's poems as narratives about the political machinations of the gods, see Clay (1989, 2003).

[10] For more on the theme of Zeus' justice in the *Theogony*, see Lloyd-Jones (1971), Blickman (1987), Clay (2003), and Lye (2009).

90   LIFE / AFTERLIFE

ἐννέα γὰρ νύκτας τε καὶ ἤματα χάλκεος ἄκμων
οὐρανόθεν κατιών, δεκάτῃ κ᾽ ἐς γαῖαν ἵκοιτο·
ἐννέα δ᾽ αὖ νύκτας τε καὶ ἤματα χάλκεος ἄκμων
ἐκ γαίης κατιών, δεκάτῃ κ᾽ ἐς τάρταρον ἵκοι.
(*Theog.* 722–725)

For a bronze anvil falling from heaven nine nights and days would reach
earth on the tenth [day]; and in turn, a bronze anvil falling nine nights
and days down from earth would arrive at Tartarus on the tenth.

In this passage, the narrator resorts to time increments as a definition of distance just as Odysseus does when he describes the journey to get to the edge
of Hades as having taken him an entire day in his ship with the urging of the
wind (*Od.* 11.11–12). The description of distance in this passage emphasizes
that a victorious Zeus created a prison for the Titans at the furthest possible point from his kingdom (χώρῳ ἐν εὐρώεντι, πελώρης ἔσχατα γαίης, "in
a dank place, [at] the very ends of the enormous earth," *Theog.* 731; see also
717–725).[11]

Hesiod's description also includes specific details about access to the
Underworld and its civilization. The audience, like a katabatic hero, is not
dropped into the middle of the Underworld but taken along as a traveler
from edge to center. The catalog of the Underworld's terrain constitutes a
good portion of the *Theogony*, which would suggest a specific purpose and
high value for this scene in the economy of a poem with just over a thousand
lines. In addition, Hesiod introduces human terms and human time frames,
taking pains to point out the difficulty and distance that a traveler must go to
reach Tartarus. The narrator locates the space of the Underworld using relatable time increments but makes a distinct change in how he describes space.
Unlike the cosmic upheaval and chaos of different aspects of the world in the
frame narrative, the Underworld is a well-ordered space which operates in a
separate *chronotope*.

In the *Tartarographia*, Hesiod shifts the audience's attention from the
primary narrative's focus on familial relationships and personalized gods
to geographical relationships so that the former become "translated into a
topographical scheme" and "all divinities referred to in the 'Tartarographia'
figure also in the pedigrees" from earlier in the poem (Solmsen 1982b, 15).

---

[11] This line echoes the description of Hermes' path into Hades with the suitors in *Odyssey* 24
(κατ᾽ εὐρώεντα κέλευθα, *Od.* 24.10).

Becoming Blessed and Underworlds of Judgment

This indicates that the landmarks listed in the Underworld scene and their relationships to each other are marked as supplying more information about previously introduced characters through a shift in poetic register. In the *Tartarographia*, the narrator takes on the first-person perspective of a man journeying through a foreign land, meeting obstacles in sequential order, to move from the edge of the unfamiliar space toward its center. Hesiod's language treats the Underworld as a three-dimensional space through which a human being is moving and looking around, a pattern reminiscent of heroic Underworld scenes of *katabasis*. He introduces each element from that single perspective, giving a tour of both natural and constructed landmarks, which is reminiscent of the *Odyssey*'s Underworld scenes.[12]

After describing the long journey to its entrance, the first point Hesiod emphasizes is that the Underworld has a distinctly unwelcoming border (τὸν πέρι χάλκεον ἕρκος ἐλήλαται· ἀμφὶ δέ μιν νὺξ / τριστοιχὶ κέχυται περὶ δειρήν· αὐτὰρ ὕπερθε / γῆς ῥίζαι πεφύασι καὶ ἀτρυγέτοιο θαλάσσης, "Around it a bronze fence is extended, and on both sides of it, triple-layered night is poured around its neck; and above it grow the roots of the earth and of the barren sea," *Theog.* 726–728). After this hostile entry point with numerous physical obstacles, the traveler next encounters a vast chasm whose dimensions are again defined in terms of human time (χάσμα μέγ᾽, οὐδέ κε πάντα τελεσφόρον εἰς ἐνιαυτὸν / οὖδας ἵκοιτ᾽, εἰ πρῶτα πυλέων ἔντοσθε γένοιτο, / ἀλλά κεν ἔνθα καὶ ἔνθα φέροι πρὸ θύελλα θυέλλης / ἀργαλέη, "It is a great gulf, neither would a man reach the ground at the end of an entire year, once he was inside the gates, but cruel storm upon storm would carry him here and there," *Theog.* 740–743). The fence, chasm, and storms are challenges that would seem impossible for an ordinary person to overcome.[13] This portrayal gives the impression that the poet is giving a "behind the scenes" tour of the cosmos from a human perspective. The obstacles are natural ones, for the most part, and of a type that are

---

[12] In the *Odyssey*, the Underworlds are also described from the single-viewer human perspective by Circe (Book 10), by Odysseus (Book 11), and by the narrator (Book 24). Petrovic and Petrovic (2018, 72) ascribe this first-person perspective to the Titans, arguing that the *Tartarographia* is focalized from their perspective after they are imprisoned and bound in Tartarus. By following the defeated Titans into Tartarus, the narrator is able to give a vision of the Underworld, whose structure maps out Zeus' victory and subsequent distribution of honors to his allies during his reign.

[13] In the passage about the origins of the divine oath, Iris easily traverses the distance to fetch water from Styx on Zeus' command (*Th.* 784–785). Petrovic and Petrovic (2018, 73) argue that the description in this passage is focalized from the perspective of the goddess Iris, who performs a regular *katabasis* to retrieve Styx's waters.

LIFE / AFTERLIFE

prohibitive for mortals, since gods, such as Hermes and Iris, do not see them as hindrances.

After passing these physical borders, the audience comes upon a group of dwellings for the gods. This is the first time in the poem that we hear about *non*-natural structures built for and inhabited by specific gods in a communal arrangement. The narrator, as tour guide, turns the gaze of the viewer back and forth from one house to the next, building up to the most frightful structure of all—the prison of the Titans, a physical reminder and implicit warning not to cross the will of Zeus.

After traversing the gulf, the first dwelling is the House of Night. This makes sense because the gods who dwell in it are those who must leave the Tartaran space daily:

καὶ Νυκτὸς ἐρεμνῆς οἰκία δεινὰ
ἕστηκεν νεφέλης κεκαλυμμένα κυανέῃσι. (745)
τῶν πρόσθ᾽ Ἰαπετοῖο πάις ἔχει οὐρανὸν εὐρὺν
ἑστηὼς κεφαλῇ τε καὶ ἀκαμάτῃσι χέρεσσιν
ἀστεμφέως, ὅθι Νύξ τε καὶ Ἡμέρη ἆσσον ἰοῦσαι
ἀλλήλας προσέειπον ἀμειβόμεναι μέγαν οὐδὸν
χάλκεον· ἡ μὲν ἔσω καταβήσεται, ἡ δὲ θύραζε (750)
ἔρχεται, οὐδέ ποτ᾽ ἀμφοτέρας δόμος ἐντὸς ἐέργει
ἀλλ᾽ αἰεὶ ἑτέρη γε δόμων ἔκτοσθεν ἐοῦσα
γαῖαν ἐπιστρέφεται, ἡ δ᾽ αὖ δόμου ἐντὸς ἐοῦσα
μίμνει τὴν αὐτῆς ὥρην ὁδοῦ, ἔστ᾽ ἂν ἵκηται·
ἡ μὲν ἐπιχθονίοισι φάος πολυδερκὲς ἔχουσα, (755)
ἡ δ᾽ Ὕπνον μετὰ χερσί, κασίγνητον Θανάτοιο,
Νὺξ ὀλοή, νεφέλῃ κεκαλυμμένη ἠεροειδεῖ. (*Theog.* 744–757)

And the dread halls of murky Night stand there, wrapped in dark clouds. In front of these, the son of Iapetos [Atlas], standing immovable, holds broad heaven with his head and untiring hands, where Night and Day, passing near, greet each other as they cross the great bronze threshold. And while the one is about to go into the house, the other goes out the door. And the house never holds both together inside. But always, the one goes around the earth, being outside of the house, while the other, in turn, remaining inside the house waits for the time of her departure, until it comes. And the one holds far-illuminating light for the ones on the earth, while the other, destructive Night, concealed in a misty cloud, holds Sleep in her hands, the brother of Death.

Becoming Blessed and Underworlds of Judgment 93

Three fierce figures—Atlas, Night, and Day—create the space in and around this house, and a sense of its dimensions comes from the fact that Atlas must be so large that his body spans the distance from the floor of the Underworld to the base of heaven.[14] The presence of Night and Day indicates that time does have a role in the makeup of the Underworld, even though here the description refers more to spatial rather than temporal dimension, just as the anvil did in marking time by how far it had to fall between the realms of the Olympians, earth, and Tartarus (*Theog.* 722–725).

After initializing the Underworld *chronotope* through temporal and spatial cues, the narrator guides the reader's view by using the same ἔνθα-mode of storytelling seen in the *Odyssey* and briefly catalogues the other houses both in and immediately adjacent to this Underworld kingdom:

ἔνθα δὲ Νυκτὸς παῖδες ἐρεμνῆς οἰκί᾽ ἔχουσιν,
Ὕπνος καὶ Θάνατος, δεινοὶ θεοί (*Theog.* 758–759)

And **there**, the children of dark Night, Sleep and Death—terrible gods—have houses

***

ἔνθα θεοῦ χθονίου **πρόσθεν δόμοι ἠχήεντες**
ἰφθίμου τ᾽ Ἀίδεω καὶ ἐπαινῆς Περσεφονείης
ἑστᾶσιν, δεινὸς δὲ κύων **προπάροιθε** φυλάσσει (*Theog.* 767–769)

And **there, in front**, stands the **echoing halls** of the chthonic god, of powerful Hades, and of dread Persephone, and a terrible dog [Cerberus] guards **in front**

Not only is space delineated, but it is also expanded into three dimensions through the directional synonyms πρόσθεν and προπάροιθε ("in front") as well as through the idea of "echoing halls," which suggests a certain magnitude of enclosed space and grandness to the dwelling. Moreover, the owners of this house are the *future* king and queen of the Underworld, at least from the perspective of the frame narrative, because Zeus has not yet assigned his brother

---

[14] Presumably, this is the distance the anvil had to fall between heaven and earth then from earth to Tartarus, plus the distance from the bronze gate circled threefold by night across the gulf to where Atlas is standing. The House of Night itself only needs to house one god at a time, either Night or Day, whose scale is almost beyond human comprehension.

94   LIFE / AFTERLIFE

to rule over the Tartaran space nor has Persephone yet been married to Hades. The Underworld *chronotope* temporarily synchronizes disparate time periods for the audience, giving a *telos* to the "present" chaos of the gods' genealogical succession in the frame narrative with a glimpse of future stability in the presence of the house of Hades and Persephone.

The next structures, Styx's house and the Titans' prison, further expand the Underworld spatially and also politically, since both represent Zeus' power. Styx was given her dwelling and oath-keeper role as a reward from Zeus, whereas the Titans were imprisoned for opposing him:

> **ἔνθα** δὲ ναιετάει στυγερὴ θεὸς ἀθανάτοισι,
> δεινὴ Στύξ, θυγάτηρ ἀψορρόου Ὠκεανοῖο
> πρεσβυτάτη· νόσφιν δὲ θεῶν κλυτὰ δώματα ναίει
> μακρῇσιν πέτρῃσι κατηρεφέ'· ἀμφὶ δὲ πάντῃ
> κίοσιν ἀργυρέοισι πρὸς οὐρανὸν ἐστήρικται. (*Theog.* 775–779)

And **there**, a goddess who is loathsome for immortals dwells—terrible Styx. She is the oldest daughter of back-flowing Ocean. And she dwells in a famous house, separate from the gods, vaulted over with great rocks, and around it on all sides it is propped up towards the sky with silver pillars.

***

> **ἔνθα** δὲ μαρμάρεαί τε πύλαι καὶ χάλκεος οὐδός,
> ἀστεμφὲς ῥίζῃσι διηνεκέεσσιν ἀρηρώς,
> αὐτοφυής· πρόσθεν δὲ θεῶν ἔκτοσθεν ἁπάντων
> Τιτῆνες ναίουσι, πέρην χάεος ζοφεροῖο.
> αὐτὰρ ἐρισμαράγοιο Διὸς κλειτοὶ ἐπίκουροι
> δώματα ναιετάουσιν ἐπ' Ὠκεανοῖο θεμέθλοις (*Theog.* 811–816)

And **there** are marble gates and a bronze threshold, immovable, fitted with continuous roots, self-generated; and in front of this the Titans dwell, away from all the gods, beyond gloomy chaos. But the famous allies of loud-thundering Zeus dwell in houses at the very foundations of Ocean.

The reference to the houses of Zeus' allies rounds out the *Tartarographia* and returns the poem back from the geographical to the genealogical chronotope.

The places indicated, however, are more than locations in space; they also refer to locations in historical time and to political power. Using ἔνθα as an act of deixis brings objects into existence, such that "in the act of pointing to or creating such objects, deixis establishes orientation points between points which the characters of the textual universe move" (Felson 2004, 254). The audience must use these fictive landmarks introduced by ἔνθα in interpreting and understanding the larger context of the Underworld journey. The narrative's deictic gestures, therefore, invite interpretations by inferring connections between different realities—that of the audience and the one presented in the story.

The beginning of the *Theogony*'s Underworld, therefore, follows a similar pattern and function to the Underworld scenes in the *Odyssey*. Since there are no human characters in it, the *Tartarographia* demonstrates how temporal-spatial information early in a scene cues the reader to the author's transition into the Underworld *chronotope*. In this episode, the chronotopic elements overlap with the author's commentary since the very nature of the universe as it is described in this scene gives evidence for and reflects the theme of Zeus' proper rule, reinforcing the poet's stated purpose at the beginning of the poem. The *Tartarographia*, like the tale of Elpenor's ghost, supports an Underworld that is contiguous with the real world, although out of sync chronotopically. The established layout of this Underworld scene, describing Styx's home in relation to other chthonic gods, postdates the events occurring in the poem's frame narrative, which features the cosmos in formation. As an Underworld scene existing in a chronotope separate from the rest of the poem's temporal reality, the *Tartarographia* verifies to the audience the only ending to the *Theogony*'s story that Greek religion would allow: Zeus' ultimate triumph. The cosmic upheaval and generational wars of the gods in the *Theogony* transform, by the end of the poem, into the stable universe predicated on Zeus' system of justice, which is based on rewards and punishments for individuals' actions.

In the frame narrative of the *Theogony* before the *Tartarographia*, gods of the earliest generation whose names later refer to sections of the Underworld have a fluid role and are actively involved in the conflicts between the gods. Tartarus is the third god to come into existence (after Chaos and Earth), emerging in the innermost section of Earth (Τάρταρά τ' ἠερόεντα μυχῷ χθονὸς εὐρυοδείης, "and murky Tartarus in the innermost part of broad-pathed earth," *Theog.* 119), with the god Erebus coming soon after, an offspring of Chaos (*Theog.* 123) who also lives below the earth (*Theog.* 669). These two gods hold dangerous elements and powers that Zeus uses to consolidate his reign: Tartarus becomes the prison where the Titans are held (*Theog.* 279–731) and Erebus holds the allies who are strong enough to help overthrow the Titans once Zeus retrieves them (*Theog.* 668–675). These two gods, whose names become referents to the Underworld, are crucial to Zeus' success in the story of the *Theogony*. They also contain an archive of characters and possible paths for the cosmos that could solidify or upend the stability of Zeus' reign. In a final gesture to these unrealized possibilities, the poet again uses the Underworld to remind the audience about the boundaries of the cosmos and Zeus' absolute power. When Gaia's last son Typhoeus emerges into the light, causing chaos and challenging Zeus' fledgling reign, the poet illustrates, through myth, the dangers of multiple narratives and why his single narrative of Zeus' ascent should dominate as the authoritative version. Typhoeus, with his many voices talking at once, is the offspring of Tartarus, and thus an embodied Underworld, whose multiple stories must be harnessed and contained for the narrative to conclude. The figure of Typhoeus and his downfall at Zeus' hands become the poet's argument for his authority to choose the main story and suppress the alternatives, which come to light through the Underworld scenes. Such strong-arm tactics in containing and silencing Typhoeus resonate with the type of reign that Zeus represents and the poet lauds. The vision that the Underworld in the *Tartarographia* gives is of a finalized, static structure, representing the fulfillment of Zeus' promise of cosmic stability.

Through the poem's layout and placement of the Underworld, Hesiod infuses a distinctive morality into the fundamental makeup of the cosmos based on individuals' relationships with the gods and the ideas the divinities represent. While favoritism of certain mortals by gods appears in the Homeric poems, usually through parentage but also through patronage, Hesiod's *Theogony* promotes a vision for this proximity that is associated with individuals' life choices in addition to familial or divine connection. It infuses elements of judgment into an Underworld scene that looks at first like a heroic Underworld in its structure. Being a blessed favorite of the gods allows nondivine mortals such as the poet and his audience to access afterlife benefits previously reserved for demigods. In this new framing, the poet of the *Theogony* can, along with kings, be described as *olbios* because he is a favorite of the Muses, who bestow the gifts of song and just speech, respectively (ὁ δ' **ὄλβιος**, ὄντινα Μοῦσαι / φίλωνται· γλυκερή οἱ ἀπὸ στόματος ῥέει αὐδή, "and he is **blessed**, whomever the Muses love; sweet speech flows from his mouth,"

Theog. 96–97).[15] In this scheme, the poet, who is neither related to a deity nor a hero, can gain divine favor in other ways, through his profession and deference to the Muses, which in turn lead to his ability to produce "sweet speech." After Homer, the blessedness of mortals increasingly becomes associated with levels of closeness to the gods through individuals' choices, abilities, and actions rather than through divine birth or heroic deeds, an idea expanded even further in Hesiod's other poem, the *Works and Days*.

Counting One's Blessedness in the *Works and Days*

In the *Works and Days* (*Op.*), *olbios* is specific to the blessedness of mortals and relates to what they receive or do while alive, which is then reflected in their afterlife experience. By playing with this idea of "blessedness," the *Works and Days* proposes a vision of the afterlife that is less starkly intimidating than the one in the *Theogony* and more directly at odds with the Homeric gloomy afterlife of mindless shades. Like previous Underworld depictions, however, the information the *Works and Days'* Underworld scene contains about ghostly society strengthens and elaborates the themes of its frame narrative, which links moral values to certain actions and behaviors by individuals.

Hesiod's *Works and Days* is a didactic poem with the conceit of a poet instructing his brother (and humanity in general) as to how to live a good, even "blessed," life filled with all the rewards that go along with adhering to justice and divine will. The lessons are reiterated through multiple myths and analogies, particularly in the representation of rivalries between races of deities and of the growing tension between mortals and immortals. The myth of Pandora, with its creation of women as a punishment for the acquisition of fire (*Op.* 59–105), and the fable of the hawk and nightingale (*Op.* 202–212) both emphasize the absolute power of Zeus and his will. The myth of the "Ages of Man" (*Op.* 109–201) similarly pushes this argument by showing how each generation of man devolves further away from the gods through their unjust acts. Throughout each era, Hesiod clearly equates a mortal's afterlife experience with his actions in life, strengthening the connection between finite life and eternal afterlife by elaborating on the specific rewards

---

[15] de Heer (1969, 20) observes that there is no association at all in this passage between *olbios* and material wealth. The skills of a poet, however, would put him in good standing with patrons.

98 LIFE / AFTERLIFE

and punishments different types of mortals can expect after death. This element of judgment tied to the willful actions of the individual and the idea of "sorting," while not new ideas, were not something explicitly emphasized in the Homeric poems.[16] Such ideas may even have been downplayed to push the focus toward the importance of gaining *kleos* among communities of the living rather than the necessity of accruing benefits that apply only to single individuals after death in a hidden, distant place like the Underworld.[17]

The "Ages of Man" section of the *Works and Days* (*Op.* 109–201) goes further than the Underworld scenes of the Homeric epics and *Theogony* in describing how human actions during life directly relate to afterlife outcomes. The episode emphasizes aspects that point to an Underworld based on the judgment of individual blessedness. These features include the persistence of consciousness after death, the centrality of the soul's afterlife experience, and the landscape of the Underworld as reflective of an individual's fate. The different status in life and death for each race of humans suggests a more compartmentalized afterlife for mortals and a richer experience for souls than indicated anywhere else in the extant Archaic poems. Justice and the rewards that come from just deeds are implied by what earns a certain race its positive or negative afterlife. This information in the *Works and Days* underpins the variety of afterlife narratives in later poetry, whose Underworld passages are variations on the central theme of "just deeds in life lead to a blessed afterlife."

The *Works and Days* highlights the afterlife existences of several generations of humanity, with varying levels of reward and punishment after death. Each afterlife is directly related to a race's actions while alive and is also tied to ideas of justice, reward, and punishment. The Silver and Bronze races, for example, commit *hubris*, dishonor the gods, and live in violent lawlessness leading to them being sent into darkness below the earth (*Op.* 140–142 and

---

[16] Martin (2014) makes a convincing argument that the sorting of the dead in *Odyssey* 11 corresponds to levels of honor and that status among the dead is suggested by which souls have the chance to drink the blood from Odysseus' pit offering. Martin's conclusion supports the argument of this chapter that status based on judgment and sorting is embedded in afterlife society representations.

[17] The idea of judgment has not received a large role in discussions of the Homeric epics because the *Nekuia* emphasizes an equitable afterlife for souls with little differentiation or awareness after death, one which scholars refer to as the "negative" view. Sourvinou-Inwood (1981, 22–25) first challenged the idea that Homer was unaware of a positive, blessed afterlife by taking into account the Underworld depictions outside of the *Nekuia*, arguing that contradictions between them were reflective of actual eighth-century BCE social and religious debates, which were fossilized in the Homeric poems, whose written form coincided with this very debate.

Becoming Blessed and Underworlds of Judgment 99

152–156, respectively). Their Underworld landscape is described as gloomy, lightless, and dank, similar to the one Odysseus encounters as he approaches Hades in Book 11 of the *Odyssey*, but with the further suggestion that it is a place of punishment. The fourth race of heroes is split into two locations. Some simply die and go to a place either neutral or dark, with the implication that their afterlives are substantially different from the select few who are allowed to go to another place called "the Isles of the Blessed."[18] The fifth race of Iron, however, seems fated to end in the dark, gloomy Underworld, which is attributed to their *hubris*, a word appearing in line 191 of the Iron race section in the accusative singular form (ὕβριν) as an internal echo to the same word and form in line 134 (ὕβριν), describing the earlier Silver race's offenses.

The Iron race's end is not explicitly described but there are hints that it may be split in a similar way to that of the heroic fourth race, perhaps due to an awareness that there are different afterlife possibilities that are triggered by individuals' actions. There is no question that the fifth race is heading toward a bad end on a path of self-destruction like the Silver and Bronze races. The poet is careful to note, though, that there are glimmers of good (ἀλλ' ἔμπης καὶ τοῖσι μεμείξεται ἐσθλὰ κακοῖσιν, "but, nevertheless, even for those men, good things will be mixed with evils," *Op.* 179). The mingling of good and evil suggests that there are choices in an individual's behavior that have implications for status.[19]

For the hubristic Silver race, however, there is no hope of redemption except after death. Through the ritual actions of living, mortal men, who give them honor and call them the "blessed dead under the earth" (τοὶ μὲν ὑποχθόνιοι μάκαρες θνητοί, *Op.* 141), the Silver race experiences a change of status along with their state of being, in that they are no longer associated exclusively with *hubris* (*Op.* 134) but with the type of blessedness associated with the gods. Although their lives were unjust and unrestrained from *hubris*

---

[18] There is some dispute over whether the heroic race goes to two locations or one, mostly by scholars who argue for a ring composition, dividing the four initial races as just or unjust in balance with each other (Querbach 1985). This reading often excludes the Iron race as an exception or later addition to an original myth of races. The reading of a bifurcated afterlife for the heroic race makes more sense when including the Iron race as part of the progression because it allows for the idea of agency in actions, which in turn determines afterlife outcome. Differentiation between heroes and their afterlives is also more representative of how status is portrayed among the heroes, particularly in the Homeric poems.

[19] The heroic race is the only other race that shows different treatment for different members, with Zeus granting special privileges to certain members.

100 LIFE / AFTERLIFE

(*Op.* 134), the spirits of the Silver race are ultimately treated as divinely blessed by the community of living men:

ὕβριν γὰρ ἀτάσθαλον οὐκ ἐδύναντο
ἀλλήλων ἀπέχειν, οὐδ' ἀθανάτους θεραπεύειν (135)
ἤθελον οὐδ' ἔρδειν **μακάρων** ἱεροῖς ἐπὶ βωμοῖς,
ἢ **θέμις** ἀνθρώποις κατὰ ἤθεα. τοὺς μὲν ἔπειτα
Ζεὺς Κρονίδης ἔκρυψε χολούμενος, οὕνεκα τιμὰς
οὐκ ἔδιδον **μακάρεσσι** θεοῖς οἳ Ὄλυμπον ἔχουσιν.
αὐτὰρ ἐπεὶ καὶ τοῦτο γένος κατὰ γαῖα κάλυψε, (140)
τοὶ μὲν **ὑποχθόνιοι μάκαρες θνητοὶ** καλέονται,
δεύτεροι, ἀλλ' ἔμπης τιμὴ καὶ τοῖσιν ὀπηδεῖ. (*Op.* 134–142)

For they were not able to restrain themselves from wicked *hubris* against each other nor were they willing to worship the immortals nor offer sacrifice on the holy altars of the **blessed** ones, as is **just** for men, according to custom. In anger, Zeus, son of Cronus, then concealed them because they did not give honors to the **blessed** gods who hold Olympus. But since the earth covered up this race also, they are called the **blessed dead under the earth**; they are second in rank, but honor, nonetheless, attends even them.

The term *makar* features prominently in this passage to define both the gods and the Silver race after it has been given posthumous honors by later mortals. There are no details about whether the Silver race's actual experience in the afterlife changes based on being called *makares*, but their conversion from being hubristic to blessed in the *makar* sense is definitely tied to the honors, or *timai*, they receive from mortal men who call them (and the gods) *makares* (*Op.* 141 and 136, respectively).[20]

As Claude Calame (2009, 74) observes, "without being assimilated to the gods, these men of silver end up having a form of immortality," attaining an afterlife that lets them be called "blessed" in the divine sense (μάκαρες, *Op.* 141), even though they dwell underground. The juxtaposition here of μάκαρες with θνητοὶ and ὑποχθόνιοι is particularly remarkable—Cornelis de Heer (1969, 21) calls the grouping an "oxymoron" —since *makar* more commonly appears with *theoi* and, somewhat rarely, with *athanatoi* (e.g., ἀθανάτων μακάρων, *Op.* 706; μακάρεσσι ἀθανάτοισιν, *Hom. Hymn Apoll.* 315). This picture gives hope

---

[20] According to Currie (2005, 72–84), the term *time* implies literal immortality through cult.

Becoming Blessed and Underworlds of Judgment

to Hesiod's audience because it has implications for them, as members of the Iron race. Although the Iron race's prospects are generally grim, the presence of any good to punctuate their evils during life gives an opening that the afterlife might yet have hope, whether through special selection by divine edict, as in the Heroic race (*Op.* 167–168), or posthumous honors by mortals, as are given to the Silver race.

In contrast to the Silver race, the afterlives of the Golden race and a select group from the race of heroes are blessed with godlike existences in life and death. The phrases and landscape features in these descriptions later become watchwords for activating links between Underworld texts. They tell of humans approaching the level of gods in their eternal lifestyles:

Χρύσεον μὲν πρώτιστα γένος μερόπων ἀνθρώπων
ἀθάνατοι ποίησαν Ὀλύμπια δώματ᾽ ἔχοντες. (110)
οἳ μὲν ἐπὶ Κρόνου ἦσαν, ὅτ᾽ οὐρανῷ ἐμβασίλευεν·
ὥστε θεοὶ δ᾽ ἔζωον ἀκηδέα θυμὸν ἔχοντες
νόσφιν ἄτερ τε πόνων καὶ ὀϊζύος, οὐδέ τι δειλὸν
γῆρας ἐπῆν, αἰεὶ δὲ πόδας καὶ χεῖρας ὁμοῖοι
τέρποντ᾽ ἐν θαλίῃσι, κακῶν ἔκτοσθεν ἁπάντων· (115)
θνῆσκον δ᾽ ὥσθ᾽ ὕπνῳ δεδμημένοι· ἐσθλὰ δὲ πάντα
τοῖσιν ἔην· καρπὸν δ᾽ ἔφερε ζείδωρος ἄρουρα
αὐτομάτη πολλόν τε καὶ ἄφθονον· οἳ δ᾽ ἐθελημοὶ
ἥσυχοι ἔργ᾽ ἐνέμοντο σὺν ἐσθλοῖσιν πολέεσσιν.
αὐτὰρ ἐπεὶ δὴ τοῦτο γένος κατὰ γαῖα κάλυψε, (121)
τοὶ μὲν δαίμονες ἁγνοὶ ἐπιχθόνιοι τελέθουσιν
ἐσθλοί, ἀλεξίκακοι, φύλακες θνητῶν ἀνθρώπων,
οἵ ῥα φυλάσσουσίν τε δίκας καὶ σχέτλια ἔργα
ἠέρα ἐσσάμενοι πάντη φοιτῶντες ἐπ᾽ αἶαν, (125)
πλουτοδόται· καὶ τοῦτο γέρας βασιλήιον ἔσχον. (*Op.* 109–126)

The deathless gods who have homes on Olympus made the very first race of mortal men golden. These were the ones who lived in the time of Cronus, when he ruled the sky. And **just like gods**, [the Golden Race of men] lived with a carefree heart, aloof and apart from toils and sorrow, and neither did wretched old age oppress them at all; but they, always the same as ever with respect to their hands and feet, delighted in feasts, far away from all evils. And they died as if subdued by sleep; and they had all goods things: the grain-giving field bore plentiful fruit of its own accord, abundantly and ungrudgingly, and they willingly and

LIFE / AFTERLIFE

peacefully distributed the [fruits of their] labors with many good things. But when at length [Zeus] hid this race under the earth, **they became in the end the holy *daimons* upon the earth**—noble, protectors from evil, guardians of mortal men—the ones who watch over judgments and cruel deeds, while they flit above the earth clothed in air and give wealth; and this kingly honor they received.

A supernatural setting, similar to the home of the gods, provides their material needs while they are alive (*Op.* 109–120). Then this race of men actually becomes gods, or *daimones*, after they die, and they have the honors of overseeing justice and distributing wealth.[21] Their good life and honorable afterlife are connected to each other. Although the term *makar* is not used explicitly, the descriptions of space are meant to give details of the existence for those designated as *makares*, such as a heart free from toils, sorrow, and illness and a home in a fertile land that needs no cultivation. Additionally, the presence of Cronus and ongoing camaraderie and joyful feasting are tropes frequently associated with this blessed existence.

The race of heroes borrows the distinctive status markers of blessedness presented in the previous two races of men. Select heroes are imagined to have an afterlife experience separate from the other dead (as occurred in some of the Homeric Underworld scenes) and similar to the gods' *makar* way of life. The blessed heroes' afterlife is marked by a lack of cares and the involvement of Cronus in a kingly role:

Αὐτὰρ ἐπεὶ καὶ τοῦτο γένος κατὰ γαῖα κάλυψεν,
αὖτις ἔτ᾽ ἄλλο τέταρτον ἐπὶ χθονὶ πουλυβοτείρῃ
Ζεὺς Κρονίδης ποίησε, δικαιότερον καὶ ἄρειον,
ἀνδρῶν ἡρώων θεῖον γένος, οἳ καλέονται
ἡμίθεοι, προτέρη γενεὴ κατ᾽ ἀπείρονα γαῖαν. (160)
καὶ τοὺς μὲν πόλεμός τε κακὸς καὶ φύλοπις αἰνὴ
τοὺς μὲν ὑφ᾽ ἑπταπύλῳ Θήβῃ, Καδμηΐδι γαίῃ,
ὤλεσε μαρναμένους μήλων ἕνεκ᾽ Οἰδιπόδαο,
τοὺς δὲ καὶ ἐν νήεσσιν ὑπὲρ μέγα λαῖτμα θαλάσσης
ἐς Τροίην ἀγαγὼν Ἑλένης ἕνεκ᾽ ἠυκόμοιο. (165)
ἔνθ᾽ ἦ τοι τοὺς μὲν θανάτου τέλος ἀμφεκάλυψε
τοῖς δὲ δίχ᾽ ἀνθρώπων βίοτον καὶ ἤθε᾽ ὀπάσσας

---

[21] There is a similar idea in *Homeric Hymn to Demeter* (488–489) of the bequest of wealth by supernatural favor. In this poem, Persephone and Demeter are portrayed as givers of wealth to those described as *olbios* ("blessed").

Ζεὺς Κρονίδης κατένασσε πατὴρ ἐς πείρατα γαίης.
τηλοῦ ἀπ᾽ ἀθανάτων· τοῖσιν Κρόνος ἐμβασιλεύει.
καὶ τοὶ μὲν **ναίουσιν ἀκηδέα θυμὸν ἔχοντες** (170)
ἐν μακάρων νήσοισι παρ᾽ Ὠκεανὸν βαθυδίνην,
ὄλβιοι ἥρωες, τοῖσιν μελιηδέα καρπὸν
τρὶς ἔτεος θάλλοντα φέρει ζείδωρος ἄρουρα. (*Op.* 156–173)

But when the earth also covered up this race, Cronus' son Zeus again made still another race upon the all-nourishing earth, a fourth, more just and noble god-like race, who are called demi-gods, the race just before [ours] on the boundless earth. Evil war and the dread call to battle destroyed them, some when they struggled under seven-gated Thebes, Cadmus' land, for the flocks of Oedipus, and others brought in ships over the great expanse of the sea to Troy for the sake of lovely-haired Helen. And there, the finality of death enshrouded some, but for others, father Zeus, son of Cronus, granted a life and habitations apart from men and settled them at the ends of the earth. They are far from the deathless gods, [and] Cronus rules them as king. In fact, they dwell **with a carefree heart on Isles of the Blessed alongside deep-swirling Ocean. They are the blessed heroes, for whom the grain-giving field bears honey-sweet fruit, blooming three times a year**.

This passage not only mimics the idea of a fertile earth and carefree heart but also *names* the location the "Isles of the Blessed" (μακάρων νήσοισι), ensuring that the audience recognizes it as the *makar* lifestyle associated with the divine realm. Calling the heroes of the fourth race *olbioi* (ὄλβιοι, *Op.* 172) emphasizes the unique relationship that the gods had with these particular men. Through the intercession of Zeus (*Op.* 167–168), these *olbioi hēroēs* enjoy a *makar*-type blessed afterlife. These particular heroes get the gods' notice, according to Calame, because they are from a hybrid race (ἡμίθεοι, "half-gods," *Op.* 160) that is capable of performing glorious deeds. Calame argues that because heroes are between gods and men by nature, they "can attain the happiness experienced by immortals through the brilliance of *kléos*" (Calame 2009, 191). Because of these religious and cultural resonances, the terms *olbios* and *makar* are active links that emerge in this time period and recall Underworld scenes through coded language to encourage certain beliefs and rituals by the living with promises for the future. This development is illustrated in the next section's examination of the *Homeric Hymn to Demeter*.

IV. Lifestyles of the Blessed in the Homeric Hymn to Demeter

The Homeric and Hesiodic epics offer our earliest examples of how different Underworld locations are segregated and how afterlife experiences in each relate to valuations of the blessedness of their denizens. In relation to Underworld scenes, states of blessedness are determined both before and after death by one's *arete* ("excellence") as judged by actions in life, proximity to the gods through birth or favor, and access to a way of life akin to that experienced by the gods. These states are indicated by words such as *olbios* and *makar* but also by descriptions of afterlife experiences in Underworld scenes that visually reflect these states. The *Homeric Hymn to Demeter (Hom. Hymn Dem.)*, like the *Theogony*, describes an Underworld kingdom already ruled by Hades but at the moment when he first takes his bride Persephone (see Figure 3.1).

Although the mortals in the *Homeric Hymn to Demeter* do not go to the Underworld, their relationship to the queen of the dead, through the cult and rituals prescribed by Demeter at the end of the poem, relies on an Underworld

FIGURE 3.1 Hades kidnapping Persephone in his chariot to be his wife while Hermes (left) observes. Red figure volute krater painted by the Iliupersis Painter. Apulian (Greek), 370–350 BCE Courtesy of © The Trustees of the British Museum.

scene as a platform to introduce the possibility of human control over their afterlife. This detail, while only a small part of the story and poem overall, is of critical importance to future formulations of Underworld scenes, as later authors expand on the strategies that different types of individuals can take to gain access to more blessed states after death.

The *Homeric Hymn to Demeter* is a song of praise to the goddess Demeter that also gives the origin myths for important phenomena in ancient Greek religion, including the marriage of Hades to Persephone and the founding of the Eleusinian Mysteries. As Demeter moves between divine and human society, the audience receives a window into the customs, practices, and interests of each as well as instructions that affect future interactions. In the course of the poem, the audience receives a vision of the Underworld when Hermes goes to retrieve Persephone and when Persephone describes her experience with Hades during her reunion with Demeter. We know from Hermes' descent and later ascent that Hades lives in a house deep under the earth in Erebus, a region within the gloom of the Underworld from which he can only depart with his charge using Hades' special immortal horses (*Hom. Hymn Dem.* 375–376). While there, Hades entertains his bride with comfort (*Hom. Hymn Dem.* 342–343) and later offers her both food (*Hom. Hymn Dem.* 372–373) and promises of "having the greatest *timai* among the immortals" (τιμὰς δὲ σχήσησθα μετ᾽ ἀθανάτοισι μεγίστας, *Hom. Hymn Dem.* 366) through the rites and offerings given to her as his bride by mortals. These details, along with references to the company of the gods earlier in the poem, reinforce ideas about the removed, divine lifestyle, whether on Olympus or in Hades, as being desirable and carefree (at least when Demeter is not causing a famine and thus disrupting mortals' ability to propitiate them with ritual offerings). The alternative to this existence is the one mortals experience on earth, filled with uncertainty and constant deference to the more powerful divine beings.

By portraying Demeter mingling among mortals and giving them direct instructions for how to perform her *timai*, the author of the *Homeric Hymn to Demeter* shares vital information about the importance of the Eleusinian mysteries and the intent of its rituals, showing audiences and future worshippers how to develop bonds with gods who, in this case, have direct influence over both life and afterlife, through Demeter's control over food-stuff and Persephone's power as queen of the dead. This hymn presents an Underworld that is directly pertinent to human audiences and almost completely removed from heroic interest. It depicts an Underworld scene with promises of a blessed afterlife accessible to those individuals who can gain divine favor through proper rituals at Eleusis *before* death, thus allowing them to presort themselves to a more blessed afterlife through such initiation.

This turn to eschatology and prescriptive blessedness occurs at a shift in the hymn, when the narrator concludes his story of the goddesses and turns to advertising the implications of Demeter's new rites for the audience both on earth and in the afterlife. After Demeter gives ritual instructions to the leaders of Eleusis (see Figure 3.2),

FIGURE 3.2 Eleusinian relief
Great Eleusinian Relief portraying Demeter (left) and Persephone (right) with Triptolemos (center). Roman copy of a Greek original, which was found in the sanctuary of Demeter at Eleusis, the site of the Eleusinian Mysteries. Early Imperial, Augustan, ca. 27 BCE–14 CE. Marble, H. 89 3/8 in. (227 cm). Rogers Fund, 1914 (14.130.9). Courtesy of © The Metropolitan Museum of Art. Image source: Art Resource, NY.

Becoming Blessed and Underworlds of Judgment

she collects her daughter and ends her self-imposed exile, finally returning to Olympus and stabilizing the cosmic balance between the realms of Olympus, earth, and Hades. Her interaction with humans, however, gives nonheroic mortals the ability to achieve a state on earth in which they will be called *olbios* ("blessed"). In the context of the hymn, then, *olbios* implies blessedness of the material sort, a visible, tangible indicator of proximity to the supernatural type (*makar*), which is also referenced in the poem (Foley 1994, 63n486–89).

In the *Homeric Hymn to Demeter*, the term *makar* is used three times in reference to the gods as a defining epithet, along with the deictic ἔνθα. Each reference to the deities as "blessed" occurs in relation to their location or movement to or from their dwellings with other gods, clearly marking the term as having a sacred connotation. In the first instance, μακάρων is a substantive adjective used to refer to the gods living in a state of blessedness, which implies that they are in a carefree existence on Olympus:

> . . . ἀτὰρ ξανθὴ Δημήτηρ
> **ἔνθα** καθεζομένη **μακάρων** ἀπὸ νόσφιν ἁπάντων
> μίμνε πόθῳ μινύθουσα βαθυζώνοιο θυγατρός (*Hom. Hymn Dem.* 302–304)

> But fair-haired Demeter remained **there**, sitting [in her temple at Eleusis] apart
> from all the **blessed gods**, wasting away with longing
> for her deep-girdled daughter . . .

Describing the gods as *makar* in this instance emphasizes that Demeter has shunned not only their company but also their state of blessedness as she languishes in grief and remains in the human realm.

The second reference to the gods as *makar* also has a spatial aspect. After Iris unsuccessfully pleads with Demeter to return to Olympus at Zeus' behest, he orders all the other gods to try to persuade her, forcing them to leave the comforts of their home to go to Eleusis with the sole purpose of begging her to return with them to Olympus:

> Ὣς φάτο λισσομένη· τῆς δ᾽ οὐκ ἐπεπείθετο θυμός.
> αὖτις ἔπειτα πατὴρ **μάκαρας θεοὺς αἰὲν ἐόντας**
> πάντας ἐπιπροΐαλλεν· ἀμοιβηδὶς δὲ κιόντες
> κίκλησκον καὶ πολλὰ δίδον περικαλλέα δῶρα,
> τιμάς θ᾽ ἅς κ᾽ ἐθέλοιτο μετ᾽ ἀθανάτοισιν ἑλέσθαι. (*Hom. Hymn Dem.* 324–328)

LIFE / AFTERLIFE

Thus [Iris] beseeched her, but [Demeter's] heart was not persuaded.
Next, the father sent all the **blessed, eternal gods,**
one after the other. And going in succession,
they called upon her and gave many beautiful gifts and whatever honors
among the immortals she might want to take.

In this passage, almost all the epithets used to describe the gods in the *Hymn*
are crowded into a few short lines: μάκαρας (πάντας), θεοὺς, αἰὲν ἐόντας, and
ἀθανάτοισιν. Individually, each of these can be translated simply as "gods,"
but in proximity, they force the audience to consider different aspects of the
beings referred to as "gods." Although αἰὲν ἐόντας ("always existing") and ἀθ
ανάτοισιν ("undying") mean essentially the same thing, the emphasis differs.
The former focuses on time and existence as having an eternal quality, while
the latter's alpha-privative draws attention to the lack of the milestone event
of "death," which is the unique identifier of mortals as a category and brings
them much pain, grief, and anxiety. The word θεοὺς is the term specifically
meaning "gods," but the term μάκαρας ("blessed") more properly describes the
gods' culture and way of life as opposed to their natures.

This suggestion of culture as opposed to nature seems to hold true as well
in the third reference to the gods as *makares*. It appears in a section of text
that is hopelessly corrupt but that can still give hints about the particular
word's usage. The received text includes it in the phrase θεῶν μακάρων ("of the
blessed gods," *Hom. Hymn Dem.* 345) in the section of the poem describing
Persephone in the Underworld with Hades. The line is untranslatable and
may have been misplaced (Foley 1994, 54); the sense of *makar*, however, in the
received text again seems to denote the gods living in a state of blessedness *as
opposed to* the locations of Persephone or Demeter, which are "far away." Foley
(1994, 20) translates the line ἡ δ' ἀποτηλοῦ ἔργοις θεῶν μακάρων ‿‿– μητίσετο
βουλῇ (*Hom. Hymn Dem.* 344–345) as the following: "Still she, Demeter, was
brooding on revenge for the deeds of the blessed gods." The word ἀποτηλοῦ,
which Foley does not translate, can also be understood with θεῶν μακάρων to
mean "far away from the blessed gods." Although the exact transcription and
translation are unclear, the sense seems to be that Demeter has excluded her-
self from the environment of the blessed gods while she broods.[22]

---

[22] For a more detailed discussion of these lines and the corruption of the text here, see
Richardson (1974, 266n344–345).

Becoming Blessed and Underworlds of Judgment

For humans in the earthly plane, the dyad of earthly qualities attached to the *olbios* designation (i.e., material wealth and divine favor) in the Archaic epic context is reflected and reinforced in the *Homeric Hymn to Demeter* when the mortal initiate attains the designation of *olbios*. In the following passage, this is explicitly paired with a projection beyond death into the afterlife status of the initiated individual:

ὄλβιος ὃς τάδ' ὄπωπεν ἐπιχθονίων ἀνθρώπων· *(480)*
ὃς δ' ἀτελὴς ἱερῶν, ὅς τ' ἄμμορος, οὔ ποθ' ὁμοίων
αἶσαν ἔχει φθίμενός περ ὑπὸ ζόφῳ εὐρώεντι.
Αὐτὰρ ἐπεὶ δὴ πάνθ' ὑπεθήκατο δῖα θεάων,
βάν ῥ' ἴμεν Οὔλυμπον δὲ θεῶν μεθ' ὁμήγυριν ἄλλων.
ἔνθα δὲ ναιετάουσι παραὶ Διὶ τερπικεραύνῳ (485)
σεμναί τ' αἰδοῖαί τε· μέγ' ὄλβιος ὅν τιν' ἐκεῖναι
προφρονέως φίλωνται ἐπιχθονίων ἀνθρώπων·
αἶψα δέ οἱ πέμπουσιν ἐφέστιον ἐς μέγα δῶμα
Πλοῦτον, ὃς ἀνθρώποις ἄφενος θνητοῖσι δίδωσιν. (*Hom. Hymn Dem.*
480–489)

Blessed is he of earth-bound men who has seen these things; but he who is uninitiated in these holy rites, and who takes no part in them, never enjoys a similar fate even after he is dead, wasting away in the dank gloom. But indeed when the splendid goddess established all these [rites], she and Persephone went to Olympus to join with the host of other gods. And there they, revered and honored, dwell near Zeus, who delights in the thunderbolt. Greatly **blessed** is he of the men on earth whom those goddesses particularly love. Straightaway they send [the god] Pluto to him upon the hearth at his great house, who gives wealth to mortal men.

The repetition of *olbios* in this passage signals its importance. As the first word in this passage, *olbios* gives a promise to initiates of a better hope for the afterlife by hinting at the soul's bifurcated path to Hades, with the one for the uninitiated leading to "wasting away in dank gloom" (φθίμενός περ ὑπὸ ζόφῳ εὐρώεντι, *Hom. Hymn Dem.* 482). This is a reference to a sorting that will occur upon death, although actual judgment is not mentioned. After this sorting, initiates can expect to receive something special in the afterlife from which noninitiates are forever excluded. The latter "**never** enjoys a similar fate" (οὔ ποθ' ὁμοίων αἶσαν ἔχει, *Hom. Hymn Dem.* 481–482) to the initiates

LIFE / AFTERLIFE

when they are both in Hades. Even though all souls lose their physical, earthly wealth and attributes, they still maintain differentiation in their afterlife environments. Actions in life, such as participation in initiation, thus convey status extending beyond the living world. In addition to escaping a gloomy afterlife, the *olbioi* initiates also get to enjoy their blessed state by being a favorite of Demeter and Persephone, who will send them material wealth. In the *Homeric Hymn to Demeter*, there are thus competing "negative" (mindless) and "positive" (conscious) views of the afterlife. Parallel existences for the dead are brought to the audience's awareness when the poet delineates the new "insider" group of special souls, who have access to an afterlife that seems to be located in a place similar to the one previously reserved for heroes.

Eventually, the term *olbios* comes to cover a larger range of experiences than its original meaning and seems to have been applied to heroes in general, particularly those associated with hero-cult. Linking Odysseus to Achilles through the title *olbios* in Book 24 of the *Odyssey* also means linking the hero Odysseus to the narrative traditions surrounding the *Iliad*'s main hero. These might even be alluding to myths about a blessed afterlife existence for Achilles on Leuke, given the immediate context of ghosts in conversation.[23] Similarly, the use of *olbios* to describe the Eleusinian initiates, a title applied to Homeric heroes, has implications for the perception of both their lives and afterlives. In the case of the *Homeric Hymn to Demeter*, the god Pluto, who is "wealth" personified, is mentioned as the conveyor of earthly, particularly agricultural, wealth to initiates in life at the request of the goddesses (Bremmer 2014a, 19). *Both* Persephone and Demeter send the god Pluto to initiated mortals who perform their cult.[24] Persephone's good will and status as a goddess of life and afterlife translate such a boon into a promise of reward after death. Since Persephone has power in both realms, there is also the implication that afterlife benefits would be equivalent to wealth acquired during

---

[23] The ghost of Achilles in Book 24 accepts the title of "blessed" (ὄλβιε, *Od.* 24.36) without issue, whereas the ghost of Achilles presented in Book 11 strongly objects to being described as "most blessed" (μακάρτατος, *Od.* 11.483) by Odysseus. His later acceptance of the title "blessed" could be interpreted as an evolution in his acceptance of his fate or that he is being honored by a fellow ghost as opposed to a person still alive. I argue that the Underworld scene in Book 24 is activating a different set of *para-narratives* from the one in Book 11 so that the audience will interpret Odysseus' recent victories in battle at Ithaca as suitable for elevating him to the same heroic and blessed status as Achilles. For more on myths of Achilles' afterlife, see Burgess (2009).

[24] In the *Homeric Hymn to Demeter*, Pluto and Hades are distinct but associated gods who were later interchanged with each other in literature and art due to their many overlapping functions and representations with Persephone. For more about the distinctions between Pluto and Hades, see Mackin Roberts (2020, 43–46).

life. The Underworld scenes in the *Homeric Hymn to Demeter*, through such language around blessedness, both create and reinforce the soteriological element to the Eleusinian Mysteries. As scholars such as Michael Cosmopoulos (2015, 164–165) have shown, the transition of the cult of Demeter at Eleusis to a mystery cult with the promise of a positive afterlife through earthly action occurs in the archaeological record around the seventh century BCE, coinciding with the time frame of the hymn's composition.[25] The poet uses the hymn's Underworld scenes and the ideas surrounding blessedness, which are associated with such scenes, to project this shift and give guidance to audiences on the levels of both belief and ritual action.

In its application as an honorific title to Eleusinian initiates (as well as to Achilles' soul and to the living Odysseus), the term *olbios* activates a complex of references that implies a form of heroic "blessedness" in the afterlife (a *makar* state of being) in addition to visible prosperity during life. As shown in these Archaic examples, conferring the title *olbios* on an individual had a specific meaning with eschatological resonance. Although the actual words of the Eleusinian mysteries' *makarismos* are unknown, it can be assumed from the hymn's strict dichotomy between the gods' *makar* existence and humans' designation as *olbios* via the Eleusinian rites that any *makarismos* probably used the title *olbios*. Calling someone "blessed" in a *makarismos* "echoes a ritual pronouncement of eternal bliss bestowed upon the initiates in a religious ritual involving preparation for the afterlife" (Dova 2012, 54–55n78). As one of the Eleusinian Mysteries' closing rituals (Richardson 1974, 313), the *makarismos* would echo the final address to Odysseus and Achilles by the ghostly Agamemnon in *Odyssey* 24 as their ultimate titles in the timeless realm of the dead. Thus, the traditions represented by the epic poetry of Homer, Hesiod, and the *Homeric Hymn to Demeter* all similarly use Underworld scenes as a convenient vehicle for transmitting their authors' perspectives on and prescriptions for the proper behavior of mortals.

IV. Conclusions: Underworld Scenes as Inflected Language

The Underworld scenes of post-Homeric Archaic poetry begin to emphasize the idea of afterlife judgment and the postdeath segregation of souls. These

---

[25] For more on the late addition of soteriological elements to the cult at Eleusis and the initiation process, see Sourvinou-Inwood (1983), Clinton (1992), and Bremmer (2014b).

scenes self-consciously connect to well-known heroic Underworlds in the Homeric epics with links and language that can be traced to specific afterlife issues and themes that appear in early Underworld scenes. They also explore the various paths available to mortals to influence their afterlife outcomes while alive, whether through divine favor, initiation, or other just actions. Over time, the imagined connections between the prosperity of a person in life (in the form of wealth and divine favor) to the potential for a good afterlife become stronger. Comparisons of human and divine states of blessedness are increasingly defined by the terms *olbios* and *makar*, which poets begin to apply across different contexts, breaking down the separation between the realms of mortals and immortals and establishing multiple connections based on shared interests. These specialized terms, along with certain phrases and ideas such as "Isles of the Blessed" become links between Underworld representations, constituting a coded language between author and audience, which uses geographical landmarks in the chthonic realm as watchwords implying afterlife status and blessedness based on a distinct moment of judgment for each individual.

The positive afterlife hinted at in the description of Menelaus' afterlife in Elysium (*Od.* 4.561–569) and in the little *nekuia*'s account of the Greek heroes' afterlife (*Od.* 24.1–204) depicts the Underworld as a place inhabited by self-aware, sentient beings who are often concerned with the activities of the living. The *makares* gods on Olympus are similarly portrayed in their divine realm across the extant works of the Archaic poets. Each poet borrows elements of the gods' *makar* way of life on Olympus to fill out sections of the Underworld space, a practice which expands further with later authors, who add even more details. Authors then merge elements from the vague, inherited descriptions of the Homeric Underworlds with the utopian qualities of an imagined divine realm to create a blessed region of the Underworld reserved for special souls (e.g., the Isles of the Blessed). The *Homeric Hymn to Demeter* takes this even further by giving mortals instructions for how to transition between forms of "blessedness" through specific actions during life. The blessed souls of the Underworld are shown to have attained the best afterlife possible for mortals, just short of deification (as happened to Heracles). Further, the *makar*-like existence is described in terms of the physical comforts this group of souls can expect, even though they do not technically have mortal bodies any longer (except, perhaps, Menelaus). The *Homeric Hymn to Demeter*'s portrayal of the relationship between initiation and afterlife status supports the poet's religious message and argument for the importance of initiation into the Eleusinian cult.

Through different configurations of Underworld scenes, ancient authors comment on the actions and beliefs of their audiences by imagining forms of afterlife blessedness based on individual choices to do just or unjust deeds during life, particularly in relation to the gods and ritual practices. The location of a soul in an Underworld scene is a coded communication by an author as to how the audience should evaluate it in relation to the larger narrative. Underworld scenes recall experiences and ideas from lived religion, and they assume familiarity and knowledge of Greek eschatological myths and religious rituals. As a part of their original function, the references may have also reinforced certain existing beliefs but then continued to be relevant for future audiences because they so pertinently serve the narratives in which they appear.

Later poets such as Pindar and Bacchylides expand the idea of a segregated afterlife by borrowing Underworld poetics from their predecessors, combining aspects of heroic and judgment-based Underworld scenes to fine-tune differences in status between their patrons and other mortals. With these two major categories of Underworld scenes to work with (i.e., heroic and judgment-based), certain elements in Underworld scenes could be employed as a quick shorthand for poets to emphasize important themes in their poems, reinforce community values and beliefs, and situate their works against a larger backdrop of poetic accomplishment. Poets could project states of "blessedness" in the *olbios* and *makar* senses through Underworld scenes by characterizing their patrons in a similar way to katabatic heroes. This use of an Underworld scene and its moral geography, when applied to living people, could serve to establish them as unique individuals whom others should treat with reverence during life, since their status was assumed to continue into the afterlife. The poet's authority to do this would be affirmed by the successful performance of his song, the reaction of his immediate audience, and the expected actions of the community, whether through gifts, esteem, repetition of his song, or cult worship. In the next few chapters, I will explore how such poetic manipulation of Underworld scenes, particularly in the elaboration of chronotopic details, led to results directly affecting the real world of the living.

4

Crafting Heroic Blessedness through Underworld Scenes

I. Introduction

The authors who composed Underworld scenes after Homer changed the nature of both the landscape and the agents who moved in them by borrowing and amplifying afterlife elements related to heroic quest and moral judgment. The realm of the dead was also put on public display in different social contexts. The Homeric epics were popular and well-known, having been produced and reproduced in various performance and competitive contexts across Greek-speaking settlements. Additionally, the rise of new religious and philosophical practices influenced how the afterlife was perceived and how Underworld scenes were configured. In the works of lyric and epinician poets, the dead and their imagined society became actively consulted resources for the living. As Emily Vermeule (1979, 4) explains, the Greeks viewed death as a multistage process, and the poet's work was to keep the dead alive "by quotation and interview." The result of this was a sense that "figures of the past were still on call for mortals of the present" (Vermeule 1979, 23). The dead themselves were often assumed to benefit from continual interaction with the world of the living. With the emphasis on reciprocity and exchange in eschatological poetics, special individuals were portrayed as achieving a hero-like status in the afterlife, thereby maintaining awareness of their identities and continuing their availability to their communities after their deaths.

Underworld scenes became a tool for assimilating mortals to epic heroes, both before and after death. By evoking an Underworld scene, authors were able to analogize an individual to an epic hero whose *kleos* transcended the life–death barrier, either directly by comparing deeds or indirectly by

Life / Afterlife. Suzanne Lye, Oxford University Press. © Oxford University Press 2024.
DOI: 10.1093/9780197690239.003.0005

presenting visions of blessed afterlife landscapes, thereby linking the individual with blessed heroes. In each case, Underworld scenes were the platform for building associations between regular mortals and famous heroes, whose uniquely special status and *kleos* seemed to extend beyond their deaths. Heroizing a living person with the types of honors and *kleos* that traditionally belonged to epic heroes was possible because of three cultural developments. First, changes in afterlife conceptions and religious practices led to the rise of a tripartite Underworld structure, in which the dead were segregated after death by judgment based on their status and deeds in life. This structure created more ways to honor the dead, particularly through cult rituals and poetic songs glorifying individuals. Second, new media and methods emerged, which created more access points and opportunities for contact between the living and the dead. For example, epinician poetry, Orphic Gold Tablets, and dirges honoring the dead all used Underworld scenes to analogize their subjects with heroes and those living a Golden Age-style afterlife. Finally, poets and politicians in the fifth century BCE increasingly employed myths of the past to promote their agendas by claiming authority and hidden knowledge about the one supernatural realm that almost all mortals had a personal stake in. Underworld scenes provided a perceived point of access to important people and events of the past. Built through a web of associations between the living and mythic heroes, Underworld scenes of the post-Homeric period show a pattern of increasing engagement between the worlds of the living and the dead that ultimately promoted a more open, accessible, and permeable afterlife.

The Underworld scenes presented in this chapter share the common goal of heroizing individuals by analogizing them to epic heroes who were then honored both in memory and in practice.[1] Epinician poetry and speeches praising the dead were two particularly effective avenues for analogizing mortals to heroes of the past and situating human efforts against the cosmic backdrop through Underworld scenes. Case studies from these genres lean more heavily on heroic Underworld scenes from the past but integrate judgment and morality into the setup of their Underworlds. Often, the goal of these works was to make a "special hero" out of a contemporary mortal so that they and their relatives might enjoy the benefits of this status *before*, not just after, death. These poets used the Underworld to amplify their subject's victory both in the local context of their communities and beyond in the

---

[1] In this period, individuals and heroes could be honored through poetry and cult worship.

Panhellenic and cosmic landscapes. Creating such status was often a political move that benefitted the subject of praise as well as the author, who could be credited as being a conveyor of *kleos* and even immortality. The epinician poets Pindar and Bacchylides, for example, breached the life–death barrier in their poems to emphasize a continuum of interaction between the living and the dead. Pindar asserts this intent in *Nemean 4*:

> . . . ὕμνος δὲ τῶν ἀγαθῶν
> ἐργμάτων βασιλεῦσιν ἰσοδαίμονα τεύχει
> φῶτα· κεῖνος ἀμφ᾽ Ἀχέροντι ναιετάων ἐμὰν
> γλῶσσαν εὑρέτω κελαδῆτιν, Ὀρσοτριαίνα
> ἵν᾽ ἐν ἀγῶνι βαρυκτύπου
> θάλησε Κορινθίοις σελίνοις. (*Nem.* 4.83–88)

> . . . And a song praising good deeds
> makes a man equal in fortune to kings:
> Let that man who dwells by Acheron
> find my voice proclaiming loudly, where
> in the contest of the loud-roaring trident-wielder,
> he bloomed with the [crown of] Corinthian
> celery leaves.

Pindar proclaims here that his song, an epinician, makes men as prosperous as kings, conveying the type of blessedness (i.e., prosperity) that contextually overlaps with the concept of being *olbios* or "blessed," which seems to be an essential component for achieving a heroic afterlife. The verb τεύχει connotes something crafted through art and skill, which is what the poet does literally and figuratively with his song of praise. Furthermore, Pindar asserts that a song containing such honors breaks across the barrier of the Underworld, which means it can be heard in the afterlife by a soul near Acheron. In turn, the "sneak peek" of the Underworld reassures the audience about the persistence of the honors and benefits of *kleos* after death. The repetition of words referring to the "loudness" of the Underworld space (κελαδῆτιν, βαρυκτύπου, *Nem.* 4.86–87) is additionally reminiscent of the phrase "the echoing halls of stalwart Hades and dread Persephone" (δόμοι ἠχήεντες ἰφθίμου τ᾽ Ἀΐδεω καὶ ἐπαινῆς Περσεφονείης, *Theog.* 767–768) in Hesiod's *Theogony*.

Pindar thus suggests that his song will boom across his world and past its boundaries into the Underworld. Indeed, his and others' epinician poems were circulated to a Panhellenic audience. The assimilation of patrons to heroes by both advertising the former's wealth (*olbia*) through aristocratic display and conflating their stories with those of mythic heroes was an effective strategy for athletic victors because their honors were tied to a particular place and community whose actions would support the everlasting relevance of the hero to that locale and beyond (whether through song or cult honors).

Similarly, mystery cult initiation made the case for special status after death, giving the promise to individuals of being sorted into a blessed afterlife, if they followed certain ritual actions before and sometimes even after death. While these Underworlds lean heavily on the idea of judgment after death, they also incorporate the idea of going through certain trials, as a hero might, in the form of an initiation, which would gain the favor of the Underworld gods and gatekeepers. As seen in the previous chapter, the *Homeric Hymn to Demeter* implies particular afterlife benefits and the favor of Demeter and Persephone for initiates who complete specific ritual actions in the Eleusinian Mysteries. Likewise, the Orphic Gold Tablets offer a unique and positive existence after death for initiates, who perform rituals both while alive and also after death as sentient souls following the instructions on the Orphic Gold Tablets. In a fourth-century BCE Tablet from Petelia, Italy (see Figure 4.1), for example, the initiate's soul is given explicit instructions for retaining its wits when navigating the Underworld:

FIGURE 4.1 Gold lamella from Petelia incised with Greek text guiding the owner to the Underworld. This is one of a set of such tablets referred to as Orphic Gold Tablets. Roman Imperial, third/second century BCE. Courtesy of © The Trustees of the British Museum.

Εὑρήσσεις δ' Ἀίδαο δόμων ἐπ' ἀριστερὰ κρήνην
πὰρ δ' αὐτῆι λευκὴν ἑστηκυῖαν κυπάρισσον·
ταύτης τῆς κρήνης μηδὲ σχεδὸν ἐμπελάσειας.
Εὑρήσεις δ' ἑτέραν, τῆς Μνημοσύνης ἀπὸ λίμνης
ψυχρὸν ὕδωρ προρέον ... (no. 2 / B1 / *OF* 476)[2]

You will find a spring on the left of the halls of Hades,
and standing by it is a white cypress.
Do not approach this spring at all.
You will find another from the lake of Memory,
pouring forth cold water ...

This Orphic Gold Tablet describes entry into the Underworld as a human-scaled, hero-type, individual journey through physical space, and the text presents itself as a travel guide to navigate this foreign land unscathed. It also suggests a choice between a negative and positive afterlife with its ominous, specific language to avoid the spring on the left. As an amulet that was found on the body of the deceased within a tomb, this tablet acts as a "passport" of sorts for a new immigrant into the Underworld, identifying the individual as an initiate of a mystery cult religion with special afterlife privileges. This tablet is intended to bridge the border between the living and the dead, promising that a mortal's actions—both in life through initiation and after death by following the instructions—will influence the afterlife sorting that is treated as inevitable. Moreover, it suggests implicitly that the special knowledge it presents can guide the initiate successfully through the unknown landscape and possible horrors of Hades, a journey only able to be told by or in relation to special heroes who have undergone a *katabasis* or survived encounters with ghosts.

In the following, I examine in more detail how Underworlds in the post-Archaic period were used to leverage and expand upon earlier heroic and judgment-based Underworlds to make afterlife society more permeable and

---

[2] Greek texts of the Orphic Gold Tablets in this chapter are from Graf and Johnston (2007), and the first number refers to their numbering. I also include their identification numbers as well as two others commonly used in classifying them. The texts of the corpus of Orphic Gold Tablets have most recently been published in both Graf and Johnston (2007) and Edmonds (2011b), with slight variations. My translations of the Orphic Gold Tablets are informed by those from both Graf and Johnston (2007) and Edmonds (2011b).

familiar. I also look at how blessed, hero-type afterlife outcomes were increasingly perceived to be more accessible to the living. I argue that Underworlds were used to heroize mortals, sometimes even before death, by prefiguring their future afterlife home as an Underworld of the type usually reserved for special heroes of Greek myth who are described as "blessed" (*olbios/makar*). Unlike the Underworlds of Archaic epic, which already had mythic source materials and a set of famous individuals to draw from, later Underworld scenes, appearing in media such as lyric poetry, inscriptions, and speeches, were used to create heroes out of everyday mortals by convincing their communities and future audiences to give them the same regard and status as heroes. Of course, this was not always straightforward and had to dovetail with religious beliefs and cultural practices. Through epinician poetry, mystery cults, and ritual associations, however, it became increasingly possible to heroize any mortal and bring them into quasi-equivalence with famous epic heroes. To demonstrate this process, I first show how the Underworld space itself was expanded conceptually into a tripartite structure. I then show how this reconceived space was leveraged by the epinician poets Pindar and Bacchylides as well as by religious cults, such as the one producing the Orphic Gold Tablets.

Consistency in the application of such scenes across the Greek world demonstrates that neither single authors, locations (like Athens or Sicily), nor religious practices can be isolated as the only origin for the new, expanded Underworld model that dominates in the fifth century BCE. This shift in representation of the Underworld, therefore, was not the work of a few individual poets acting independently or in response to specific religious practices, but rather a Panhellenic phenomenon that occurred across media and contributed to the authority of each author's work. In the following examples, we can observe with further clarity how poets and artists used Underworld scenes to engage in active dialogue with each other, their audiences, and a wide range of source material for the singular purpose of making mortals blessed.

II. Shifting to the Positive: Awareness and Identity in a Tripartite Underworld

In Archaic poetry, life in the Underworld is presented as being "lived" by souls in a society that parallels the world of the living. The Underworld is also a space where imagined outcomes for individuals could be proposed, projected, and produced artistically.[3] The Underworlds in the earliest extant poetry are depicted as distant, separate, and frighteningly different. The dead are generally seen to be living only a partial, limited existence, often without full consciousness, sensations, or bodies. Poets in the Archaic period, however, increasingly portrayed the kingdom of the dead as continuous with that of the living as well as approachable under certain circumstances: through rituals, divine dispensation, or the designation of "blessedness."

As the heroic and judgment-based Underworld types began to emerge and crystallized as the two dominant types, authors borrowed features from their predecessors' Underworlds to construct Underworld scenes that often had some elements of both but tended toward one, depending on the messages they wanted to convey. In these combined Underworlds, three configurations emerge, which are based on the idea of an individual's blessedness on the *olbios/makar* scale: negative, positive, and "positive-plus." In Underworld scenes of judgment, these three designations refer to the soul's experience in the afterlife and whether it is being punished or is receiving some sort of reward on a sliding scale based on its level of blessedness (*olbios*). There were two main ways for mortals to be considered *olbios*—and therefore eligible for the most pleasant type of afterlife (positive-plus)—either by nature, through birth and favor from the gods (as with heroes), or by performing deeds that gain *arete* and are worthy of *kleos*, as determined by the poet and individual's community. With these as the options and Underworld scenes as the means, the challenge for the author was how to signal to the audience that his patron, the subject of his poem, was worthy (i.e., *olbios*) enough to be placed in the highest status of humanity akin to the most exceptional heroes of myth. The earliest poetic attempts to do this simply analogize a living person to a special hero. This is the strategy seen in the *Nekuia* when the poet presents Odysseus and Heracles in the narrative as heroic equals. An alternative strategy is to place the living person in an idyllic, blessed afterlife, implying that he or she had been judged *olbios* by the ultimate divine arbiters of this, the Underworld judges. Besides predicting an individual's attainment of an *olbios* designation among the dead, this second strategy also makes the case for giving him or her proleptic honors in life, similar to that of mythic heroes, in anticipation of such an afterlife. This can most clearly be illustrated in epinician poetry, but

---

[3] In Homer, the dead are not able to interact with the living nor are they generally sentient except through necromantic rituals, as shown in the *Nekuia* of *Odyssey* 11. Pindar's epinician poems and *threnoi* depict the dead, especially heroes, enjoying blissful afterlives without direct interaction with the living.

it also occurs elsewhere, in both literature and art. In both of these scenarios, a tripartite Underworld becomes necessary to make room for a new class of mortals within the existential scheme, who are more like heroes than like other mortals but still come from the ranks of the latter (i.e., ordinary people). The elaboration of a tripartite Underworld supports the idea of a range of existential statuses for regular mortals who could not claim to be *olbios* by birth, as most heroes could, but who still wanted to differentiate themselves as exceptional in this world and beyond.

Poets, politicians, and religious rituals celebrating a living patron or the valorous dead jumped on this idea to reflect differences in status between people in their communities by portraying them in Underworld settings. To do this, they expanded on the notion of a segregated Underworld, which had already been suggested by their predecessors, and on the ways that individuals could gain special status or recognition through *kleos* or initiation. Certain details in Underworld scenes became a quick shorthand for poets to communicate the meanings of their poems, and extensive visions or new combinations of chthonic elements could convey additional nuances of meaning to the shorthand references. Epinician poets could project their patrons' states of blessedness and, therefore, their immortality by describing the specific features that would mark their patrons as blessed in both the *olbios* and *makar* senses. A poet who describes his subject with the characteristics contained in the lifestyles of the *olbioi* heroes and *makares* gods relies heavily on the audience's knowledge of multiple mythic narratives and willingness to believe in the poet's crafting of immortality. The poet's authority to do this would then be affirmed by the performance of his song, the reaction of his immediate audience, and the expected actions of the community (e.g., in gifts, esteem, or cult worship).

Blessedness and The Rise of the Tripartite Underworld

While a gloomy death made the acquisition of epic *kleos* in life paramount in the Homeric epics, other factors contributing to earthly *kleos* (such as being a just ruler, succeeding in athletic competition, gaining immortality in song, or becoming an initiate) created pressures on poetic portrayals of the Underworld and afterlife society to account for exceptional humans who were not traditional heroes. Poets after Homer attempted to accommodate an expanded view of the afterlife, increasingly focusing on the positive afterlife and whether consciousness and sentience in souls was a blessing or a curse. Their Underworld scenes, therefore, have certain common features that arise from the basic assumption of the soul's self-awareness: a persistence of identity, the segregation of souls based on earthly status, and afterlife judgment leading to punishment or reward. These, in turn, led to ideas of the increased importance of deeds throughout an individual's entire life and the gods' favor, evidenced most visibly by their earthly wealth, since such status would extend into eternity.

To account for this shifting perception and portrayal, scholars have typically categorized Underworlds into three major types, which have generally been labeled "negative," "positive," and "positive-plus."[4] The negative Underworld is associated with the *Nekuia* in Book 11 of the *Odyssey*. Based on the descriptions of the souls as "feeble heads of the dead" (νεκύων ἀμενηνὰ κάρηνα, *Od*. 11.29) and "witless" (ἀφραδέες, *Od*. 11.476) in this episode, many scholars have described the Homeric Underworld as "negative" and the more hopeful ones that came later as "positive." In a negative Underworld, souls live a seemingly purposeless existence in a semiconscious or completely mindless state, surrounded by gloomy darkness. They are said to exist without consciousness unless extraordinary means are applied, such as drinking the blood ritually offered by Odysseus or being given a special dispensation by the gods (re. Tiresias, *Od*. 11.90–137). In this vision, the Underworld is seen as an impersonal "holding pen" for souls, including notable heroes such as Achilles, who may be temporarily revived for information but otherwise leads a sad existence.

By contrast, in the positive Underworld, souls have consciousness, maintain their earthly identities and personalities to a certain degree, and often dwell in supernaturally enhanced landscapes. Because of the authority of Homer, the negative afterlife was thought to be the dominant view of Greeks in the Archaic Period, a position that has been challenged in more recent scholarship.[5] Although souls in the *Nekuia* were not automatically separated into "good" and "bad" based on their deeds in life, as was regularly the case

---

[4] See Graf and Johnston (2007, 100–108) for an overview of the tripartite division.

[5] Within the discussion about the negative Underworld, scholars disagree about whether the *Nekuia* represents a more traditional belief or an innovation and to what extent elements of the positive Underworld can be found in Homer (Page 1955; Sourvinou-Inwood 1981; Tsagarakis 2000; Vernant 1991; Edmonds 2011a, 2004). Indeed, when one considers all the Underworld representations in Homer and Hesiod as a whole, the exclusively negative afterlife of the *Nekuia* seems to be an anomaly. As discussed in previous chapters, the Homeric epics contain many, often competing visions of the afterlife that have been overshadowed by the focus on *Odyssey* 11's *Nekuia*. See Sourvinou-Inwood (1981) and Edmonds (2011a) in particular for more on this debate.

in later Underworlds, there are hints that some form of judgment existed in the afterlife, even in the mindless, "holding pen" model for all the dead. The identification of Minos as a judge among the dead (*Od.* 11.568–570) suggests that even the negative afterlife of the *Nekuia* was more complex than has been typically described by those who focus on the gloominess of the space and the souls' lack of awareness.[6]

The *Odyssey* shows awareness of the positive (i.e., sentient) afterlife and incorporated versions of it, demonstrated by the description of Menelaus' future in Elysium in Book 4 and also in Book 24, where the souls are imagined to be living in eternal, amiable companionship. Indeed, the Homeric texts offered much raw material for later poets to expand the Underworld in both positive and negative directions. Even the "negative" *Nekuia* of Book 11 portrays differences between certain figures in the Underworld, such as eternal punishment for famous sinners and the retention of self-identity for Tiresias. The earthly deeds of humans here did not, however, determine where they ended up in the afterlife nor was the designation of Underworlds as negative or positive based on the souls' experiences. Rather, scholars based these designations on whether consciousness would be retained by the dead. Thus, a positive afterlife, as it has been described in scholarship, means simply that souls would retain a persistent sense of their identity and an awareness of their surroundings as if they were alive.

The main epic template for the positive vision of the Underworld, which was expanded in post-Homeric poetry, particularly in Pindar, appears to be the introductory Underworld episode in Book 24 of the *Odyssey*. In this scene, referred to as the "little *nekuia*," the ghosts of famous Greek heroes are envisioned in a scenario that is often evoked in later Underworld scenes. With fully realized and remembered identities, the souls of the Greek heroes Achilles and Agamemnon meet in the Underworld and converse with each other in leisurely fashion on a range of topics, particularly their deaths and heroic deeds, while their companions sit around them in attendance (*Od.* 24.1–204). These souls of Greek leaders greet the newly arrived souls of the dead suitors, who are also self-aware and only just being led to their new home in Hades. The heroes and newcomers strike up a conversation with a familiarity

---

[6] Odysseus' reference in the *Nekuia* to the "great sinners" Tityus, Tantalus, and Sisyphus also suggests Underworld judgment (*Od.* 11.576–600). As has been noted in the previous chapter and elsewhere (Edmonds 2011a, 12–13), the Homeric epics seem to be aware of the positive afterlife and incorporate versions of it. For more on the internal contradictions in the Homeric Underworlds, see Sourvinou-Inwood (1981, 22–25) and Edmonds (2011a, 13).

based on a personal relationship that is not only remembered but also persists across the life–death barrier (*Od.* 24.103–104). The soul of Agamemnon recognizes Amphimedon and uses their *xenos* relationship, retained across the life–death barrier, as justification for approaching the latter (*Od.* 24.106–119). Once the relationship is reaffirmed, Amphimedon recounts the events in Ithaca, indicating Odysseus' deeds there as worthy of immediate immortalization in song (*Od.* 24.120–190).

Homer's presentation of a positive Underworld is a closed system with new information moving in one direction—from the world of the living to the world of the dead.[7] The souls in this Underworld scene only remember details from their personal experiences and learn updates about the world of the living from the souls of the newly deceased who arrive after them. Afterlife society here is imagined to be like the Greek society of the living: institutions and relationships like those of *xenia* continue to be important and honored. Moreover, the interactions between the souls of the Greek leaders mimic the conversations these leaders had while fighting the Trojan War. Their conversations in the afterlife suggest continuity with the interactions they had while alive in the Greek camp of the *Iliad*, and the rapprochement between Achilles and Agamemnon that started near the end of the *Iliad* is finalized in the afterlife, with the latter giving due honors to the former. In this positive Homeric Underworld, the ghosts of heroes remember their identities after death, exist as sentient beings who retain their earthly honors, and cultivate their relationships in the afterlife, even without their physical bodies.

Based on this possibility for the consciousness of individual identity and the continuity of relationships, a range of afterlife outcomes emerged in post-Homeric poetry, including an expansion of the positive afterlife and a reconfiguration of what negative and positive afterlives entailed. With the positive-plus afterlife as a possibility, a negative afterlife no longer meant an egalitarian society of souls lacking awareness after death; rather, it evolved to mean an unfavorable outcome in the afterlife, which included punishment for souls who would maintain awareness after death and the ability to suffer as if they were still alive. In light of this, scholars recognized that a positive

---

[7] The exception to this is Achilles' necromantic dream in Book 23 of the *Iliad* (23.69–101). In that scene, Patroclus' ghost gives Achilles details of the Underworld and how the experience there is affected by proper burial. The ghost implies that souls in the afterlife remain conscious, since he retains his self-identity and experiences pain at being excluded from the company of souls outside the gates of Hades. This Underworld scene visualizes Achilles' grief and performs the same function of authorial commentary as the scenes from the *Odyssey* by projecting Achilles' particular concerns about death and the fate of his friend.

afterlife referred to a wide range of afterlife existences, from simple awareness and the absence of punishment to having an elevated existence similar to that of the blessed heroes.[8] To distinguish along this range, scholars designated the latter as a "positive-plus" afterlife, which features a Golden Age type of environment with feasting and a carefree existence in company with mythic heroes, as described in Hesiod's Isles of the Blessed (*Op.*, 170–173).

With this shift in postdeath possibilities, certain types of wealth and status gained in life were perceived to be transferrable into the afterlife, presenting the possibility of an unbroken continuum of privilege and blessedness across the life–death divide. Visible wealth in life, which was used to heroize an individual, whether through patronizing a poet to gain *kleos* or being initiated into a cult, could, therefore, prognosticate a carefree existence for an individual in the afterlife. Reversals of fortune were possible as well because a wealthy individual or king could face punishment for oath-breaking or other unjust acts. More likely for the elite, however, was a further elevation of rank and status from life to afterlife because they were imagined not only to maintain divine favor but also to join a company of select heroes living a blessed afterlife and to achieve immortality through song, as the Homeric heroes did. Equating the person being praised, or *laudandus*, in song to such heroes as Achilles and Peleus gave the individual a status that could cross over from the mortal realm into the eternal one. In this way, a *laudandus* was marked as "larger than life," just like these special heroes.

Making Mortals Blessed

In the positive and "positive-plus" Underworld scenes, a major categorizing principle for both mortals and chthonic space is the idea of "blessedness," a designation that leads to the sorting and different experiences of souls in the afterlife. This idea of blessedness, often represented by the terms *olbios* and *makar*, permeates the physical landscape of the Underworld as well as the identities and experiences of individuals who live there, whether ghosts or chthonic figures. The society of the dead is segregated by levels of blessedness, a concept that becomes associated with divine favor, earthly wealth, and certain lifestyles. Hesiod's *Theogony* (775–806), for example, portrays an Underworld

---

[8] Johnston (Graf and Johnston 2007, 100–108) describes the three categories of souls as "bad, good, and good-plus" corresponding to afterlives of punishment, reward, and extra rewards after metempsychosis. See also the description of these three states in *Olympian* 2 in Willcock (1995, 137–140).

space that holds an organized society, containing the eternal prison of the Titans in Tartarus, homes for chthonic gods, undesirable monsters or deities such as Styx (described as "loathsome to the gods"), and, of course, ghosts with preternatural powers assigned to different areas.[9] The "Ages of Man" passage in his *Works and Days* (109–201) describes different afterlives based on each race's closeness to the gods. From such inherited Underworld scenes, later poets chose elements to clarify what immortality might mean, how being blessed fit into different visions of immortality, and who would be able to attain the quasi-immortal status of being called "blessed" (*olbios*) in life and death. Epinician poetry promises widespread *kleos* and projects a blessed afterlife for patrons who spend their wealth on items of cultural value, such as poetry and athletics, which brings them the designation of *olbios* on top of having *kleos*. Mystery cult initiates end up in a similarly happy afterlife with the designation of *olbios* because of their ritual actions, which gives them *kleos* within their community of initiates.

While the *makar* existence of the gods and the almost equivalent *olbios* designation for humans were a clearly defined distinction in Archaic poetry, the two terms became more intertwined in later references, particularly in cult rituals and in poetry honoring individuals for exceptional deeds.[10] An Orphic Gold Tablet discovered in Thurii, for example, greets the initiate as *olbie* and *makariste*: ὄλβιε καὶ μακαριστέ, θεὸς δ᾽ ἔσηι ἀντὶ βροτοῖο (5 / A1 / *OF* 488). Most scholars translate this as "happy and blessed, you will be a god instead of mortal" (Graf and Johnston 2007, 12–13; Dova 2012, 14; Torjussen 2014, 38).[11] The use of *olbios* or *makar* to describe a mortal or initiate in the

---

[9] For a discussion on the geography of the Underworld and its residents, see Lye (2009).

[10] Hero cult could also convey a type of blessedness, but not one for which Underworld scenes would be useful. A community would have expectations of local involvement by the hero honored in a hero cult, including that he care about and be present in the lives of his people. This would be somewhat at odds with an Underworld scene representation of that hero living a carefree existence in a far-off place, like the Isles of the Blessed. Of course, some individuals may have been honored with both poetic praise and hero cult, but not all cult heroes were poetic subjects and vice versa. For a discussion about the relationship between hero cult and epinician, see Currie (2005).

[11] While this particular Orphic Gold Tablet is dated to the 4th century BCE, the oldest one discovered dates to the 5th century BCE (Graf and Johnston 2007, 4–5). The length and formulaic language of the Orphic Gold Tablets' poetics suggest they were modeled on much older sources than are extant. The double honorific of *olbie* and *makariste* could indicate an original use of *makar* for initiates as a ritual designation, but it is equally likely that it is because of slippage between the terms in the centuries leading up to the tablet's composition.

makarismos greeting linguistically indicates the existential conversion of the individual through initiation and projects the soul's "positive-plus" future in the afterlife. This initiation, in turn, informs the community about how it should perceive that person's status both in life and after death.

The interplay between such technical terms shifted ideas about heroes, heroism, and *kleos* because it expanded who might have access to the benefits of blessedness that were traditionally reserved for special or semidivine mortals. The increasingly inclusive nature of the Eleusinian mystery cult, for example, coincided with a widening of the blessed afterlife space in literary and visual portrayals to accommodate nontraditional heroes. Combined, these linguistic, cultural, and religious trends seem to have provided interest in and pressure to redefine the landscape of the Underworld to reflect what was happening in belief systems in the real world. The Eleusinian Mysteries were open to a wide range of initiates: men, women, free, slave, Greek, and non-Greek. Its main limiting factor was economic, since there were costs in terms of time and money for completing each phase and paying the fees associated with the initiation process (Bremmer 2011, 376–377). Thousands of initiates made their way from Athens to Eleusis each year throughout the long history of this particular cult, and Walter Burkert (1983, 249) underscores the close, long-term connection between Athens and Eleusis when he asserted that "Athenians were, as a rule, mystai."[12] Therefore, as Athens and the Eleusinian Mysteries rose in influence during the late Archaic and early Classical periods, so too did the idea of a blessed afterlife as a result of individual deeds.[13] This impulse to seek the special level of *kleos*, which katabatic heroes often enjoyed, or gain an *olbios* status through deeds spread across power centers in the Greek world during this period. The potential for gaining the *olbios* status on earth through deeds, just as Achilles, Odysseus, and mystery cult initiates

---

[12] Bremmer (2011, 376) concludes that the Eleusinian Mysteries lasted about a millennium and argues that its basic format remained intact, although specific details must have changed over such a long span of time. The connection between Athens and Eleusis is attested in the archaeological as well as literary record. Francis Walton (1952, 112–113) points to an Athenian decree concerning the cult in the early fifth century BCE as further archaeological proof of Athenian control over and association with the Eleusinian Mysteries. Additionally, Walton notes the discovery of a Mycenean megaron as evidence that the sanctuary originated as far back as Mycenean times.

[13] Cosmopoulos (2015, 165) even ties the development of the *polis* and the emergence of individualism to the soteriological addition and expansion in the Eleusinian Mysteries, arguing that the "angst caused by the political instability in Athens, coupled with the increasing awareness of the uniqueness and separateness of the individual, was a major factor in a shift of attitudes toward death, as the Homeric idea of the soul as an unconscious and empty entity gave way to the view of the soul as an immortal being worthy of a better afterlife."

did through their actions and rituals while alive, gave all mortals some level of control in determining their afterlife fates.

Poets simultaneously aided the heroizing process by portraying their patrons in songs just as earlier poets did for heroes, making the honors and *olbios* status afforded to the latter equally applicable to their own earthly patrons. For both the epic hero and epinician *laudandus*, *kleos* in song was thought to be a compensation for death (Currie 2005, 72). Heroizing an individual in this way was achieved by juxtaposing a *laudandus* with a famous hero such as Achilles, who had achieved that positive-plus afterlife (as happens in Pindar's *Olympian* 2), or by writing mortals into known heroic or divine storylines that involve *katabasis* or similar encounters with death. Thus, the *laudandus* and the hero could be equated in both poetic renown (*kleos*) and earthly honors (*timai*).[14] A second, more subtle strategy involved how a poet labeled his subject, using the specialized terms for blessedness as links that would indicate a promise for the future of a positive-plus, heroic afterlife. Because *olbios* and *makar* each refer to a way of life, with the former being primarily associated with mortals and the latter more linked to the gods, slippage between the two terms by post-Homeric poets was one way that the barriers to heroic immortality were ideologically weakened.[15]

The terms *olbios* and *makar* in Underworld scenes softened the strict cosmic divisions between mythic heroes of the past and regular mortals by evoking a supernaturally pleasant afterlife existence where divine and mortal agents intermingle. This did not happen automatically, however, and Underworld scenes started to promote this new vision for the life–afterlife transition by representing a range of experiences for sentient souls in the Underworld. Starting in the late Archaic period, these new Underworld scenes lean heavily on judgment-based Underworld configurations, which emphasize the positive and positive-plus afterlife scenarios and explore multiple ways for mortals to achieve the latter's blessed states. They also, however, include certain elements from the heroic Underworlds, such as a focus on an individual's actions and earthly *kleos* as the key to achieving a good afterlife judgment. Starting with the epinician poets, the following sections examine

---

[14] Currie (2005, 72–84) argues that *time* ("honor, esteem") implies literal immortality through cult as opposed to *kleos*, which describes the metaphorical immortality of song. He observes that the latter was favored in the Homeric poems to the exclusion of the former, but that Pindar seems to interweave the two types of immortality.

[15] The terms and their derivatives become more interchangeable by the fourth century BCE, although *makar* was always more closely associated with the uniquely blessed state of the gods and exclusively so in the Archaic period (de Heer 1969, 56).

case studies that show these efforts to use Underworld scenes to confer a blessed, hero-like status onto living people.

III. Crafting Heroic Blessedness in Pindar's Underworlds

Early literary evidence for the post-Homeric expansion of the positive Underworld appears in Pindar's Underworld scenes in his *threnoi* (funerary dirges) and epinicians, such as *Olympian* 2 (*Ol.* 2) and *Nemeans* 1 and 9 (*Nem.* 1 and 9). As a group, these poems demonstrate that his engagement with Underworld motifs is part of a larger program for claiming poetic authority and assimilating his patrons to heroes. *Olympian* 2, an epinician celebrating the tyrant Theron of Acragas as *laudandus*, presents a distinctly tripartite Underworld in which the poet suggests that his patron might achieve not only a sentient afterlife but also a state of blessedness among the dead equivalent to that of Homeric heroes who live in a carefree ghostly society. This is all premised on the idea that souls are judged and segregated. Within the positive afterlife scheme of this poem, it appears that a negative experience is no longer defined solely by lack of awareness but rather by punishment in the Underworld. Furthermore, the positive afterlife hints at a state not only of simple sentience and remembrance but also one that has gradations of rewards, up to and including the possibility of a positive-plus experience, that is, a blissful, Golden Age–type afterlife in the company of revered Homeric heroes. Scholars ascribe Pindar's positive afterlife to an evolution in religious belief, possible "extrinsic additions" such as metempsychosis from Pythagorean influences in Sicily, and a poetic strategy of appealing to an aristocratic audience who wanted to maintain their upper-class status after death (Currie 2005, 40).[16] Because of Pindar's prominence and his seeming rejection of the *Nekuia*'s picture of the afterlife in his *Olympian* 2 and *threnoi*, Pindar is frequently pitted against Homer, as they seem to present conflicting eschatological visions.[17]

---

[16] See Lloyd-Jones (1990), Nisetich (1988), and Woodbury (1966) for further discussion on the influence of Acragas and the Pythagoreans.

[17] Gazis (2021, 80) most recently argues that Pindar's other epinician poems follow the negative, Homeric view of the afterlife and that *Olympian* 2 is an outlier by a poet who incorporates local religious beliefs he does not fully understand to please his Sicilian audience. See also Willcock (1995) for an analysis of the tripartite Underworld in *Olympian* 2 and possible local resonances, particularly with Orphic beliefs. Pindar's deft wielding of the tripartite Underworld scene follows a similar strategy to the one used in the *Odyssey* to give Odysseus katabatic status through analogy and proximity to special heroes, suggesting

The direct, almost exclusive comparison between Homer and Pindar in scholarship has promoted the perception of a simplistic dichotomy between negative and positive afterlives, which does not cover the complexity of afterlife visions that exist in Greek literature. Almost all post-Homeric authors, including Pindar, use intertextual linking in their Underworld scenes to both negative *and* positive versions in order to direct their audiences through a network of myths and texts, bringing authorial guidance and external context to the audience's view. Overlooking such links has led to a failure in seeing how Underworld scenes respond to and support societal shifts, such as the consolidation of a political power in an individual or the rise of democracy and the *polis*.[18] While Pindar's influence may have expanded a positive version of the afterlife, he did not invent it. He relied heavily on earlier sources, including Homer and Hesiod, using a network of Underworld scene sources as a platform for his version. Because of its direct allusion to the afterlife description in Hesiod's *Works and Days*, Pindar's *Olympian* 2 most clearly represents the phenomenon of creating a blessed status for a living individual through Underworld poetics, although this also occurs elsewhere for the similar purpose of elevating a mortal's status.

The juxtaposition of Pindar and Homer with respect to myth and eschatological beliefs is ubiquitous in scholarly literature but has tended to lead to reductionist or teleological conceptions of afterlife accounts, primarily involving direct comparisons between only these two authors.[19] Deriving the

---

continuity rather than divergence between Homer and Pindar in relation to Underworld scenes.

[18] Edmonds (2004) attempts to mitigate this to some degree in his analyses of Underworld journeys but looks at each author and work as separate phenomenon as opposed to the continuum of interlocking imagery for which I argue. For a discussion of how Pindar's epinicians contributed to a cultural program to consolidate Syracusan monarchy, see Morgan (2015).

[19] Currie (2005, 44) writes that "the view of mortality presented in Pindar's odes is strikingly at odds with that of the *Iliad*." Nisetich (1989, 30) refers to *Olympian* 2.56–80 as "Pindar's *Nekyia*," in order to emphasize Pindar's indebtedness to the *Odyssey* and claim to poetic authority. Nagy (1990, §2) weighs in on this debate by arguing that "Pindar's lyric poetry treats Cyclic heroes as equivalents of Homeric heroes," which is why heroes from Homer and the epic cycle appear in *Olympian* 2's Isle of the Blessed. The more inclusive treatment of Cyclic heroes extended into Pindar's treatment of his patrons. Ehnmark (1948, 12–13) views Pindar's poetry as representing "a transitional stage in the belief" of immortality between Homer and later writers. Solmsen (1982a, 20–21) describes Pindar as adopting a Homeric motif—Thetis' intercession with Zeus to increase Achilles' glory—to remove Achilles to the Isles of the Blessed, countering Homer's seeming abandonment of the hero to an unhappy fate in Hades. Finally, more recently, Gazis (2021) argues that Pindar's view of the Underworld was Homeric, discounting the anomalous ones as temporary local influence.

eschatological passage in *Olympian* 2 solely from the Homeric poems, as most scholars have done, has missed the larger phenomenon of Underworld scenes' hypertextuality in Greek literature (and culture). Such scenes create strong bilateral connections between earthly deeds and afterlife experience as a way to influence behavior and belief, often for social commentary and political ends. As shown in the previous chapter, the idea that human agency and actions determine states of afterlife blessedness is manifest in many forms from different authors well before Pindar. Pindar's Underworlds, with their references to multiple sources beyond Homer's *Nekuia*, therefore, are hardly an anomaly; rather, they reflect continuity and expansion in afterlife representation. Although setting up Homeric and Pindaric Underworld scenes in opposition to each other has been important for pointing out cross-genre connections and offering a picture of how the ancient Greeks used the Underworld scene, the limited scope of the debate has missed links that Pindar seems to have expected his audiences to make, ones that go beyond pleasing a local Sicilian audience. Such narrow focus has also caused scholars to overlook connections in Pindar's poetry to the more positive-type Underworlds presented outside of the *Nekuia* in the Homeric epics and also in other Archaic poetry.

In *Olympian* 2, Pindar structures his Underworld scene both to mirror his patron's society and to map onto familiar geography. More importantly, Pindar makes his patron Theron's special status and afterlife on the Isle of the Blessed accessible to others by tying his ascension to human actions. Of course, entrance to its idyllic, positive-plus afterlife still applies most aptly to the elite, or *esloi* (ἐσλοί, *Ol.* 2.63), but Pindar creates an opening to allow his patron, a historical figure, to determine his afterlife outcome through his deeds as proclaimed through the poet's song for his community.[20] The Underworld scene in the poem presents a mythology that activates several known sources to serve the poem's goal of praising Theron of Acragas for his chariot race victory. The poem portrays a segregated Underworld with several distinct outcomes for the soul that counterbalance each other logically and spatially. The epinician's Underworld is based on the basic premise of punishment for the bad (*Ol.* 2.56–60) and reward for the good (*Ol.* 2.61–65) but adds a third option of metempsychosis, or reincarnation (*Ol.* 2.68–70) leading eventually to an even more idyllic afterlife location ("positive-plus"). This third part was

---

[20] As Solmsen (1968, 503–504) observes, Pindar allows the *esloi* who keep their oaths a positive afterlife by default, which is free from human suffering (*Ol.* 2.61–67), then gives them the extra bonus of the idyllic afterlife after three cycles of just living. This spoke directly to the aristocratic audience for Pindar's epinician in Theron's court, whose members would have viewed themselves as the *esloi*.

132   LIFE / AFTERLIFE

an eschatological innovation already in the Homeric poems, also attributed to Pythagoras, and seemingly part of the local Sicilian religious and cultural milieu, potentially with Orphic religious resonances. The presocratic philosopher Empedocles of Acragas, who was a prominent Sicilian contemporary when Theron commissioned *Olympian* 2 (Willcock 1995, 134),[21] adopts a similar philosophy of rebirth in his poems. Since Empedocles also includes the idea of rebirth in his philosophical poems, dated not long after Pindar's *Olympian* 2, Willcock (1995, 139) argues that the setting itself was a catalyst for the exchange of this unusual idea, concluding:

> It is reasonably assumed that the isolated assertion of such a doctrine in *O.*2 has more to do with Theron than with Pindar; and the connection with Empedocles supports that. Such ideas being current in the west, perhaps we are hearing an echo of a local cult in Akragas.[22]

As Willcock points out, Underworld scenes probably link not only to other literary texts that we can trace but also to narratives assumed in local practices and rituals. *Olympian* 2, therefore, may reference Pythagorean doctrines as well as the poems of Hesiod and Homer to support Pindar's argument that his patron belongs with the blessed host of heroes in a *makar*-type afterlife, reflective of both figurative and literal belief.

In *Olympian* 2, souls are allowed to live in a place called the "Isle of the Blessed," after spending three virtuous cycles living on earth and in the Underworld:[23]

> οἵτινες ἔχαιρον εὐορκίαις, ἄδακρυν νέμονται
> αἰῶνα· τοὶ δ' ἀπροσόρατον ὀκχέοντι πόνον
> ὅσοι δ' ἐτόλμασαν ἐστρὶς
> ἑκατέρωθι μείναντες ἀπὸ πάμπαν ἀδίκων ἔχειν
> ψυχάν, ἔτειλαν Διὸς ὁδὸν παρὰ Κρόνου τύρσιν· ἔνθα **μακάρων**
> **νᾶσον** ὠκεανίδες αὖραι περιπνέοισιν. (*Ol.* 2.66–71)

---

[21]   *Olympian* 2 was commissioned by Theron in 476 BCE to celebrate his victory in the chariot race at Olympia (Willcock 1995, 134).

[22]   Willcock (1995, 138–139) also refers to Plato's later adoption of metempsychosis as having been influenced by his journeys through this region, using the events in the distant future to support his claims for Pindar's times.

[23]   In this case, being one of "the good," who have a chance to achieve the blessed afterlife, means keeping one's oaths (εὐορκίαις, *Ol.* 2.66).

Those who took pleasure in keeping their well-intentioned oaths live their lives without tears, while others suffer unspeakable pain.
And all those people who steadfastly held their souls completely away from all injustices three times on either side traveled the road of Zeus along the tower of Cronus; and there the ocean winds blow around the **Isle of the Blessed.**

Pindar takes the detail of "Islands of the Blessed" from Hesiod, but curiously makes it singular rather than plural so that the blessed dead are consolidated into one place. Moreover, the emphasis on oaths (εὐορκίαις) also hearkens back to Hesiod, where they were central to the mechanism of Zeus' justice in the *Theogony*, since almost all serious injustice entailed broken oaths or perjury.[24] By combining these ideas with elements from the Homeric Underworlds, Pindar manages to place this exceptional afterlife experience within the reach of regular mortals (Nisetich 1989, 62–63). Both Homer and Hesiod are meant in his poem, therefore, to be recalled simultaneously and not exclusively. The depiction of souls living with enough consciousness in the Underworld as well as in the world of the living to "stay away from all injustice on either side" (ἑκατέρωθι μείναντες ἀπὸ πάμπαν ἀδίκων, *Ol.* 2.69) makes Pindar's conception of the Underworld a positive, judgment-based one, binding it solidly to the idea of justice as determined by Underworld judges.[25]

The "road of Zeus" reminds the audience that proximity to Zeus is a key feature for entrance into a blessed state in the *makar* sense (as in the case of Menelaus' Elysian fate, *Od.* 4.561–569). The subsequent reference to Rhadamanthus a few lines later (*Ol.* 2.75) strengthens this Homeric connection (cf. *Od.* 4.564). The "tower of Cronus" in turn recalls the Golden Age period in Hesiod over which Cronus ruled (*Op.* 111) as well as the "Isles of the Blessed" where Zeus made Cronus the king to oversee the blessed state of select heroes (*Op.* 169).[26] The "ocean winds" confirm that Pindar is talking

---

[24] For more on the power of the oath as a foundation for justice under Zeus' reign, see Lye (2009).

[25] Willcock (1995, 158) offers a brief discussion and summary of the debate surrounding whether ἑκατέρωθι ("on either side," *Ol.* 2.69) means that souls can live just or unjust lives in the Underworld.

[26] The term for tower τύρσιν (*Ol.* 2.70) can refer to a single tower in a fortification wall or to an entire walled city. It implies a contained society that has a central organizing government. When paired with the name of a powerful ruler, the phrase "Cronus' tower" suggests a kingdom administered by Cronus. See also Gazis (2021, 83–85) for a discussion of these lines.

about a similar location to Hesiod's, near Ocean (cf. ἐν μακάρων νήσοισι παρ' Ὠκεανὸν βαθυδίνην, *Op.* 171). The constructed features of a road and tower are rather puzzling, but they, along with Pindar's reference to "people 'in the know'" (συνετοῖσιν, *Ol.* 2.85),[27] echo similar language seen on the Orphic Gold Tablets.[28]

In her volume with Graf on the Orphic Gold Tablets (Graf and Johnston 2007, 103–104), Johnston points out that Pindar supports a tri-partite Underworld not only in *Olympian* 2 but also in his Fragment 133 (Fr. 133) *threnos*.[29] Pindar's Fr. 133 specifies that Persephone will send certain souls back to the world of the living after nine years of atonement in the Underworld. After this period, these souls become kings and warriors, then ultimately "holy heroes":

οἶσι δὲ Φερσεφόνα ποινὰν παλαιοῦ πένθεος
δέξεται, ἐς τὸν ὕπερθεν ἅλιον κείνων ἐνάτῳ ἔτεϊ
ἀνδιδοῖ ψυχὰς πάλιν, ἐκ τᾶν βασιλῆες ἀγαυοὶ
καὶ σθένει κραιπνοὶ σοφίᾳ τε μέγιστοι
ἄνδρες αὔξοντ'· ἐς δὲ τὸν λοιπὸν χρόνον ἥροες ἁ- (5)
γνοὶ πρὸς ἀνθρώπων καλέονται. (Pindar, Fr. 133)

And for those from whom mistress Persephone will accept recompense for an ancient woe, to the sun above she sends their souls back up in the ninth year, and from these will arise splendid kings and men swift with strength and with the greatest wisdom. And in the future, they are called holy heroes by men.

The wider application of the term "hero" to include the souls of certain his-torical individuals expands access to the type of glory previously reserved for

---

[27] For a discussion of this phrase and passage, see Most (1986), who suggests a translation that would place the poet in the role of Muse-inspired oracular announcer whose messages were intended for a select audience, including Theron.

[28] The earliest date of an extant Orphic Gold Tablet is fifty years later, but its complexity suggests a much earlier provenance for its concepts and, potentially, an Orphic source poem for which the tablet itself may have been a mnemonic device (Graf and Johnston 2007, 103–104). Richard Janko (2016) has argued for a date of late sixth/early fifth century BCE for the "archetype" text for the Orphic Gold Tablets, a date which concurs with the argument of this chapter of an increased interest and more active engagement in projecting blessed afterlives for select individuals.

[29] For more of the *threnoi* fragments, see Maehler (1975).

Crafting Heroic Blessedness through Underworld Scenes

traditional heroes, who were often linked to a god by birth or favor.[30] The shift is particularly pertinent for rulers such as Theron, who have earthly prosperity (*olbos*) and want to translate their state of being from *olbios* in life to *makar* in the afterlife.[31] Moreover, Theron, Pindar's patron and the protagonist of *Olympian* 2, wants his people to know it. Indeed, Theron went on to receive posthumous hero-cult honors according to the historian Diodorus Siculus (11.53.2), a form of literal immortality conveyed by his successors and the community at large. The establishment of this cult not only validated the legitimacy of his heirs but also affirmed the honors predicted by the poet in portraying Theron's future achievement of *makar*-level status (Currie 2005, 74–84).

Pindar promotes the elevation of a human ruler to the level of divinely favored hero, using an Underworld scene as a poetic shortcut. Such a scene, with its traditional mythic roots, allows Pindar to present metempsychosis as a form of purification accessible to any excellent mortal. The poet's patron, or *laudandus*, is being praised with the ultimate compliment—assimilation to the heroic *kleos* that all but guarantees the eternal rewards of immortality, immediately through the song being performed and perhaps also with the promise of a blessed afterlife in the future. As Nisetich (1989, 68–71) argues, this idea of striving to complete great deeds that then lead to poetic *kleos* and the ultimate life of ease in the afterlife fits Pindar's epinician program, since it allows Pindar to create parallels between the deeds of recognized heroes, such as Achilles, and his patron's efforts on the race course.

This connection between the Underworld scene of *Olympian* 2 and its Sicilian context may go even further than has previously been suggested. The singular "Isle of the Blessed" (as opposed to Hesiod's plural "*Isles* of the Blessed") may reflect Sicily itself. The location near ocean breezes, which has a royal palace (cf. tower of Cronus, *Ol.* 2.70–71) and operates under a centralized system of just, nondemocratic rule (cf. Rhadamanthus, *Ol.* 2.75), can also be used to describe Acragas' location near the sea and Theron's court.

---

[30] The phrase "holy heroes" also recalls the phrase "δαίμονες ἁγνοί" (*Op.* 122), the title of members of the Golden Race after they die and reside in a blessed state.

[31] Although *makar* is not exclusively used of gods in Pindar's time as it is in much of Archaic poetry, Pindar is building links between his work and those that use *makar* in this sense. On Pindaric usages of *makar* and *olbios*, see de Heer (1969).

Creating a specific locality—Sicily as Isle of the Blessed—and portraying it as a land ruled by a Golden Age type of king give extra validation to Theron's rule and achievements. His athletic competitions are the obstacles that he had to overcome, and they are made analogous to a katabatic journey by their juxtaposition with an Underworld scene. He succeeds at those challenges, and his success can translate into the prosperity of the elite at Acragas. The *makar* state for heroes in the poem becomes the *makar* state of Theron, whose membership in the literary host of heroes within Pindar's epinician builds the foundation for the tyrant's *kleos*-based honors while living. Then later, further honors could be bestowed in the future through hero cult.[32]

Pindar here uses the Underworld options inherited from his poetic predecessors as the common language to argue for a vision of the Underworld as more of a "foreign land" that is an adjacent extension of one's current location rather than as a distant, closed-off divine realm (although it still retains supernatural elements and exists in the Underworld *chronotope*). In *Olympian* 2 and the *threnoi*, Pindar capitalizes on traditional features of Underworld scenes to create a positive afterlife society through hyperlinked networks of association, assuming a vast range of knowledge on the part of their audiences, as inferred by the omission of extensive details from their mythic narratives (Currie 2005, 364).

Pindar's incorporation of metempsychosis into his eschatological myth in *Olympian* 2 and his advocacy for a positive afterlife both in this epinician and in his *threnoi* have given him a central spot in discussions of ancient Greek religion and eschatology, since his influence is well-attested in the ancient sources. Pindar's importance in the discussion of Greek eschatology should be rooted, however, not only in his positive afterlife vision but also in how he changes the agents within the Underworld scene. By suggesting that nonheroic mortals, who are known historical figures, could enjoy a similar afterlife to mythic heroes, Pindar promotes a vision that expands perceived access to a blessed afterlife.

Unlike previous Underworld scenes, which describe mythic heroes undergoing an Underworld quest, Pindar centers his Underworld on what mortals can do in an everyday context to become blessed (*olbios*) in their

---

[32] Currie (2005) argues that Theron tried to establish himself as the object of heroic cult during his lifetime. Praise in the epinician would surely promote the tyrant's standing in the community, but praise given through an Underworld scene is a different kind of regard from praise through a hero cult. The latter would require the hero to continue to engage in the local community in ways that the former would not.

afterlives. Moreover, he uses this particular strategy in other epinicians besides *Olympian* 2, including in *Nemeans* 1 and 9 for Chromius of Aetna.[33] *Nemean* 1, for example, contains mythic and linguistic references to Underworld scenes, although it does not explicitly have an afterlife scene. The reader is clued into an eschatological reading of this poem by several features, none of which might be evidence on their own, but together show a pattern activating heroic Underworld *para-narratives* to heroize individuals. In line 9, the poet sings of "divine deeds of excellence" performed by a man (ἀρχαὶ δὲ βέβληνται θεῶν κείνου σὺν ἀνδρὸς δαιμονίαις ἀρεταῖς, "and the beginnings have been laid out by the gods with that man's divine deeds of excellence," *Nem.* 1.8–9).

The conflation of mortal and divine within the same thought is a bold beginning to the poem, and the proximity of certain terms weakens the distinction between man and the gods. Currie points out the oxymoronic juxtaposition of *andros daimoniais* (ἀνδρὸς δαιμονίαις, *Nem.* 1.9) and the latter word's meaning of "divine" (as opposed to the generic meaning of "marvelous") because of its proximity with θεῶν (Currie 2005, 1–2). Indeed, *daimoniais* implies not just "divine" as a state but rather something "achieved by divine favor." This challenge to existential boundaries is further underscored by the line's activation of a similar phrase in Hesiod's *Works and Days* describing the Silver race: *makares thnētoi* (μάκαρες θνητοί, *Op.* 141). In both instances, an adjective with a divine register is applied to a mortal being. Further, the reference to the Silver race, which lived in an unjust time but nonetheless gained blessed (*makar*) status after death because of community honors, is particularly applicable to the *laudandus*, a tyrant who lords over tumultuous political times and can assume similar treatment by his subjects after his death, in the form of honors, grave offerings, and, perhaps even hero cult.

A second linguistic oxymoron in the poem, which also involves the uneasy juxtaposition of the divine and the mortal, is the phrase *olbiois en domasi* (ὀλβίοις ἐν δώμασι, "in the blessed houses," *Nem.* 1.71). This refers to the place where Tiresias predicts Heracles will live when he takes Hebe as his wife in the presence of Zeus. Based on the context, the dwellings can be none other than those of immortals, and the expected phrase for houses of the gods would be "*makaron en domasi*" (μακάρων ἐν δώμασι, "in the houses of the blessed gods"). The adjective ὀλβίοις is peculiar because in this period it still has the sense of earthly riches and human prosperity. The transference of the honorific *olbios* from a person to his possessions must refer to the homes as being

---

[33] *Pythian* 3 for Hieron of Syracuse also uses a similar tactic.

138   LIFE / AFTERLIFE

elaborate, rich, or large (de Heer 1969, 37). The use of the adjective *olbios* is marked as transgressive because it applies to the divine realm an epithet that is used almost exclusively for humans and their possessions. Although there is some precedent (cf. *Homeric Hymn to Hermes* 460–461),[34] it is extremely rare at this stage and in Pindar's sources for *olbios* to be used in such fashion. This phrasing, therefore, creates a striking ending in the last section of the epinician.

Besides these two examples, a third example of Pindar playing with the boundary between life and death comes in the myth itself. The story of young Heracles' defeat of the snakes (δράκοντας, *Nem.* 1.40) anticipates his labors, particularly his greatest feat, a successful *katabasis* to kidnap the "anguiform" Cerberus, who is often depicted on vases from c. 510–480 BCE accompanied by a snake (Ogden 2013, 248).[35] As one of the mythical heroes associated with the foundation of the Nemean Games, Heracles is not an unusual figure to expect in this epinician. It is convenient, however, that he is also a katabatic figure who has achieved immortality through his prowess and fame, an association the poet evokes in service to heroizing his *laudandus*. Although Heracles' defeat of the snakes may have been a common myth, Pindar retells it using language associated with eschatological boundary crossing.[36]

Additionally, the figure of the seer Tiresias, in conjunction with the praise of a hero, recalls the *Nekuia*, an instance in which both Tiresias and Heracles appear in the Underworld as part of Odysseus' Underworld encounter.[37]

---

[34] In this hymn, Apollo describes Hermes with the epithet *olbios*, even though they are both gods (i.e., *makares*), an application of the term that de Heer (1969, 17) describes as "unprecedented."

[35] Snakes are chthonic creatures associated from the earliest Greek literature with the Underworld and the dead. They appear on tombstones as a familiar along with heroes receiving offerings from the living in a Spartan relief from the sixth century BCE and are associated not only with Heracles but also the Dioscuri, who also have associations with Underworld scenes (Ogden 2013, 252–253).

[36] The figure of the snake is associated with movement across the life–death barrier and with reincarnation. There is evidence from that period of snake cults and the veneration of snakes, partly because of the belief that "heroes revisit the world of the living from under the earth in the form of a creature that divides its life between the earth and the surface, and which ever renews its own life by sloughing" (Ogden 2013, 247).

[37] Although Aristarchus and other scholars have argued that Heracles' appearance in the *Nekuia* was a later "post-Homeric" interpolation, it would have been understood to be part of the Homeric tradition and text by Pindar's time (Nagy 1996, 65–112).

Tiresias' prophecy in *Nemean* 1 bypasses Heracles' death, instead focusing on the hero's great deeds and apotheosis, which allows him to enjoy an afterlife among the gods. Alone, the presence of these mythic figures and the snakes might not be read as having eschatological undertones, but the context is suggestive. Chromius goes beyond humans by performing divine deeds while the deified Heracles and his immortal wife live in houses described in mortal terms.

The assimilation of Chromius to heroes who enjoy a blessed afterlife by appeal to divine intervention is further supported by *Nemean* 9. In the opening verses, Chromius' house is described as *olbion es Chromiou dom'* (ὄλβιον ἐς Χρομίου δῶμ', "the blessed house of Chromius," *Nem.* 9.3) using the same phrase describing the gods' houses at the end of *Nemean* 1. This is the more appropriate application of *olbios*, but its verbal echo with *Nemean* 1.71 and the implication of the word itself indicating that Chromius is wealthy because of divine favor creates an intertextual link between two poems that feature heroes who overcome a dismal afterlife. Thus, Chromius is doubly heroized through hyperlinks set up by Underworld scene motifs.

That Pindar sees himself as conveying immortality on his patron Chromius through mythic reference is borne out in his allusion to the *kleos* of Hector (Ἑκτορι μὲν κλέος, *Nem.* 9.39) and in the celebration of Chromius for military deeds but not for death on the battlefield (cf. the hero Amphiaraus). The divine source for Chromius' earthly blessedness is reiterated by the piling on of words that all contain some aspect of supernatural involvement: *pros daimonon thaumaston olbon* (πρὸς δαιμόνων θαυμαστὸν ὄλβον, "wondrous happiness from the gods," *Nem.* 9.45). Both *thaumaston* and *olbon* have a sense of divinely induced marvel and prosperity, and *daimonon* means "of the gods." Pindar thus emphasizes that Chromius is a favorite of the gods, and both the epinician poems argue that an earthly figure can be made immortal by being celebrated in song, thereby avoiding the silence of the grave.

Pindar is not alone in his use of Underworld scenes to craft heroic immortality for his patrons through a positive-plus vision of the afterlife. The belief that deeds in life affect one's afterlife is already suggested in Hesiod's *Works and Days*, as seen in the previous chapter, and it is a theme explored by Pindar's contemporaries who are in direct dialogue with his poems. Pindar's innovation is to make the choice of a blessed afterlife rest with the mortal individual, without the direct aid of divine intercession. Other poets are less explicit in afterlife promises, but nevertheless still use their poetry to promote the idea that the living and the dead can have direct influence on each other.

140   LIFE / AFTERLIFE

IV. Epinician Expansion of Blessedness in Bacchylides

Like Pindar, Bacchylides uses epic Underworld scenes to immortalize his patrons by creating visions of heroic encounters and blessedness in the land of
the dead. *Odes* 3 and 5 clearly demonstrate a rewriting of epic material, from
Homer in particular, to reflect the expanded, positive vision of eschatological
relationships that we also see in Pindar's poems. *Ode* 3 represents Bacchylides'
direct assimilation of a patron onto a mythic figure, while *Ode* 5 demonstrates
a wholesale reimagining of Heracles' Underworld myth to promote newly
envisioned connections between the living and the dead.

In *Ode* 3, Bacchylides uses his patron's wealth to assimilate him to the
mythic story of Croesus and thus catapult him to the level of a legendary
person. The poet establishes his patron Hieron as a man of god-given wealth,
describing him as a prosperous man with the marked term *olbion* (ὄλβιον,
Ode 3.8). The poet repeats this association between earthly wealth and divine
grace at lines 22 and 92 (ὄλβων and ὄλβου, respectively). To round out his
earthly possessions, the poet defines his patron's *olbios* status in terms of how
his Panhellenic audience cheers him on:[38]

> ἁ τρισευδαίμων ἀνὴρ
> ὃς παρὰ Ζηνὸς λαχὼν πλεῖστ-
> αρχον Ἑλλάνων γέρας
> οἶδε πυργωθέντα πλοῦτον μὴ μελαμ-
> φαρέϊ κρύπτειν σκότῳ. (*Ode* 3.10–14)

> Oh, thrice-blessed man
> who was allotted from Zeus the privilege of
> ruling over the greatest number of Greeks
> and who knows how not to conceal his
> towered wealth in dark-shrouded gloom.

The phrase *triseudaimon aner* (τρισευδαίμων ἀνὴρ, *Ode* 3.10) echoes Odysseus'
address to Nausicaa when he first arrives at Scheria (τρὶς μάκαρες μὲν σοί γε πατὴρ
καὶ πότνια μήτηρ, / τρὶς μάκαρες δὲ κασίγνητοι, "while thrice blessed indeed are
your father and mistress mother, / thrice blessed too are your siblings," *Od.*
6.154–155). Although the sense of blessedness is slightly different, the concept

---

[38] See Morgan (2015) for a discussion about the importance of Pindar's Panhellenic spectators.

Crafting Heroic Blessedness through Underworld Scenes 141

of being a particular favorite of the gods remains.[39] Furthermore, the ideas of towered wealth and concealment in darkness seem to refer to the chthonic landscape. Wealth in the form πλοῦτον is associated with the ground, and the adjective πυργωθέντα, referring to a built structure, most likely means that the wealth has been bounded in a way that is both visible but inaccessible, as towers would gird but might also hide a great city. Wealth alone, although important, is not enough to make Hieron blessed, but rather he must use it appropriately now in ways that help him attain *kleos*, which is what can help him achieve the *olbios* status, and a good afterlife. Additional meanings of these references become clear with the start of the myth of Croesus, known for his great wealth and powerful kingdom Lydia. Bacchylides here identifies Hieron as a living Croesus, who each spent their wealth appropriately to show their blessings from the gods. Hieron, like Croesus, propitiated Apollo and went a step further by commissioning the epinician that is currently amplifying his *kleos* to the community. These combine to make such leaders peers with heroes and famous men of the past in terms of their blessedness. As a result, through analogy, Croesus' fate will be Hieron's.

In Bacchylides' version of the myth, Croesus is saved from the funeral pyre by Apollo through the will of Zeus. This activates a *para-narrative* of Sarpedon's death at Troy, after which Zeus orders Apollo to remove his son's body from the battlefield and preserve it so that the gods Death (Thanatos) and Sleep (Hypnos) can transport it to Lycia for proper burial and local honors from his community (*Il.* 16.666–683). After activating this *para-narrative*, Bacchylides diverges from the expected outcome by making Apollo and Zeus intervene *before* Croesus dies on the funeral pyre. Croesus and his children are transported to the land of the Hyperboreans, in "the only case of living mortals being taken to the 'Land of the Blessed'" (Maehler 2004, 94n59). Since he already assimilated Hieron to Croesus at the beginning of the ode, the audience who is "in the know" (Φρονέοντι συνετὰ γαρύω, "I utter wise words for the wise," *Ode* 3.85) will understand that the poet has also created immortality for Hieron through song and has the power to do this for anyone whose deeds are similarly pious, since those are the "greatest of profits" (Ὅσια δρῶν εὔφραινε θυμόν· τοῦτο γὰρ / κερδέων ὑπέρτατον, "gladden your spirit doing pious deeds; for this is the greatest of profits," *Ode* 3.83–84). From the perspective of the song, such deeds might include not only athletic

---

[39] *Eudaimon* is a term for human good fortune, and generally means that a god is looking out for the person's interests.

accomplishment, which brings glory to the community, but also Hieron's support for the performance of the *Ode* celebrating his victory. The poet here expects his work to be more than entertainment. He further implies that he has privileged access and authority to make pronouncements that activate connections between the living and the supernatural realm of the dead.

In *Ode* 5, Bacchylides uses a more explicitly structured Underworld scene to laud the same patron Hieron, but this time the praise is less direct and more focused on the limitations of man.[40] In the proem and introductory praise sections, Bacchylides anticipates his eschatological myth by using a series of images that activate Underworld *para-narratives* in quick succession, combining aspects of sorting that we see in judgment-based Underworlds with a strong focus on Heracles' story in order to align the *laudandus* with the hero's heroic *katabasis*. He says his song comes "from the holy island" (ἀπὸ ζαθέας / νάσου, *Ode* 5.10–11) to Syracuse, which conceptually suggests a connection to the "Isles of the Blessed." The mythic section recounts Heracles' last labor, the descent into Hades to retrieve the hell-hound Cerberus, and the end of the *Nekuia*.[41] Instead of describing the actual labor, however, the poet focuses on an imagined dialogue that Heracles has with Meleager's ghost and thereby combines the myths of two famous heroes into one story. Their meeting in the Underworld is first attested and described here. A dithyramb by Pindar on the same topic, titled either *The Katabasis of Heracles* or *Cerberus* is mentioned in the *Iliad* scholia (70bS; 61B) and may have predated Bacchylides' version but has not survived.[42] What we know is that these two poems are the "first *certain* meeting of the two" and the "first *certain* mentions of Deianeira in this context" (Burnett 1985, 198n7).

The two poems' focus on Deianeira is somewhat perplexing, although they may be referring to competing versions of Heracles' famous myth. Pindar's version is known to have had Meleager ask Heracles to marry his sister, but Bacchylides reverses this so that Heracles is the one looking for a wife. The

---

[40] The poem is dated to 476 BCE and celebrates a victory in the single horse race at Olympia. This is the same victory and patron to which Pindar devotes his *Olympian* 1, and the two poets have often been compared on the basis of the survival of these two competing poems celebrating the same event and patron (Lefkowitz 1969). *Olympian* 1 contains the myth of Tantalus but focuses on the crimes that led to his later state of eternal punishment, not the punishment itself except via an oblique reference (πατὴρ ὑπερκρέμασε καρτερὸν αὐτῷ λίθον, "the father [Zeus] hung over him a sturdy rock," *Ol.* 1.57).

[41] Heracles' *katabasis* was apparently a popular topic for lyric poets (Burnett 1985, 198n7). At least one other poet (Stesichoros) is known to have written a poem titled *Cerberus* (*PMG* 206).

[42] See scholia ABDGe on *Il.* 21.194 for a summary of Pindar's version of the story (Maehler 2004, 107).

Crafting Heroic Blessedness through Underworld Scenes

hero is so enthralled with Meleager that he wants to connect himself to the deceased hero by marrying his sister (Ἡρά τις ἐν μεγάροις Οἱ / νῆος ἀρηϊφίλου / ἔστιν ἀδμήτα θυγάτρων, / σοὶ φυὰν ἀλιγκία; "Is there any daughter in the halls of battle-loving Oineus, unmarried and similar in form to you?" *Ode* 5.165–168). H. Maehler suggests that the question and eventual outcome of Heracles' marriage to Deianeira, which would have been known to the audience but is only hinted at here, is meant to be an "illustration of [Bacchylides'] introductory statement [in *Ode* 5.50–55] that no mortal can have complete happiness" (Maehler 2004, 127n168). In both versions, the suggestion is that information gleaned (or action taken) in the Underworld influences events in the real world: the intentions and will of shades extend across the life–death boundary to affect the living.

The mythical interlude in Bacchylides' *Ode* 5, therefore, has a similar effect to the Underworld story in Pindar's *Olympian* 2, in that it imagines cross-border incursions where some action on one side will have an effect on the outcome of the individual's existence on the other side of the life–death boundary. While the Underworld scene in Pindar's version promotes a sunny vision of great deeds leading to immortality, the Underworld intervention in Bacchylides' *Ode* 5 leads to a tragedy unforeseen by Heracles and Meleager, but already known to the audience. In the latter, the tragic earthly events to come are in service to the ultimate blessed afterlife allotted to Heracles after he is deified.

Bacchylides formulates his myth to mimic the *Nekuia*'s necromantic dialogue between a ghost and a living man, generally ignoring the journey aspect of Heracles' *katabasis* but still relying on the heroic Underworld configuration such that the audience imagines a treacherous path, insurmountable to most mortals. Bacchylides uses the *entha*-mode of description that is common to Underworld scenes of Archaic epic to point out a famous landmark (Cocytus) in Hades and to describe the ghosts as flitting about:

> ἔνθα δυστάνων βροτῶν
> ψυχὰς ἐδάη παρὰ Κωκυτοῦ ῥεέ-
> θροις, οἷά τε φύλλ᾽ ἄνεμος
> Ἴδας ἀνὰ μηλοβότους
> πρῶνας ἀργηστὰς δονεῖ. (*Ode* 5.63–67)

And **there**, [Heracles] perceived the souls of
wretched mortals by the streams of Cocytus,
and they are just like the leaves the wind drives about
on the bright, sheep-pasturing headlands of Ida.

The stories evoked here are definitely Homeric in that the shades, for the most part, seem senseless and noninteractive, except for Meleager's ghost who seeks out Heracles.[43] When Odysseus seeks out the shades and instigates a necromantic encounter via rituals and blood, he also has to fend most of them off with his sword until Tiresias approaches. Echoing this scene, Heracles similarly treats the ghosts as a threat and tries to fend off Meleager with his bow (Bacchyl. *Ode* 5.71–76). The details of afterlife existence that each poet specifies create an environment of direct poetic competition between the various *para-narratives*. Although Meleager and the other ghosts do not have any hope for a better afterlife, the effect they have on Heracles' immediate future and subsequent end gives significance to the encounter.

Bacchylides analogizes his patron Hieron to Heracles by displaying the source of the Panhellenic hero's end and ultimate deification as based in an Underworld encounter that was also a capstone labor consolidating Heracles' *kleos*. Both Bacchylides and Pindar support an expanded afterlife model by moving heroes found in Homer's dark, gloomy, impersonal Underworld into a space where maintaining awareness of one's personal identity after death and of rewards for one's deeds are a prerequisite for enjoying a blessed afterlife. Both poets thus move the bar for mortals' attainment of heroic blessedness within reach of a designated "exceptional" person, such as the *laudandus* of an epinician, where he would be treated as a peer to famous heroes.

In these instances, accessibility to a positive-plus Underworld space occurs by placing the poets' aristocratic patrons in the august company of heroes as peers, a constructed heroization rooted in the idea of afterlife judgment and subsequent sorting. Such poetic assimilation through an Underworld scene proposes to break down any perceived separation between the supernatural and earthly realms. It also conceptually creates an opening for negotiating how status might be maintained by an individual across the life–afterlife boundary. By commissioning a poem with an Underworld scene, the *laudandus* could, therefore, validate and advertise his *kleos* in life as equivalent to an epic hero through analogy, since the poet can depict him as assigned to a blessed afterlife after death.

By suggesting a continuum of experience and direct interaction between the living and the dead, poets were integral to creating a sense of permeability across the life–death barrier and heroizing those who were able to translate

---

[43] The simile of wind blowing the leaves is also a poetic echo of a famous simile in *Il.* 6.146–149, further linking this passage to Homeric epic. Unlike Odysseus, Heracles does not need to do anything to call forth a shade, but rather runs into Meleager while seeking Cerberus.

their blessings across that boundary. Such assimilation of rich patrons and special individuals to heroes eventually changed perceptions about the distance of the Underworld from everyday life. Both Bacchylides and Pindar invested in making the Underworld a persistent presence, which was deeply relevant in the real world, by emphasizing the idea that people could influence their afterlives. By engaging in select eschatological imagery from their well-known predecessors, these poets validated their own authority as inheritors of the tradition to immortalize men through song and to heroize them through Underworld poetics.[44] This strategy extends across the Greek world as a more global phenomenon in different media. The pattern of heroizing through Underworld scenes occurs prominently in nonliterary texts as well, including those in the religious and political spheres. In the next section, I show how the Orphic Gold Tablets use Underworld scenes to create even more options for heroizing everyday mortals, both before and after death.

V. The Orphic Gold Tablets: Passports to a Blessed Afterlife

As epinician poetry began to portray an expanded vision of the afterlife through Underworld scenes, so too did other media, which were aimed toward different audiences across the Greek world. Religious texts like the Orphic Gold Tablets from Western Greece and funerary speeches in Athens capture additional snapshots of the seemingly universal trend of using Underworld scenes to change the perceived existential possibilities for mortals, both before and after death. Underworld scenes facilitate both the actual heroizing of mortals and the expansion of belief about the afterlife's accessibility and permeability by appearing in a variety of performance contexts, both those sponsored to celebrate aristocratic patrons and those that seem to relate to religious rituals. Like epinician poets, mystery cult initiates and those promoting various political agendas used Underworld scenes to argue that they and their followers should achieve the blessed status of heroes, a positive-plus afterlife experience, and honors among the living. In this section, I examine how the Orphic Gold Tablets and the mystery cult they represent leverage Underworld poetics to contribute to a radical shift in the ancient Greeks' perceived existential possibilities.

---

[44] Currie (2005, 84) goes further, arguing that *Olympian* 2 heroizes Theron not only by conferring *kleos* but also by predicting a hero cult for his patron that was created posthumously.

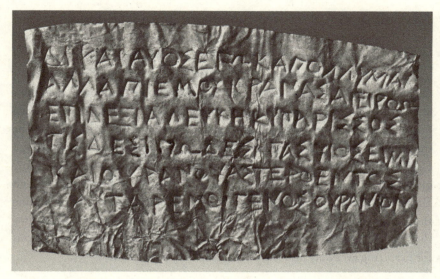

FIGURE 4.2 Gold lamella from Greece incised with Greek text guiding the owner to the Underworld. This is a similar tablet to the one in Figure 4.1. Both are referred to as Orphic Gold Tablets and associated with Orphic mystery cults. Mid-fourth century BCE. Image courtesy of Getty's Open Content Program.

Passports to the Heroic Underworld

The Orphic Gold Tablets are a set of thin gold sheets, or *lamellae*, inscribed with poetic texts that give instructions to initiates for how to gain access to a blessed, positive-plus afterlife (see Figures 4.1 and 4.2)

Found in graves across the Mediterranean dating as early as the fifth century BCE, they mark their owners as initiates into a mystery cult (or similar religious modality) that seemed to be related to the figure of Orpheus (hence the name "Orphic" cult and "Orphic" Gold Tablets).[45] The Orphic Gold

---

[45] There is much debate about whether the collection of Gold Tablets, as a group, point to a real-world mystery cult. They use formulaic, poetic language and seem related to each other, even with findspots ranging from Southern Italy to Crete. For this reason, many scholars argue that they all originated from a single source and religious group (Bernabé Pajares and Jiménez San Cristóbal 2011; Riedweg 2011; Janko 2016). Others disagree that Orphism was a religious movement or cult because of the lack of other evidence in the archaeological or literary records (besides the Gold Tablets themselves) for its existence. Edmonds (2011c, 268–270), for example, suggests that the Gold Tablets' texts could have originated from short hexameter oracle responses and been in more widespread, casual use by itinerant "magicians." For an overview of the scholarship on Orphism and Orphic texts, see Meisner (2018). Regardless of their origin, there is no question that the gold lamellae, which I will refer to as "Orphic Gold Tablets," transmit an eschatological agenda using motifs from traditional Underworld scenes. For this discussion, I refer to the mortal addressee of the Orphic Gold Tablets as the "initiate."

Tablets promise salvation after death and a better afterlife for those who are initiated into its group. They do this by presenting a vision of the afterlife landscape where the sentient soul of an individual, the initiate, is analogized to heroes and has choices on which areas and figures of the Underworld to approach. His or her actions, based on those choices, are what allow the soul's entrance into a heroic afterlife instead of the negative one for noninitiates, which is filled with either suffering or forgetfulness.

To illustrate how these religious texts employ judgment-based Underworlds to presort their initiates by analogizing them to heroes and a heroic afterlife, I will focus on four out of the corpus of over twenty extant tablets of various lengths. The oldest one, from Hipponion, is dated to the fifth century BCE, while the others from Petelia and Thurii, also in Southern Italy, and Pelinna in central Greece, are dated to the fourth century BCE. All use similar, formulaic language, as is common for ritual texts, suggesting they are related. Written for the most part in Greek hexameters, they were found in communities across the Greek world, from Sicily and Southern Italy to mainland Greece and Turkey. Some scholars have speculated that they could be from a far-reaching, popular religious tradition, potentially disseminated by itinerant religious figures (Edmonds 2011c). The more widely accepted view, however, is that the Orphic Gold Tablets come from an established "Orphic" mystery cult with texts derived from a much older source or "Ur-text" whose words may even have been used in conjunction with specific religious rituals (Obbink 2011).[46] Regardless of their origins, recurring phrases and themes link to the two types of Underworlds, using a tactic similar to what we see in the epinician poems to heroize particular mortals, namely, the initiates. Each of these texts, found in the graves of individuals, both male and female, offer instructions to their bearers for what to do when they find themselves in the Underworld. The Hipponion tablet gives directions and warnings to the newly dead initiate, exhorting him to enter the gates of Hades and identify himself to chthonic guardians as an individual worthy of a blessed afterlife existence:

Μναμοσύνας τόδε ἔργον, ἐπεὶ ἂν μέλλησι θανῆσθαι
εἰς Ἀΐδαο δόμως εὐήρεας. ἔστ᾽ ἐπὶ δ<ε>ξιὰ κρήνα,
πὰρ δ᾽ αὐτὰν ἑστακῦα λευκὰ κυπάρισος·

---

[46] Several scholars have attempted to reconstruct the archetype poem by combining overlapping elements from the extant Orphic Gold Tablets (Riedweg 2011, 248–252; Janko 2016, 123–124).

LIFE / AFTERLIFE

ἔνθα κατερχόμεναι ψυχαὶ νεκύων ψύχονται.
ταύτας τᾶς κράνας μηδὲ σχεδὸν ἐνγύθεν ἔλθηις. (5)
πρόσθεν δὲ εὑρήσεις τᾶς Μναμοσύνας ἀπὸ λίμνας
ψυχρὸν ὕδωρ προρέον· φύλακες δὲ ἐπύπερθεν ἔασι.
τοὶ δέ σε εἰρήσονται ἐν φρασὶ πευκαλίμαισι
ὅ τι δὴ ἐξερέεις Ἀΐδος σκότος ὀρφήεντος.
εἶπον· ὑὸς Γᾶς ἤμι καὶ Ὡρανῶ ἀστερόεντος. (10)
δίψαι δ᾽ ἤμ᾽ αὖος καὶ ἀπόλλυμαι· ἀλὰ δότ᾽ ὦ[κα
ψυχρὸν ὕδωρ πιέναι τῆς Μνημοσύνης ἀπὸ λίμν[α]ς.
καὶ δή τοι ἐρέωσιν ὑποχθονίωι βασιλῆϊ·
καὶ δή τοι δώσωσι πιῆν τῆς Μναμοσύνας ἀπὸ λίμνα[ς].
καὶ δὴ καὶ σὺ πιὼν ὁδὸν ἔρχεα<ι>, ἄν τε καὶ ἄλλοι (15)
μύσται καὶ βάχχοι ἱερὰν στείχωσι κλεινοί. (no. 1 / B10 / *OF* 474)

This is the work of Memory, when you are about to die,
you will go to the well-built halls of Hades. There is a spring on the right,
and a white cypress standing by it;
There the souls of dead, descending, refresh themselves.
Do not go too near this spring. (5)
Ahead you will find, from the lake of Memory,
pouring forth cold water; and guards are in front of it.
They will ask you, with keen perception,
what you are asking for from the gloom of murky Hades.
Say: "I am the child of Earth and starry Sky, (10)
I am thirsty and I perish; but quickly allow me
to drink cold water from the lake of Memory."
And then indeed they will speak to the chthonian king,
and then indeed they will allow you to drink from the lake of Memory,
and then also you, having drunk, will go along the sacred road, which
other (15)
famous initiates and Bacchics march in a line.

In this text, the retention of memory across the life–death divide and the ability to follow the instructions are what distinguish the individual from the other souls entering Hades and also allow for him or her to keep company with blessed individuals who took similar action. Memory and specialized knowledge are, therefore, crucial to the initiate's fate. This focus is true across many of the Orphic Gold Tablets and is reminiscent of *Olympian* 2's reference to "those in the know" (συνετοῖσιν, *Ol.* 2.85). As Alberto Bernabé Pajares and

Ana Jiménez San Cristóbal (2011, 86) have concluded, "the concept of knowledge is inherent to the nature of Orphic *teletai*." Forgetting, a form of mindlessness that happens in a negative Underworld, is the main obstacle for the dead in the religion of the Orphic Gold Tablets (Bernabé Pajares and Jiménez San Cristóbal 2011, 75–76; Betz 2011, 104–105). Memory gives access to an Elysium-type afterlife that will also allow the individual to join the august company of other initiates on a sacred road (ὁδὸν. . . . ἱερὰν, 1/B10/*OF* 474, 15–16). This recalls the reference in *Olympian* 2 to a road of Zeus which leads to the tower of Cronus (ἔτειλαν Διὸς ὁδὸν παρὰ Κρόνου τύρσιν, "they follow the road of Zeus near the tower of Cronus," *Ol.* 2.70). Although these texts come from different settings and their audiences might be different, they are clearly tapping into a commonly held expectation of a special path for select individuals that leads to a unique and blessed section of the Underworld. Moreover, both the epinicians and this Orphic Gold Tablet assume that the mortal they refer to has the ability to enter this blessed space because of their deeds during life, which include athletic accomplishment and ritual initiation, respectively.

The Petelia tablet (see Figure 4.1) starts with similar assumptions about the initiate and his or her potential place in the afterlife but goes even further, proclaiming that the individual will not only be among heroes but rule over them:

Εὑρήσσεις δ' Ἀΐδαο δόμων ἐπ' ἀριστερὰ κρήνην, *(1)*
πὰρ δ' αὐτῆι λευκὴν ἑστηκυῖαν κυπάρισσον.
ταύτης τῆς κρήνης μηδὲ σχεδὸν ἐμπελάσειας.
εὑρήσεις δ' ἑτέραν, τῆς Μνημοσύνης ἀπὸ λίμνης
ψυχρὸν ὕδωρ προρέον· φύλακες δ' ἐπίπροσθεν ἔασιν. (5)
εἰπεῖν· Γῆς παῖς εἰμι καὶ Οὐρανοῦ ἀστερόεντος,
αὐτὰρ ἐμοὶ γένος οὐράνιον· τόδε δ' ἴστε καὶ αὐτοί.
δίψαι δ' εἰμὶ αὔη καὶ ἀπόλλυμαι. ἀλλὰ δότ' αἶψα
ψυχρὸν ὕδωρ προρέον τῆς Μνημοσύνης ἀπὸ λίμνης.
καὐτ[οί] σ[οι] δώσουσι πιεῖν θείης ἀπ[ὸ κρή]νης, (10)
καὶ τότ' ἔπειτ' ἄ[λλοισι μεθ'] ἡρώεσσιν ἀνάξει[ς].
[Μνημοσύ]νης τόδ<ε> ἔ[ργον – – –
θανεῖσθ[αι – –] τόδε γραψ[– –
– –]τογλωσειπα σκότος ἀμφικαλύψας. (no. 2 / B1 / *OF* 476)

You will find a spring on the left of the halls of Hades,
and standing by it is a white cypress.

150   LIFE / AFTERLIFE

Do not approach this spring at all.
You will find another from the lake of Memory,
pouring forth cold water; and guards are in front of it. (5)
Say: "I am the child of Earth and starry Sky,
but my race is heavenly. You yourselves also know this.
I am thirsty and I perish; but quickly allow me
to drink cold water from the lake of Memory."
And they themselves will allow you to drink from a divine spring, (10)
And then after **you will rule over the other heroes**.
This is the work of Memory. When you are about to die . . .
Write this . . .
. . . darkness enfolding . . .

The phrase *a[lloisi meth'] eroessin anaxei[s]* (ἄ[λλοισι μεθ'] ἡρώεσσιν ἀνάξει[ς], "you will rule over the other heroes") line 11 is notable for several reasons. Along with the "hall of Hades" in the first line, it situates the narrative in the traditional Greek Underworld, attesting to the presence of heroes and confirming the initiate's place among them in this space because they performed the correct ritual actions. The verb *anaxeis* (ἀνάξει[ς]) is also interesting in this context because it implies a prominent role for the addressee and recalls Odysseus' greeting to Achilles' ghost as one who rules over the dead (κρατέεις νεκύεσσιν, *Od.* 11.485).[47] In this way, the Petelia tablet places the individual initiate in the position of a blessed hero in relation to the other dead. Furthermore, the initiate is labeled a ruler of heroes, perhaps another subtle reference to Achilles, who calls himself the "best of the Achaeans" (ἄριστον Ἀχαιῶν, *Il.* 1.244).

Corroborating the Orphic Gold Tablets' interest in heroes and a heroic Underworld, some tablets seem to make even more direct reference to the Homeric Underworld. The first Orphic Gold Tablet from Thurii also recalls the heroic Underworld of the *Nekuia*:

Ἀλλ᾽ ὁπόταμ ψυχὴ προλίπηι φάος ἀελίοιο, | *(1)*
δεξιὸν Ε.ΘΙΑΣ δ᾽ ἐξιέναι πεφυλαγμένον | εὖ μάλα πάντα·
χαῖρε παθὼν τὸ πάθη|μα τὸ δ᾽ οὔπω πρόσθε ἐπεπόνθεις.

---

[47] The verb *anaxeis* (ἀνάξει[ς]) could equally be from the verbs *anago* (ἀνάγω) or *anasso* (ἀνάσσω). The former, in a ritual setting, means "to lead [the rites]" or "celebrate," which is the way Edmonds (2011b, 22) interprets it. Based on its line position in the hexameter line, however, it most likely comes from the verb ἀνάσσω, a word which regularly appears in this closing position of a line in both the *Iliad* and *Odyssey*.

Crafting Heroic Blessedness through Underworld Scenes

θεὸς ἐγ|ένου ἐξ ἀνθρώπου· ἔριφος ἐς γάλα | ἔπετες.
χαῖρ<ε>, χαῖρε· δεξιὰν ὁδοιπόρ[ει] | (5)
λειμῶνάς τε ἱεροὺς καὶ ἄλσεα | Φερσεφονείας. (no. 3 / A4 / *OF* 487)

But when the soul leaves the ray of the light of the sun,
Go to the right, after having been very vigilant about all things;
Hail! Having suffered an experience that you had not yet suffered before,
Be born as a god from a human; a kid, you fell into milk
Hail! Hail! Travel the road on the right
To the holy meadows and groves of Persephone.

In this reference to the "holy meadows and groves of Persephone," there is an echo of Circe's description of Odysseus' Underworld destination as at "a fertile promontory and the groves of Persephone" (ἔνθ᾽ ἀκτή τε λάχεια καὶ ἄλσεα Περσεφονείης, *Od.* 10.509). The adjective "fertile promontory" suggests a flat shore not too different from a meadow. The phrase *kai alsea Persephoneies* (καὶ ἄλσεα Περσεφονείης) appears in both works to close out the line with a specific location. Although it might be familiar as a Homeric formula, it is not so common a phrase, and Persephone takes on the role as intercessor between the individual mortal hero and the chthonic world in both instances. In another Orphic Gold Tablet from Thurii, Persephone is again confirmed as an intercessor, and the *makarismos* greeting uses both *olbios* and *makar* to refer to the state of the initiate:

Ἔρχομαι ἐκ κοθαρῶ<ν> κοθαρά, χθονί<ων> βα|σίλεια,
Εὐκλῆς Εὐβωλεύς τε καὶ ἀ|θάνατοι θεοὶ ἄλλοι.
καὶ γὰρ ἐγὼν | ὑμῶν **γένος ὄλβιον** εὔχομαι | εἶμεν.
ἀλά με Μο<ῖ>ρα ἐδάμασε | καὶ ἀθάνατοι θεοὶ ἄλλοι (4a)
καὶ ἀσ|στεροβλῆτα κεραυνόν. (4b)
κύκλω | δ᾽ ἐξέπταν βαρυπενθέος ἀργα|λέοιο, (5)
ἱμερτῶ δ᾽ ἐπέβαν στεφά|νω ποσὶ καρπαλίμοισι·
Δεσσποί|νας δὲ ὑπὸ κόλπον ἔδυν χθονί|ας βασιλείας.
ἱμερτῶ δ᾽ ἐπέβαν | στεφάνω ποσὶ καρπαλίμοι|σι.
ὄλβιε καὶ μακαριστέ, θεὸς δ᾽ ἔσ|ηι ἀντὶ βροτοῖο.
ἔριφος ἐς γάλ᾽ ἔπετο|ν. (no. 5 / A1 / *OF* 488)

I come pure from the pure ones, Queen of those below the earth,
Eucles, Euboleus, and the other immortal gods.
For I too boast to be of your **blessed race**.

But Fate defeated me and the other immortal gods
and the lightning-throwing thunderer.
I flew out of the circle of painful, heavy grief,
I stepped up to the desirable crown with swift feet;
I sank into the bosom of the Mistress, the Underworld queen.
"You, **happy and divinely blessed**, will be a god instead of a mortal."
A kid, I fell into milk.

The declarations of the individual's identity and the focus on his or her deeds and honor create conceptual overlaps between the initiate and famous heroes, both in this poem and the others to varying degrees. As Miguel Herrero de Jáuregui (2011) has observed, the Orphic Gold Tablets use language that seems to intentionally link to and apply Homeric speech patterns and a *kleos*-based honor system to their initiates. In particular, Herrero de Jáuregui (2011, 288) identifies the frequently used term *eukhomai* in the Orphic Gold Tablets' invocations, the regular identification of one's superior ancestry or *genos*, and the action-oriented, agonistic language as three consistent points of similarity, concluding that "the (Orphic) poets of the *katabasis* of the soul turned a traditional epic tale into a soteriological program." Moreover, the narrative echoes that of Patroclus' death and the subsequent rituals by the Greeks to support his crossing over into the Underworld. Beyond the greeting and narrative pattern, the conversion from mortality into immortality is underscored further by the use of both terms for blessedness (*olbios* and *makar*) in the vocative, which refers to the initiate's state and location among the dead (Bernabé Pajares and Jiménez San Cristóbal 2011, 93–94).

By addressing the dead initiate as the audience or expressing the unique passwords for him or her to access a blessed afterlife, the Orphic Gold Tablets assume the soul's sentience and a continuity of identity and self-awareness across the life–death barrier. Moreover, the celebratory nature of the initiate's success is suggested by the presence of certain phrases of welcome, references to blessedness, and assumptions of the "happy privilege" the initiate has received, which all come together in a tablet from Pelinna:[48]

Νῦν ἔθανες | καὶ νῦν ἐγ|ένου, **τρισόλβ|ιε**, ἄματι τῶιδε. *(1)*
εἰπεῖν Φερσεφόν|αι σ᾽ ὅτι Β<ακ>χιος αὐτὸς | ἔλυσε.
τα{ι}ῦρος | εἰς γάλα ἔθορες,

---

[48] See Bernabé Pajares and Jiménez San Cristóbal (2011, 82–83) for a discussion on the connection between wine and the rites it may be referencing.

Crafting Heroic Blessedness through Underworld Scenes 153

αἶ|ψα εἰς γ<ἀ>λα ἔθορες,|
κριὸς εἰς γάλα ἔπεσ<ες>. (5)
οἶνον ἔχεις εὐ|δ<α>ίμονα **τιμή**<ν>
κἀπιμένει σ' ὑπὸ | γῆν **τέλεα** ἄσσαπερ **ὄλ|βιοι ἄλ|λοι**. (no. 26a / D1 / *OF* 485)

Now you have died and now you have been born, **thrice blessed one**,
on this very day.
Say to Persephone that Bacchios himself freed you.
A bull, you rushed into milk.
Quickly, you rushed into milk.
A ram, you fell into milk.
You have wine as your fortunate **honor**,
And there remains for you beneath the earth the **rewards (or rites)**,
as the **other blessed ones** [enjoy].[49]

Key words in this passage, such as *trisolbie*, *time*, *telea*, and *olbioi alloi* (in bold),
evoke a network of narrative links that show the overlap between the religious
beliefs in the Orphic Gold Tablets of a tripartite, judgment-based afterlife
existence and the heroic Underworld journey of Archaic epics. Each tablet
refers to a harrowing journey through the physical Underworld space for the
purpose of heroizing an individual, with the term "blessed" underscoring this
new state. The Orphic Gold Tablets are thus intended by their users to bridge
the border between the living and the dead and suggest implicitly that its special knowledge can make mortals blessed.

VI. Conclusions

The case studies of this chapter show a pattern of use for Underworld scenes
across the Greek-speaking world, which, through poetic and community
commemoration, helped to expand the perceived existential boundaries and
honors everyday mortals could achieve in both life and afterlife. Authors drew
from a wide range of ancient and contemporary sources, particularly the epic
Underworld portrayals of heroes and judgment after death, to develop and
expand on each other's strategies for creating a more inclusive Underworld.

---

[49] Edmonds (2011b, 36) chooses a slightly different reconstruction, yielding the translation
"and you will go beneath the earth, having celebrated rites just as the other blessed ones."
Both versions support the idea of the initiate entering into a company of blessed souls
whose location is related to their actions (i.e., rites, either in life or after death).

Pindar, while perhaps shaping works to appeal to local audiences, still would not have limited his poem to only apply to one performance, since he aspired to be a Panhellenic poet and promoted himself as fit to compete with Homer.[50] His poems, therefore, needed to resonate outside of the Sicilian context. They, however, allow only certain elite members of society (the *olbioi*) into the august company of heroes who spend an eternity as *makares* through honors (*timai*). This is a fundamental shift in the portrayal of mortals' access to spaces that used to be exclusive to those with divine ties by blood or favor. Epinician poetry allowed a specific, exceptional mortal to achieve special heroic status. In the newly detailed Underworld for the blessed, he was thus eligible to be a peer among the Homeric heroes and worthy of honors given by the living. The Orphic Gold Tablets expanded this trend further to encompass any individuals, not just rulers, who performed certain praise-worthy actions based on the mystery cult's religious beliefs.

As the fifth century BCE progressed, the people allowed to inhabit the circle of blessedness expanded. Furthermore, both the literary and artistic products of this period emphasize that several solutions for obtaining a favorable afterlife existed besides heroic deeds or celebration in song. A familiarity with Underworld scenes, such as the idea of afterlife blessedness and the continuity of a sentient existence, was developed through regular interactions with and reminders of the relationship between the living and the dead in everyday objects, large and small, as well as through the educational process of public performances and visual storytelling. The public nature of civic funeral orations and grave *stelai* as well as the wide-spread availability of white-ground lekythoi for funerary rites suggest a larger and more sophisticated audience with whom authors and artists negotiated to frame the relationship between the living and the dead. Recalling and reimagining Underworld narratives on a regular basis provided a framework for authority, intervention, and self-identity throughout a time of tremendous social and political change. The next chapter looks more closely at how cultural, religious, and political transformations were negotiated through Underworld scenes on stage and in other civic venues.

---

[50] For more on how Pindar and his poetry interacted with Homeric epic in the larger Panhellenic context, see Nisetich (1989, 28) and Nagy (1990).

5

World and Underworld

DEMOCRATIZING THE AFTERLIFE THROUGH UNDERWORLD SCENES

I. Introduction

The fifth century BCE has often been described as a period of drastic reorientation for the ancient Greek world. During this time, authors refocused their stories to align with the new reality after the shocks of the Persian War, which included the sack of Athens and the allied Greeks' eventual victory. The people living in Athens during those times experienced "a philosophical and religious, as well as a political, revolution," which occurred against a backdrop of multiple wars and imperial expansion (Herington 1986, 20). Francis Dunn (2007, 3) describes the phenomenon ancient Athens experienced as a form of "present shock," leading to a change in focus in which "the locus of authority came to reside less in the heroic past and more in present human experience." Poets, thinkers, and artists throughout the fifth century BCE, particularly in Athens, used Archaic literary language and familiar mythic motifs to describe and engage with their changing cultural and political realities. They scrutinized their myths, religious rituals, political norms, and gods, while also challenging and reformulating them to meet and reconceptualize their reality. In this chapter, I first discuss the idea of a democratized afterlife. I then examine how Underworld scenes contributed to changes in thought and identity by analyzing case studies in three major areas: (1) in personal, everyday spaces; (2) in the political sphere; and (3) in public, religious, and performative venues. Through these examples, I demonstrate how Underworld scenes became an alternative platform in public performances and private rituals for revolutionizing traditional beliefs and for negotiating power dynamics and

Life / Afterlife. Suzanne Lye, Oxford University Press. © Oxford University Press 2024.
DOI: 10.1093/9780197690239.003.0006

community values among the living. I argue that Underworld scenes in fifth-century BCE Athens democratized the Underworld, making its perceived borders more permeable and its benefits more accessible to people from different classes and backgrounds.

II. Democratizing the Afterlife

Alongside Athens' rise to prominence starting in the fifth century BCE, authors and artists reworked famous myths to emphasize the affinity between the worlds of the living and the dead, which reinforced representations of Underworld scenes across media. The nonsentient afterlife of the *Nekuia* seems to have disappeared, so that souls were almost universally considered to be conscious as they experienced a range of punishment or reward in the afterlife. Along with this consciousness, souls increasingly appeared in situations and conversations that mimicked those among the living. This was part of a larger trend in postwar, fifth-century BCE Athens, during a time when Athenians and their allies seemed to have become particularly concerned with making connections to their mythic past as a way to give context to their democracy and to promote their newfound Panhellenic influence (Dunn 2007, 67–85). It is during this period that we see three major trends: (1) the rise of the Theseus myth to a status of central importance coinciding with the rise of Athens (Calame 1990; Walker 1995; Mills 1997); (2) the emphasis on the Trojan War as a Panhellenic venture of Greek-speakers being paralleled to the Greek alliances against the Persian invasion (L. G. Mitchell 2007; Green 2010); and (3) the "invention" of the non-Greek barbarian as a reliable, often feminized "other" against which to define Greek identity (Hall 1989; S.P. Morris 1992).

This unique historical moment influenced the codification and standardization of Underworld scenes as a rhetorical strategy and created a vital impetus for an increase in Underworld scenes as communicative devices across media to process political, religious, and societal changes. Athenian power and democracy, with its rhetoric of individuality and rule of the people, shifted the Underworld's representation so that it was rewritten as a space where individuals on all levels of society had some direct power over the supernatural realm. Authors and artists maintained the basic framework and language of Underworld scenes, established by Homer and his immediate successors, so that the Underworld was not only a political space ruled by Hades and Persephone but also a geographic and cultural space inhabited by souls segregated into neighborhoods of punishment and reward based on their actions in life. Increasingly during the fifth century BCE, Underworld scenes began to promote the idea of afterlife society as a reflection of contemporary society and were constructed to emphasize deeper connections between the experiences of souls in the afterlife and the actions of the living, particularly their kin.

As a result of Athenian assertiveness in appropriating its mythic past, Underworld motifs and images appeared as propaganda in a variety of public, civic venues meant for mass consumption. Literature, art, and ritual converge in their portrayal of a democratized Underworld. While making offerings to the dead at tombs by family members was common from the Archaic period, the idea of the dead coming back to respond and commingle directly with the living, either to haunt or to help, emerged in the early Classical period (Johnston 1999, 31). Furthermore, ordinary men, mostly (but not exclusively) citizens, began to be heroized for their deeds in war through funeral orations and civic monuments, in a similar way to the *laudandus* of epinician poetry. References to Underworld motifs and specific scenes from earlier literature became more abbreviated and centered on specific aspects of the afterlife, allowing for the rapid activation of several narratives through hypertextual linking from single phrases or figures. The appearance and references to the afterlife across genres in more compact (but no less impactful) forms indicate that creating links to a network of Underworld scenes was viewed as a familiar, accepted, and understood rhetorical strategy in which the audience was heavily invested and deeply informed. In this period, Underworld scenes were presented to audiences in small, upper-class gatherings, such as symposia, as well as during large-scale civic performances or festivals. They also persistently appeared on monuments in public spaces, so that everyone who lived in or visited Athens or its sphere of influence could be considered an audience able to decode the compressed language of Underworld scenes. Formal education was not required to understand the intertexts between newly composed afterlife narratives and older sources, however, since the general public would have been aware of the Homeric and Hesiodic Underworld myths. Those stories were reinforced regularly in festivals and rhapsodic performances, both in the competitions hosted at the Panathenaia as well as in other noncompetitive live performances around Greece.[1]

---

[1] Collins (2001, 159) observes widespread evidence for public interest in rhapsodic performance attested from the sixth century BCE down to the third century CE, arguing that the "evidence surely bespeaks the popularity of *rhapsôidia* as a mode of live performance."

A class of wandering expert called the *goēs*, or "necromancer," seemed to have had a thriving business in Athens at this time, even earning ridicule in comedy (Johnston 1999, 119). The importance of the *goēs*, a specialist in communicating with the dead through ritual actions and utterances, increased throughout the Archaic period so that by the fifth century BCE, it was considered its own profession.[2] These specialist intermediaries allowed more touchpoints for people at all levels of society to evoke and apply chthonic narratives to their daily lives.[3] This development, in turn, localized the power of contacting and controlling chthonic forces onto professional, accessible individuals. Any person could go to a *goēs* (necromancer) or *psychagogus* (soul-driver) and make contact with the dead or could appeal to Hermes, Charon, Theseus, or Heracles as psychopomps (soul-escorters), who were less intimidating perhaps than Hades and Persephone.[4]

Underworld scenes in extant tragedies and comedies offer evidence for the ways that theatrical productions reinforced and invented connections between life and afterlife at various levels of society with the goal of making

---

[2] The function of the *goēs* as translator between the living and the dead may have evolved from the early role of "chief mourner" in Archaic funeral procession, who was the "direct communicant with the dead" (Vermeule 1979, 17). Foreign elements may have been incorporated into the *goēs'* rituals but must always have been balanced by "homegrown needs and incorporating native ideas" (Johnston 1999, 83). Necromantic sanctuaries and oracles of the dead, administered by specialists (*goēs* and *psuchagogoi*), had already popped up around Greece during the Archaic period, but the terms referring to these places for communication with the dead (*nekuomanteion, psuchagogion*) are first found in the fifth century BCE (Ogden 2001, 17). The necromantic ceremony in plays such as the *Persians*, therefore, would have been familiar to Aeschylus' audience, either through direct experience or through collective knowledge (Jouan 1981, 419).

[3] Johnston points out that Greeks adopted new ways of communicating with the dead, including the art of *goeteia* ("invocation of the dead"), as funerary laws became more restrictive and sees this professionalization of necromancy to be a further example of distancing the dead from the living (Johnston 1999, 102–104). I argue instead that the rise of the *goēs* and the additional power that he had to both call up souls and persuade the gods allowed for *more* access to the realm of the dead for anyone who wanted it by giving clearer, more specific avenues for communication.

[4] In the fifth century BCE, "*goēs*" and "*psychagogus*" seem to be technical terms for professional necromancers. According to Johnston, "there was in fact a thriving business in manipulating the dead," a topic which appealed to tragedians who featured them in several plays (Johnston 1999, 119; Bardel 2005, 86–87). Heracles, Theseus, and Pirithous were popular characters in tragedy. Gantz (1980, 162) names at least four plays by Aeschylus about Heracles; there were several plays with the title *Theseus*, and another called *Pirithous* is ascribed to Critias. The ferryman Charon was a later addition to this set, appearing in the epic *Minyas* and only becoming established as a regular part of Underworld imagery in the fifth century BCE (Johnston 1999, 96).

World and Underworld   159

spaces for the dead in the world of the living and vice versa. These new genres translated traditional literary material onto the stage to make sense of emerging political and social realities (while also reaffirming religious beliefs), particularly related to the rise of democracy, the *polis*, and Athenian power. Ghosts and Underworld scenes created a bridge across space and time between a heroic past and the present, using the time-bending nature of the Underworld *chronotope* to make mythic stories reflect the present and to cast current events against a backdrop removed from daily reality.

The emergence of new professions in relation to the dead, the Underworld, and their representation demonstrates that Athenians were interested in more clearly defining the parameters with which the living would engage with the dead. Minor, relatively weak deities and even ghosts were thought to be ubiquitous and to bridge the gap between mortals and immortals (Vermeule 1979, 126). Negotiating with the dead began to mimic the *polis'* actions related to domestic and foreign policy. This idea that an ordinary mortal could negotiate with death and chthonic powers, either through force (physical/persuasive) or legislation (designating sites of contact), as one might with another city-state through battle or diplomacy, marks a shift in the perceived power dynamics between mortals and immortals. Admetus' grief in Euripides' *Alcestis*, for example, persuades Heracles to battle for the life of Alcestis with Death himself (Thanatos), who was depicted in a speaking role on stage alongside Apollo. Thanatos argues for the strict rules of obligation that men must die in their time, while Apollo and Heracles are portrayed as advocates for men who are willing to confront death, even when it goes against strict legal codes of justice (Golden 1970–1971, 117). The play portrays death as negotiable rather than final, blurring the border between life and death.

The mythic figures of Sisyphus, a sinner undergoing eternal punishment in Hades, and Theseus, a katabatic hero, also became emblematic to a certain degree of this newly conceived relationship between the living and the dead. The Sisyphus story, first recorded in Homer and popular in satyr-plays, was portrayed on stage multiple times throughout the fifth century BCE, indicating a fascination with his ultimate demise and the idea of a mortal duping the gods.[5] Envisioning the society of the dead in real-world terms across literary and visual media—and also expecting the dead to act predictably in response

---

[5] Aeschylus was known to have staged at least one and perhaps even two plays about Sisyphus' escape from Hades and death via trickery (Gantz 1980, 162; Sutton 1980, 27–28; Goins 1989, 401). A fragment from Euripides' version (415 BCE), originally attributed to Critias, asserts that man created the gods, a somewhat shocking theological assertion that attempts to reframe the power dynamic between humans and immortals (Kahn 1997, 249).

to the actions of the living—made the supernatural less abstract, less dangerous, and less distant from everyday reality. Underworld scenes were crucial in this reframing because they provided a landscape outside of time to imagine meaningful encounters and interactions between the living and the dead that could have immediate impact and existential significance.

The use of traditional Underworld elements in new scenes and through new media is a further indication that Greeks in fifth-century BCE Athens and beyond were attempting to assert control over the narratives of their self-identity and democratize the Underworld by putting reminders of the society of the dead in the spaces of the living. Using newly conceived traditional narratives, Underworld scenes promoted and helped support political and cultural revolutions in the public sphere and in private practices. For example, the episode depicted in the famous Elpenor Vase scaffolds its meaning by linking to multiple other Underworld scenes as *para-narratives* (see Figure 5.1).

On the vase is a moment from Homer's *Nekuia*, in which Odysseus talks to the ghost of his dead companion Elpenor while waiting for the soul of the seer Tiresias. Hermes is also present, however, which does not match the *Nekuia* but activates other scenes, such as the one in Book 24 (among others), in which Hermes plays a lead role guiding souls to Hades. The artist clearly relies on the viewing audience to supply the story and necessary context. Underworld scenes like this were particularly suited for capturing the changing conceptions of the individual's relationship to aspects of his world, both seen and unseen. Their easily recognizable features allowed the rapid activation of narratives involving a specific set of familiar images, which could be applied across a variety of media and extended through both space and time. The reliance on this type of intertextual linking seems especially true in Underworld scenes that people might encounter in everyday life, particularly those appearing in private spaces and on personal objects.

III. Making Space for the Dead: Underworld Scenes in Everyday Life

Private spaces and objects show the normalization of Underworld scenes in everyday settings as a strategy for commemorating and engaging with the dead. These visual representations rely on the same intertextual networks that literary Underworld accounts use. Images of Underworld scenes on objects such as funerary cups and white-ground lekythoi activate and engage with

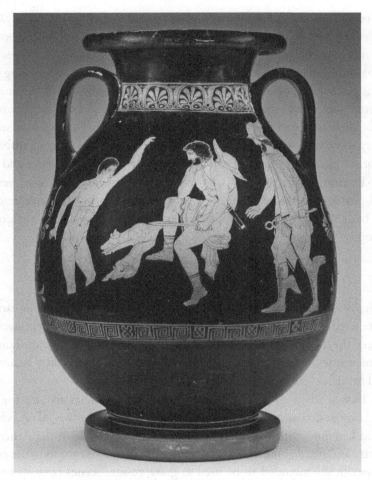

FIGURE 5.1 The Elpenor Vase by the Lykaon Painter portrays Odysseus (right) and the ghost of his dead comrade Elpenor (left) in the Underworld, a meeting described in *Odyssey* 11. An added element is Hermes (right) in his role of psychopomp. Greek red-figure jar (pelike). Greece, 440 BCE. Photograph courtesy of © 2023 Museum of Fine Arts, Boston.

literary Underworld scenes as *para-narratives*. Through such scenes, they were able to frame dead loved ones against a backdrop of a positive afterlife and imagine them as peers to heroes such as Theseus and the Tyrannicides, who fought for and died to protect the state. The hypertextual poetics of the Underworld made the realm of Hades and a blessed afterlife more accessible to the living by familiarizing them through mundane objects and settings.

162   LIFE / AFTERLIFE

Greek vases and monumental displays, as artifacts of everyday life, did on the personal level what dramatic performances and political speeches were doing at the civic level. Alexandre Mitchell (2009, 4) compares the vase paintings in which gods are mocked to Aristophanes' *Frogs*, arguing that the images on such objects give indications of the commonly held values of Athenian society and that the comic representations on vases were an extension of what appeared on the comic stage. Although they might represent a literary scene from epic or drama, Underworld scenes on objects reinforced the larger message of a persistent connection between the living and the dead. By moving the possibility of contact into everyday life, such vessels could promote the close connection between real life and the afterlife on a daily basis through media that were accessible and affordable to a majority of people.

Everyday Underworlds: Small Scale Representations

Underworld scenes appear on several types of Athenian vases and in various private settings with the common purpose of creating a perceived connection between the living and the dead. White-ground lekythoi are the most famous Athenian vases and are uniquely associated with fifth-century BCE Athenian burial practices (see Figure 5.2 and 5.3).

A lekythos is a container that held oils and perfumes to care for the dead body and that sometimes stored condiments and olive oil. A white-ground lekythos, which is the same shape but found only in the Athenian funerary and ritual context, is a type of lekythos distinctive for its white color and specifically intended to be used as grave goods. Scenes relevant to the life–death transition, including images of Charon, Hermes, Thanatos, and Hypnos, were common on such lekythoi (Arrington 2015, 246). Their popularity and use peaked in the fifth century BCE with a precipitous decline around 400 BCE (I. Morris 1992a, 110–111).[6] Buried with the dead, these lekythoi held supplies that were thought to be needed for the afterlife, and

---

[6] For more on the production of white-ground lekythoi and their associations with different types of burial, see also Walton et al., (2010).

their contents mirrored the perceived necessities and appetites of the living. In funerary rituals, they were first displayed around the corpse in the home then transported and buried with it (Arrington 2015, 247). Even after burial, family members brought additional lekythoi on such occasions as the Genesia and Anthesteria, annual festivals related to contacting and appeasing the dead (Humphreys 1980, 100–101; Johnston 1999, 43–46 and 63–71). These offered

FIGURE 5.2 This white-ground lekythos depicts a woman bringing offerings to the tomb which separates her and the dead youth (left). Attica, 460–450 BCE. Courtesy of © The Trustees of the British Museum.

FIGURE 5.3 This white-ground lekythos is attributed to the Timokrates Painter or Vourni Painter. It depicts family members preparing to visit a tomb with a woman (left) gathering the standard funerary offerings, ribbons, wreaths, and aryballoi in a basket. The youth (right) is holding a pomegranate, a symbol of death. Attica, 470–460 BCE. Image courtesy of Getty's Open Content Program.

additional regular occasions beyond public or state funerals for the living and the dead to interact—and in a more personal way. A lekythos used on such occasions "evokes that which has been lost" and operates as a visible token specifically associated with the dead (Arrington 2015, 267). Its imagery of the afterlife activates narratives in which the audience imagines the dead for purposes of both consolation and protection. The dead who did not receive proper burial or sufficient honors from the living were often thought to intend harm (Johnston 1999, 127–129). Creating spaces through analogy and Underworld scenes, therefore, served the specific purpose of keeping the dead in their realm and in designated places where they could receive due honors and be appeased. Painted funerary vases gave a central position to the dead to keep them integrated in the community and "convey the sense of a personal relationship between the dead and the mourner" (Humphreys 1980, 113).

The popularity of white-ground lekythoi as grave goods throughout the fifth century BCE and their specialized association with funerals and tombs are indicators of the narratives that ordinary people used to define the life–death relationship (Oakley 2004, 6–11).[7] In one lekythos, the figure of Hermes leads a woman along while an *eidolon* (soul) flutters near his knees, identifying the god in his role of psychopomp (Oakley 2004, 139). By recalling Hermes in this role from Book 24 of the *Odyssey*, the vase ties this woman's soul to an afterlife that is marked by consciousness, like the dead suitors experience in the epic. Similar vases showing Thanatos and Hypnos are visual intertexts to the narrative of Sarpedon's death in the *Iliad*, in which his body is rescued from the battlefield by these two gods and taken back to his homeland to be esteemed in future hero cult (*Il.* 16.666–683). The juxtaposition of a regular mortal in the tomb, alongside objects that activate the Sarpedon story as a *para-narrative*, sends a message that while the person is deceased, he or she can expect honors and special favors from the gods—and from the living—after death.

These representations are also found on another type of grave good: white-ground cups. A series of these cups attributed to the Sotades Painter also portrays scenes reminiscent of Underworld visits and include chthonic figures

---

[7] White-ground lekythoi, often found in and around graves, were affordable, widely available, and, therefore, accessible to non-elites, which may explain their ubiquity (Arrington 2015, 179). Although some were used in the actual funeral rites and buried with the dead, others were put on display at tombs during private and public occasions honoring the dead (Oakley 2004, 11). The vessels themselves, with their images of both domestic and afterlife motifs, seem to be addressed to the dead as consolation and a reminder of continued care and commemoration by the living (Humphreys 1980, 113).

FIGURE 5.4 This white-ground drinking cup (kylix), a grave offering, is attributed to the Sotades Painter. It depicts Glaucus (right) and Polyeidos (left) in a conical tumulus tomb. In the scene, Polyeidos is using a spear to thrust down at one of two snakes on the floor of the tomb. Attica, 460–450 BCE. Courtesy of © The Trustees of the British Museum.

such as Elysian apple-pickers and serpents (Hoffmann 1997, 1989).[8] Although there is some debate about the identity of the figures, except where they are actually named, scholars have reached a consensus that the imagery deals with life after death. Herbert Hoffmann has identified the primary figures as Glaucus and Polyeidos and sets the scene around the moment the latter resurrects the former (see Figure 5.4).

The myth of Minos' son Glaucus, who was restored to life by the seer Polyeidos, is depicted in this set of cups along with this afterlife imagery (Griffiths 1986). A snake helped the latter find a special herb that allowed

---

[8] Apple-pickers and apple trees in funerary contexts may refer to an idyllic afterlife as well as the apples in the garden of the Hesperides and Heracles, all of which would point to Underworld narratives. A funerary base from Kallithea shows similar apple-picking imagery, and Kosmopoulou (1998) sees evidence in this of an overall shift in attitude from negative to positive Underworld depictions over the course of the fifth century BCE. She argues that various factors, such as war and the plague, caused an increased concern over the transition and survival of one's memory.

the resurrection of Glaucus, recalling the Underworld stories about a mortal's escape from death (or capture through consumption of food, as in the case of Persephone). [9] Glaucus is thus set up as a paradigm for a mortal undergoing both a *katabasis* and an initiatory transformation (Hoffmann 1997, 120–121). As with the white-ground lekythoi, the Sotades cups need only a few figures or signs to activate multiple Underworld narratives that inform the viewing experience. The Sotades cups, therefore, fall into a fifth-century BCE trend expanding the concept of "hero" to include the Dionysian mystery initiate (Hoffmann 1997, 15). The Underworld scene depiction can also be interpreted as an example of a genre of myth in which humans test the boundaries between the mortal and immortal worlds (Vermeule 1979, 128–132). This assimilation of humans to heroes through a ritual initiatory process to determine their afterlife outcome further underscores the perceived permeability and accessibility of the Underworld, by bringing the mythical and historical together into another, more personal point of contact within the Attic context. Like the Orphic Gold Tablets used in the mystery cult setting, the Sotades cups, which were also buried with the dead, suggest a belief that messages and knowledge cross the borders of the Underworld.[10] The phenomenon of personalizing the Underworld and making it seem more accessible was, therefore, ubiquitous. Representations on everyday objects and at regular events framed the dead as maintaining aspects of their humanity and sustaining their long-standing community ties beyond the grave. The Sotades cups and white-ground lekythoi point to the practice of trying to create personal relationships between the living and the dead on the individual level.

Outside of the grave setting, different vessels brought mythic Underworld scenes into the living spaces of ordinary people. The famous calyx-krater by the Niobid painter ("Niobid Krater," Louvre G341), which dates to the mid-fifth century BCE, contains a scene with Heracles and Theseus as central figures surrounded by other great heroes, such as Achilles and Odysseus.[11] In a single glance, the scene links to multiple Underworld narratives whose stories

---

[9] See Ogden (2013), Stansbury-O'Donnell (1999, 177), and Krappe (1928, 267) for more about the association of snakes with chthonic powers and special knowledge.

[10] For more on the Orphic Gold Tablets, see previous chapter.

[11] There has been much debate over the scene, but recently scholars have interpreted the scene as set in the Underworld, with various heroes surrounding the easily identified figure of Heracles (Simon 1963, 43–44; McNiven 1989, 192). Simon (1963, 44–45) argues convincingly that the recumbent figure is Theseus, using comparisons with the *Nekuia* calyx-krater in New York featuring the group of Heracles-Theseus-Pirithous in the Underworld dated to the same time period.

must be recalled by the viewer in order to make sense of the figures. The object itself, a container for mixing wine, would have been stored nearby or placed on direct display in an intimate space of conviviality, creating an intrusion of the mythic dead into the space of the living on a regular (perhaps even daily) basis. In turn, the living who interact with the vessel would be caught up in its narratives as witness and participant, perhaps even as a proxy for the dead themselves that would have been imagined to surround the figures shown in the Underworld scene. This krater was found in a tomb in Etruria, suggesting the widespread influence of Athenian beliefs about how afterlife society mirrors that of the living. The findspot of the krater also suggests that those who left it there imagined the krater being used by the dead in the afterlife in a similar way to how such a vessel would be used by the living.

The Niobid Krater is additionally interesting because of its connection to early Classical monumental paintings. The krater itself is thought to be a replica of a monumental painting, put in miniature, since "all of the known monumental paintings of the early Classical period which could possibly have been the model for the scene on the Niobid krater have been recognized in it," albeit with some problems (McNiven 1989, 192). One such known monumental paintings is Polygnotus' *Nekuia* in the Lesche of the Cnidians, which featured a large-scale wall painting of an Underworld scene in a building where the Cnidians could gather and feast. Such a setting created an opportunity for extended personal contemplation of the Underworld scene by visitors in a private space but on a larger scale than the white-ground lekythoi, Sotades cups, and Niobid Krater would allow.

The Underworld, Large as Life: Fraternizing with the Dead

The Lesche of the Cnidians, described by Pausanias in the second century C.E., contained a visual representation of epic myths by the famous fifth century BCE painter Polygnotus. The Lesche was built to be a local gathering spot or "club house" for the Cnidians at Delphi. Inside the building, the visitors were imagined to share space with the dead, drawn to life-size in this well-known example of monumental art. Although the Homeric Underworld is the most dominant source for the Polygnotus scene and has been assumed to be its inspiration, several figures on the Lesche do not appear in the Homeric epics but can be traced to other narratives of the Underworld. Polygnotus' Underworld, therefore, is a visual index hyperlinking to a wide network of *para-narratives* whose details the audience was expected to provide through their knowledge of multiple Underworld stories. Recent reconstructions

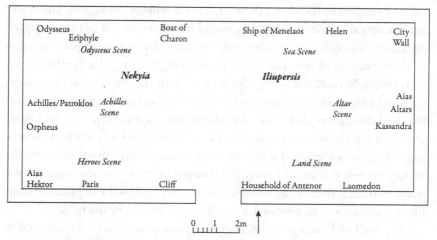

FIGURE 5.5 Reconstruction of the interior of the Lesche of the Cnidians at Delphi. The walls depicted a monumental painting of the *Nekuia* and *Iliupersis* by the famous painter Polygnotus, who used *Odyssey* 11 as his primary inspiration for an Underworld scene, which he combined with figures from other katabatic myths. This figure originally appeared in Stansbury-O'Donnell (1990, fig. 2). Image courtesy of the author, the Archaeological Institute of America, and the American Journal of Archaeology.

agree on the elements which bear on our discussion, and I rely on the ones by Mark Stansbury-O'Donnell (1990, 1999), which divide the Lesche symmetrically into Odysseus' *Nekuia* on the left wall and the *Iliupersis* on the right (see Figure 5.5).

Upon entering the Lesche, it would be immediately clear to the visitor that time and space were being intermingled on both the physical and cognitive levels. The viewer, faced with the monumental paintings of the two scenes in a closed environment, would be put in the roles of both actor, participating in various rituals with his peers, and audience, looking at the scenes on the walls. On one side, the *Iliupersis* freezes the actions of heroes in life as they battle at the Fall of Troy, while the *Nekuia* across from it represents mythic heroes in death, after having been judged. Between the representations of these two extremes—life and afterlife—would stand the audience members, who fill the liminal space and interact with the worlds of the living and the dead equally. The display of the *Iliupersis* opposite the *Nekuia* makes the latter into an Underworld scene, which focuses on the implications of actions in life on afterlife outcome in the same way that Achilles' presence in the *Odyssey*'s Underworld scenes comments on the meaning of heroic action and the afterlife of blessed heroes. The spatial arrangement for the Lesche and Polygnotus'

Underworld scene plays with time by forcing the viewer to participate with figures in various temporal and narrative frames.

The artist of an Underworld scene, like an author, brings the viewer into the Underworld chronotope within seconds through strategically placed figures, such as Sisyphus (Stansbury-O'Donnell 1990, 215). Upon entering the Lesche and turning left, the visitor begins a quasi-*katabasis* and can be analogized to the *Nekuia*'s Odysseus. Both witness what is in the Underworld and are allowed to return to the land of living outside of that space to tell the tale. Visitors in the Lesche must simultaneously be in the Underworld of Polygnotus (through physical presence) and also in any Underworld *para-narratives* that they recall to make sense of what they are viewing. Each visitor modulates his or her own experience and the narrative section they can view at any one time as they participate in activities within the space.[12] The Underworld scenes on the Lesche's walls, therefore, foster a sense of accessibility and interaction between the worlds of the living and the dead. The Lesche paintings also show that such Underworld intertextuality at the narrative level was present beyond the immediate Athenian context as a Panhellenic phenomenon.

As objects representing encounters with Underworld scenes in private spaces, the Lesche of the Cnidians, Niobid Krater, white-ground lekythoi, and Sotades cups all suggest that individuals of this time period wanted to feel like they were in direct contact with the dead and could bridge the life–death barrier. Through Underworld scenes on everyday objects, the afterlife came into contact with individuals on a more personal level, appearing as an enhanced and sometimes distorted reflection of everyday life projected against the backdrop of heroic tales. Each representation, whether in text or image, continued to rely on the audience's understanding of the basic mythic framework and image set of the Underworld chronotope as developed and used in Archaic poetry dating back to the Homeric epics. The messages about the afterlife conveyed through these usable, everyday, commonly held objects tied into larger cultural debates about the relationship between the living and the dead. Through the Underworld scenes on these objects, ideas about death and a blessed afterlife remained present in the lives of people of all classes, backgrounds, and levels of society. This message was further amplified by Underworld scenes in public and communal settings. In the next section, I discuss Underworld scenes in civic space and how they promoted the idea

---

[12] For more on the viewing experience, see Stansbury-O'Donnell (1999, 87).

of a democratized Underworld in ways that supported political and religious agendas.

IV. The Politics of the Afterlife: The Underworld in Civic Space and Propaganda

Starting in the late sixth century BCE, Athenians gave legislative and legal priority to regulating the relationship between the living and the dead. At stake in this were ideas related to the physical location of the dead, ways to access the Underworld, and the perceived proximity of the Underworld space to the world of the living. Through legislation, Athenians designated limitations on mourning and specific places for the private burial of the dead while at the same time honoring the war dead publicly by *deme*, or tribe, in grand civic events. Ian Morris (1987, 209–210) describes a drastic change in burial patterns moving from the Archaic to Classical periods that tracks with changes to social structures and the rise of the *polis*, particularly noting the reforms of Cleisthenes in 508/7 BCE, which diminished aristocratic strongholds on power through proactive legislation reorganizing the living citizen body and funerary laws dictating the dispensation of the dead. Along the same vein, Robert Garland (1989, 15) argues that the corpse, in particular, became a focal point to express partisan sentiment and activity such that funerary legislation "was thus one of the chief weapons by which democracy in its early days sought to establish itself as an effective means of government and to encourage the growth of democratic sentiments." He concludes that newly empowered citizens may have wanted clarification on the treatment of corpses during funerals and afterwards as part of the larger reordering of society. The relationship between living individuals inside the walls was mirrored in the placement of their remains, both in their locations outside the walls and their organization.[13] These societal changes were processed culturally through representations of the dead using Underworld scenes, which reflected similar ideas about the continuity of community across the life–death barrier in various literary and artistic genres. During this time, the dead were often portrayed as being separated by a slim barrier, whether just under the earth or on the other side of a tombstone, rather than far away at the edge

---

[13] See Humphreys (1980), Closterman (2007), and Shea (2021) for more about changes to the layout and placement of family tombs in Classical Athens.

of the world as in Homeric epic. This made them potentially more accessible through necromantic rituals by experts, who could be hired both in the city or at nearby cave sanctuaries (Ustinova 2009; Ogden 2001). With the emphasis on the physical placement and location of the dead, both in the real world and the Underworld, the visible, horizontal proximity of the living and dead in the city began to mirror the envisioned vertical proximity between the living in the real world and the dead in the Underworld. With the metaphorical shortening of the vertical and horizontal distances between the living and the dead, the paths for communication and connection between these two communities were made clearer and more consistent.

Furthermore, the physical presence of tombs within the city itself became less important because commemoration and invocation of the war dead could occur simply by naming them in a centrally located public memorial (Arrington 2015, 125–127), a practice that relies on *hypertextuality*'s notion that a simple name or image could recall an entire narrative about the dead. This practice and expectation seem to have occurred at Sparta as well, particularly after the battle of Thermopylae. In that case, the dead were buried far away from the city, but could be evoked simply by listing them on state-sponsored memorials in the city and celebrating them at these sites through commemorative speeches, away from their actual remains (Low 2011, 4–6). This indicates that, even when tombs were outside of the city walls or the immediate visual field, the dead could still be considered actively present in the daily public spaces of the living across time and space.

In Athens, the living could also see the tombs while walking along the main thoroughfare of Academy Road during a festival, in the procession to Eleusis, or while shopping for amphorae (Arrington 2015, 90). Contact with the dead could occur throughout the year directly and casually outside the city in the cemetery, since the dead were thought to congregate around tombs (Johnston 1999, 27). The funerary laws, which focused on maximum limits for the public display of mourning and funeral costs, did not appear to be excessively prescriptive or prohibitive (Sourvinou-Inwood 1995, 289; Johnston 1999, 40–41). As public funerals for the war dead (as a collective) became more prominent in the mid-fifth century BCE, the state created a narrative of sacrifice to the state and of "shared struggle" by the living and the dead (Arrington 2015, 122). Against this backdrop, politicians could heroize certain citizens by using Underworld scenes to draw comparisons between them and heroes of the past, both through poetry, as epinician poets did for their patrons, and through public, civic displays for the citizenry.

Heroizing the Polity through Underworld Scenes

Outside of the epinician and religious contexts, other authors also were able to heroize individuals using Underworld scenes. Whether performing to large audiences or small, they aimed to make grander political statements about their realities and confer a status on their subjects, which was denied in regular political discourse. An anonymous, sixth-century BCE poem shows that the Underworld scene strategy Pindar and Bacchylides were using in Sicily to publicly heroize their patrons was also being used across the Greek-speaking world. The following poetic fragment, one of the earliest and most explicit politicizations of an Underworld scene, applies epic language to heroize the Athenian tyrant-killer Harmodius, who had been killed in 514 BCE:

(893) ἐν μύρτου κλαδὶ τὸ ξίφος φορήσω
ὥσπερ Ἁρμόδιος καὶ Ἀριστογείτων
ὅτε τὸν τύραννον κτανέτην
ἰσονόμους τ᾽ Ἀθήνας ἐποιησάτην.
(894) φίλταθ᾽ Ἁρμόδι᾽, οὔ τί πω τέθνηκας,
νήσοις δ᾽ ἐν μακάρων σέ φασιν εἶναι,
ἵνα περ ποδώκης Ἀχιλεὺς
Τυδεΐδην τέ †φασι τὸν ἐσθλὸν Διομήδεα. *(PMG 893–894)*

(893) I will carry my sword in a myrtle branch,
just as Harmodius and Aristogeiton
when they killed the tyrant
and made Athens a place of equal laws
(894) Dearest Harmodius, surely you have not yet died,
but they say you are on the **Isles of the Blessed**,
where indeed swift-footed Achilles is
and [also] Diomedes, the noble son of Tydeus.

This anonymous poem directly connects actions that serve the cause of justice with the blessed afterlife of the hero, using familiar Underworld imagery to make its argument that Harmodius be considered a heroic equal to the great Iliadic heroes Achilles and Diomedes.

The insertion of an Underworld reference into a praise poem associated with justice and assessing deeds leans on a judgment-based afterlife by establishing a strong link between one's actions in life and subsequent fate in the afterlife. As Edmonds (2004, 199) argues, "the assassination of

World and Underworld

Hipparchus ranked, at least for some, with the epic heroism of Diomedes and Achilles, and such heroic deeds sufficed for admission to a better place after the mortal life was over." The phrase "Isles of the Blessed" (νήσοις δ' ἐν μακάρων, *PMG* 894) gestures to the judgment-based Underworld of Hesiod's *Works and Days*. This poet, however, doubles down on the segregated aspect of the Underworld by activating a second narrative specifically associating the blessed isles with the afterlife location of the famous heroes Achilles and Diomedes. When this author wants to indicate the exemplary nature of individuals in short order, he does so most simply and effectively through an allusion to the "Isles of the Blessed" followed by a reference to the premier Homeric hero Achilles, thereby conflating two myths concerning blessed afterlives.[14]

The poem elevates the tyrant-killers' status by so clearly linking it to a specific source through an Underworld scene. The well-known reference points the audience toward the author's interpretation that these citizens' actions are on par with that of the blessed heroes of myth. As the audience follows the poet's praise of Harmodius, they do so explicitly through the lens of Homeric and Hesiodic poetic Underworld accounts to heroize a mortal, bringing glory not only to a local hero but also to Athens itself. This mimics Pindar's technique and phrasing in *Olympian* 2, underscoring that the strategy was Panhellenic. This intersection between the political and poetic in Underworld scenes expanded even further in the face of unforeseen political, religious, social, and cultural pressures, both from internal strife within the democratic *polis* and external attacks from enemies. We can see this in literary and artistic forms as well as in political speeches that sought to democratize the spaces of the living and the dead throughout the Classical period in Athens.

Creating Outposts of the Dead: Funeral Orations and Funerary *Stelai*

Politicians in Athens used the language and images of mythic Underworlds to activate a network of Underworld narratives that could be broadly applied to convey heroic status on any individual, such as those who served the political interests of the government. Underworld scenes featuring the society of the dead and the persistence of values after death democratized access to the mythic Underworld and blessed afterlife of heroes. At the same time,

---

[14] Achilles is not specifically mentioned in Hesiod's Underworld but is understood from other poems to have attained a blessed afterlife (Burgess 2009).

174 LIFE / AFTERLIFE

these scenes also promoted a more democratized reality for the living, since the living and the dead were seen to be in more continuous communication, thereby accessible to each other for good or ill.

In Athens, the war dead, regardless of aristocratic ties or citizenship, were given special treatment in death, and the state honors afforded them extended beyond the funeral to their living relatives. War orphans, for example, were supported by the state and treated as dignitaries (Loraux 2006, 55–57). The war dead came to represent ideal citizens—heroes of the state deserving of honor, or *time* (τιμή)—and were praised in a similar fashion to mythic heroes and the *laudandi* of epinician poetry in terms of their levels of reward and collective esteem. The honors for their sacrifice extended into conceptions of their afterlives: any soldier from a battle such as those at Marathon or Thermopylae, regardless of background, could be connected to special heroes such as Achilles and Heracles through Underworld scenes. Made worthy of such heroic *time*, the war dead could then be equated to the heroism of these venerated figures through the suggestion of a "long and ancient pedigree" (Arrington 2015, 276).

In Pericles' funeral oration from Thucydides' *History of the Peloponnesian War*, the narrative of the heroic dead is expanded from actual tombs and the physical remains of the dead to other venues—the earth, civic *stelai* with lists of the dead, commemorative speeches, and the memory of individuals (see Figure 5.6):

ἀνδρῶν γὰρ ἐπιφανῶν πᾶσα γῆ τάφος, καὶ οὐ
στηλῶν μόνον ἐν τῇ οἰκείᾳ σημαίνει ἐπιγραφή, ἀλλὰ καὶ ἐν
τῇ μὴ προσηκούσῃ ἄγραφος μνήμη παρ' ἑκάστῳ τῆς γνώμης
(4.) μᾶλλον ἢ τοῦ ἔργου ἐνδιαιτᾶται. (Thuc. 2.43.3)

For the entire earth is a tomb for extraordinary men, and not only
an inscription on *stelai* in their homeland commemorates them, but
also abroad, the memory of their resolve rather than their deed lives in
each person, unwritten.

In this passage, praise is no longer focalized around a specific site, such as a tomb. Instead, Pericles argues that the physical structure of the tomb and the names on it are a shorthand referring the audience to a specific narrative about heroism, sacrifice for the *polis*, and Athenian power. Through such a speech, the "extraordinary men" come alive in the mental landscape of the audience and connect to the stories of the heroic dead that are ingrained in cultural memory. The physical landmark of the *stele* along with any image or inscription points to a subtext, or *para-narrative*, that must be provided by the viewer's memory at the author's prompt.[15] This affects the experience of encountering the funerary monument by introducing the heroic Underworld chronotope into the real space of the viewer. The author or artist thus brings the audience into an active dialogue about the life–death barrier and the status of the dead. Such framing had existential implications for the living and put pressure on the formulations and actual religious beliefs about the afterlife at that time.

Alongside such commemorative monuments, funerary orations were performed annually by law during wartime (Frangeskou 1999, 315; Loraux 2006, 70; Arrington 2015, 35–36). A type of epideictic speech that began in Athens around 465 BCE shortly after the Persian War, the funeral oration (*epitaphios logos*), has been described as quintessentially "Athenian and only Athenian" (Loraux 2006, 25, 94–95). Although Thucydides calls the rituals surrounding the war dead "ancestral" (πατρίῳ νόμῳ, 2.34.1) in his introduction to Pericles' famous funeral oration, the ceremony incorporates elements of the Cleisthenic democratic reforms, such as the display and procession of the coffins by *deme* (Thuc. 2.34.1–7). In the public cemetery (δημόσιον σῆμα, Thuc. 2.34.5), lists of the dead by *deme* on *stelai* would surround the mourners, and rituals that used to be performed in private became part of these public burials. The state, therefore, controlled the schedule and rituals of the dead, framing their narratives of valor on behalf of the city into entry tickets for civic immortality, which, in turn, suggested positive afterlife repercussions. The state did not promise a blessed afterlife for the war dead but implied, through narrative framing and commemoration of the dead, that the war dead would achieve the type of postdeath immortality and status associated with heroes such as Achilles (Currie 2005, 89–119). The focus of such speeches was more on heroic warriors from the past than on the specific deeds of the immediate dead who were being commemorated (Arrington 2015, 110). Moreover, regular commemorations in public speeches and the persistent presence of *stelai* created space for the war dead in everyday life at Athens. The dead were thus given "double *time*," both at their public funeral and through yearly cult celebrations (Loraux 2006, 71). Their deeds, juxtaposed against those of the audience, made them, although dead, into

---

[15] For more about the form, setting, and contexts of Athenian monuments to the war dead, see Low (2012).

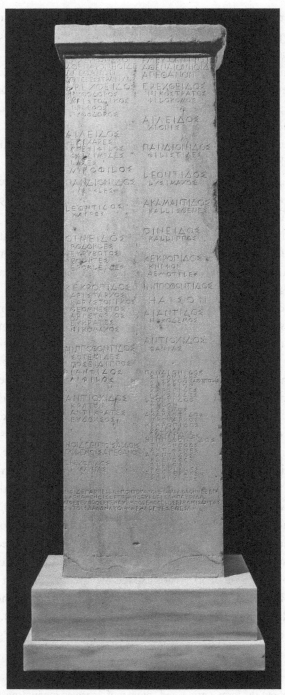

FIGURE 5.6 Grave stele (*IG* i³ 1162) of an Athenian casualty list from the 440s B.C.E. EM 10618: Epigraphic Museum, Athens © Hellenic Ministry of Culture / Hellenic Organization of Cultural Resources Development (H.O.C.RE.D). Photograph by Georgios Vdokakis.

World and Underworld 177

direct competitors with the living, who had to live up to a new standard of self-sacrifice (Arrington 2015, 111).

The public funeral oration, as a genre, was increasingly important in creating an identity for the dead in relation to the living and reasserting civic values, especially in periods of transition and war, such as the time immediately after the wars with Persia and during the Peloponnesian War. Funerary monuments from the Archaic period were, for the most part, destroyed en masse during the Persian sack of the city, "in effect wiping the landscape clean of visual testimony to the history of prominence that elite families previously had claimed in the community" (Calkins 2010, 263). As a result, when tombs were being rebuilt, people could rewrite their lineages in these "clean-slate" cemeteries to coincide more closely with the increasingly democratic ideals of the *polis*, a move supported both on tombs and in funeral orations by the use of traditional afterlife motifs, newly applied.[16] Pericles' speech offers both the rich and the poor similar opportunities for immortality through collective memory and suggests that this remembrance would impact the dead in the afterlife (Bosworth 2000, 6). The status of being considered blessed (*olbios*), previously reserved for aristocrats or heroes of the past, became more widely accessible, as "it was the state funerals for war dead which first brought the honours of heroic burial within the range of every Athenian citizen" (Humphreys 1980, 123). Further, the *epitaphios logos* and its accompanying *stelai* offered inclusivity into the civic community in death, a membership that may not always have been acknowledged or allowed in life. The names on the *stelai* were not exclusively Athenian, and speech itself tied the most recent dead to "all those of earlier wars, mythical and historical" (Loraux 2006, 64–69, 99).

This invocation of the past into the present with its concomitant prediction for a glorious Athenian future relies on the Underworld chronotope, as established by the earliest Underworld scenes. The difference in this period, compared to Homer's epics or even Pindar's epinicians, is that the narrative into which this Underworld representation is embedded is the political narrative that the rulers of the Athenian city-state formulated to promote its civic pride locally and its democracy globally. This conflation of the worlds of the

---

[16] Closterman (2007, 649) discusses the re-framing of familial ties and lineage on family tombs as a response to changes in the relationship between individuals and the state, arguing that Classical Attic peribolos tombs, which held multiple members of a family, projected a message of "unity and survival" rather than ancient lineage in their images and that these tombs were oriented to face towards the road for passers-by to see. For more on this topic, see Calkins (2010, 263).

living and the dead is highlighted in Plato's *Menexenus*, when he warns that funeral orations and their accompanying ceremonies affect the mind of the living such that even Socrates reacts to such a speech with the line: "I think that I all but live in the Islands of the Blessed: so eloquent do the orators seem to us" (οἶμαι μόνον οὐκ ἐν μακάρων νήσοις οἰκεῖν: οὕτως ἡμῖν οἱ ῥήτορες δεξιοί εἰσιν, Pl. *Menex.*, 235c4-5).

This suggests that the formalization of the funeral oration was perceived by the audience as bringing together the worlds of the living and the dead through the language of the Underworld, having "abolished the frontiers that separate reality from fantasy" (Loraux 2006, 336). Plato further says such speeches turn the city into a spectacle by making it (and its residents) "more wondrous" (θαυμασιωτέραν, *Menex.* 235b6). Athenian politicians thus used recognizable Underworld imagery to envision a reality that connects and intermingles the worlds of the living and dead by celebrating them in one breath (cf. *Menex.* 235a). The effect of this was to expand accessibility for common citizens to the more positive types of afterlives and the perceived permeability between the worlds of the living and the dead.

Funeral orations and ceremonies honoring the war dead created regular, formal occasions for the dead and living to interact. Additionally, objects such as accompanying memorial *stelai* that contained the names of the dead and reminders of both their sacrifice and blessedness also acted as incursions into everyday life by the Underworld chronotope, since they created dedicated spaces for encountering the dead. [17] With the prominent placement of such physical access points in the landscape, Underworld scenes could appear in even more subtle ways, such as on a vase with a simple image of the katabatic heroes Theseus and Heracles or on a memorial *stele* with names of the dead warriors who had been analogized to blessed heroes of the past in a funeral oration. These images tied into civic messages of heroic struggle on behalf of the state as leading to a blessed existence beyond the grave as a reward, a form of *kleos* that would be acknowledged frequently by the living at public occasions. Moreover, the treatment of the war dead and their graves was analogized to the treatment of mythic heroes, an association which Demosthenes acknowledges in his fourth century BCE funeral oration when he describes the dead as having "the same position in the Isles of the Blessed

---

[17] Frangeskou (1999, 327–328) demonstrates that funeral orations by Lysias and Demosthenes assume the blessedness of the dead by contrasting their happy afterlives with the grief of the relatives mourning them and the "lamentable state of public affairs."

as the good men who came before" (τὴν αὐτὴν τάξιν ἔχοντας τοῖς προτέροις ἀγαθοῖς ἀνδράσιν ἐν μακάρων νήσοις, Dem. *Epit.* 60.34).[18]

Underworld scenes were inserted into large-scale civic cultural events to suggest the ways that the audience should categorize the dead and their immortality. The dead were not treated as distant from the living in this scheme. This was an outlook that served the needs of the state in the fifth century BCE, particularly during times of strife. If the war dead were considered to have a continued presence among the living, then a violent death in war did not constitute an existential break separating citizens from their families and homeland. Through Underworld scenes, the loss of individuals in war was made more palatable because space was literally set aside in the city for the dead to continue their participation in civic society. This was not limited, however, to large venues and ceremonies; it also permeated literary and visual representations of Underworld scenes, particularly on the stage throughout the fifth century BCE, a period that expands the Underworld scene to give multiple avenues for people to be heroized and experience a positive afterlife.

V. Fraternizing with the Dead: The Underworld on Stage

The democratization of the Underworld occurred on multiple levels of society and was reinforced not only in the political sphere and the physical landscape, but also in religious festivals and theatrical performances. Underworld scenes appear with rather surprising frequency in surviving and reconstructed plays from the Classical period. It is unclear whether this is because of the nature of drama itself or because of the appetite of the audience for such scenes, two questions which have not been explored by scholars in a cohesive way. What becomes apparent in an examination of the dramatic corpus of the fifth

---

[18] The institutionalization of funeral orations as a genre in both form and content allows some extrapolation back to fifth–century BCE orations from later ones such as those of Demosthenes (Loraux 2006, 279). Currie (2005, 89–119) compares the commemoration of the war dead to the creation of hero-cult rituals. Arrington (2015, 115) comments on the uncertainty in extant orations as to the status of the war dead, noting that Lysias viewed their celebration in song as the chief avenue of immortality for these mortals. Sourvinou-Inwood (1995, 191–195) argues that the form of address χαίρετε on public grave monuments in the fifth century BCE suggests a heroization of the dead, as this was the common mode of address for gods and heroes.

century BCE—both the plays that have survived antiquity in their entirety and that exist in fragments quoted by ancient commentators—is that ghostly characters and scenes drawn from well-known Underworld narratives appear with some frequency and regularity. In this section, I examine Underworld scenes from both tragedy and comedy with case studies that have substantial Underworld scenes, such as Aeschylus' *Persians* and *Choephoroi*, Aristophanes' *Frogs*, and fragmentary plays which were said to have been set in the Underworld.

In plays, Underworld scenes convey social commentary not only through the inherited language of Underworld poetics but also through visual and interactive elements, which reinforced contact with the scene and its messages over an extended period of time, sometimes weeks or even longer. Underworld scenes in a stage production were present not only in the moment of the performance but also became part of the lives of the cast and crew throughout the production process. Moreover, because of the competitive and interactive aspects of dramatic performance, the audience would have had an immersive, multisensory experience (Weiss 2023, 30–33) and also have spent time contemplating an Underworld scene in comparison with the content of other plays, both through the judging process and perhaps even afterwards. Furthermore, these plays would enter the public conversation, particularly if they won, because of their prominence in the festival program, with some even being portrayed on everyday objects like vases (Bardel 2005, 100–112). Since viewing the plays was a civic and religious obligation, the plays containing Underworld scenes serve as a touchpoint for the citizenry to publicly reaffirm their shared values by mirroring the concerns of the living and to propose solutions to civic problems in the society of the dead. Aeschylus seems particularly fond of Underworld scenes, but other tragedians were also known to incorporate them into their productions, which suggests that consultation with the society of the dead was a commonplace motif in the tragic genre (Bardel 2005). Comic writers, such as Aristophanes and Eupolis, also include Underworld scenes (partly, perhaps, in response to tragedy's preoccupation with them). A common feature across plays that include Underworld scenes is that they assume an audience well-versed in Underworld narratives from earlier poetic representations as well as those that appear in contemporary civic and mystery cult practices.

Aristotle's *Poetics* refers to plays involving Hades as a regular type of stage production, which he categorizes as "spectacle." The phrase "tragedies set in Hades" appears as an oblique reference in his definition of the four types of tragedy:

World and Underworld

181

τραγῳδίας δὲ εἴδη εἰσὶ τέσσαρα (τοσαῦτα
γὰρ καὶ τὰ μέρη ἐλέχθη), ἡ μὲν πεπλεγμένη, ἧς τὸ ὅλον
ἐστὶν περιπέτεια καὶ ἀναγνώρισις, ἡ δὲ παθητική, οἷον οἵ τε
(1456a.) Αἴαντες καὶ οἱ Ἰξίονες, ἡ δὲ ἠθική, οἷον αἱ Φθιώτιδες καὶ ὁ
Πηλεύς· τὸ δὲ τέταρτον †οης†, οἷον αἵ τε Φορκίδες καὶ ὁ Προ-
μηθεὺς καὶ **ὅσα ἐν ᾄδου**. (Arist. *Poet.* 1455b–1456a)

There are four kinds of tragedy (for its divisions were also said [earlier]
to be such a number): the complex, which is essentially reversal and
recognition; the pathetic, such as the *Ajaxes* and *Ixions*; the character-
based, such as the *The Women of Phthia* and the *Peleus*; and the fourth
is †spectacle†, such as the *The Daughters of Phorcys*, the *Prometheus*, and
the ones set in Hades.[19]

Although there has been much debate about the nature of the plays labeled
"spectacle" in the *Poetics* and no specific titles are listed, there is little doubt
that they were a viable and popular form of entertainment for Athenian
audiences. Aristotle's strong and continuous criticism of "spectacle" for focusing on optical effects at the expense of plot and for being less connected
to epic because they rely on visual effects speaks indirectly to their popularity.
The importance of visual display on stage and a play's ability to impress the
audience through "spectacle" have largely been overlooked by scholars as crucial components for the success of a production and the political career of
its *choregos*, according to Helene Foley (2003, 3), who argues that "dramatic
victories might often have been awarded as much or more for the choral performance and dramatic spectacle as for the content/plot of the plays themselves, especially given the larger context of the festival, where dithyrambic
(and comic) choruses played such a central role."

By making spectacle of much lesser importance than plot or other parts
of tragedy (1450b15–20), Aristotle influenced later writers to focus attention
on the value of tragedy's ethical lessons and, until fairly recently, to remove

---

[19] The reference to "spectacle" and "[plays] set in Hades" has come under attack by scholars
because this area of the text has been labeled hopelessly corrupt. Nevertheless, it has been
strongly argued by Richard Janko, following Bywater's reconstruction (1909), that "spectacle" (ὄψις) is an appropriate restoration. Janko observes that an identical miscopying in
the MSS occurs at 1458a5 and that "spectacle" is the logical choice to be mentioned here
as the fourth type, since it is referred to as a class of plays (1453b1–11) but is not elsewhere
categorized in the text (Janko 1987, 121n56a2). See also Gilbert's (1947) discussion on how
poetic rather than visual (e.g., spectacle) considerations influenced dramatic criticism in
Aristotle and afterwards.

or downplay the impact of "spectacle" from the discussion of fifth-century BCE tragedy. At various points in the *Poetics*, he tries to distance the visual aspects of stage production that are the mainstay of creating "spectacle" from poetic composition, saying that good poets can create the terrifying and pitiable without recourse to "spectacle" (1450b15–20, 1453b1–14). He rather grudgingly admits that "spectacle" is one of the main features of tragedy that not only differentiates it from epic but also makes the same stories more palpable and vivid (ἐναργέστατα, 1462a15–17) by bringing the figures and events to life. Recent studies have shown that Aristotle's distaste for "spectacle" and his placement of it as secondary or ancillary to other aspects were not shared by original audiences. In fact, the evidence points to a strong desire and demand by Athenian theater-goers and judges for just such visual effects. Furthermore, it appears that one common route to building intensity and horror was to "put Hades on stage," either in the form of a ghost, a chthonic deity, or a katabatic journey.

Based on the regularity and normality of references to the society of the dead in the dramatic corpus, it would seem that evoking the Underworld on stage was a trope that could be activated in Aristotle's category of "spectacle." Underworld scenes might even have become a somewhat formulaic tool through which playwrights elicited a sense of horror and wonder in the audience. The visual effects involved would have allowed the poet to address his audience outside the temporal frame of his play while also linking hypertextually to similar scenes of foreboding and dread in different media. The emphasis in the surviving Underworld scenes tends to be on the distinctly gloomy atmosphere of the dead and the supernatural forces that the Underworld contains, which can be used to help or harm the living. Although the atmosphere of the dead is modeled after epic Underworld scenes, new developments are added, including the idea that ghosts kept tabs on what was going on in the world above, took an active interest in the actions of the living, and had the ability to haunt or reprimand the living in the real world. Their persistent interest in the living and the threat of their continued presence on earth made the souls of the dead into a political entity with a "voice" in society, particularly after they were brought into the interactive, civic, and religious space of the theater. Furthermore, the device of a "ghost on stage" would not have become such a regular trope if the audience were not already primed by elements in popular culture and on public display to accept and incorporate chthonic motifs into daily life.

Until a more recent focus by scholars on the "visual and performative dimensions" of tragedy, the staging of ghosts and the Underworld has largely

World and Underworld 183

been overlooked or ignored (Bardel 2005, 84).[20] Of the extant tragedies, Aeschylus' *Persians* and *Eumenides* as well as Euripides' *Hecuba* feature ghosts with speaking roles, and Euripides' *Alcestis* stages Death himself (Thanatos).[21] In comedy, Aristophanes' *Frogs* is set almost entirely in the Underworld, and his competitors were known to include Underworld scenes and ghostly consultations. The dead on stage, as a ghost or a body, acted as a "point of focus" and a "means of generating further dramatic action" because of the shock value they could provide both to the audience and to the characters in a play (Whitehorne 1986, 60). Many more instances of Underworld motifs appear in textual and visual fragmentary evidence, which leads to the conclusion that Underworld scenes on stage were quite popular and even a regular feature of the dramatic genre, as were kings, heroes, gods, and war narratives.

Only in recent decades has the topic of "ghosts on stage" started to gain attention (Bardel 2005; Martin 2012). Based on extant plays and fragments, staged ghost scenes were popular, and ghosts themselves were "an integral part of theatrical performances from Aeschylus onwards" (Bardel 2005, 84). For ghostly motifs to be useful devices across such a wide range of plays, Underworld and necromantic scenes must have been familiar to Athenian society. The imagined intermingling of the living with the dead did not occur solely on the stage, however, and the theater was only one venue for large-scale, popular, civic and religious engagement with Underworld scenes. Vernant describes dramatic performances as history made "live" and immediately relevant to their viewers:

> As I have pointed out, neither the characters nor their destinies are fictitious to the Greek audience. They really have existed, but in other times, in an age now gone forever. They are men of the past belonging to a sphere of existence quite different from that of the audience. By being set on stage, they are made to seem present, characters truly there, although at the same time they are portrayed as figures who cannot possibly be there since they belong to somewhere else, to an invisible beyond. What the public sees before it in the theater is not a

---

[20] The last comprehensive study of ghosts on stage was Ruby Hickman's *Ghostly Etiquette on the Classical Stage* from 1938 (Hickman 1938).

[21] Although only 33 tragedies survive in full, five of them engage with Underworld entities directly (*Persians, Choephoroi,* and *Eumenides* by Aeschylus; *Hecuba* and *Alcestis* by Euripides). The ghosts of Darius, Clytemnestra, and Polydorus are speaking characters on stage as is Thanatos himself.

184

poet recounting the trials withstood in ancient times by men now gone whose absence is, so to speak, implied by the very narration. Instead, those trials take place before its very eyes, adopting the form of real existence in the immediacy of the performance (Vernant and Vidal-Naquet 1988, 243).

The problems addressed on stage, therefore, were the problems faced by the Athenian audiences, with enough abstraction to be palatable.[22] The myths of the "other" (in this case, dead heroes or kings from familiar stories) were seen as models and analogues to present situations (Dunn 2007, 4). The gods and the dead (in the form of ghosts) were at times put on stage, and they justified their actions to mortals through the course of a dramatic performance, shifting the power of interpretation to the audience and judges. Although they might be used to escape a particularly difficult point in the plot through the device of *deus ex machina*, gods still had to explain their decisions and actions in the performance context in front of a human audience. Through otherworldly scenes with gods and ghosts, poets and populace negotiated their power and place in the cosmos. The regular occurrences of ghosts and Underworld motifs in tragedy—and their prominent role in the action of plays devoid of other supernatural intervention—reflect the relationship the Greeks felt they had, not only with their past but also with the dead and the gods, both chthonic and Olympian. In the following, I give more detailed readings of tragedies and comedies to demonstrate how Underworld scenes further broke down the life–death barrier and simultaneously supported the democratization of the *polis* and the Underworld.

Consulting the Dead in Tragedy

In Attic drama, the mythology surrounding afterlife society was used to inform the reality of the protagonists and, by extension, Athens itself. Further, a recognizable pattern in the appearance of Underworld motifs linked them to well-known Archaic Underworld scenes. As in Homer, contact with the world of the dead in tragedy occurs at crucial points in the plot, but direct

---

[22] In a famous exception, Herodotus talks of how Phrynichus staged a tragedy called *The Fall of Miletus*, which was based on a Persian attack. It so disturbed the audience for its literal depiction of historical events close to their own personal experiences that the poet was fined for upsetting his audience (Hdt. 6.21). See also Dova (2020, 161–174) and Vernant and Vidal-Naquet (1988, 244).

World and Underworld 185

engagement with the Underworld realm remains largely embedded in scenes that do not actually advance the action of the story. The plot is put on hold to allow internal space for consultations with chthonic powers on important themes, and the lasting effect is a reorientation of the narrative in light of fresh information, which gives added meaning to the plot and a direction to proceed. This functions similarly to the Underworld scene in the *Odyssey*'s *Nekuia*, linking the scenes together. Every time an Underworld reference is made, therefore, the scope of the text widens. Current actions and choices are pitted against a more expansive time frame, either past or future, as well as against a wider frame of authority, traceable all the way back to the Homeric poems, which were embedded in Athenian society's collective, cultural consciousness.

In the *Persians*, the earliest extant play with a ghostly visitation (472 BCE), Aeschylus uses the language of the Underworld to present a conversation between the Persian Queen Atossa and the ghost of her husband Darius (*Pers.* 681–842). Queen Atossa and the chorus perform a necromantic ritual combining libations, hymns, and dance in a loud and frenzied climax (*Pers.* 598–680). In this scene, they call up the dead with the following words:

βαλήν, ἀρχαῖος βαλήν, ἴθι ἱκοῦ, *[στρ. 3]*
ἔλθ᾽ ἐπ᾽ ἄκρον κόρυμβον ὄ-
χθου κροκόβαπτον ποδὸς εὔ- (660)
μαριν ἀείρων βασιλείου τιή-
ρας φάλαρον πιφαύσκων·
βάσκε πάτερ ἄκακε Δαριάν· οἴ·
ὅπως κοινὰ γᾶι κλύηις νέα τ᾽ ἄχη, *[ἀντ. 3]*
δέσποτα δεσποτᾶν φάνη- (666)
θι. Στυγία γάρ τις ἐπ᾽ ἀ-
χλὺς πεπόταται· νεολαία γὰρ ἤ-
δη κατὰ πᾶσ᾽ ὄλωλεν· (670)
βάσκε πάτερ ἄκακε Δαριάν· οἴ·
αἰαῖ αἰαῖ· (*Pers.* 658–672)

King, ancient king, come, draw near,
come to the topmost point of your tomb,
raising your feet in their saffron-colored slippers
[and] showing the tip of the royal crown.
Come, guileless father Darius – oh!
so that you may hear the new commonly shared suffering;

186   LIFE / AFTERLIFE

> master of masters, appear.
> For some Stygian fog hovers upon us; for all the youth
> of the nation have recently perished
> Come, kindly father Darius, oh!
> Aiai! Aiai!

Discussing this passage, Edith Hall (1996, 152–153) suggests that this invocation might refer to the entrance of Darius' ghost onto the stage, especially because it describes Darius' clothing in such detail (*Pers.* 660–661). She observes that Darius' speech indicates the chorus must have performed violent physical movements, such as "pounding and scratching the earth," during this ghost-raising scene.

The necromantic invocation of Darius' ghost is similar to the beginning of Book 11 of the *Odyssey* when Odysseus and his crew must also attract an individual ghost, that is, Tiresias, for privileged information about the future. In both cases, the rites are rewarded by the appearance of the requested ghost. Darius' ghost acknowledges the efforts of his wife and her court, saying that the "ground groans, having been beaten and scratched up with pounding" (στένει, κέκοπται, καὶ χαράσσεται πέδον, *Pers.* 683) and that, even though among the dead, he "gladly accepted the drink-offerings" (χοὰς δὲ πρευμενὴς ἐδεξάμην, *Pers.* 685). Besides linking to the necromantic scene in Homer, the opening speech of Darius' ghost also alludes to details from other Greek Underworld scenes and myths, which rely on the audience to supply multiple *para-narratives* to understand Darius' words:

> . . . ἐστὶ δ᾽ οὐκ εὐέξοδον,
> ἄλλως τε πάντως, χοὶ κατὰ χθονὸς θεοὶ
> λαβεῖν ἀμείνους εἰσὶν ἢ μεθιέναι.
> ὅμως δ᾽ ἐκείνοις ἐνδυναστεύσας ἐγὼ
> ἥκω. τάχυνε δ᾽ ὡς ἄμεμπτος ὦ χρόνου. (*Pers.* 688–692)

> And there is no especially easy way out (of the Underworld),
> And besides, the gods below the earth are better at seizing than releasing.
> But, nevertheless, I have come, since I have authority among them.
> But hurry up so that I will not be blamed for spending too much time here.

This brief description of the afterlife recalls the Greek Underworld in Archaic literature, configured as a place of internal hierarchies, in which souls are interested in the affairs of the living and sometimes available to the living for consultations in special situations. The emphasis on the power of the Underworld gods and their somewhat uncompromising nature fits into the idea of Hades as a god who cannot easily be appealed to and the Underworld as a place of punishment and reward. Further, the continuity of Darius' high status after death (ἐνδυναστεύσας ἐγώ, *Pers.* 691), which allows him to return to the land of the living for brief visits, implies an Underworld similar to those of Pindar in which a special mortal maintains his identity and status after death. Darius' ghost, despite being sentient and privileged among the dead, still must return to Hades' gloomy landscape, which recalls the dark Underworlds of Homer and Hesiod (ἐγὼ δ᾽ ἄπειμι γῆς ὑπὸ ζόφον κάτω, "but I depart the earth down under the gloom below," *Pers.* 839).

After first establishing a hybrid Underworld space, the subsequent dialogue between the living and Darius' ghost contains further assumptions about ghosts and their society that are also rooted in Homer. Like most ghosts, the soul of Darius has a blind spot for present events and must be informed by his wife about Xerxes' campaign against Greece. This conceit allows the playwright, supported by the *choregos*, to give an update of the current state of affairs for the audience—from the *Athenian* point of view. In turn, Darius' ghost recounts the past to her (and the audience), reminiscing about Persia's rise to power and his own failed campaign against the Greeks. He also gives a prophecy about the immediate future (the rout of Xerxes' army and his shameful arrival in tattered rags). This ghost episode uses the Underworld chronotope to display the past, present, and future before the audience's eyes in a single, synoptic scene.

Removing the necromantic scene with Darius' character would not significantly affect the plot. The chorus' song reacting to the messenger's news of Xerxes' defeat places the events in the Persian political context (as the Greeks conceived of it) and could easily have introduced the appearance of Xerxes himself as a failed leader (*Pers.* 907). The ghost's appearance, however, both offers the chance for a stunning visual effect and gives the playwright the additional opportunity to influence audience opinion by situating the plot against the backdrop of a larger historical and moral context.[23] In this way, Aeschylus

---

[23] The effusive chants, frenzied movements, and loud singing to which Darius' ghost refers must have created the type of spectacle that Aristotle thought was of lesser importance in tragedy (Hall 1996, 152–153). Also, the use of βαλήν, the Persian word for king, would have further exoticized the scene. Incorporating foreign or foreign-sounding words, particularly when summoning chthonic powers, was also common practice on curse tablets, which started to become popular in the fifth century BCE (Gager 1999; Eidinow 2013).

188   LIFE / AFTERLIFE

was able to use an Underworld scene to create and reinforce Athenian and, more generally, "Greek" identity in opposition to his Persian characters.

Through the necromantic scene, Xerxes' defeat is framed as a crushing blow that struck to the heart of the Persian Empire and threatened its dominance on the world stage. The unspoken implication is that an emerging power—Athens—is ripe to take on a leadership role, particularly because of its democratic ideals. Further, the Persian defeat is seen as a righteous one because of Xerxes' *hubris*, which called down the wrath of the gods upon him. Aeschylus uses Darius' ghost, therefore, not only as a foil to Xerxes but also a mouthpiece for the gods: Darius is a reflective ghost who evaluates his own son's deeds as hubristic (Papadimitropoulos 2008, 456–457). The speeches of Darius' ghost promote a certain view of Xerxes as having been ripe for divine retribution since he acted as an arrogant, hot-headed youth, who wielded power over an unstable, enslaved constituency without proper respect for the gods (Hall 1996, 15–16). This is exactly the message that Aeschylus seems to have wanted his democracy-practicing audience to take home. The play supports such an assessment visually and morally with references to the Underworld and its stark imagery, which represent cosmic truth and an ultimate authority.

Despite the attention the Darius ghost scene has received, it is not the only instance in the *Persians* in which Aeschylus uses the rhetoric of the Underworld. The first invocation of an Underworld scene comes much earlier in the play and is used to situate the Underworld and its power in relation to man. After Queen Atossa enters and recounts her first dream in the play, the chorus of elders and advisors to the royal court tells her to propitiate equally the gods above and below the earth. The blessings of the gods above are only asked for in a general way (*Pers.* 215–219), however, while the ones below must be treated with greater care. The chorus gives specific instruction in how to approach Underworld deities, what should be requested, and to whom any requests should be addressed:

> δεύτερον δὲ χρὴ χοὰς
> γῆι τε καὶ φθιτοῖς χέασθαι. πρευμενῶς δ' αἰτοῦ τάδε, (220)
> σὸν πόσιν Δαρεῖον, ὅνπερ φὴις ἰδεῖν κατ' εὐφρόνην,
> ἐσθλά σοι πέμπειν τέκνωι τε γῆς ἔνερθεν ἐς φάος,
> τἄμπαλιν δὲ τῶνδε γαίαι κάτοχα μαυροῦσθαι σκότωι. (*Pers.* 219–225)

But, secondly, you should pour libations to the earth and to the dead. And graciously ask for these things: that your husband Darius, whom you say you saw during the night, sends good things to you and your son from under the earth into the sunlight and that the reverse of these things [i.e., bad fortune] be held fast under the earth and made obscure by darkness.

In this passage, ἐσθλά, meaning good fortune and prosperity, is a form of blessedness and synonymous with the idea of *olbios*. As a gift from powers under the earth, its connotation is *material* wealth, since that is where the god Pluto dwells. As discussed in previous chapters, earthly prosperity that derives from direct intervention by supernatural powers implies afterlife blessedness for the recipient. Darius' continuation of wealth and status after death is reaffirmed in his ghost's opening speech (*Pers.* 688–692). The ghost's appearance orients the play within its historical and political context in a way that plot and character do not while also offering the stamp of authority. The source of its authority originates in two attributes associated with the Underworld: religious ritual and literary precedence. By including Underworld scenes, Aeschylus calls on the supernatural power of the divine in a controlled way via established, traditional necromantic rituals and also connects his play intertextually to specific literary forbears, claiming their authority as his own.[24]

This passage sets before the audience four basic assumptions: (1) the Underworld is a political kingdom directly under the earth with a somewhat thin barrier between the living and the dead that should be approached delicately; (2) a person can communicate with the dead through intermediaries and make special requests of individuals who have an interest or connection to events in current time; (3) ghosts maintain their earthly ties and have influence over chthonic powers, allowing them to act as intercessors similar to certain gods (e.g., Hermes, Persephone); and (4) earthly prosperity or misfortune can be directly controlled (or withheld) by Underworld deities.

We see this same pattern in the *Choephoroi*, also by Aeschylus, when Orestes and Electra, in conjunction with the chorus, attempt to raise Agamemnon's ghost. They use both song and ritual acts to appeal first to the intermediary Hermes:

---

[24] Both Homer (*Odyssey* 11; *Iliad* 23) and Bacchylides (*Ode* 5) contain extended necromantic scenes, which were performed widely at public events. This necromantic scene points directly to those as opposed to stories of *katabasis*.

LIFE / AFTERLIFE

κῆρυξ μέγιστε τῶν ἄνω τε καὶ κάτω *(124a)*
Ἑρμῆ χθόνιε, κηρύξας ἐμοὶ (124b)
τοὺς γῆς ἔνερθε δαίμονας κλύειν ἐμὰς (125)
εὐχάς, πατρῴων δωμάτων ἐπισκόπους,
καὶ γαῖαν αὐτήν, ἡ τὰ πάντα τίκτεται
θρέψασά τ᾽ αὖθις τῶνδε κῦμα λαμβάνει.
κἀγὼ χέουσα τάσδε χέρνιβας νεκροῖς
λέγω καλοῦσα πατέρ᾽ "ἐποίκτιρόν τ᾽ ἐμὲ (130)
φίλον τ᾽ Ὀρέστην φῶς τ᾽ ἄναψον ἐν δόμοις. (*Cho.* 124–131)

***

Ορ. ὦ γαῖ, ἄνες μοι πατέρ᾽ ἐποπτεῦσαι μάχην.
Ηλ. ὦ Περσέφασσα, δὸς δέ γ᾽ εὔμορφον κράτος. (*Cho.* 489–490)

***

Ορ. ἤτοι Δίκην ἴαλλε σύμμαχον φίλοις (497)
ἢ τὰς ὁμοίας ἀντίδος λαβὰς λαβεῖν,
εἴπερ κρατηθείς γ᾽ ἀντινικῆσαι θέλεις. (*Cho.* 497–499)

Electra: Greatest messenger of the ones above and below, (124)
Chthonic Hermes, call for me the gods from inside the earth
to hear my prayers, the ones who watch over our patrimonial household,
and the earth itself, which bears all things and, in turn, after
nurturing takes back the flood of these [creatures].
And I, while pouring these libations to the dead, call my father
and say, "Pity me and my beloved Orestes and in these halls kindle light.

***

Orestes: Oh, Earth, send up for me my father so he may look upon the
battle (489)
Electra: Oh, Persephone, give him [to us] well-formed and mighty.

***

Orestes: Either send forth Justice as an ally to your loved ones (497)
or allow them instead to seize upon similar [devious] snares,
if, indeed, having been defeated in the past,
you want to conquer in return.

These ritual libations and invocations are not successful in bringing Agamemnon's ghost up from the dead, so his children conclude that they themselves must be the instruments of their father's vengeance (*Cho.* 500–513). As a compromise, they ask Agamemnon to send help to them from the netherworld, assuming that he can hear their pleas and come to their aid. Although they fail to get Agamemnon's ghost to appear and directly intervene, the characters frame their future actions as having been blessed and even conceived by chthonic powers.

The vision of the afterlife as having a direct and immediate correspondence to individual action is the underlying message of this failed necromantic attempt.[25] Agamemnon is seen in this play as reaching beyond the grave to affect the living, just as the living are seen to plead for such aid with the sure expectation of succor, whether visible or invisible, because they have performed certain rites. Their actions and expectations fall under the contract of reciprocation ("dō ut dēs") that is fundamental to the idea of Greek religious ritual, particularly sacrifice. As Burkert (1985, 57), says, "the sacrifice, it is known, creates a relationship between the sacrificer and the god; poets recount how the god remembers the sacrifice with pleasure or how he rages dangerously if sacrifices fail to be performed." This same relationship seems to have been extended in the fifth century BCE to the dead, who make demands of piety similar to those previously reserved for the gods or deified individuals (Seaford 1994, 106–143).

Aeschylus uses Underworld scenes as a global strategy in his plays, as can be seen in several tragic fragments. The largest and most relevant fragment comes from the *Psychagogoi* ("Soul-drivers"), a recreation of stories from Homer's *Odyssey*. The *Psychagogoi* was thought to be the first of two plays dealing with the dead in a single tetralogy, and it is known to be a dramatization of the *Nekuia*, the episode in which Odysseus consults the souls of the dead at the edge of the Underworld (*Od.* 11).[26] The title refers to a class of professional necromancers, the *psychagogoi*, who used wailing to raise the dead (Bardel 2005, 86–87), and the play's action is centered on Odysseus' ritual

---

[25] Both Johnston (1999, 98) and Sourvinou-Inwood (1995, 420–421; 1981, 38–39) comment on an increasing tendency during the classical period to view the living and the dead as individuals. In his analysis of this scene, Shilo (2022, 104–109) argues that the characters' expectations for contact across the life–death barrier is because of their personal desires rather than an understanding of any supernatural continuation of identity and consciousness.

[26] Scholars have speculated that the order of this tetralogy is *Psychagogoi, Penelope, Ostologoi*, and the satyr-play *Circe* (Gantz 1980, 151–153; Bardel 2005, 85).

to raise the dead. The *Psychagogoi*'s chorus consists of experts in calling the dead, mortals who live near the edge of the Underworld, like the Cimmerians from the *Nekuia*. Their role in the play is to instruct Odysseus in necromantic rituals:

ἄγε νῦν, ὦ ξεῖν', ἐπὶ ποιοφύτων
ἵστω σηκῶν φοβερᾶς λίμνας
ὑπό τ' αὐχένιον λαιμὸν ἀμήσας
τοῦδε σφαγίου ποτὸν ἀψύχοις
αἷμα μεθίει (5)
δονάκων εἰς βένθος ἀμαυρόν.
Χθόνα δ' ὠγυγίαν ἐπικεκλόμενος
χθόνιόν θ' Ἑρμῆν πομπὸν φθιμένων
[αἰ]τοῦ χθόνιον Δία νυκτιπόλων
ἑσμὸν ἀνεῖναι ποταμοῦ στομάτων, (10)
οὗ τόδ' ἀπορρὼξ ἀμέγαρτον ὕδωρ
κἀχέρνιπτον
Στυγίοις να[σ]μοῖσιν ἀνεῖται. (Fr. 273a, Radt)[27]

Come now, stranger, stand on the grassy precincts
of the terrifying lake and, when you have cut the
throat sinews of this sacrificial victim, let the blood fall (5)
to the shadowy depths of the reeds
as a drink for the lifeless ones.
After calling upon primeval Earth and chthonic Hermes,
the guide of the dead, ask chthonian Zeus to send up
a swarm of night-roamers from the mouths of the river, (10)
from which this wretched water that washes no hand comes, a branch
rising up from Stygian streams.

The similarity between this scene and Homer's version are clear: both place Odysseus in a sacred space near a body of water to make a sacrifice of blood for the dead to drink and both imagine chthonic deities as driving up a crowd of dead from the Underworld depths. Indeed, as Katerina Mikellidou (2016) has argued, the play appears to have been a dramatized adaptation of the *Nekuia*. The differences, though, are perhaps more notable because they

---

[27] The tragic fragments referred to in this chapter come from *Tragicorum Graecorum Fragmenta* (Radt 1977, 1985; Kannicht and Snell 1981).

World and Underworld 193

indicate Aeschylus' activation of details from *Odyssey* 24's *nekuia* (*Od.* 24.1–204) as well, thus conflating Homer's two famous Underworld scenes into a new version of this myth for a fifth-century BCE audience. These details include the presence of Hermes as a guide and also the comparison of the dead to a "swarm" of nocturnal animals (cf. simile comparing the dead to bats, *Od.* 24.5–14). Multiple narratives are at play in the Aeschylean version of Odysseus' consultation with the dead and connect the two texts together with interlocking references.

The playwright chooses to emphasize the supernatural powers (i.e., Hermes the soul-guide and Chthonic Zeus, the male ruler of the dead) and then portrays them as the instigators for Odysseus' upcoming necromantic scene. [28] The evidence suggests that this passage preceded the appearance of Tiresias' ghost (Fr. 275, Radt) and that the dead seer gives a prediction about Odysseus' death (although different from the one in the *Odyssey*). Since Fr. 273a refers to the gods sending up a "swarm" of dead and we know Aeschylus' scene links hypertextually to Homer's *nekuiai*, it is not too great a leap to conclude that other ghosts besides Tiresias also appeared on stage to converse with Odysseus and that they were probably used to review his past deeds and set up the conditions of his return to Ithaca, as the ghosts of the *Odyssey* did.

The tetralogy's third play, the *Ostologoi* ("Bone-gatherers") seems to have been set after the suitors were slain.[29] The title very likely refers to the suitors' families coming to collect their slain sons' bodies from Odysseus' home or a funeral pyre (Grossardt 2003). There is not enough evidence to know whether the suitors' ghosts appeared on stage. The scene itself, however, and its performance so closely after the *Psychagogoi* (in which at least one ghost and possibly more appeared on stage) suggest that the play had strong intertextual ties to the *katabasis* of the suitors' ghosts in *Odyssey* 24 (1–204) and probably included details from that scene, including multiple ghosts. At the very least, the audience, well-versed in Homer from rhapsodic competitions and festivals, would have made the connection, and their knowledge of the epic's

---

[28] Persephone is the Underworld god more commonly evoked as intercessor, and it is she who sends up the dead in the *Odyssey* (11.226) after Odysseus enters her grove and performs the ritual sacrifice for the dead. A later fragment of the *Psychagogoi* (Fr. 277, Radt) does refer to Persephone (Δαῖρα), who may have also been involved in sending up ghosts, but this is speculative because of the fragmentary evidence. Chthonian Zeus is most likely Hades here, as the two are not distinctly differentiated in the earliest sources (Evans 1974, 116).

[29] The second play in the tetralogy, *Penelope*, is presumed to present the events in Ithaca after Odysseus' arrival when the hero reclaims his kingdom, perhaps even from Penelope's perspective (Gantz 1980, 152).

194 LIFE / AFTERLIFE

portrayal of the suitors' ghosts would have informed the viewing process. Homer's Underworld narrative, therefore, would have "shadowed" the events of the play as a persistent *para-narrative*, providing a means of subtextual communication between playwright and audience. As the final tragedy in this set before the satyr play, the *Ostologoi* would have had to give some resolution to the events and issues raised in the *Psychagogoi*. The fact that there were bone-gatherers suggests that closure would involve funeral rites and other forms of lament giving the dead their due.

Of all the possible episodes to borrow from the *Odyssey*, Aeschylus chose to dramatize the most titillating stories that would have the most visceral impact as spectacles for the audience. His links to the *Odyssey's* Underworld narratives in these plays was not described by ancient commentators as unusual nor was the tetralogy produced at a particularly early, experimental stage in the history of tragedy.[30] Linking to epic Underworld scenes on stage does not seem to have been surprising or disturbing to ancient audiences, who may have valued the spectacle of visualizing the Underworld and the dead as well as the resonances created by allusions to well-known epic scenes. A fragment thought to be from the *Psychagogoi* supports the notion that some aspect of the Underworld would be on stage and that it was meant to be terrifying for everyone but the speaker: Ἀιδην δ' ἔχων βοηθὸν οὐ τρέμω σκιάς ("having Hades as my ally, I do not tremble at the shades/ghosts," Fr. 370 K-.Sn.).[31]

---

[30] The date of the first official performance of tragedy as chorus and a single actor at Athens is given as 534 BCE and associated with Thespis (Storey and Allan 2005, 8). Moreno (2004, 20) observes that the *Odyssey's Nekuia* (Book 11) was not a popular topic for dramatization (or for vase painters) as compared to the *katabaseis* of Heracles and Theseus, which were widely portrayed. I argue that it does not matter how often and in what forms the specific events of Homer's *Nekuia* are explicitly presented, only that they are evoked whenever an Underworld scene appears.

[31] This translation follows Moreno's excellent argument for construing Ἀιδην as the actual "lord of the Underworld" (instead of "death") and "σκιάς" as "ghosts/shades" (instead of "shadows/dark places/hell"), since these were the more common definitions of these terms in the classical tragic corpus (Moreno 2004, 7–17). The line is unassigned in Kannicht-Snell's *Tragicorum Graecorum Fragmenta* (1981), but Moreno (2004, 17–29) makes a good case for its belonging to Aeschylus' *Psychagogoi*, probably from the prologue in which Odysseus announces his intention to go to Hades. Of course, the fact that it was not specifically attributed to Aeschylus could mean that it occurred in a different, unknown tragedy, potentially even one centered on Heracles, which Moreno (2004, 18) argues is unlikely. This would further support my argument for Underworld scenes as a normal trope in dramatic performance. As a part of the *Psychagogoi*, the line further reinforces the notion of the "Underworld on stage" and, at the very least, must have come from a tragedy with either a *katabasis* or a necromantic scene.

World and Underworld 195

Similarly, in the fragments of Sophocles' *Polyxena*, the ghost of Achilles appears on stage and describes the Underworld as a fearful place of darkness akin to the descriptions by Odysseus in the *Nekuia* but with the sentience and negative atmosphere implied by Patroclus' ghost (*Il.* 23.69–74). Although staging for this scene is unknown, the ghost was most likely on stage in front of Agamemnon's tent to make its demands for Polyxena's sacrifice (Bardel 2005, 93–94) and perhaps even made a second appearance later in the play to warn Agamemnon of his upcoming, sordid death, as has been conjectured from some seemingly prophetic fragments (Calder III 1966, 42–43, 49). The ghost, by demanding the sacrifice of Polyxena, brings into the theatric space of the living a feeling of the dark horrors of the afterlife and the wrath of the supernatural as well as the hope that human action can mitigate it:

ΨΥΧΗ ΑΧΙΛΛΕΩΣ
ἀκτὰς ἀπαιωνάς τε καὶ μελαμβαθεῖς
λιποῦσα λίμνης ἦλθον, ἄρσενας χοὰς
Ἀχέροντος ὀξυπλῆγας ἠχούσας γόους (Fr. 523, Radt)

Achilles' Ghost:
I have come leaving the cheerless and darkly deep headlands
of the sea, the mighty streams of Acheron, which echo the
wails that accompany fierce blows. . .

The purpose of the sacrifice is twofold: to appease Achilles' ghost with blood before the Greeks' departure from Troy and to influence the gods' favor for the return from Troy. Indeed, the ghost of Achilles does seem to give predictions for the future, including a cryptic reference to gloomy clouds (λυγαίου νέφους) and a new tunic for Agamemnon, "cloaked in evils" (χιτών σ' ἄπειρος, ἐνδυτήριον κακῶν, Fr. 525–526, Radt).[32] The phrasing of this passage recalls Odysseus' journey to a headland (ἀκτή, *Od.* 11.509) of Ocean near the dank house of Hades (εἰς Ἀΐδεω δόμον εὐρώεντα, *Od.* 11.512) where the "streams of Pyriphlegethon and Cocytus flow into Acheron" (εἰς Ἀχέροντα Πυριφλεγέθων τε ῥέουσι Κώκυτός θ', *Od.* 11.513–514).

---

[32] The reference in the fragment to Agamemnon's garments wrapped around him may allude to his death through ensnarement by his wife Clytemnestra. It also produces an intertextual link with the πέπλος of Agamemnon in Aeschylus' *Oresteia* as both a garment and funeral shroud. See Lee (2004, 263–269) for a discussion of how words for different garments, including πέπλος, may intersect with and refer to Agamemnon's fate.

LIFE / AFTERLIFE

Achilles' ghost in this play also seems to have been a direct model for Polydorus' ghost in the prologue of Euripides' *Hecuba*, produced decades later in the second half of the fifth century BCE. In the latter case, there is no doubt that Polydorus appeared on stage, and several scholars have proposed possible entry points, either from a particular *eisodos* or a subterranean space (Lane 2007). Finally, the popularity and importance of Underworld scenes is supported by their very survival in manuscripts and testimonia. The recurrence of the "ghost-on-stage" device with interlocking echoes through hyperlinks across generations and authors demonstrates the persistent appeal of Underworld scenes as a mode of communication between authors and audiences in tragedy well into the fifth century BCE.

Parodying the Underworld in Comedy

In Old Comedy, a further breakdown of the barrier between the mortal and the supernatural occurs on stage, but for the purpose of parodying societal practices and beliefs through direct, biting commentary. The most famous extant example of Underworld motifs on the comic stage is Aristophanes' *Frogs*, produced nearly 67 years after Aeschylus' *Persians*.[33] Comedies in the fifth century BCE already took everyday situations to the absurd as a form of social commentary. The fact that "a trip to the Underworld" was adopted as a comic subject at all, much less the centerpiece of the action, shows that by the time of *Frogs*, the premise was already a cliché. Aristophanes' *Frogs*, in particular, amplifies this effect by using the conventions of Underworld scenes to mock Athens' political situation and leaders by presenting afterlife society as an alternate version of real life in which solutions to the problems of reality can be found. *Frogs* portrays the Underworld as a place teeming with life and commerce, mirroring contemporary Greek society. Dionysus is the protagonist and wants to perform a *katabasis* on behalf of Athens in order to resurrect a poet who can give good advice to the leaders of the city regarding the war with Sparta. With him as a companion is his slave Xanthias, whose lines both poke fun at his master and communicate context to the audience. The god is characterized as a buffoon who asks Heracles, the most famous katabatic hero from myth, for directions to Hades so he can bring back the soul of a dead poet to help guide Athens out of its war with Sparta.

---

[33] *Frogs* won first prize at the Lenaia in 405 BCE (Dover 1997, 1).

World and Underworld 197

The presence of Dionysus, a god, on stage is already jarring, although not unique. Gods had been brought onto the stage already in such plays as Aeschylus' *Eumenides* and Euripides' *Alcestis*. Dionysus was a featured character in numerous plays, although usually in the guise of a human: as Paris in the *Dionysalexandros* of Cratinus, a soldier in the *Taxiarchs* of Eupolis, and an effeminate young man in the *Bacchae* of Euripides (Dover 1997, 23).[34] In *Frogs*, however, he appears as himself, an Olympian god and, more specifically, the god of the theater, albeit a buffoonish one. As a result, Dionysus' stage presence signals to the audience that the god is looking out for Athenian interests and that the play will fracture the boundaries between the realms of gods and men by bringing an imagined supernatural realm into the real space of the theater. The fantasy of boundary-crossing gods would have been familiar to the audience from earlier plays, thus making the buffoonish Dionysus and the opening jokes about paths into Hades even funnier. The presence of a god and the hero Heracles, also a boundary-crosser, reaffirms the breakdown of space as does the subsequent staging of the Underworld, which envisions afterlife society as a reflection of the Athenian city-state.

In his meeting with Heracles, Dionysus asks how to get to the Underworld. Heracles first suggests suicide as the quickest way, but Dionysus rebuffs him. The joke is that the latter is a god so it would be impossible for him to commit suicide, and the conversation highlights the different pathways into Hades. Dionysus finally decides to perform a *katabasis* like Heracles and specifically asks for the "harbors, bakeries, brothels, rest stops, detours, fountains, roads, cities, lodgings, and hostesses" (λιμένας, ἀρτοπώλια, πορνεῖ, ἀναπαύλας, ἐκτροπάς, κρήνας, ὁδούς, πόλεις, διαίτας, πανδοκευτρίας, *Ran.* 112–114). This creates a vision of the Underworld that ties it closely to human society by representing the dead as having similar needs and appetites to the living. In response, Heracles tells Dionysus to enter Hades by crossing a large lake (*Ran.* 137) and then describes the strange sights the god will see: great snakes and countless monsters, a sea of filth, and finally a mystic band of initiates who live near Pluto's gate (*Ran.* 142–163). Although Aristophanes may have exaggerated and distorted certain aspects of his Underworld for comedic effect, this exchange between Dionysus and Heracles evokes the Archaic poets' vision of the Underworld as a geographical, segregated place that can

---

[34] Dionysus is presumed to have appeared as a character on stage in several more plays, although his role in each is unclear. These plays include the *Babylonians* and the *Dionysus Shipwrecked* by Aristophanes, the *Dionysus* by Magnes, the *Dionysus* by Aristomenes, and the *Dionysoi* of Cratinus (Dover 1997, 22–23).

be accessed from the real world by uniquely qualified individuals who could survive the obstacles of the journey. The humor comes from the disconnect created between the expected unreality of the traditional Underworld and Dionysus' suggestion that the afterlife mirrors everyday life in Athens.

After approaching the liminal figures of Heracles for advice on performing a *katabasis* (*Ran.* 38–163) and seeking the corpse of a recently dead man to hire him to carry his luggage (*Ran.* 172), Dionysus chooses to take Charon's ferry to Hades. The dialogue between Charon and Dionysus and the subsequent boat ride is rich in references that recall other Underworld scenes to fill out the ferryman's back story (*Ran.* 181–270).[35] Charon's presence emphasizes the difficulty of crossing to the Underworld but also its accessibility *if* the correct procedures are followed and he receives proper payment.[36] He highlights class structures by refusing to ferry the slave Xanthias and further ties such treatment of the latter in the Underworld back to a controversial issue in contemporary Athenian politics. The ferryman compares Xanthias to the slaves who fought for Athens at sea to gain their freedom and citizenship, with seeming reference to those at the Battle of Arginusae in 406 BCE, saying "I won't take a slave, unless he had fought at sea to save our skins" (δοῦλον οὐκ ἄγω, / εἰ μὴ νε ναυμάχηκε τὴν περὶ τῶν κρεῶν, *Ran.* 190–191).[37] With this line, Aristophanes uses his Underworld scene to link his play to a controversial political narrative in the city, making an "inside joke" with his contemporary audience. Charon is portrayed as being aware of and responsive to the current political situation in Athens. He is knowledgeable of events, therefore, in the worlds of both the living and the dead. Since Xanthias cannot claim the citizenship status of the Arginusae survivors, Charon directs him to walk around the lake on foot and pass by the "Withered Rock" (τὸν Αὐαίνου λίθον, *Ran.* 194). In this reference, there is a faint but nonetheless present link to the "White Rock" (Λευκάδα πέτρην, *Od.* 24.11), along which Hermes leads the suitors' ghosts in

---

[35] The figure of Charon is a "modern" addition to the Underworld landscape whose role overlaps with that of Hermes Psychagogus to a certain extent. The earliest literary reference to him as a ferryman of the dead may have been in the epic poem *Minyas* (sixth century BCE), and the earliest image dates to the late sixth century BCE (Oakley 2004, 113). Most extant images of him are on white-ground lekythoi from fifth-century BCE funerary contexts (Dover 1997, 113; Oakley 2004, 108–125).

[36] *Frogs* contains the first written reference to Charon's fee (*Ran.* 137–142, 269–270). An image of a youth paying this fee to Charon is also depicted on a white-ground lekythos from 420 BCE (Oakley 2004, 123–124). The depictions of the figure Charon and the practice of giving him payment are, thus, culturally reinforced across contemporary media.

[37] See Hale (2009, 224–234) for more on the events at Arginusae and the enfranchisement of slaves who fought in naval battles for Athens.

World and Underworld 199

the *Odyssey* before reaching the entrance to Hades. Aristophanes and his audience would be attuned to this connection between the two rocks as similar Underworld landmarks.[38]

The two choruses of Aristophanes' *Frogs* also embed political and social statements in the Underworld space with specific motifs from other Underworld narratives to underscore their messages. Dionysus performs a *katabasis* to help Athens find a successful solution to the war and its hardships, thus tying the Underworld scene to current events. With this premise, the playwright suggests to his audience that the Underworld is a place to comment on Athenian policies and practices, using experts from different time periods and stations in life (and death) as advisors to frame the audience's views of contemporary affairs in the democratic *polis*. Through Dionysus' *katabasis*, Aristophanes indicates that everything (and everyone) the god encounters in the Underworld should be examined with this purpose in mind.

This extends further to another unique feature of the *Frogs*: its two, seemingly unrelated choruses. Once the frog chorus exits, it is not heard from again and does not interact with the second chorus. Furthermore, ancient and modern sources have argued that, unlike the second chorus of initiates, the frogs chorus was not seen by the audience and only heard from off-stage (Dover 1997, 29; Allison 1983, 8–9).[39] Of course, the invisibility of the frogs could easily be explained by the fact that they are swimming below Charon's boat in the lake at the boundary of the Underworld, where darkness and gloom would be expected.[40] I would suggest, however, that Aristophanes draws on the idea of a cacophonous Underworld borrowed from Homer's *Odyssey* in

---

[38] Stanford (1948, 412n11) refers to the "White Rock" (*Od.* 24.11) as "another of the mysterious crags of the infernal regions, like the Rock of Withering in *Frogs* 194" and notes several instances in addition to these that particular rocks appear as landmarks in the Underworld.

[39] Dover (1997, 29–32) argues that a hidden frog chorus would fit with the economical nature of the productions during cash-strapped war times and may even have led to further jokes about the production being "economical." Allison (1983, 9) observes that there is no reference by Charon, Dionysus, or the frog chorus itself to any visual element of the frog chorus, a typical practice for comedies upon entrance of a chorus. Indeed, the second chorus describes themselves as wearing "flip-flops and rags" (τόδε τὸ σανδαλίσκον καὶ τὸ ῥάκος, *Ran.* 405–406), which would support the argument for an unseen frog chorus because of economic constraints. Allison (1983, 8–11) also points to the repeated aural references in the text of the play as evidence for a focus on sound over sight. Sifakis (1971, Ch. 10) and Corbel-Morana (2012, Ch.3), on the other hand, argue for a visible frog chorus.

[40] The initiates in the second chorus refer to carrying torches during their procession (λαμπάδας, λαμπάδι, *Ran.* 340 and 351, respectively), indicating an environment either dark or dimly lit.

which the sense of sound is foregrounded while sight becomes unreliable.[41] When Hermes leads the dead suitors to the Underworld, they make a lot of noise, squeaking like bats (*Od.* 24.5–6). The idea of animal sounds echoing around the entrance into the Underworld thus further links the Underworld scenes of Aristophanes and Homer.[42]

Moreover, having a chorus of frogs is particularly marked because their amphibious qualities relate to the Athenians' vision of themselves as powerful on land and sea. The marsh frog, which is the most likely species Aristophanes imitates in his chorus, is a species of green frog that is more closely associated with water than land and was known for being particularly loud (Allison 1983, 16; Dover 1997, 119). The amphibious and vociferous qualities of these frogs can be mapped directly onto Athenian self-identity and pride. Like the frogs, Athenians were known for their adaptability to land and sea and obstreperousness as a democratic *polis* open to the voices of many. Moreover, as creatures that swarm and move in groups, they can also be associated, according to Page duBois (2022, 92), with democracy and the masses that make up the *demos*. The chorus of frogs (and the later chorus of initiates) in the Underworld space, therefore, acts as a proxy for the audience in the Underworld, visualizing it as a democratized space (duBois 2022, 96). The frogs' defeat in song by Dionysus could also be connected to the recent disappointment of the Athenians related to their sea battle at Arginusae (406 BCE). Although they defeated the Spartans, the Athenian generals were unable to retrieve the survivors and the dead from the sea battle because of inclement weather, and most of these leaders were subsequently executed for this abandonment after a controversial group trial. The frogs whose voices are quelled and who disappear back into the water after their shining moment of full-throated song could be compared to the sailors who were lost at sea in their moment of greatest triumph.

The frogs are liminal figures, and it is this feature that connects them to the second chorus of initiates.[43] This only becomes clear, though, through the

---

[41] The emphasis on the darkness and removal of sight in *Odyssey* 11 is discussed in more detail in Chapter 2.

[42] The audience might also associate the two scenes because it was already cued to thinking of the *Odyssey* during the appearance of Heracles earlier in the play. Moreover, both the *Odyssey* and the *Frogs* share the idea that a returning "hero," clever with words, can save his native city from disastrous ruin.

[43] Scholars have been at a loss to explain why there are two choruses and how they relate to each other. My analysis suggests solutions to both these questions.

World and Underworld

hypertextual interconnections that are possible in an Underworld scene. If the frogs represent the Athenians, so too do the initiates who identify themselves with the Eleusinian mysteries through their cries of "Ἴακχ' ὦ Ἴακχε" (*Ran.* 316–317) and their outfits of rags (Allison 1983, 15). Iacchus was the god carried from Athens to Eleusis during the celebration of the Eleusinian Mysteries, the mystery cult that was one of the most inclusive and also particularly associated with Athens (Dover 1997, 30–31).[44] In the play, the inclusiveness of the cult adds another dimension to the enfranchisement debate in Athenian politics that is directly addressed in the following passage:[45]

τὸν ἱερὸν χορὸν δίκαιόν ἐστι χρηστὰ τῇ πόλει
ξυμπαραινεῖν καὶ διδάσκειν. πρῶτον οὖν ἡμῖν δοκεῖ
ἐξισῶσαι τοὺς πολίτας κἀφελεῖν τὰ δείματα (*Ran.* 686–688)

It is fitting for the holy chorus to recommend and teach what is useful to the city. First, then, we think it best to make citizens equal and remove their fears.

The chorus asserts its role as advisor to the city and recommends the restoration of citizenship rights to those who had been a part of the oligarchic revolution.

The trope of people beyond the grave giving advice to the living is strengthened by the hyperlinked *para-narratives* activated through references to their identities as Eleusinian initiates and Athenians. The initiates connect to the *polis*, not only because of the ties between Athens and Eleusis but also because this theatrical chorus, composed of actual citizens in the civic setting of the theater, is literally advocating for enfranchisement.[46] As representatives of mystery cult initiates, they bring the idea of a blessed afterlife into the civic space, promoting the belief that proper actions in life lead to eternal reward.

---

[44] Burkert (1983, 249) suggests that a great number of Athenians had been initiated into the cult at Eleusis, stating "Athenians were, as a rule, mystai." The Eleusinian Mysteries were open to a wide range of initiates—men, women, free, slave, Greek, and non-Greek. Judging by this inclusiveness, the main limiting factor was most likely an economic constraint (Bremmer 2011, 376–377).

[45] Scholars have long debated about the identity, function, and meaning of the chorus of initiates in the *Frogs*, particularly their associations with Dionysian and Eleusinian mystery cults (Segal 1961; Allison 1983; Moorton 1989; Brown 1991; Dover 1997; Lada-Richards 1999; Edmonds 2004).

[46] Choruses consisted of Athenian citizens. For more about choral identity, see Foley (2003).

LIFE / AFTERLIFE

Their success in initiation is analogized to the Athenians' actions during the war and how proper actions and divine direction might bring a successful aftermath. In his staging of the Underworld and Eleusinian initiates, Aristophanes thus plays with the idea of living people metaphorically being inserted into the Underworld as a chorus of the dead and then "returning" from the dead once the performance ends to lead their lives as citizens, having been transformed by this civic, religious experience. What happens in the Underworld reflects and comments on events in real life, justifying Dionysus' *katabasis* in the main narrative frame. In the end, Dionysus successfully brings a poet back from the dead, showing the realm of the dead as a source for solutions to the present, real-world problems of Athens.

Likewise, the comic playwright Eupolis employs the "embassy to the Underworld" motif in his play *Demes*, produced several years before *Frogs*.[47] Through fragments and testimonia, we know the play was set either in or near the Underworld and that four dead leaders (Solon, Miltiades, Aristeides, and Pericles) were brought back to help Athens during a time of dire need to advise on which laws to pass or repeal (Rusten 2011, 81).[48] Scholars agree that the *Demes* opens with an Underworld scene. Whether it was a *katabasis* or a necromancy by the title character Pyronides, however, has been a topic of debate. Ian Storey's argument for the latter is convincing based on practicality and the precedent of the *Nekuia*. Additionally, none of the ancient sources mention a scene in Hades for the play (Storey 2003, 121–124).[49] Even if the *Demes* was partially set in Hades, Aristophanes might have wanted to take the "embassy to the Underworld" idea further than Eupolis for comic effect by treating a *katabasis* as an ordinary trip, setting the majority of *Frogs* in Hades, and using a god rather than a mortal as the protagonist. Furthermore, Aristophanes may have already used the embassy idea in another play. The fragments of his *Gerytades* suggest a play with the premise of sending an embassy of poets to the Underworld, chosen from "those whom we know are frequenters of

---

[47] Eupolis' *Demes* is thought to have been produced between 417-410 BCE. While most scholars like the date of 412 BCE, Storey (2003, 112–114) argues for the earlier date of 417 BCE, and Telò (2007, 16–24) argues for a later date of 410 BCE.

[48] *Demes* may have borrowed the theme from Cratinus' *Cheirons*, an earlier play that resurrected Solon (Rusten 2011, 25). Another play that may have shared an Underworld setting is Nicophon's *Return from Hades*, which has not survived (Rusten 2011, 28).

[49] Telò (2007, 24–33) argues for a *katabasis* in the *Demes*. Because of the nature of hypertextual linking, my argument applies regardless of the staging for the scene, since both a necromancy and a *katabasis* could activate the same Underworld *para-narratives*.

Hades and enjoyed going there often" (οὗ ς ἤσμεν ὄντα ς ᾀδοφοίτα ς καὶ θαμὰ ἐκεῖσε φιλοχωροῦντα ς, Aristophanes, *Gerytades* Fr. 156).[50] The reference to a class of poets who were known to be "frequenters of Hades" suggests that Underworld scenes were a regular preoccupation in the works of playwrights in festival competitions and that people generally knew that about them.[51]

The various figures brought on stage recall both the socio-political hierarchy of fifth-century BCE Athens and famous characters of myth, making these Underworld scenes meaningful to audiences through their connection to both past and present. Like others before them, they track time by recognizable landmarks, both mythological and mundane and maintain the basic structure of the Underworld as established in traditional and contemporary media, linking the play to heroic *katabaseis*, religious authority, and democratic ideology.

In all these stage performances, playwrights adhered to the idea of the Underworld chronotope as a place at the borders of the known world, alien yet reflective of human thought and activities in their contemporary contexts.[52] The performative medium of drama, like funerary orations and public grave markers, filled the physical and mental landscape of Athenians with interactive Underworld scenes in regular community activities relating to political and religious celebrations. Together, these holistic, three-dimensional Underworld scene experiences made the society of the dead more present, available, and accessible to the living.

VI. Conclusions

In the fifth century BCE, poets, playwrights, and artists promoted new ideas of accessibility and permeability between the realms of the living and the dead within the constraints of traditional stories and religious beliefs. They

---

[50] See Farmer (2017, 197–212) and Olson (2020) for a reconstruction of the fragment and a full discussion about the play and its setting in Hades. Olson argues against Farmer's conclusion that the play dated before *Frogs* and was set in Hades. Regardless of its setting on stage, its engagement of an Underworld scene and reference to *katabasis* uses the Underworld's hypertextual poetics to activate a network of similar scenes.

[51] Farmer (2017, 200–203) argues that the embassy consisted of poets who were living Athenians and contemporaries of Aristophanes, who each represented one of the competitive categories at the City Dionysia (i.e., tragedy, comedy, and dithyramb).

[52] Other comic plays set in Hades, for which there is only fragmentary evidence, include: Pherecrates' *Miners*, dated to the 420s BCE (Aparisi 1998, 80–81) and Aristophanes' *Frying-Pan Men (Tagenistai)*. Both contain utopian Underworlds free from toil with an easy life (Constantakopoulou 2007, 164).

found a convenient language in Underworld scenes for such communication with their audiences and elaborated on several key features to envision new connections between the living and the dead. These included the ideas of heroic blessedness, the continuity of existence after death, and afterlife segregation through judgment. By enhancing traditional landscapes of the dead but keeping the fundamental idea of the Underworld scene as a vehicle for communication between creator and audience, authors and artists in Athens made the dead relevant to the living in a way that shaped beliefs about immortality and the power of mortals to influence their own honors (*timai*). Underworld scenes appearing in political, cultural, and religious discourse leveraged their connections to each other and to works of the past to change the way everyday people perceived both life and the afterlife.

Underworld imagery and myths in fifth-century BCE Athenian sources dealt with the dead as persistent members of the community, framing their change of existential state (i.e., death) as one of continuity rather than disruption. Through interactive representations of the afterlife in public and private spaces, Underworld scenes in texts and on objects became mirrors reflecting the concerns of their audiences and platforms on which their creators and audiences could contemplate solutions to societal problems. Regular references in various media to a vibrant afterlife and the popularity of new intermediaries, particularly Charon, Heracles, and Hermes, indicate a shift in perception during the fifth century BCE to a more permeable and accessible Underworld for all levels of society. Authors and artists drew from a wide range of ancient and contemporary sources to craft this more inclusive, democratized vision of afterlife society that matched the aspirations of Athenian democracy. In the next chapter, we will see Plato's backlash to these changes in Underworld portrayal and explore how he used Underworld scenes to undermine the idea of a democratized afterlife and promote afterlife blessedness as a status reserved primarily for the select few who pursued philosophy and the philosophical lifestyle.

6

Plato's Underworlds

REVISING THE AFTERLIFE

I. Introduction

As an inheritor of the public discourse about the Underworld and a critic of popular trends in his world, Plato uses Greek Underworld scenes to challenge the democratized afterlife depictions prominent among authors and artists in late fifth-century BCE Athens. In this pursuit, he composed multiple Underworld scenes that often contradict each other to create new limits and relationships between its internal structures and how the worlds of the living and dead connect. While pre-Platonic Underworld scenes have some variety and support each author's agenda, they are generally consistent in their theological grounding and do not stray too far from each other in their makeup, relying heavily on the Archaic models first seen in the epics of Homer and Hesiod. Plato's Underworlds, however, are quite different from each other and those of their predecessors. Despite having great variety in their details and referent points, Plato's Underworlds promote his ideology of the superiority of philosophers by using Underworld poetics to reframe traditional beliefs about heroes, heroism, and afterlife judgment and rewards. By employing a seemingly contradictory variety of Underworld scenes, Plato shows that their attributes, whether heroic or judgment-based, all point toward a different locus of meaning and belief than those found in the traditional myths he engages. In short, he uses hypertextual Underworld poetics to redirect the links in mythic Underworld scenes to *para-narratives* that portray a different cosmic paradigm and valorize a new set of "heroes"—philosophers.

Plato, like his predecessors, configures his Underworld scenes to promote a particular agenda. In his dialogues, Underworld scenes support immediate

Life / Afterlife. Suzanne Lye, Oxford University Press. © Oxford University Press 2024.
DOI: 10.1093/9780197690239.003.0007

dialectic arguments and also an overall worldview about the importance of philosophy by showing how it interacts with the widely known myths and religious beliefs that are inherently referenced in such scenes.[1] Thus, one might still see familiar figures such as Odysseus and Minos or landmarks such as Acheron and Styx, but their effects on the philosophical soul are different from what other humans or even the heroes of the past would experience. By shifting the bricolage of Underworld scenes, Plato emphasizes that they are rhetorical tools for communication rather than representations of reality, simultaneously using their visceral impact on audiences and authority within his culture while also devaluing the original systems of belief they depict.[2]

From this perspective, the Underworld scenes Plato portrays do not need to be consistent as long as they engage with broadly known afterlife beliefs to promote philosophers as the most blessed of mortals in the cosmic scheme. To accomplish this, he manipulates certain fundamental aspects of Underworld scenes. In particular, he alters the Underworld *chronotope* and the premise of afterlife judgment to challenge traditional beliefs about the types of actions and activities that achieve the best afterlife outcome with a release from earthly cares.[3] He situates the Underworld much more firmly within the timeline of the real world than his predecessors did and removes the traditional isolation of the Underworld *chronotope*. As a result of this change, afterlife existence is converted into a stage within human chronology. In his scheme, death is no longer a separate, parallel, simultaneous, and permanent existence for a soul. Rather, Plato's Underworld scenes portray life and death as interchanging states of a person's soul. To create these scenes, he appropriates a variety of

---

[1] Annas (1982), Bernabé Pajares (2013), and Edmonds (2012, 2014) have discussed the differences between Plato's Underworld scenes and possible reasons behind them, including influences from Orphic eschatologies. These scholars and I overlap in our conclusion that Plato uses his various Underworlds for the purpose of argument and support for his theory of philosophy. This chapter places Plato's strategy within a broader context of the use of Underworld scenes by Greek authors and points out specific interventions he makes in such scenes to reframe the entire network of Underworld scenes he activates so they appear to support his views.

[2] Plato underscores his engagement with his predecessors' Underworld scenes and doubt about their veracity with hedging comments, such as "if indeed what we are told is true" (εἴπερ γε τὰ λεγόμενα ἀληθῆ, *Apol.* 41c6–7) and "indeed this, or something like this, is true about our souls and their dwelling places . . ." (μέντοι ἡ ταῦτ᾽ ἐστὶν ἢ τοιαῦτ᾽ ἄττα περὶ τὰς ψυχὰς ἡμῶν καὶ τὰς οἰκήσεις, *Phd.* 114d2–3). For more on the different systems of belief that Plato incorporates into his Underworld scene, see Edmonds (2004, 2014).

[3] For more on the general idea of the "chronotope," see Bakhtin (1981), Gary Morson and Caryl Emerson (1989), and Andrea Nightingale (2002). For more on the chronotope in Underworld scenes, see the Introduction.

afterlife myths from traditional sources, rewriting them in great detail and from multiple angles to reimagine the Underworld as a place whose order, hierarchy, and integration into the world of the living come at a very specific and ongoing cost to the individual, one that does not end at death. While this strategy of using Underworld scenes to promote ideology is not new, Plato uses them to transform the hierarchy of the "blessed," altering which actions people can take to have the greatest chance of attaining the best afterlife. In his formulation, neither heroic action, assimilation to heroes, nor ritual initiation are privileged paths to achieving the blessed (*olbios*) status which would lead to a positive-plus, Golden Age afterlife where one's soul would feast eternally with heroes of the past. Rather, those like him and his mentor Socrates, who practice philosophy and live according to what he defines as the philosophical lifestyle, would exceed the status of heroes and gain the most blessed afterlives.[4] Indeed, Plato redefines the notion of "blessed heroes" so that the new figures to emulate are the philosophers, whose lifestyle purifies the soul to such an extent that it earns a pleasurable state of existence beyond what original positive-plus judgment promises. Plato thus uses Underworld scenes to challenge the status quo of traditional beliefs and to create a new hierarchy of blessedness, which still includes just and heroic men of the past but makes their actions worth less in the cosmic scheme of blessedness. To do this, he borrows the imagery and concepts of famous Underworld scenes, particularly those of Homer and Hesiod but also those of cult (Bernabé Pajares 2013), as tools to undermine and overwrite their messaging so that their configuration fits his ideology.

In the following, I first give an overview of the major changes that Plato makes to Underworld scenes. I then examine how he incorporates afterlife depictions from Homer, Hesiod, and others in the Underworld scenes of four works (the *Apology, Gorgias, Phaedo,* and *Republic*) to situate his arguments and idiosyncratic eschatology about the fate of the soul firmly within Greek tradition. I argue that Plato uses Underworld scenes to challenge the fifth-century BCE trend of democratizing the Underworld and that he tries to

---

[4] Plato's character Socrates refers to a philosophical lifestyle as one in which he discusses virtue and other things and examines himself and others on a daily basis (*Apology* 38a). Based on Plato's descriptions across his dialogues, "living a life according to philosophy" involves the pursuit of wisdom through discussion and argument and also self-improvement through active reasoning and dialogic inquiry. These pursuits happen through self-examination and dialogue with others about important topics, such as virtue and justice, so that one always knows and does what is right and best in a given situation. For a discussion about Plato's definition of philosophy and the philosophical lifestyle, see Cooper (2012, 50–54).

reestablish a hierarchy of blessedness with a higher bar for who can have access to the newly defined, positive-plus afterlife. In Plato's reformulation of the afterlife, philosophers have the best chance to achieve the afterlife outcome previously reserved for heroes of the past and those in the present who have been assimilated to mythic heroes by deeds, *kleos*, or cult. Running contrary to traditional religious beliefs and cultural practices, Plato privileges philosophers as the most blessed (*olbios*) of mortals because they use philosophy as an enabler in finding a secure path to the highest status in the afterlife. In Plato's scheme, the excellence in warfare that gained *arete* and lasting *kleos* for Homeric heroes is no longer enough to achieve true excellence, which can only come through a well-examined life based in reason and just acts (i.e., the philosophical lifestyle).

To make this case, Plato uses Underworld scenes to dismantle the meaning and assignment of blessedness from the inside, undermining traditional myths of the afterlife by weaponizing their own poetics. While his Underworld scenes might have a similar structure to ones of the past and thus look familiar, he changes the types of actions that differentiate an individual's status among the dead and lead to the most privileged, positive-plus afterlife. While Plato, like his contemporaries, employs the poetics of Underworld scenes to make societal commentary, his purpose is vastly different in that he attempts to make the Underworld seem more distant than the ones appearing in other media. As a result, Plato's Underworlds look more like the hierarchical ones portrayed in Hesiod and Pindar than the ones in Athenian funeral orations. While his system theoretically might be open to anyone, only people of Plato's own sphere had both access to his ideas and the resources to follow his particular tenets for living the sort of philosophical life that would most expeditiously allow them to attain the status of a philosopher worthy of a blessed afterlife. By subordinating traditional heroic accomplishment to philosophical practice, Plato makes the greatest rewards of the afterlife less accessible to most people, thus counteracting the democratizing trends in the afterlife poetics of the fifth century BCE.

General Features of Plato's Underworld Scenes

Although Plato has characterized the traditional stories of myth from poets as harmful to the young, saying he would exclude them from his ideal city (*Resp.* 607b), he nevertheless uses their Underworld scenes to support his dialectic argumentation. Through the variability of his Underworld representations, Plato deftly demonstrates that Underworld myths are moldable to suit any

Plato's Underworlds   209

given situation, thus undermining the credibility of traditional ideas about the afterlife as any sort of truth. He further devalues popular beliefs about the Underworld by explicitly characterizing Underworld scenes as narratives and treating them as a tool or exercise in rhetoric, deployed like dialectic argumentation, to support his truths rather than to represent the actual nature of the cosmos. In *Republic* 588c–d, Socrates calls the creation of mythic figures "the work of a clever sculptor" (Δεινοῦ πλάστου, ἔφη, τὸ ἔργον, *Resp.* 588c11) and says that "accounts of such myths are more malleable than wax" (εὐπλαστότερον κηροῦ καὶ τῶν τοιούτων λόγος, *Resp.* 588d1). With such phrases in mind, Kathryn Morgan (2000, 185–186) has argued that "myth" in Plato is a technique that gives a "short-cut" for an analytic process and reflects a mode of discourse that has validity primarily when proper argumentation has already taken place, although it might also replace it. Myths in Plato are an intuitive leap that work best, according to Morgan, when they are firmly grounded in rational, philosophical analysis because they do not have the one flaw that causes similar myths by poets to be rejected, namely that they are "Muse-inspired." Instead, because they are grounded in argument and the recollection of the soul's nature, all the Underworld myths that Plato's Socrates crafts claim to elucidate the unknowable aspects of the soul's journey after death. Each dialogue's Underworld scene uses a different register of argument to compensate for failures in the dialectic process, such as a shortness of time, the ethical shortcomings of his interlocutors, and the lack of verifiability in a line of argument (K.A. Morgan 2000, 180–184). In this reasoning, the Underworld myths can be interpreted as "a metaphorical expression of the content of the dialectic path" (K.A. Morgan 2000, 180).[5] Plato uses myth, therefore, for the sake of argument. This strategy is not unique: he borrows it freely from the very poets that his character Socrates denigrates and excludes from his ideal state. By appropriating the poets' own rhetoric to subvert their power, Plato demonstrates how easy it is to create an Underworld *muthos* as a representation of one's argument, even when one might not believe in it. Furthermore, by focusing on the effects of such narratives on the soul, he shifts the cultural dialogue around Underworld scenes, adapting their

---

[5] Morgan (2000, 180) argues that beliefs portrayed by myths about the soul are also represented in the dialectic sections and that Socrates does not rely on these myths alone to make his argument. She writes, "When myth is deployed in connection with the transcendent and incorporeal world of the Forms, it expresses a belief about them and about the incorporeal soul which is either justified (although not verified) by dialectical argument or which must be so justified on a subsequent occasion."

familiar myths to support his novel, philosophy-based understanding of the cosmos and the soul's journey through it.

Across the dialogues, Plato, through Socrates, uses the common language of Underworld scenes to reimagine the nature of blessedness and create new models for assigning souls and making a case for why they deserve those assignments.[6] He describes landmarks and famous inhabitants that make his Underworlds recognizable (e.g., the placement of Tartarus, the presence of well-known sinners) and sets up these familiar features against his audience's collective knowledge of ancient Greek eschatological myth. Moreover, Plato centralizes the afterlife narrative around the individual soul's experience as it moves through the Underworld space, bringing in the first-person point of view of a katabatic hero or mystery cult initiate by using the language and framework of a heroic Underworld.[7]

The first inherited feature of Underworld scenes that Plato preserves is the idea that an individual might be specially favored by the gods (i.e., "blessed" or *olbios*), thereby giving him or her access to the positive afterlives previously associated exclusively with heroes. Second, Plato adopts the idea of a geographic location for the Underworld whose regions map morality and represent the idea of "justice" as bound to the physical landscape. For example, Tartarus is an area of the Underworld reserved specifically for the unjust. Finally, he embraces the idea that actions in life determine the afterlife experience.

On the other hand, Plato also makes some important changes within this framework to counter the democratized Underworld of his contemporary context. First of all, heroes, while still respected, are superseded by philosophers on the scale of blessedness. Second, deeds, glory in battle, athletic prowess, and the celebration of *kleos* by poets or a community are no longer sufficient to achieve the most blessed afterlife status. Finally, to underscore his argument for philosophy as the path to the most blessed afterlife outcome, Plato folds the Underworld *chronotope* into that of the real world and underpins both with the same underlying system of justice that particularly rewards the philosophical soul. In doing so, he diminishes the

---

[6] For more on Plato's re-use of traditional Underworld motifs in the *Phaedo*, see Edmonds (2004, 207–219) and Bernabé Pajares (2013).

[7] The Orphic Gold Tablets, discussed in Chapter 4, is one example that offers a glimpse of how mystery cult initiates viewed the soul's journey in the afterlife from the individual soul's experience. They also show how initiation and individuals' choices were perceived to lead to a blessed afterlife (Edmonds 2004; Graf and Johnston 2007; Bernabé Pajares and Jiménez San Cristóbal 2008).

Underworld's fundamental alterity by making any time spent in it into a corrective recompense for events that happened in life. In the case of the *Apology* and *Gorgias*, for example, Plato envisions the afterlife as a space where ultimately better judgments about an individual soul's character are made than in the real world, where it might have been rewarded or punished unjustly. In his dialogues with metempsychosis, such as the *Phaedo* and *Republic*, death becomes a phase in a soul's lifecycle as opposed to a final destination of no return, except for those who have been able to live a philosophical lifestyle sufficient to escape this cycle. The alterity of the Underworld, therefore, is not because it is unknowable except to special heroes, but rather because of the transparency with which justice—reward or punishment—is deployed. Through such framing, he makes the pursuit of philosophy the most important activity an individual can do during life to achieve the afterlife status previously associated with heroes because it develops skills and insights needed by the soul to overcome obstacles in the Underworld.

The soul's movement through the geography of the Underworld represents the soul's character and can be used as a visible diagnostic of its condition. This physicality makes the blessed Underworld more accessible to certain people (especially philosophers), but it also takes it out of reach from the majority of individuals who do not have the means or ability to live the type of philosophical lifestyle promoted by Plato and Socrates. Such changes hinge on the idea of a judgment-based Underworld with the expectation of heroic Underworld outcomes for those who can attain the highest afterlife status. Furthermore, such status becomes predetermined by persistent actions in life rather than single actions or agonistic encounters on a battlefield. This perceived accessibility and ability to cause direct effects in the afterlife makes the Underworld present in daily life beyond what was already in the visual landscape of his world, but in a looming, admonitory way because every action or thought in life, even hidden ones, becomes linked to a certain result in the afterlife in a cause-effect relationship. In this way, Plato uses Underworld scenes to highlight certain strains of religious and cultural belief and redirect their networks of links from traditional paradigms of heroism and initiation to his philosophy-based one.

In his Underworlds, Plato often focuses on how the soul's encounters and experiences in the afterlife are determined primarily by choices it made during life when it had agency. What happens to a soul in the Underworld is, therefore, presented as a correction meant to cosmically balance its actions during life by making the soul the object rather than subject of its fate for an allotted time. Plato continues, and even expands on, the popular premise of a "positive," sentient afterlife with strong connections across the life–death barrier.[8] In the *Apology* and the *Gorgias*, two of his earlier works, Plato presents this premise using a primarily judgment-based Underworld as the terminal location for souls. Souls practicing philosophy while alive, like Socrates', can earn their place after death with great men and heroes of the past (*Ap.* 41a), sometimes even on the Isles of the Blessed after being sorted by qualified, experienced judges (re. *Grg.* 526c). These scenes draw from the Underworlds of *Odyssey* 24, *Works and Days*, and *Olympian* 2, in which the souls of dead heroes are separated from others after death and live in congenial companionship for eternity. In the *Apology*, Plato's Socrates predicts that he will have access to such heroes after death, thus assuming the democratized afterlife prevalent among his contemporaries. In the *Republic* and *Phaedo*, however, Plato shifts that vision to incorporate and emphasize metempsychosis as part of the soul's experience, applying it even to the souls of dead heroes, such that their eternal access to the most blessed afterlife is threatened. As the narrator proposing this reconfiguration, Socrates describes souls going through phases of life and afterlife in order to relate both the joys and horrors they encounter. The same familiar "neighborhoods" of a segregated Underworld are present (e.g., Tartarus for punishment, Isles of the Blessed for reward), but he changes their layout, their relationship to each other, the make-up of their denizens, and the administration of reward or punishment by chthonic powers.

Generally introduced through the voice of the character Socrates, Plato's Underworld scenes are intermingled into his dialectic arguments at key moments. Like the Underworlds of his predecessors, they engage the audience in metatextual moments to emphasize the significance of the surrounding frame narrative. In the case of the dialogues, the local narrative in which they are embedded is dialectic argumentation, usually about the nature of justice and the impact of philosophy on the soul's experiences in life and death. Although they often seem contradictory, the Underworld scenes in Plato share a few key features. First, the society of the dead is regimented, with laws akin to the natural laws of the world.[9] Second, topographical features in the Underworld act on the soul as the means by which Underworld

---

[8] For more about the heightened contact and greater accessibility for individuals across the life–death divide, see Chapter 5.

[9] For more on the idea of the continuity of status in the afterlife as a default mode in Plato, see Edmonds (2020a, 547–552).

Plato's Underworlds   213

judgment is executed. Thus, the morality of individual souls is reflected in the very spaces that they inhabit: good souls go to pleasant, sunny climates to enjoy the Golden-Age type, "*makar*" afterlife of heroes with no more cares or striving, while evil ones live in regions that are dark, dangerous, and full of painful punishments. Third, the soul has a heightened physicality, allowing it to perceive pain and pleasure. Any violence or bliss experienced in the different environments of the Underworld reminds the soul (and the audience) of its character during life and why it finds itself in a particular location. Finally, in most of Plato's Underworld scenes, there is no escape from the environment, since the landscapes of the afterlife are contiguous with the world of the living, as in the *Phaedo*, or exist specifically for the purpose of rewarding or punishing souls, as in the *Republic*. As a general rule, the upper realms of the Underworld are locations for reward while the lower levels are focused on punishment. Souls then move between these levels during different phases of their life cycles.

Another shared feature of Plato's Underworld scenes is that they often explicitly relate themselves to the famous Underworld scenes of Homer and Hesiod. By referencing these influential poets in almost every Underworld scene, Plato signals that he views his scenes as equivalent to theirs and that those should be the references for the audience to use as points of comparison. These signals serve as a starting point from which to compare Socrates' reimagined Underworlds and allow Plato to incorporate ideas of the afterlife from other authors as well as from ritual practices and religious beliefs. Picking up on Hesiod's representation of the Underworld as a moral geography, for example, Plato's Underworlds map each soul's level of blessedness directly to its physical location in the Underworld space, with those undergoing punishment inhabiting one part, at least temporarily, while others are assigned to feast with famous heroes on the Isles of the Blessed. This explicit juxtaposition invites direct comparison between the philosopher's Underworld scenes and those of his predecessors to support his argument for the importance of philosophy over religious beliefs, superstition, or cultural practices. Creating such overt connections to well-known Underworld scenes is both an acknowledgment of his predecessors and a challenge to their authority because he uses their inherent poetics to overwrite the meaning of their messages in support of his perspective.

Socrates makes philosophical training a crucial element for navigating one's life *and* afterlife. Although most of the preparation toward a blessed afterlife must occur during a person's lifespan, souls are, for the most part, not released from earthly responsibility or obligations after death, particularly when metempsychosis is a possibility. For example, souls must also make correct choices in the afterlife to improve or maintain their position, by following their divine guide correctly (*Phdr.* 250b–c) or by choosing the correct future life before they are reborn (*Resp.* 10.620c). The soul's agency in the afterlife and the repercussions of afterlife choices are particularly apparent in the examples when souls choose their next incarnation (*Leg.* 903c–905b) and negotiate with their victims for forgiveness when given the opportunity to escape from infernal punishment (*Phd.* 114a). In Socrates' attack on his predecessors' beliefs, Underworld scenes become key forms of commentary and argument against practices that, he contends, injure the soul in its journey through life and afterlife. Through Underworld scenes, Plato brings the weight of eschatological myths into his argumentation and demonstrates that his philosophical program extends both beyond the real world and beyond the rational arguments of dialectic inquiry into different *chronotope*s and existential states. Employing the Underworld's alternate register of communication bolsters his arguments beyond the immediate discussion into an eternal, cosmic time frame by relying on the rhetorical features of Underworld scenes that already exist in authoritative sources and can be assumed to be understood by his audiences.

A comparison of the different Underworld scenes across the Platonic dialogues highlights their rhetorical nature and their flexibility in supporting seemingly conflicting narratives. As Stephen Halliwell (2007, 460) observes, the reader of Plato leaves with the impression of "uncertainty about an afterlife—uncertainty tempered by hope." By creating a familiar backdrop against which to visualize the superiority of the philosopher in this life and the next, Plato's Underworlds ultimately refute the idea that the most blessed afterlife can be granted or guaranteed by poetic immortalization, community honors, religious rituals, or divine favor. In the place of these, he offers philosophy as an expeditious, initiatory path and the primary means for his audience to overcome the worst aspects of death. In the following case studies, I show how Plato changed his Underworld scenes over time to challenge the prevailing views about life and the afterlife. I start with the *Apology* and *Gorgias* to show how he borrows and restyles myths that are clearly borrowed from Homer and Hesiod. Then, I discuss how Plato's *Phaedo* configures Underworld scenes to create a moral landscape that emphasizes judgment, punishment, and reward. Finally, I examine the *Republic*'s "Myth of Er" and discuss how this Underworld scene attempts to promote radical change to the fundamental beliefs of his times about life and the afterlife.

II. Plato's Underworlds as Argument in the Apology and the Gorgias

Across Plato's dialogues, the character Socrates generally describes a vibrant Underworld landscape full of sound and activity as souls traverse it undergoing various fates, whether enduring punishment in its harsh environment or interacting with their fellow souls. When introducing Underworld scenes to his interlocutors, Socrates prefers to give pictures of the afterlife through landscapes rather than through necromantic conversations that often privilege the first-hand, heroic perspective. This is significant because it points to a shift in the emphasis within Underworld scenes from famous, larger-than-life, sentient individuals, such as mythic heroes, to a more vibrant environment and community, which includes souls of various backgrounds. Detailed descriptions by a quasi-omniscient, impersonal narrative voice such as that of Socrates also lends authority to the account because the experience of the space is divorced from the limits of a katabatic hero's perspective.[10]

In his Underworld scenes, Socrates employs a distinct pattern to challenge traditional sources. He first recalls an Underworld scene through direct reference, often with an additional assumption or declaration that he has received it from a reliable source or via accepted tradition. He uses similar motifs and the same language found in revered, well-known poets such as Homer and Hesiod so that it appears at first as if he is merely recounting their Underworld visions. His conclusions about the Underworld, however, often end with a very different orientation and set of beliefs from the sources he references. Indeed, he uses the language of the Underworld to refute three major claims of mystery cults and poets from previous generations: (1) that great deeds lauded in song can make a mortal equivalent to a blessed hero in the eyes of the community, (2) divine favor and wealth in life can lead to a blessed afterlife (i.e., the direct translation of an individual from a high-status, prosperous (*olbios*) life to a Golden Age, supernaturally blessed (*makar*) type of existence in the afterlife), and (3) initiation through cult rituals marks an individual for a blessed afterlife. Instead, he makes the practice of philosophy into a surer path and form of initiation that can lead to the most positive outcome in the afterlife because it most directly helps people to live just lives. This adds an additional level of status in the cosmic scheme

---

[10] The exception to this is the *Republic*'s "Myth of Er," which is explicitly set up as a narrative by an "everyman" figure taking on the role of katabatic narrator.

for philosophers to occupy above that of traditional heroes, which shifts the identity of the group that would be considered most blessed. In this scheme, the most *olbios* are those who display their philosophical rather than physical prowess, which translates into a soul that is most ready for the moment of judgment. For Plato, the true heroes of his generation are the philosophers, and an individual's dedication to cultivating his soul through philosophy is the key activity for ensuring a blessed afterlife judgment.

In the *Apology,* one of Plato's earliest works, the character Socrates describes death as a change in location for the soul:

κατὰ τὰ λεγόμενα μεταβολή τις τυγχάνει οὖσα καὶ μετοίκησις τῇ ψυχῇ τοῦ τόπου τοῦ ἐνθένδε εἰς ἄλλον τόπον (*Ap.* 40c7–9)

As they say, [death] happens to be some sort of change and relocation for the soul from the place here to another place

The Underworld in this dialogue is a separate place in a different region, like a foreign country, where all the dead congregate and live in a parallel society, undergoing judgment by supernatural judges and conversing with mythical and historical figures (*Ap.* 40c–41c). Like his predecessors, Plato borrows the basic premise of a geographical Underworld where the dead are sorted into groups. In Homer's Underworld of mindless dead in Book 11 of the *Odyssey,* the souls that Odysseus encounters come to him in separate groups that do not intermingle. The Greek leaders of the Trojan War do not appear with the dead heroines or with mythic Underworld figures like Minos. Book 24 of the *Odyssey* also portrays this segregation, with heroes congregating together as a distinct group to discuss their lives. Similarly, Hesiod's Ages of Man in the *Works and Days* presents different afterlife experiences for each generation of men. In this work and others, like Pindar's *Olympian* 2, certain heroes are allotted a privileged afterlife with a pleasant, carefree existence separate from other souls. With only a few allusions to these and other predecessors, Plato's character Socrates creates a fully realized Underworld scene in the *Apology,* which emphasizes that his Underworld portrayal of segregated souls is inherited from this long tradition. When he repeats the phrase τὰ λεγόμενα ("the things being said," *Ap.* 40e), Plato creates rapport with his audience as part of an insider group who already knows the references (cf. Pindar's συνετοῖσιν, "those in the know," *Ol.* 2.85). Moreover, the disclaimer of personal responsibility for the Underworld myth he presents deflects attention from his eschatological originality by coloring his entire mythic account with

Plato's Underworlds

the guise of ancient authority.[11] Such disclaimers give his stories authoritative status by making them impersonal. They are simply accepted as "things that are said" or "handed down" by a tradition and not invented by a single individual. Socrates' argument here is one by consensus, constructed so that the audience cannot blame or attack him for inconsistencies between his stories of the afterlife and others' because he denies any claim to being their author. Socrates never endorses the details, and he relies on this vagueness to underscore the authority of things that are "more or less true." In short, he gives little ground on which his critics can contend so his version stands.

Similarly, in his reference to judgment in the Underworld, Socrates combines strategic specificity with vague generality regarding who the judges are and how they work together, which mimics to some extent, the type of jury he faced in the real world (*Ap.* 41a). The specific judges he names are all mythic figures famous for being just leaders and favorites of the gods: Minos, Rhadamanthus, Aeacus, and Triptolemus (*Ap.* 41a3–4). The order is significant since Minos can be traced back to the *Odyssey* (11.568) as the golden-sceptered judge among the dead, whom Odysseus saw at a distance as he was about to leave the Underworld. Rhadamanthus, like Minos, has a prominent position among the dead for his abilities as a judge and was originally associated with those who received favorable judgments and lived in a blessed state with famous heroes. In Homer's *Odyssey*, he dwells in the Elysian plain where Menelaus eventually goes after death (*Od.* 4.561–569). In Pindar's *Olympian* 2, he issues decrees in the Isle of the Blessed, where heroes such as Achilles dwell in a blissful afterlife (*Ol.* 2.75–84). The two other judges mentioned do not appear as early as Minos and Rhadamanthus, and their addition speaks to Socrates' point that Underworld judgment occurs in a quasi-democratic style, with many opinions contributing to the outcome of judgment. All these judges, including the ones not explicitly named, are famous for being just kings when living and seem to continue these prominent roles in the

---

[11] Plato shows a similar pattern in two other Underworld scenes where he shifts responsibility from himself and his character Socrates for any idiosyncrasies onto unnamed, authoritative figures: (1) when he concludes the Underworld description in the *Phaedo* (τὸ μὲν οὖν ταῦτα διισχυρίσασθαι οὕτως ἔχειν ὡς ἐγὼ διελήλυθα, οὐ πρέπει νοῦν ἔχοντι ἀνδρί, "It's not fitting for the rational man to rely on the things I have described to be true," *Phd.* 114d1–2) and (2) when he is about to introduce the myth of the charioteer in the *Phaedrus* (οἷον μέν ἐστι, πάντῃ πάντως θείας εἶναι καὶ μακρᾶς διηγήσεως, ᾧ δὲ ἔοικεν, ἀνθρωπίνης τε καὶ ἐλάττονος, "[to describe] what [the soul] is, would be a very long account and a task entirely for the gods, but [to describe] what [the soul] is like, is humanly possible and of shorter duration," *Phdr.* 246a4–6).

218   LIFE / AFTERLIFE

afterlife, having been preselected based on their exemplary lives and discernment (Μίνως τε καὶ Ῥαδάμανθυς καὶ Αἰακὸς καὶ Τριπτόλεμος καὶ ἄλλοι ὅσοι τῶν ἡμιθέων δίκαιοι ἐγένοντο ἐν τῷ ἑαυτῶν βίῳ, "Minos, Rhadamanthus, Aeacus, and Triptolemos and as many other demigods who were just during their life," *Ap.* 41a3–5).[12] Through them, Socrates emphasizes a connection between just deeds in life and rewards in the afterlife, since these judges were famous partly for having uninterrupted favor with the gods and prestige among men, a status they carried with them after death.

In this list of judges, Socrates projects the type of Underworld that his audience is already familiar with from the famous Underworlds in Archaic poetry while also shifting the focus to "afterlife judgment and justice," a popular theme in fifth century BCE visual and dramatic representations, particularly in comedy. Socrates tries to reclaim the blessed afterlife from the expectations of privilege and divine favor, focusing instead on individuals' deeds in life and whether they adhere to practices that are just and part of a philosophical lifestyle. He then provides an Underworld model in which he, a private individual, interacts with famous men, including mythic heroes *because* of the decision of the judges. Through the network of Underworld scenes he evokes, Socrates presents a vision of himself as having been favorably assessed by the Underworld judges and enjoying a blessed eternity mingling with famous poets and heroes. By such a portrayal, Plato shows that a philosopher such as Socrates can have an afterlife outcome and level of glory through philosophical inquiry equivalent to what Homeric heroes attained through deeds on the battlefield.

Cultivation of the soul during life is presented as particularly important in the *Apology* because judgment is treated as a capstone experience to life—a single chance for correct afterlife assignment. In the final sections of the *Apology*, Socrates describes an Underworld society that "corrects" the injustices of the real world through characters that are associated with the mythic afterlife:

ἀφικόμενος εἰς Ἅιδου, ἀπαλλαγεὶς τουτωνὶ τῶν φασκόντων δικαστῶν εἶναι, εὑρήσει τοὺς ὡς ἀληθῶς δικαστάς, οἵπερ καὶ λέγονται ἐκεῖ δικάζειν,

---

[12] Although Aeacus is a famous king and ancestor of Greek heroes as early as *Nemean* 8.6–12, he does not appear as a judge of the Underworld until the fourth century BCE in Plato's *Apology* and *Gorgias* and in Isocrates' *Evagoras* 9.15. Triptolemus is one of the lords of Eleusis to whom Demeter shows the Eleusinian rites in the *Homeric Hymn to Demeter* (473–479). He is said to give true judgments and administer justice but is not mentioned as doing so in the Underworld until Plato.

Μίνως τε καὶ Ῥαδάμανθυς καὶ Αἰακὸς καὶ Τριπτόλεμος καὶ ἄλλοι ὅσοι τῶν ἡμιθέων δίκαιοι ἐγένοντο ἐν τῷ ἑαυτῶν βίῳ ... (*Apology*, 41a1–5)

When anyone arrives in Hades, after having escaped from those calling themselves jurymen here, he will discover the true jurymen, who indeed are said even to pass judgment there—Minos and Rhadamanthus and Aeacus and Triptolemos and the other demigods who were just during their own lives [on earth] ...

After alluding to an Underworld of judgment, Socrates asserts that he expects to be placed by the judges among revered individuals and blessed heroes in the afterlife, claiming that he would both "keep company further with Orpheus and Musaeus and Hesiod and Homer" (*Ap.* 41a6) and converse regularly with "Palamedes and Ajax son of Telamon and many others of old" to compare their similar experiences of unjust conviction while alive (*Ap.* 41b1–4).[13] The long list of mythic figures rhetorically implies that the names mentioned are only a sample of the many people with whom Socrates sees himself conversing in the afterlife.

In this passage, Socrates presents the idea of a segregated Underworld society, similar to that of the heroic race in Hesiod's Ages of Man (*Op.* 156–174), in which some heroes are taken to the Isles of the Blessed, while others are not. There are also echoes here from the *nekuia* of *Odyssey* 24 (*Od.* 24.1–204), in which the souls of famous figures congregate to discuss their lives. In this example, Underworld society is portrayed as superior to that of Athens because only there in the chthonic realm would true justice for Socrates' case be accomplished. This blessed Underworld, therefore, is not just Socrates' reward for leading a good life; it is also a correction to the injustice of his conviction (Annas 1982, 122–123).

Through the "positive" afterlife motif of newly arrived souls conversing with famous mythic figures in the afterlife and the naming of poets associated with famous Underworld scenes, Socrates links the *Apology* to the Underworlds of earlier poetry. In this dialogue, he starts from the premise that life and afterlife are inevitably connected so that actions in one affect

---

[13] No specific Underworld story involving Musaeus is known, but he is thought to have written a Hymn to Demeter, as had Orpheus, which would have involved the story of Persephone and the Eleusinian Mysteries (Currie 2011, 190). Besides being a poet pre-dating Homer, Orpheus was also famous for his *katabasis* to Hades. By generating an Underworld scene himself, Socrates joins their ranks and further equates himself with them, taking on similar authority as both an author and protagonist.

outcomes in the other. Unlike Pindar's patrons, however, Socrates does not seek heroization with song or cult to be considered worthy of that *makar*-type afterlife akin to the lifestyle of the gods. He expects a blessed afterlife because he anticipates that the judges of the afterlife will reward him for the way he lived his life (i.e., as a philosopher), and he will thus enjoy an eternity with famous figures from myth and history, untroubled by the pressures of time or access. No other known source configures the Underworld quite as Socrates does in the *Apology*, and he consolidates the patchwork of elements from different authors even further in the *Gorgias*.

The Importance of Judgment in the *Gorgias*

Plato expands on his vision of afterlife judgment further in the *Gorgias* by having the character Socrates introduce an Underworld scene with a quote from Euripides that creates the equation "death = life and life = death" (*Grg.* 492e–493a). The impact of such a statement is that a person who crosses the boundary between the two states of existence remains essentially intact, carrying all his psychic faculties, strengths, and foibles with him.[14] Furthermore, at this point in the dialogue, Socrates uses this equation to argue that one can predict afterlife experiences through examination of the living. To demonstrate this concept fully, he introduces two very different Underworld scenes in the *Gorgias*, whose common denominator is the fact that a person's afterlife depends on his actions in life. In the earlier Underworld scene, Socrates describes a folktale that he says originated in Italy or Sicily and features water-bearers whose leaky jars represent the soul:

> καὶ ἡμεῖς τῷ ὄντι ἴσως τέθναμεν· ἤδη γάρ του ἔγωγε καὶ
> ἤκουσα τῶν σοφῶν ὡς νῦν ἡμεῖς τέθναμεν καὶ τὸ μὲν
> σῶμά ἐστιν ἡμῖν σῆμα, τῆς δὲ ψυχῆς τοῦτο ἐν ᾧ ἐπι-
> θυμίαι εἰσὶ τυγχάνει ὃν οἷον ἀναπείθεσθαι καὶ μεταπίπτειν
> ἄνω κάτω, καὶ τοῦτο ἄρα τις μυθολογῶν κομψὸς ἀνήρ, ἴσως (5)
> Σικελός τις ἢ Ἰταλικός, παράγων τῷ ὀνόματι διὰ τὸ πιθανὸν
> τε καὶ πειστικὸν ὠνόμασε πίθον ... (*Grg.* 493a1–7)

---

[14] This idea of the persistence of identity and self-awareness after death became popular during the fifth century BCE at all levels of society as spaces were made for the dead in the daily life of the living (re. Chapter 5). By making death and life equivalent, Socrates creates an analogy between the uninitiated in the myth and the unphilosophical among the living (Linforth 1944, 7). These negative states point to faults in the souls of these groups.

Plato's Underworlds 221

And we likewise are dead in reality; for I've even heard already one of the wise men [saying] that now we are dead and our body is a tomb, but that the part of the soul in which our appetitive desires happen to be is the type of thing which is persuadable and shifts to and fro; and therefore this [part] some clever, mythologizing man, perhaps some Sicilian or Italian, named a *pithos* jar, misleading by means of the name, because of its plausible and persuasive character... [15]

At face value, this passage does not seem connected to the famous Underworld scenes of Homer and Hesiod, yet there are strong hints of such a connection, especially when Socrates claims authority for his account by referring to "wise men" as well as a "clever" Sicilian or Italian man. While the phrase "wise men" indicates a group of people who are not only learned but also in agreement, the latter reference may point to Pythagoreanism in light of Plato's own recent journey to Italy (Linforth 1944, 305–311; Blank 1991, 28).

Plato seems to have invented this Underworld tale wholesale. Ivan Linforth (1944, 311–312) argues that Plato presents it as a secondhand report of an allegorical myth because Socrates elsewhere opposes such mythical allegories as the work of an "exceedingly clever" man (λίαν δὲ δεινοῦ, *Phdr.* 229d3–4) who also happens to be unfortunate in his creative storytelling abilities. In this line of thinking, Plato might prefer to show Socrates hedging instead of caught in a contradiction with something he said elsewhere.

Another explanation for this roundabout introduction to an Underworld scene, however, is that Plato has no such qualms about presenting contradictory language but instead uses often opposed elements from the afterlife image set to build a network of intertextual links to other familiar Underworld accounts. His choice of a "Sicilian or Italian" protagonist, for example, recalls the Pythagoreans and Orphics whose eschatological beliefs flourished in those regions.[16] Since Socrates' myth focuses on the fate of the soul, the audience can be expected to connect it to the most famous eschatological ideas of that region.

Although he deviates from the Homeric Underworld scene framework in this passage, Socrates still subtly evokes it through his characterization of the myth's source. His focus on the identity of the man in this passage—his

---

[15] I follow Blank's (1991, 25–26) interpretation of this difficult phrase.

[16] For a discussion on possible Orphic influence in Plato's Underworlds, see Bernabé Pajares (2013).

cleverness (κομψός), story-telling ability (μυθολογῶν), nationality, and lack of a name—coupled with the eschatological theme creates an allusion to another clever storyteller, who often does not self-identify at first: the many-wiled (πολύτροπος), cunning (πολύμητις) Odysseus, whose heroic status is tied to his persuasive speech and audience-adapted identities. David Blank's (1991, 24–25) observation that the word Plato uses for cleverness (κομψός) has the negative connotation of "trickiness" further supports this man's resemblance to Odysseus, who uses his wits to trick those he encounters. Furthermore, the word μυθολογῶν (*Grg.* 493a) also brings Homer and his epics to mind, as it seems to be a technical term for Socrates when referring to poets. Elsewhere, Socrates castigates poets like Hesiod and Homer by name for being "myth-tellers," using a similar expression to describe what they do (e.g., μυθολογητέον, *Resp.* 2.378c4; μεμυθολογημένα, *Resp.* 2.378e3). By classifying this unknown Sicilian or Italian with the same word for "myth-teller," Socrates associates him with other myth-tellers, such as Homer and Odysseus, and trusts his readers to do the same.

Socrates has an ambivalent relationship with such myth-tellers across his dialogues, but here in the *Gorgias* he uses one to support his argumentation, counting on the reader to see the connection. Although the introduction of the water-carrier myth at this point may be "more a rhetorical gambit than a part of the argument" (K.A. Morgan 2000, 189), it lays a foundation of intertextual links for the subsequent Underworld passage. For example, the leaky jar motif links to the myth of the Danaïds as a *para-narrative*, with the image of the appetitive soul mirroring these sinners' eternal punishment of forever carrying leaky jars. Plato's Underworld myths thus work as embedded rhetorical strategies not only because they are supported by logical inference but also because they provide a separate register of discourse via a common language to communicate the values encoded in his arguments.

In the *Gorgias'* second Underworld scene, Socrates uses the more recognizable features of the mythic Greek Underworld, depicting it as the same geographical and political place that his poetic predecessors did.[17] He describes an afterlife that has elements from Homer and Hesiod but does not exactly match the original sources. He alters and embellishes the details in a similar fashion to the "clever, mythologizing man" of the earlier Underworld myth, alluding to several traditional concepts such as the division of the cosmos, the Golden Age of man, the Isles of the Blessed, and judgment by Minos and

---

[17] For a discussion on the political structures represented in Underworld scenes, see Herrero de Jáuregui (2021).

Plato's Underworlds

Rhadamanthus. This index of familiar topoi activates narratives from several epic sources in a rapid, dizzying succession that obscures his alterations.

Socrates introduces his second afterlife myth with the phrase "just as Homer says" to describe the division of the three cosmic realms after the Titans' defeat (*Grg.* 523a), yet he does not pursue the Homeric representation of the afterlife:

> ὥσπερ γὰρ Ὅμηρος λέγει, διενείμαντο τὴν ἀρχὴν ὁ Ζεὺς καὶ ὁ Ποσειδῶν καὶ ὁ Πλούτων, ἐπειδὴ παρὰ τοῦ πατρὸς παρέλαβον. (*Grg.* 523a3–5)

> For just as Homer says, Zeus, Poseidon, and Pluto divided the realm, when they took it over from their father.

In this passage, Socrates refers to the generational struggle familiar from Hesiod's *Theogony* but then recasts it by presenting the relationship between Cronus and Zeus as more collaborative than antagonistic. Without pause or closure between the Homeric quote and his own account, Socrates describes the divine succession as a continuum between the two eras of Zeus and Cronus rather than a strict division. This transition of power from the Titans to the Olympians is framed as a simple matter of inheritance (ἐπειδὴ παρὰ τοῦ πατρὸς παρέλαβον, "when they took it over from their father," *Grg.* 523a5). The verb παρέλαβον means "take over or inherit" in the context of succession and does not suggest the violence and cosmic upheaval with which such succession occurred, as told in Hesiod's *Theogony*. By altering the relationships under the guise of authority, Socrates sets up the reconciliation between the divine generations that allows an afterlife dually governed, with different sections for the sinners and the "blessed," even to the present day (*Grg.* 523a5–b4). By placing the quote in the introduction of the myth, he extends the influence of the phrase "just as Homer says" and the authority that the poet's name conveys over his entire narrative.

The division of the three realms to which Socrates refers, however, is verifiable and can be traced to Homer's *Iliad*:

> τρεῖς γάρ τ' ἐκ Κρόνου εἰμὲν ἀδελφεοὶ οὓς τέκετο Ῥέα
> Ζεὺς καὶ ἐγώ, τρίτατος δ' Ἀΐδης ἐνέροισιν ἀνάσσων.
> τριχθὰ δὲ πάντα δέδασται, ἕκαστος δ' ἔμμορε τιμῆς·
> ἤτοι ἐγὼν ἔλαχον πολιὴν ἅλα ναιέμεν αἰεὶ (190)
> παλλομένων, Ἀΐδης δ' ἔλαχε ζόφον ἠερόεντα,
> Ζεὺς δ' ἔλαχ' οὐρανὸν εὐρὺν ἐν αἰθέρι καὶ νεφέλῃσι. (*Il.* 15.187–192)

224 LIFE / AFTERLIFE

> For we are three brothers, sons of Cronus, whom Rhea bore—Zeus
> and I, and the third is Hades, who rules the ones below.
> And everything was divided into three parts, and each received his
> share of honor;
> and I indeed, when the lots were shaken, obtained the grey sea to
> dwell in always,
> but Hades obtained by lot the murky gloom, and Zeus won the broad
> heaven in the air and clouds.

By looking at this passage, it becomes apparent that Socrates alters the quote from the *Iliad* and in Hesiod's narrative account of divine succession. In Homer, the three gods who divide the realm are Zeus, Poseidon, and Hades. As he starts his myth, Socrates makes one small, but significant change, replacing Hades with Pluto as the lord of the third realm. Although Hades and Pluto by this period were thought of as the same god, Socrates chooses to diverge from the original name to privilege the latter, with its slightly different connotations of meaning. By activating the link referring to the Iliadic passage but altering the language from the source, Socrates rewrites Homer's divisions of the cosmos, introduces the idea of allotment creating separate outcomes for different individuals, and highlights that the proper place for Pluto is in the Underworld, where true wealth is a reward given to the souls of the pious in the form of a blessed afterlife.[18]

Although the two are associated, Hades and Pluto are not interchangeable in the Archaic myths to which Socrates alludes.[19] Homer never refers to Pluto the god, and the first mention of this divine embodiment of "wealth" comes in Hesiod. In the *Theogony* (969–975), Hesiod describes Pluto as a son of Demeter who bestows much wealth (ὄλβον) on any man he encounters (*Theog.* 969–973). The substitution cannot be careless on Socrates' part, a

---

[18] Afterlife judgment is only implied in Homer when Odysseus mentions glimpsing Minos and eternally punished sinners at the end of Book 11 of the *Odyssey*, but no vision of a positive afterlife is offered to regular men there. In the *Odyssey*, Menelaus alone escapes the gloomy Underworld of his peers and only then because he is related to Zeus by marriage.

[19] The idea of Pluto as "wealth" comes up later in the myth during the era of improper judgments. From Cronus' through the beginning of Zeus' reign, living men donned the visible trappings of wealth right before they died, distracting the afterlife judges from their sinful lives to the point that they were not able to categorize men correctly for punishment and reward (*Grg.* 543b–544a). Beautiful bodies with visible signs of riches were deemed to be the problem because judges could not see past these superficial adornments, so Zeus changed the system to post-mortem judgment of souls *without* bodies, removing material wealth from the equation of judgment. "Wealth" as related to bodies was cosmically problematic because it obscured the truth about the soul's piety during life.

Plato's Underworlds 225

close reader and critic of his sources.[20] Instead, Socrates likely links his narrative to this second passage from Hesiod and reads it in conjunction with the one from Homer. The word *olbon* in the latter, while simply meaning "wealth" in its Archaic context, had a different connotation for Plato's audience. It not only meant "wealth" in the earthly sense but also in afterlife blessedness coming from divine favor.[21]

This allusion to the Pluto passage of Hesiod is further supported by the next sentence in which Socrates makes direct references to Isles of the Blessed and the "Ages of Man" passage from Hesiod's *Works and Days*:

> ἦν οὖν νόμος ὅδε περὶ ἀνθρώπων ἐπὶ Κρόνου, καὶ ἀεὶ καὶ νῦν ἔτι ἔστιν ἐν θεοῖς, τῶν ἀνθρώπων τὸν μὲν δικαίως τὸν βίον διελθόντα καὶ ὁσίως, ἐπειδὰν τελευτήσῃ, εἰς **μακάρων νήσους** ἀπιόντα οἰκεῖν ἐν πάσῃ εὐδαιμονίᾳ ἐκτὸς κακῶν ... (*Grg.* 523a5–b2)

> This was the law then concerning men during the reign of Cronus, and even still now among the gods it is ever [the law], that when a man who has lived his life justly and devoutly dies, he goes to the **Isles of the Blessed** to live in complete happiness apart from ills ...

In this passage, Socrates conflates Hesiod's Golden Race, which occurred under Cronus' rule, with the Race of Heroes. In the latter period, some heroes were sent by Cronus' successor Zeus to the Isles of the Blessed where existence and ease of living were similar to what Golden Age men experienced (*Op.* 168–173).

Another connection between these two ages of men in Hesiod is that Cronus is established by Zeus to be the sovereign over the Isles of the Blessed, a fact which Socrates glosses over later by referring only vaguely to the rulers of this place as "the minders from the Isles of the Blessed" (οἱ ἐπιμεληταὶ οἱ ἐκ μακάρων νήσων, *Grg.* 523b7–8), who act as counterpoint to Pluto, the ruler of the "sinner" section of the Underworld. By not naming Cronus the ruler of the Isles of the Blessed as in the Hesiodic source, Socrates weakens Cronus' prominence and emphasizes a strong difference (with a more peaceful transition) between the times of Cronus and Zeus, presenting the latter as overseeing a

---

[20] See Boys-Stones and Haubold (2010) for an exploration of Plato's deep, often overlooked connections to Hesiod, particularly as a practitioner of didactic myth.

[21] See the discussion of *olbios* versus *makar* in Chapter 3.

more just system of afterlife judgment. In short, Plato gives a "parable of progress" (Sedley 2009, 56–58). Moreover, by linking to the Race of Heroes and Isles of the Blessed as *para-narratives*, Socrates gains access to the combined ideas of afterlife judgment and continued existence for a chosen few, which only occurs during this epoch. In the other ages, death does not lead to sorting or individual judgment, and all the dead of a certain race, save that of heroes, share the same fate.

With these revisions to the Homeric and Hesiodic afterlife myths, Socrates then creates an original myth of judgment that has just enough direct and indirect references to keep it tied to traditional sources, thereby giving it the sheen of authority. With such clear allusions to Homer, Hesiod, and other sources, it is easy for his reader to forget that Socrates' myth has almost no traditional basis in them, since these sources do not give the same solution to favorable judgment that he does: the practice of philosophy.

At various points, Socrates even seems to find it necessary to reiterate a claim of authority for his new Underworld account, using the repetition as a form of argumentation. He says, "Homer too bears witness to these things" (μαρτυρεῖ δὲ τούτοις καὶ Ὅμηρος, *Grg.* 525d6) and later directly cites a line from the *Nekuia* (*Od.* 11.569) at the close of the myth, after repeating the names of the places and Underworld judges one more time (*Grg.* 526b–d). Socrates' insertion of these citations borrows epic authority to support a new, broader vision of afterlife judgment that he has just invented and applies it by granting special status to those who have lived justly, particularly philosophers. Since the Archaic epics do not approach the same level of detail concerning Underworld judgment or the fate of the soul, Socrates' narrative is able to fill in areas of the Underworld's murky space without seeming to disrupt it, even while also redirecting its links to promote living a philosophical life as a new form of heroic *arete*.

Finally, although he has just done the type of mythologizing through slight changes of meaning that the "clever" Italian or Sicilian man does in the first Underworld scene, Socrates denies his story as an act of mythologizing. He recategorizes what he creates from *muthos* to *logos*, introducing his second Underworld myth by saying it is specifically a *logos* and not a *muthos* (Ἄκουε δή, φασί, μάλα καλοῦ λόγου, ὃν σὺ μὲν ἡγήσῃ μῦθον, ὡς ἐγὼ οἶμαι, ἐγὼ δὲ λόγον, "Listen, indeed, as they say, to a very fine account, which you will think a myth, but I think is an account," *Grg.* 523a1–2).[22] Midway through,

---

[22] This designation echoes Hesiod's introduction to the Ages of Man passage, which is also introduced as a *logos* (Εἰ δ᾽ ἐθέλεις, ἕτερόν τοι ἐγὼ λόγον ἐκκορυφώσω εὖ καὶ ἐπισταμένως, "and if you want, I will summarize for you another account well and skillfully," *Op.* 106–107)

Plato's Underworlds 227

Socrates gives additional force to his Underworld account by saying that he trusts his portrayal of the afterlife to be true because it is what he himself has "heard" (Ταῦτ' ἔστιν, ὦ Καλλίκλεις, ἃ ἐγὼ ἀκηκοὼς πιστεύω ἀληθῆ εἶναι, "This is, Callicles, what I have heard and trust to be true," *Grg.* 524a7–b1). The unnamed source and the inclusion above of an unnamed "they" can be interpreted as a reference to traditional Athenian education or, at the very least, Socrates' reliance on inherited wisdom that is authoritative.

To drive home the point, Socrates concludes the scene by again calling it a *logos* that has convinced him, even though he himself invented it (ἐγὼ μὲν οὖν, ὦ Καλλίκλεις, ὑπό τε τούτων τῶν λόγων πέπεισμαι, "Callicles, I indeed have been persuaded by these accounts," *Grg.* 526d2–3). The use of the passive without a named agent allows Socrates' authorship to disappear. He thus sets up Callicles, his interlocutors, and his readers in such a way that any objection to the Underworld myth of judgment he just proposed would sound like a direct attack on the authority of Homer and Hesiod as well as on the official sources from whom he has allegedly heard such accounts. Because he has linked these authoritative narratives to his own, dismissing his would create a chain reaction that would dismiss the others operating in the background as well. Socrates' message is that while Homer and Hesiod write *muthoi, he* presents *logoi,* a more rational, accurate account. Knowing the importance of *muthoi,* he leverages them to support his *logoi* and covers his bases by suggesting that anyone who challenges his reasoning would also have to contend with tradition itself. [23]

In both the *Apology* and the *Gorgias,* the Underworld acts as a place where true justice is meted out. The Underworld configurations in these two dialogues, particularly the *Gorgias,* may be because of the concern with Socrates' trial and its unjust verdict (Annas 1982, 122). Socrates presents himself as unafraid of afterlife judgment because he knows he has cultivated his soul properly through philosophy and will acquit himself well before the judges (*Grg.* 524d). He connects his pure life to a blessed afterlife since his soul is unblemished. This is unlike the souls that are whip-scarred by their

---

[23] Lincoln (1999, 37–40) notes that Plato rarely uses *muthoi* because he sees them as connected to poetry, which he views as inferior to philosophy. Lincoln further notes that Plato thinks poetry "appeals to the basest part of the human soul" and that their *muthoi* are meant for those who cannot engage in philosophic reasoning, such as "women, children, and the lower strata." Edmonds (2012, 166), on the other hand, argues that Plato's employment of mythic details in Underworld scenes are crucial illustrations in "vivid and graphic terms" of the workings of Socratic *elenchos* because the myths help clarify the dialectic argumentation.

acts of perjury and injustice, whose marks stay on their soul into the afterlife (*Grg.* 524c–525a). In the Underworld scene he himself has created, Socrates writes himself into the narrative of a hero enjoying a carefree afterlife on the Isles of the Blessed.

Although Socrates' arguments challenge some aspects of the underlying ideologies of the Homeric and Hesiodic Underworld scenes, he maintains the basic configuration of his cultural and literary predecessors: a "positive" Underworld containing a stratified society in a different *chronotope* that exists in parallel to the real world. In the *Apology* and *Gorgias*, he highlights actions in life as important factors in afterlife outcome, as does Pindar, but he moves away from the Classical Athenian model of continuous, regular inter-action between the living and the dead. Plato's additions and modifications to afterlife society expand the Underworld-scene network by inserting new points of connection between existing Underworld scenes and his uniquely configured afterlife scheme, which reflects his dialectic arguments privileging philosophers. In these dialogues, Plato creates links that cast philosophers as the new "heroes"—and Socrates the premier "special hero"—replacing the demi-gods of myth, the divinely favored wealthy, the poetically immortalized *laudandus*, and the cult initiate. The demarcation between life and death, however, remains binary, and individuals can expect only a single life and af-terlife, two states separated by a single judgment.

III. *Mapping Morality into the* Phaedo's Underworld Chronotope

In the *Phaedo*, Plato adjusts his messages about the soul's afterlife existence, moving further away from his sources as he starts to introduce and incorpo-rate the idea of metempsychosis into his Underworld scenes. Nevertheless, he still refers to the traditional mythic Underworld throughout his narratives as a start to lay claim to their authority and give implicit sanction to his own eschatological accounts. With metempsychosis, the soul's lifecycle extends beyond a single life and afterlife. Plato may have borrowed this idea from the Pythagoreans, but he, like Pindar, places his souls in a setting that resembles the Underworld of heroes, as described by Homer and Hesiod.

To synthesize these traditional Underworld images, Plato's Socrates makes adjustments to the Underworld *chronotope* to compensate for the fact that each soul will repeat its journey to the afterlife many times and can adjust its location there by how it chooses to act during its cycles of life on earth. Although rewards in a blessed afterlife and severe punishment in Tartarus still remain, as in his earlier sources, Socrates adds new temporary states of existence within the afterlife to represent a range between these extremes and also makes a soul's residence in any of these levels less permanent—even for those who achieve the afterlife of the "blessed." In the course of these dialogues, it emerges that the philosopher's soul is most suited to mitigating the negative aspects of the cycle.

In tinkering with the traditional Underworld, Plato calibrates its topography and temporality to the human scale so that the chronotopes of the real world and the Underworld are experienced in a chronological cycle, which can be tracked through the movement of souls through space. Socrates anchors the Underworld firmly to real time so that decisions in each phase of existence have results across the life–death boundary.[24] Rather than making history "ephemeral" in light of the eternal fate of the soul (Shilo 2013 Section 53), Plato's configuration locks the migration of souls to time, writ large, in a positivist structure where individual evolution can occur but the past continues to have a hold on the present and future.

In earlier authors, the literary Underworld offered entry into a different chronotope, and souls were generally depicted as having a parallel but nonoverlapping existence with the living. Of course, circular and repetitive time still exists in Socrates' accounts, as incurable sinners undergo an endless loop of suffering and souls continue to cycle through Underworld punishment or reward until eventual rebirth. These processes, however, are subject to deadlines that are calculated in chronological time in the dialogues featuring metempsychosis, such as the *Phaedo* and *Republic*.

Unlike in most early Underworlds, souls in the *Phaedo* are subject to aspects of time and challenges of space that are familiar to the living. Despite each person's potential to ensure his soul a good afterlife, once he arrives in the Underworld, the processes applied to souls—time, judgments, punishments, and rewards—move like clockwork: they are carried out impersonally with almost no loopholes or chances for appeal. Moments of opportunity are built into the system but appear infrequently at designated intervals, allowing escape only on rare occasions under predetermined conditions. For example, souls whose sins are curable undergo punishment in Tartarus for exactly one year (ἐνιαυτόν), after which a current carries them out to appeal their cases

---

[24] Shilo (2013 Section 53) argues that "history becomes the ephemeral as opposed to the eternal fate of the soul." I argue instead that Plato's main goal in the *Phaedo*'s Underworld myth is to align the soul's fate to its history in the world, even when that history occurs over eons.

(*Phd.* 114a). Any special treatment for souls is based more on their personal actions, rather than their pedigree or divine favor. Socrates asserts that following one's guardian spirit without vacillation gives souls a chance to avoid unpleasantness on the initial journey to judgment (*Phd.* 108a–c). Those souls, in turn, are most likely to escape the darker regions of the world to dwell on the pure surface of the earth, although they may still be subject to rebirth since they have bodies (*Phd.* 114b–c). The only souls who completely escape the cycle are those purified by philosophy, who attain a higher level of existence in the hollows of the earth than any other group, including traditional heroes (*Phd.* 114c).

Additionally, Plato references Archaic sources in the *Phaedo*'s Underworld scene, as he did in the *Apology* and *Gorgias*, but he adds elements that make them vastly different. He borrows just enough detail to link his myth of a blessed, misty race of mortals to that of Hesiod's Golden Race, suggesting to his audience that the two myths should be read together. Then, through his character Socrates, he recalibrates a timeline borrowed from Hesiod's "Ages of Man" in the *Works and Days* by presenting members of different races as existing simultaneously rather than chronologically. A Golden Age in which humans interact with gods thus exists during the *same* timeframe as that of regular mortals living now (*Phd.* 111). In Hesiod's scheme, mortals living now would be in the Iron Age with the Golden Age only a distinct memory and completely inaccessible. In the *Phaedo*, however, there is just one epoch instead of successive ages of man. After saying that he and his audience "live in a certain hollow of the earth while imagining [they] live on the surface of it" (οἰκοῦντας γὰρ ἔν τινι κοίλῳ τῆς γῆς οἴεσθαι ἐπάνω αὐτῆς οἰκεῖν, *Phd.* 109d6–7), Socrates goes on to describe the actual surface, where a different group of men lives in a purer, more beautiful environment (*Phd.* 111a–c). The marker that such a place is blessed is that immortals also dwell there, using the temples as second homes (*Phd.* 111b).

In addition, some of these lucky mortals live on islands in the upper realm surrounded by air (τοὺς δ' ἐν νήσοις ἃς περιρρεῖν τὸν ἀέρα πρὸς τῇ ἠπείρῳ οὔσας, *Phd.* 111a6–7). This passage echoes Hesiod's description of the Golden Race, whose men live "just as gods live without a care in their hearts" (ὥστε θεοὶ δ' ἔζωον ἀκηδέα θυμὸν ἔχοντες, *Op.* 112). After their deaths, the Golden Race's fate was to become guardians of men who are "clothed in air going everywhere on the earth" (ἠέρα ἑσσάμενοι πάντη φοιτῶντες ἐπ' αἶαν, *Op.* 125). Socrates downplays the change in state of the Golden Race between their blessed lives and misty afterlives but preserves the recognizable attributes

Plato's Underworlds

of this god-like society of mortals, such as their carefree existence and association with the medium of flowing air (ἀήρ). Thus, in his description of the earth's many layers, he borrows Hesiod's idea of the succession of races as a hierarchy of mortals who are defined by the places where they live and their relationships to the gods. After creating a sense of déjà vu and authority through descriptions linking to this famous source, Plato completely changes the narrative by stacking the races in a simultaneous, interconnected space so that all are subject to the same chronology and tied to the same cosmic locality. The purer or more blessed men are not from the past but are simply the ones residing "above" in the upper realms with the gods, while lesser creatures, such as regular men, animals, and the dead, are assigned to hollows and lower regions.

The descriptions of each location of men and their lifestyles resonate with the common language of traditional Underworld scenes enough to lull the audience into complacency. Socrates' versions end, however, with a fundamental rearrangement of the narrative chronotope that drastically changes the meaning of each detail so that the audience exits with a vision of the Underworld that is different from the one they had upon entering. This "ecological eschatology," as Andrea Nightingale (2002) calls it, rearranges the relationship between man and his world by embedding ethical meaning into the landscapes through which the souls move. In such an environment, significant nonhuman beings and inanimate entities, such as those found in the natural world, "have histories of their own, most of which predate human history" (Nightingale 2002, 241–242). Further, this movement through space marks and is marked by temporal intervals. Socrates formulates the *Phaedo* with the basic assumption that the immortal soul is an entity subject to chronological time. This seems like a small detail, yet it has significant repercussions for the Underworld chronotope and its premise that the cosmos is constituted of separate realms. Because the soul is the protagonist of his Underworld scenes, its chronological experiences are tied to its movement through the physical world during its life and afterlife. The time it takes for a soul in the afterlife to improve its standing is analogized to the time the soul devotes to improving itself through just deeds and activities, including the practice of philosophy, during life. The soul's awareness of time and space thus strongly anchors and connects the Underworld chronotope to human time, giving extra weight to how men spend their time on earth.

On entering his Underworld discussion in the *Phaedo*, Socrates first makes the experience of the soul relatable and personal to his listeners by

232   LIFE / AFTERLIFE

showing that their souls are an extension of their living identities and that people can cultivate their souls while alive to control which path they take in the Underworld:

οὐδὲν γὰρ ἄλλο ἔχουσα εἰς Ἅιδου ἡ ψυχὴ ἔρχεται πλὴν τῆς παιδείας τε καὶ τροφῆς, ἃ δὴ καὶ μέγιστα λέγεται ὠφελεῖν ἢ βλάπτειν τὸν τελευτήσαντα εὐθὺς ἐν ἀρχῇ τῆς ἐκεῖσε πορείας. (*Phd.* 107d2–5)

For the soul goes to Hades having nothing else except its education and upbringing, which indeed are said to most benefit or harm the one who died, right at the beginning of his journey there.

In this passage, Socrates envisions the soul, fortified only with its training, as having the same reactions, emotions, and sensations as if it were still in a body. The soul even feels the passage of time because it must go through stages of punishment and reward on its way to rebirth. He claims through the passive λέγεται to have received this fact about the soul through an authoritative source, one who is a universally known (although unnamed) individual. This passage additionally suggests that the soul's whole experience is based on where it starts its journey, since it is sorted into a specific neighborhood after judgment. Afterlife location thus corresponds to the state of a person's soul when he was alive during his most recent incarnation.

Instead of the traditional portrayal of three equidistant realms as separate, stacked layers that are generally inaccessible to each other (except for boundary-crossing gods and special heroes), Plato's Socrates describes vertical incursions between the layers in the form of "hollows," which create an interwoven landscape connecting different layers of topography as well as different states of being, regardless of whether a particular level houses the living or the dead (*Phd.* 111c–d). By presenting these conduits as a fact of nature and reality, the philosopher can refute the binary category of life versus death and argue that the soul's immortality allows continuous movement through these natural environments and states of being.

Thus, the pock-marked sphere of Plato's Underworld has a purpose, with hollows that are interconnected to each other and that correspond to different states of existence for mortals (*Phd.* 109a–111c). When he comes to explaining the nature of the hollows in the Underworld, Socrates inserts a quote from Homer's *Iliad* to tie his description of the cosmos to an authoritative source. The purpose of this is to link the two geographies so that Homer's myth of the Underworld acts as a *para-narrative*, shadowing the forthcoming one:

Plato's Underworlds

μέγιστον τυγχάνει ὂν καὶ διαμπερὲς τετρημένον δι᾿ ὅλης τῆς γῆς, τοῦτο ὅπερ Ὅμηρος εἶπε, λέγων αὐτό "**τῆλε μάλ᾿, ἧχι βάθιστον ὑπὸ χθονός ἐστι βέρεθρον**: ὃ καὶ ἄλλοθι καὶ ἐκεῖνος καὶ ἄλλοι πολλοὶ τῶν ποιητῶν Τάρταρον κεκλήκασιν. εἰς γὰρ τοῦτο τὸ χάσμα συρρέουσί τε πάντες οἱ ποταμοὶ καὶ ἐκ τούτου πάλιν ἐκρέουσιν: γίγνονται δὲ ἕκαστοι τοιοῦτοι δι᾿ οἵας ἂν καὶ τῆς γῆς ῥέωσιν. (*Phd.* 112a1–6)

One of the hollows, which is also the biggest, is bored right through the entire earth. This is the one of which Homer spoke, when he said the following: "**very far away, where the deepest pit under the earth is**"; and which elsewhere he and many other poets have called Tartarus. For all the rivers flow together into this void and out of it they flow back again; and they each have the nature of the land through which they also flow."

Besides Homer, Socrates refers here to "many other poets" whom he enlists as authorities in naming this Underworld region "Tartarus." Socrates asserts a connection between the space called Tartarus by an unnamed multitude of famous poets and the great hollow he just described, which the audience is invited to think of as the *same* Tartarus. The audience is then introduced to a topography that has other names familiar from Archaic descriptions of the Underworld, such as the rivers Acheron, Styx, Pyriphlegethon, and Cocytus (*Phd.* 113a–c). In reference to Cocytus, Socrates says that the river he describes is the same one "as the poets say" (ὡς οἱ ποιηταὶ λέγουσιν, *Phd.* 113c8), again reiterating the coincidence of his Underworld geography with that of Underworld scenes from traditional myth. This affirms that Socrates' description is within his audience's knowledge base and suggests he is only reminding his interlocutors of things they already know rather than introducing something new.

The details surrounding Socrates' corresponding landmarks, however, differ greatly from its referenced source. Socrates presents the Homeric quote as concordant with the one he is describing by removing the larger context of the allusion. The full quote refers to a vast expanse between the sky, earth, and Tartarus:

ἤ μιν ἑλὼν ῥίψω ἐς Τάρταρον ἠερόεντα
τῆλε μάλ᾿, ἧχι βάθιστον ὑπὸ χθονός ἐστι βέρεθρον,
ἔνθα σιδήρειαί τε πύλαι καὶ χάλκεος οὐδός,
τόσσον ἔνερθ᾿ Ἀΐδεω ὅσον οὐρανός ἐστ᾿ ἀπὸ γαίης (*Il.* 8.13–16)

234 LIFE / AFTERLIFE

Or I will seize and hurl him to murky Tartarus
Very far away, where the deepest pit under the earth is,
[And] there the gates are iron and the threshold bronze,
as far below Hades as the sky is from the earth.

In this passage, Zeus threatens to punish any gods who insert themselves into the Trojan War against his plans by bodily removing them from the divine realm to the farthest point in space from the company of gods: the pit of Tartarus, deep under the boundary of Hades, which itself is a great distance from the heavens. The earth is placed equidistant between the Underworld and Zeus' domain, which only emphasizes the breadth of space separating the cosmic landmarks of sky (realm of the gods), earth (home of mortals), and Hades (kingdom of the dead). The Homeric layout for the cosmos seems to reflect the one described in the *Apology*, in which the living are in one location and the dead are somewhere else (*Ap.* 40c). In this scheme, the world for mortals is binary: alive, dead; here, there.

The *Phaedo*, however, envisions interlocking tunnels between these cosmic landmarks, through which water oscillates, flowing down from different regions of earth to converge in the Underworld before returning to the surface (*Phd.* 111d–e). The contiguousness of these hollows where mortals of different status live in a terraced geography emphasizes the continuity between the states of the living and the dead. The souls of the dead differ from the living through their location in lower regions of the earth. They are, however, able to aspire to (and eventually achieve) a dwelling near or on the surface of the earth through piety and may even escape from their bodies altogether, if they happen to have practiced philosophy sufficiently (*Phd.* 114c). The integrated geography of the real world and the Underworld reflects the integration between life and death that happens for a soul undergoing reincarnation (a concept foreign to the Homeric epics). Souls move back and forth between life and death through the very same regions that the oscillating water regularly flows back and forth. Although calling on the authority of poetic predecessors, Plato sharply diverges from traditional myth to superimpose his own myth of the Underworld by redefining its actual and moral geography. Through his Underworld scenes, Plato "redefines Hades as an image for the eternal divine realm of ideal realities" (Edmonds 2020b, 66). Elements in the Underworld become a shorthand for communicating about the hidden ideal realities through language and patterns of action that are recognizable to the audience from their cultural and religious contexts.[25]

By refining the Underworld environment's spatial map of morality, Socrates allows the reader to categorize souls he presents along a new spectrum of blessedness. Moreover, by emphasizing topographical features, Socrates also indicates that a soul's unembodied, postdeath experience can bear physical similarities to its earthly, bodily existence. He describes the landscapes of the Underworld hollows in sensual terms, imagining how different features would affect a human body moving through space, with extra attention to the sounds, sights, and feel of the physical environment. The streams that flow into Tartarus, the lowest level, are not only wet but also hot and cold, muddy and turbulent (καὶ ἀενάων ποταμῶν ἀμήχανα μεγέθη ὑπὸ τὴν γῆν καὶ θερμῶν ὑδάτων καὶ ψυχρῶν, πολὺ δὲ πῦρ καὶ πυρὸς μεγάλους ποταμούς, πολλοὺς δὲ ὑγροῦ πηλοῦ καὶ καθαρωτέρου καὶ βορβορωδεστέρου, "an extraordinary magnitude of everflowing rivers of both hot and cold water flow eternally under the earth, and much fire and great rivers of fire, and many [rivers] of wet mud, both purer and muddier," *Phd.* 111d5–e1). Souls witness various sights and colors as they are swept along various waterways to judgment, reward, or punishment. For example, Styx is noted for being "dark blue" (κυανός) in color (*Phd.* 113 b–c). This dark, harsh climate is also accompanied by a great clamor of sound. On the shores of the Acherusian lake, a crowded throng of souls waiting for rebirth hear the shouts and cries of other souls swept in a continuous swirling agitation of water while begging for forgiveness (κατὰ τὴν λίμνην τὴν Ἀχερο υσιάδα, ἐνταῦθα βοῶσί τε καὶ καλοῦσιν, "at the Acherusian harbor, [the souls] there shout and call out," *Phd.* 114a7–8).

The souls caught in such riptides feel the dizzy disorientation of the water's pull and are desperate to escape. The environment of this Underworld scene corresponds to the sensual experiences of the world in the upper levels

---

[25] Edmonds (2020b, 66) points out that wordplay in the *Phaedo* underscore Plato's doublespeak: "The singing (ἀίδειν) of the nightingale (ἀηδών) links together the realm of Hades (ἀίδου) with the unseen (ἀιδῆ) and eternal (ἀίδιον) realm of the Forms (εἴδη), which the soul can perceive by knowing (εἰδέναι) when it makes itself without the pleasures (ἀηδές) and pains of the body . . . All of these words, with their combination of a, i/e, and d sounds, resemble each other sufficiently to remind the reader of each other whenever they appear in the dialogue, in the same way that (as the interlocutors discuss) certain phenomena trigger the process of recollection through their resemblances and the chain of associations."

of the earth. A bright array of multiple colors (ποικίλη, χρώμασιν διειλημμένη), which include purple (ἀλουργῆ), golden yellow (χρυσοειδῆ), and pure white (λευκή), can be seen on the surface of the earth in contrast to the darker hues of the hollows (*Phd.* 110b7–c6). The men who live in this realm have superior senses, particularly their eyesight and hearing, and they mingle with each other and the gods in a happy (εὐδαιμονίαν) existence (*Phd.* 111b3–c3). Their reality and the societies of the living and the dead in the hollows are synchronic and syntopic, existing on the same earth in the same time frame. Moreover, the landscapes are also experienced in the same way, with or without a body.

The *Phaedo*'s landscape organizes competing ideas about "blessedness" into a hierarchy of value by visualizing them from various angles in the fates of souls as they move through space over preset time increments (*Phd.* 113d–114c). Souls can improve their lot and live in regions closer to the surface of the earth, depending on their level of sinfulness. Only philosophers, however, receive the ultimate reward of escaping bodily form and live in a place beyond the pure location on the surface where men who lived holy and just lives dwell (*Phd.* 114c). The *Phaedo* treats different groups of souls not as individuals but as examples that play out Plato's hierarchy of blessedness and punishment. Each soul that his character Socrates mentions, particularly the famous examples, calls upon a range of familiar narratives that give depth to his argument. The Underworld scene, therefore, acts as a common language that bridges understanding between people on different sides of Plato's dialectic argument. Its details are a dynamic index of narratives that complement the message and purpose of the dialectic argument.

Further, the arrangement of this index builds the experience of the reader to rewrite his or her assumptions using the new information and linked *paranarratives*. Socrates creates new connections and links that promote his argument by using comprehensive, concrete details whose expression overwrites the existing codes, which are more vague. It is one thing, for example, to imagine parricides as generally being held to account as in Aeschylus' *Eumenides*:

ὄψηι δὲ κεῖ τις ἄλλος ἤλιτεν βροτῶν
ἢ θεὸν ἢ ξένον τιν᾽ ἀσεβῶν
ἢ τοκέας φίλους,
ἔχονθ᾽ ἕκαστον τῆς δίκης ἐπάξια.
μέγας γὰρ Ἅιδης ἐστὶν εὔθυνος βροτῶν
ἔνερθε χθονός,
δελτογράφωι δὲ πάντ᾽ ἐπωπᾶι φρενί. (*Eum.* 269–275)

Plato's Underworlds 237

And you will see also, some other mortals as have sinned, dishonoring either a god or some guest or his dear parents, each one receiving deserved punishment; for Hades is a great judge of mortals below the earth, and he observes all things keeping a record in his mind.

This passage trusts in judgment and Hades' accounting system but only vaguely refers to what constitutes "deserved punishment." Socrates, on the other hand, describes precisely what punishments sinners might expect, in real and relatable terms, which has a very different impact. For example, those who have done violence against their parents or committed murder but repent are thrown into Tartarus for a year, after which they get caught up in a current that separates them based on their crimes: murderers go to Cocytus and parricides to Pyriphlegethon (*Phd.* 114a). Regardless of their path, they all end up at the Acherusian lake where they have an opportunity to persuade their victims to forgive them. If they fail, they must cycle through Tartarus and back to the Acherusian lake at regular intervals until they succeed. When they do convince their victims to forgive them, they are allowed to wait with all the other souls for rebirth (*Phd.* 114a–b).

By giving sinners a path for expiating their sins, Socrates removes the totalitarian, arbitrary power of capricious gods and the finality of Underworld judgment. He transfers agency and choice to humans, both to victims who later become judges against those who wronged them and also to sinners who must use their wits, knowledge, and eloquence to escape further punishment. Socrates uses his interlocutors' (and the poets') basic belief that sinners are punished in the afterlife but builds on that by making the punishment both surmountable and real in human terms and timeframes. He rewrites the narrative of Underworld punishment by giving mercy to the damned that the traditional accounts do not seem to offer, underscoring his argument that punishment be educational (cf. *Grg.* 525b).[26] He also frames the exchange between sinners and victims as an exercise in persuasion (πείσωσιν, *Phd.* 114b), similar to the real-world convention of wrongdoers negotiating with victims' families to avoid prosecution.[27]

The myth, therefore, argues that the development of one's persuasive abilities, as developed by philosophical training, is important because it can

---

[26] As Shilo (2013, Section 46) puts it, "he is addressing his contemporaries in the prevalent vocabulary of myth, simultaneously warping mythic situations into ideas that radically question Greek cultural assumptions."

[27] Cf. the discussion of this practice in Demosthenes 37.58-60.

give reprieve from extended punishment to a wrong-doer, should he find himself on the wrong side of judgment in the afterlife, even if he commits a serious crime. In this way, Plato converts the common language of "punishment in Hades" into an argument for the development of one's philosophical abilities by making punishment for most sinners only one, temporary stage of the afterlife experience. In the *Phaedo*'s Underworld, punishment is rehabilitative for sinners, who could have avoided painful afterlife punishments with more attention to their souls' philosophical development during their lives. Metempsychosis, as described here (as well as in other dialogues, such as the *Republic*'s "Myth of Er," and the *Laws* [903c–905b]), gives multiple opportunities for mortals to "get it right," but it also forces the living (i.e., Plato's audience) to take the long view of their existences, since the afterlife phases of the soul are much longer than the incarnate ones.[28]

Furthermore, Plato suggests that the soul's journey to the Underworld would be seen as pleasurable to the philosophically trained, even if it has to go through multiple stages of afterlife existence. In the *Phaedo* (85ab), Socrates tells his followers that, because most men fear death, they think swans and other birds sing mournfully at their death. He goes on to say that this is the opposite of what is happening and that the birds are actually singing to rejoice the coming of death because they know that good things await them in Hades. Philosophers, like these birds, have special insights that help them recognize that the name for the realm of Hades (ἀιδου) refers to the "unseen things" (ἀιδῆ) of reality. These include the Forms (εἰδη), which can only be known to the soul through philosophical practice and knowledge.[29] At death, a fully philosophically trained soul, like Socrates', is released from the appetitive senses of the body to a state of pleasure analogous to the blessed afterlife of myth. In this case, Socrates remaps the word "Hades" itself into a link to the unseen Forms and relates the pleasure of a philosophical soul after death with the blessed afterlife of heroes. In this way, Socrates redirects the link associating a "journey to Hades" with something fearful, as Odysseus and his crew perceive it at the beginning of the *Nekuia* (*Od.* 11.5), into something

---

[28] In the "Myth of Er," the period that a soul spends in either punishment or reward is one thousand years, ten times the lifespan of a man, which is described as only a century (*Resp.* 10.615a–b). Before this, Socrates says that the time from childhood to old age is short, and argues that an immortal thing like the soul should not be as concerned with it in relation to the whole of time (*Resp.* 608c–d).

[29] For more on Plato's word play of these terms and their relation to views of the afterlife in the *Phaedo*, see Edmonds (2020b).

pleasurable that a soul should be eager to attain: a potentially higher state of blessedness than envisioned for heroes in traditional Underworld scenes.

By altering the meanings and functions of temporal and spatial elements he borrows from predecessors' Underworld scenes, Plato's Socrates changes the relationship between the chronotopes of the real world and the Underworld. As a result, he also changes the nature of the relationship between life and afterlife on a conceptual level. No longer is the afterlife a mirror to life that can be manipulated and negotiated through ritual or patronage. Instead, the afterlife becomes another phase of the human lifecycle, like childhood or old age. This extension of the human lifecycle is further elaborated in the *Republic*, a dialogue in which the challenge to traditional sources and eschatological beliefs is even more pronounced.

IV. Rewriting the Afterlife in the Republic

The *Republic* begins and ends with a *katabasis*, one historical and one mythical. The first word of the dialogue is κατέβην, or "I descended" (*Resp.* 327a), spoken by the character Socrates in the first person about his descent to the Piraeus the day before. The word proves to be programmatic for the dialogue in the way that Plato's first words often are (Burnyeat 2012, 316). To kick off the conversation, Socrates says he met friends and went to the house of Cephalus, an old man who is the father of his companion Polemarchus. While there, Cephalus describes wealth across the generations of his family as an equilibrium and defines a concept of justice that is tied into having enough personal wealth banked to pay back gods and men for favors given (*Resp.* 330a–331c). Cephalus' earthly wealth is a result of his character, which allows him to maintain and grow his wealth, and he shows ethical concern for how his actions affect others—he does not want to cheat, deceive, or short-change others (*Resp.* 331b). He attributes his peaceful old age to the fact that he has managed his wealth and his life in an orderly, decent fashion so he does not have the same fear of Hades that other old people have from stories of how the unjust are punished in the afterlife (*Resp.* 330d–331b). He implies, therefore, that he and his audience believe that deeds in life affect their allotted afterlife. Additionally, this opening discussion quickly turns to a reflection on justice and just living more generally with a series of references to Hades and the *Nekuia* by several different interlocutors (Cephalus, *Resp.* 330d–e; Adeimantus, *Resp.* 363c–d; and Socrates, *Resp.* 386c–387a) as *para-narratives* to illustrate the high stakes of cultivating one's soul properly through philosophical inquiry during life.

In parallel to his opening, Plato closes the *Republic* with the story of Er, a mythic descent and literal *katabasis* that explores these very themes but presents them more explicitly against the eschatological backdrop of an Underworld scene. Cephalus' description in the opening scene of the variability of wealth in his family—his grandfather made a fortune, his father lost it, and then he mostly reacquired it (*Resp.* 330b)—is similar to the fate of the soul which Er describes as going back and forth between cycles of punishment and blessedness in the afterlife between successive incarnations. The success of the soul in the *Republic*'s Underworld is grounded in the soul's character and a sense of justice nurtured through its philosophical education (cf. *Phd.* 107d).[30] In this eschatology, "we choose to be good, or not, against the background of a cosmos that is indifferent to individuals' concerns and does not necessarily guarantee rewards for our being just" (Annas 1982, 138). The *Republic*'s Underworld scene closes the dialogue by expanding on the opening scene dialogue through a transformed afterlife myth, bringing the argument full circle to highlight the importance of justice and the practice of philosophy on a man's soul across its many lives, regardless of the details of fortune within individual cycles of life.

In the introduction to the "Myth of Er," the final episode of the *Republic*, Plato activates a specific Homeric Underworld scene as a *para-narrative* and then uses it to promote his new belief system. In the "Myth of Er," Socrates starts by saying he is not creating "a tale of Alcinous" (Ἀλλ' οὐ μέντοι σοι, ἦν δ' ἐγώ, Ἀλκίνου γε ἀπόλογον ἐρῶ, *Resp.* 614b2), yet he seems to be doing just that, presenting a "reinvented myth" (Halliwell 2007, 447).[31] In the passage immediately preceding this phrase, there is no mention of Odysseus, but the hero's figure looms over the final myth with this introductory reference to Alcinous and the presence of Odysseus himself at the end of the Underworld scene as the final soul Er encounters, recognizes, and names.

Socrates' initial denial of Homer as a model does the opposite by intentionally bringing the epic poet into the discussion. Additionally, the subject matter of an Underworld journey can only make this citation of "a tale of Alcinous" refer to the *Odyssey*'s *Nekuia* in Book 11 out of the range of tales

---

[30] The soul (and Cephalus' family) could in theory avoid the shift between bad and good generations of lives but only with proper care of the soul, which would require strict attention and development of character.

[31] Halliwell (2007, 447) argues that story patterns in the "Myth of Er" contain elements not only from the myths of Odyssey, Orpheus, and Heracles, but also the myths in the *Phaedrus*, particularly the combination of *katabasis* and *anabasis*.

that Odysseus tells to the Phaeacians in Books 9-12 of the *Odyssey*.[32] Through rhetorical sleight of hand, therefore, Socrates creates proximity between the two myths via the allusion to Alcinous, even while repudiating the connection. Moreover, this denial of a Homeric connection is used to emphasize the relative truthfulness of his own subsequent tale about Er, since he has already referred to poets' tales as generally false earlier in the *Republic* (377a) and has also said he would expunge large parts of the *Nekuia* for being neither true nor beneficial for men intending to be warriors (*Resp.* 386c).

It would not make sense, therefore, for him to engage in the type of Homeric mythmaking about the afterlife that he earlier denigrates. Nevertheless, by name-dropping Alcinous, the king of the Phaeacians, Socrates understands his audience will read the upcoming story of Er as a myth *like* Odysseus' but one that has more claim to truth than Homer's stories. It could, therefore, act as a replacement for the parts he wants to eliminate (*Resp.* 386a–387c). The distancing that Socrates requests is an intentional failure since the allusion thrusts the Homeric Underworld story into the reader's consciousness at the very moment of his denial and invites his audience to read and interpret the "Myth of Er" and the *Nekuia* in parallel.

Before beginning the "Myth of Er," therefore, the character Socrates suggests that Glaucon and other listeners should view it as the type of story the many-wiled Odysseus would tell. The effect of this is to draw the authority of the Homeric poet into the story. Centering the allusion on the figure of Alcinous in the "Myth of Er" draws out the aspect of judgment contained in the *Nekuia*. Alcinous, king of the Phaeacians, is the main figure that Odysseus needs to convince through his fantastic storytelling in order to get support for his return home, and the heart of the hero's tales to his Phaeacian judge is his visit to the shades in Hades (Most 1989). Glaucon, therefore, is analogous to Alcinous, since Socrates already established himself as the storyteller, the role of Odysseus. This pattern of Socrates styling himself as Odysseus occurs at various moments throughout the *Republic*, as David O'Connor (2007, 60–61) observes, so it is not too surprising here.[33] What is worth pointing out is

---

[32] By Plato's time, a "tale of Alcinous" had the meaning of a lengthy and possibly false story (Montiglio 2005, 95–97, 154n59). Socrates here uses this proverbial meaning to emphasize his own truthfulness, while also evoking Homer's *Nekuia*. This is the very episode that, earlier in the *Republic*, he says he would excise because its representation of the Underworld instills an unhelpful fear of death in the young (*Resp.* 386c).

[33] The connection between Socrates and Odysseus as narrators of multiple tales is further reinforced by the opening of the *Republic*, in which Socrates presents himself as a first-person narrator to the audience and describes a series of conversations and events culminating in an Underworld scene.

242 LIFE / AFTERLIFE

that Socrates extends the roles from the myth into reality by referring to his myth as didactic.

Both the *Nekuia* and the "Myth of Er" are first person accounts by a narrator who can describe the society of the dead and bring back wisdom when they return to the living. Er says that the judges ordered him to be a messenger to humanity who could tell the tale of his katabatic journey there after seeing and hearing everything in that place:

... ὅτι δέοι αὐτὸν ἄγγελον ἀνθρώποις γενέσθαι τῶν ἐκεῖ καὶ διακελεύοιντό οἱ ἀκούειν τε καὶ θεᾶσθαι πάντα τὰ ἐν τῷ τόπῳ. (*Resp.* 10.614d1–3)

[They said] that he must be a messenger to men of the things there, and they ordered him to listen and observe all the things in that place as a spectator.

This command echoes Anticlea's final exhortation to her son Odysseus in the *Nekuia* before her soul fades from view: ἀλλὰ φόωσδε τάχιστα λιλαίεο· ταῦτα δὲ πάντα / ἴσθ᾽, ἵνα καὶ μετόπισθε τεῇ εἴπῃσθα γυναικί ("but struggle as fast as you can to the light of day and behold all these things so that sometime later you may tell your wife," *Od.* 11.223–224). With the encouragement to "tell what he has witnessed," the katabatic hero then has a duty to instruct the living.

By referring to Odysseus' storytelling as "a tale of Alcinous," Socrates refocuses the account of Er away from Odysseus the storyteller onto Alcinous as the judge assessing the tales of the hero's wanderings. The peculiar reference to the *Nekuia* as the story told to Alcinous, who holds power over the storyteller, foreshadows the importance of judges, judgment, and justice in the upcoming "Myth of Er," which relates back to the discussion on the nature of a just man in the opening scene of the *Republic*. Through this simple phrase that links the two texts, Plato primes his audience through his chosen messenger Socrates to see the myth from the perspective of assessment and argument by activating the *Nekuia* narrative in the background hypertextually as a source of simultaneous comparison. Through its rhetorical framework and intertextual references, both the internal and external audiences become invested in the eschatology Er describes, thereby extending the myth beyond the immediate dialogue.

Additionally, the term *apologon* itself in the phrase Ἀλκίνου ἀπόλογον (*Resp.* 314b) feeds into this recasting of the tale as one of judgment and justice

Plato's Underworlds   243

in the afterlife by framing it with a technical term from Athenian courts. The simple definition of *apologon* here is "story" because we know, in this case, that it refers to the stories told by Odysseus. For Plato's audience, however, the word has other connotations besides a simple tale, particularly as it relates to the idea of judgment, since *apologia* is also the technical term for a defendant's speech in court.[34] In light of the succeeding myth, the word *apologon* cannot simply mean "a story"; rather, it has a legal flavor, since it is also being supplied as evidence to prove the conclusions of his arguments in the dialogue. The term both reminds the audience that Odysseus is being judged when he tells the *Nekuia* to Alcinous and also cues the reader to Plato's forthcoming story of Underworld judgment.

This association seems further supported by the fact that Socrates could have used a different term to refer to his Underworld myth. He elsewhere refers to Underworld scenes as *muthoi*, but not again as *apologoi*. In the *Phaedo*, when Socrates describes the true nature of the earth and sky, he calls it "telling a *muthos*" (μῦθον λέγειν, *Phd.* 110b) and then follows this statement with details about the regions of the sky and the Underworld. Similarly, in the *Gorgias* (493a, 523a), Socrates introduces the two Underworld passages as productions of people who create *muthoi*.[35]

Introducing the "Myth of Er" as an *apologos* rather than a *muthos* (or even a *logos*, as in the *Gorgias*), despite its similarity to the eschatological content that he calls *muthoi* in other dialogues, marks it off as different even though, at face value, he seems to be equating the two terms. Perhaps he did not want to undermine his myth by using the latter term before telling it, since he had already cast the term *muthoi* in a negative light earlier in the dialogue. He must have realized that the subject matter would bring his other afterlife accounts into an intertextual dialogue with the current one, however, and he acknowledges this by referring retrospectively to the Er myth as a *muthos*, so it is categorized with his other tales:

---

[34] Socrates refers to his defense as an *apologia* in the *Apology* (28a).

[35] In the latter example, Socrates says he would rather call the upcoming Underworld account a *logos* to designate its truthfulness, demonstrating the particular care he takes with applying terminology. He acknowledges, however, its categorization as a *muthos* by (1) saying that Callicles (and therefore other listeners) would interpret it as such and (2) introducing the account itself with "As Homer says . . ." (ὥσπερ γὰρ Ὅμηρος λέγει, 523a). Socrates here calls a *muthos* a *logos* to promote its veracity, but he does not deny that he is essentially mythmaking.

Καὶ οὕτως, ὦ Γλαύκων, μῦθος ἐσώθη καὶ οὐκ ἀπώλετο,
(c.) καὶ ἡμᾶς ἂν σώσειεν, ἂν πειθώμεθα αὐτῷ, καὶ τὸν τῆς Λήθης
ποταμὸν εὖ διαβησόμεθα καὶ τὴν ψυχὴν οὐ μιανθησόμεθα. (*Resp.* 621b8–c2)

And thus, Glaucon, the *muthos* was preserved and not destroyed,
and it would save us, if we were persuaded by it; and we shall
pass through the river of Lethe well and not pollute our souls.

This recategorization of his tale as *muthos* is somewhat surprising, since it contradicts his insistence before the account that he was not telling a tale like the ones found in the *Odyssey.*

Socrates explains his aversion to such tales earlier in the *Republic* when he calls *muthoi* the stories first told to children, which he describes as generally false but also containing some element of truth (*Resp.* 377a). By now calling the Er story a *muthos* and making it the final word in support of his argument of the ideal city, Socrates highlights another level of communication that is occurring between him and his audience, one that uses the language of *muthos* to add enough authority to a new story in order to give it the force of argument. The source of this power is the network of texts that are automatically activated by linking across the Underworld myths and using their common language to redefine traditional myths.

In addition to the phrase "tale of Alcinous," Plato reinforces the hypertextual connections to other Underworld myths by having Er describe the fates of Orpheus, Ajax, and Odysseus, who each appear in famous Underworld narratives, as well as the outcomes of Thamyris, Epeius, and Thersites, whose stories are marked by their souls' natures being judged as flawed. Their deficiencies manifest themselves in less desirable incarnations in their next lives (*Resp.* 10.620a–d).[36] Also appearing before Er is Atalanta, a problematic heroine not unlike the ones Odysseus met in the *Nekuia.*[37]

Although connecting to these traditional myths, Socrates also makes his Underworld conform to the vision he presented in the *Phaedo* of an ecological eschatology that is connected to the real world's *chronotope.* In the "Myth

---

[36] Thamyris was punished by the Muses for hubris and became a nightingale; Epeius built the Trojan horse and became a craftswoman; and Thersites was beaten by Odysseus for speaking against his leaders and became a monkey.

[37] Atalanta's connection via the Calydonian Boar Hunt to Meleager, who made a famous ghostly appearance in Bacchylides (*Ode* 5), would have been an additional layer of connection between her and Underworld scenes.

of Er," human timeframes intrude more frequently and at more regular stages than seen in the *Phaedo*. After souls complete their cycles of reward in the heavens or punishment under the earth, they gather in a meadow for exactly seven days (ἑπτὰ ἡμέραι), then leave by foot on the eighth day (τῇ ὀγδόῃ) for a journey lasting four days (τεταρταίους) to reach a spot where they see a bright light (*Resp.* 10.616b). At that point, they walk for an additional day (ἡμερησίαν) to reach the source of the light (*Resp.* 10.616b).

By including such specificity in measurable time, Socrates makes this Underworld scene spill beyond the structures of its own narrative so that it appears to occur in the real world. With such a distinct timeframe, it is clear that this Underworld scene is being constructed for the benefit of the reader at large and not solely to convince Socrates' immediate interlocutors. The proof of this comes from the fact that the *Republic* ends with this Underworld myth, not waiting for a response from Socrates' companions in the dialogue. Like the *Gorgias*, the *Republic* never returns from its final Underworld scene to the original conversation for reactions from Callicles and Glaucon, respectively, to see whether Socrates' myths and his conclusions about their meanings have convinced them of his argument. The audience is left hanging on that score and has no recourse but to take on the role of Socrates' interlocutors (O'Connor 2007, 72).

Instead of simply following the argument as an eavesdropper to the conversation, the reader is invited to become actively engaged in the dialogue, formulating imagined responses to Socrates that Plato does not provide through his characters. This essentially expands the dialogue outside the boundaries of the text and extends the mythic Underworld chronotope into the reality of the audience. Readers must compare the Underworld story just presented to the ones they already know from poetry, art, and ritual. A set of competing narratives appears in the mental landscape, shadowing each element that is introduced in Socrates' afterlife portrayals. Each reader might have a slightly different set of afterlife stories corresponding to the mythic allusions, but Socrates solves this problem by making his text the anchor against which the other recalled versions must be compared. He does this by specific reference to other versions, such as the Underworld scenes found in Homer and Hesiod, showing his knowledge and mastery of the well-known accounts, which he then mimics, subsumes, and refutes in his own version. In the *Republic*'s "Myth of Er," for example, he puts Er into the role of a storytelling Odysseus giving witness to an Underworld journey, since "he was telling what he had seen there" (ἔλεγεν ἃ ἐκεῖ ἴδοι, *Resp.* 614b7–8). Socrates then specifically names Odysseus as a character in Er's afterlife narrative, who must follow the same cosmic laws as other souls without special treatment from his traditional status as a hero (*Resp.* 620c).

In the "Myth of Er," souls that are well-versed in philosophy can achieve a more positive experience while they undergo the timed stages of the afterlife (*Resp.* 619d–e). Socrates makes the point in this myth, however, that no one is exempt from the cycle of rebirth, not even a hero such as Odysseus, with a glorious past or divine favor (*Resp.* 620c). Socrates, therefore, brings up the famous Greek hero to dilute the relationship between afterlife blessedness and material wealth or heroic honors that previous poets had emphasized in their Underworld depictions. Thus, *kleos* from battle and a successful *nostos* are no longer sufficient sources of immortal glory and heroic blessedness. In Socrates' Underworld, the best recourse against a bad afterlife is a philosophical education. When describing the allotment of lives, he interrupts his Underworld tale in the middle to address Glaucon and his larger audience directly:

ἔνθα δή, ὡς ἔοικεν, ὦ φίλε Γλαύκων, ὁ πᾶς κίνδυνος ἀνθρώπῳ, καὶ
διὰ ταῦτα μάλιστα (c.) ἐπιμελητέον ὅπως ἕκαστος ἡμῶν τῶν ἄλλων
μαθημάτων ἀμελήσας τούτου τοῦ μαθήματος καὶ ζητητὴς καὶ μαθητὴς
ἔσται, ἐάν ποθεν οἷός τ᾽ ᾖ μαθεῖν καὶ ἐξευρεῖν τίς αὐτὸν
ποιήσει δυνατὸν καὶ ἐπιστήμονα, βίον καὶ χρηστὸν καὶ πονη-
ρὸν διαγιγνώσκοντα, τὸν βελτίω ἐκ τῶν δυνατῶν ἀεὶ πανταχοῦ αἱρεῖσθαι·
(*Rep.* 618b7–c5)

There, indeed, dear Glaucon, it seems that this is the greatest danger for man, and for these reasons especially, we must pay attention to how each of us, neglecting other subjects, will be both a seeker and learner of this subject, if perhaps it would be somehow possible to learn and to seek someone who would make him able and knowledgeable at distinguishing the good life and the worthless one and make him always choose the very best out of the possibilities.

The deictic ἔνθα at the beginning of this passage is characteristic of descriptions in Underworld scenes (re. Chapter 2). This interlude also recalls Odysseus' interruption to address his Phaeacian hosts in the *Nekuia*, a link that Socrates further establishes by describing the afterlives of famous mythic figures and heroes, including Thamyris, Agamemnon, Ajax, Atalanta, Thersites, and finally Odysseus. The emphasis on famous Greek warriors from Homer plus a female heroine, even in this abbreviated list, recalls Odysseus' Underworld

Plato's Underworlds

account in the *Nekuia*, which also features women and Greek heroes from the Trojan War. In both, Homer and Plato activate a set of narratives that give further depth to the viewer's general observations about Underworld society. Having Odysseus himself as the final soul Er encounters strengthens the connection between the two versions.

Socrates concludes the "Myth of Er" with a second reminder: the soul's uninterrupted existence across the life–death barrier signifies that "practicing justice with reason in every way" (δικαιοσύνην μετὰ φρονήσεως παντὶ τρόπῳ ἐπιτηδεύσομεν, *Resp.* 621c) while alive means that its good experience on earth will be mirrored after death on the thousand-year journey, leading to a positive afterlife (καὶ ἐνθάδε καὶ ἐν τῇ **χιλιέτει πορείᾳ**, ἣν διεληλύθαμεν, εὖ πράττωμεν, "both here and in the **thousand-year journey**, which I have recounted, we would fare well," *Resp.* 621d). In this instance, although he subjects the Underworld to chronological time, Socrates makes its time frame almost impossibly long considering that he counts the human life span at about one hundred years (*Resp.* 615a–b). This serves to emphasize the burden and urgency of preparing the soul during the short period of life when man has the greatest agency over his soul's cultivation.

By being so particular about time frames, Socrates tries to convince his audience that time in the Underworld and real world are implicated in each other. When Er leaves the Underworld, time in the real world has passed and he reappears at a later time and at a different place from which he entered. His *katabasis*, therefore, does not occur as a node in the plot outside of time that could be removed without affecting his story. This is markedly different from other extant Greek Underworld scenes. By including the Underworld in chronological time, Socrates makes the myth into another piece of evidence for his argument that corresponds to his other arguments about the soul. He portrays extreme permeability across the life–death barrier by applying human time constraints to the denizens of the afterlife, giving further proof to the equation he originally introduced in the *Gorgias* that "life is death and death is life." At the same time, he cuts off access to afterlife blessedness for most people, or at least delays their progress significantly, by introducing obstacles to make the road much more difficult.

V. Conclusions

In his Underworld scenes, Plato found an effective tool with which to challenge and rewrite the perceived relationship between life and death. He centers his scenes on the immortal soul's journey through phases of life and afterlife, undermining tradition by using its tool, the Underworld scene, to create authority and promote an alternative value system, which privileges philosophy and those who practice it. By using Underworld scenes in this manner, he calls into question their status as being "true" in an absolute or religious sense while at the same time arguing that they are a vehicle to transmit truths about human choices and the human condition.

Alluding to familiar myths throughout his Underworld scene, Plato urges his readers to make the connections and engage with his radical arguments about the superiority of philosophy over traditional beliefs by presenting them within a familiar language. By anchoring his argument into generally familiar structures, he is able to present revolutionary ideas about blessedness, heroic deeds, the value of *kleos*, and the nature of the cosmos. This is the case in the *Phaedo* when Socrates casually refers to one of the hollows of his larger geography as the Tartarus from Homer and other poets (*Phd.* 112a). By bringing this up in the middle of an elaborate Underworld scene, Plato gives his own myth authority and makes it the central reference point from which to explicate the more cryptic traditional one. He further suggests that his Underworld, with its greater specificity of information, is more reliable than the older one he references because it more clearly presents the relationships between things. The confidence with which he presents his account in turn implies to the audience that his surrounding details are accurate, even though his larger point contradicts the religious beliefs embedded in the accounts of the very poets he says he is citing.

The inconsistencies in his Underworld depictions underscore the fact that Plato treats Underworld scenes not as truth but rather as a tool that supports his arguments by communicating information that cannot be conveyed by other means. Plato identifies his eschatological material in the *Phaedo* as a *muthos* (not *logos*), which "places it in dialogic relation to the other genres of discourse in the dialogue" (Nightingale 2002, 235).[38] Using the Underworld image set, Plato activates the narratives that he needs by highlighting certain myths of the soul's journey in the afterlife: in the *Apology*, he discusses the survival of memory beyond the grave, in which the soul can have dialogue with famous people, as seen in Homer and Pindar; in the *Gorgias*, he describes multiple myths of judgment; and in the *Phaedo*, the *Laws*, and the

---

[38] See also McCabe (1992), who argues that Plato's eschatological myths complement, but do not necessarily reiterate, the claims of their parent dialogues by suggesting new directions for interpretation.

Republic, he details the segregation of souls in the afterlife and their fate of metempsychosis.

In this way, Plato follows the tradition of authors using Underworld scenes as commentary to promote their views. He is radical because he uses Underworld scenes to depart from the religious and cultural views of the past that centered on heroes and the favor of the gods. While his predecessors made shifts within the frame of inherited Greek religion, Plato uses their strategies to change the baseline meaning of the nature of heroes, heroism, and blessedness such that philosophers become the true heroes. Plato does not completely abandon traditional heroes or features of the Underworld but rather gives them new roles. Traditional heroes, therefore, appear and still receive special status in the Underworld, but their position in the cosmic hierarchy is lower than that of philosophers who now have the most blessed outcome. Plato's Underworlds, therefore, use his audience's cultural understanding of Underworld scenes to institute new dogma about the state and journey of the soul through the afterlife.

By moving a narrative into the Underworld, authors are able to offer a view of time and space removed from the pressures of the plot. Plato's innovation was to keep the pressure on by extending chronological time and the plot of a human life into the Underworld space. For Plato, therefore, the move to the Underworld is not a "grasp backwards" to recover events that are decisive for understanding the present action (Bettini 1991, 136–137). Instead, his Underworld scenes create a backdrop for arguing why the cultivation of the soul in one's present life through a philosophical lifestyle is so important. In this sense, Plato does not advocate a complete replacement of poetic and mythic tradition with other forms of speech like dialectic. In the hands of a philosopher like himself, he shows that such traditional speech can be wielded as an effective rhetorical tool to dovetail with his more privileged types of argumentation (i.e., dialectic). By making Underworld space and time tangible through the movement of souls and by bringing landscape elements to life for the reader in showing their impact on souls, Plato's later dialogues stress continuity between life and afterlife as part of a single cycle of existence. While this might be reassuring to the privileged few that can practice philosophy, it creates more inequality between souls who have more obstacles to overcome and more locations in the newly created Underworld levels to get stuck. In this way, his Underworld scenes work to make the most blessed afterlife more inaccessible overall. Through the variety of Underworld scenes he presents in his works, Plato shows his fluency in afterlife poetics and ability to use the hypertextuality of Underworld scenes to claim authority in

250 LIFE / AFTERLIFE

support of his radical reconstruction of reality and reassignment of the most blessed status to philosophers.

Throughout his works, Plato revolutionizes Underworld scenes by disconnecting them from traditional religious practice and belief and moving them into a literary-imaginative frame, which, removed from the earthly concerns of everyday life, supports a vision of the cosmos based on the primacy of philosophers and the Forms. Under Plato's influence, later authors build on this idea and use Underworld scenes to promote their own perspectives and assessments of their societies in a much more direct, self-conscious, and critical way within the safety of Underworld scenes. In the next chapter, I discuss the afterlife of Greek Underworld scenes and their stability across time as a form of authorial commentary.

7

Epilogue

THE AFTERLIFE OF THE AFTERLIFE

I. Introduction

As a phenomenon in ancient Greek storytelling and myth, Underworld scenes appear in different genres and time periods, starting with our earliest written sources, the Homeric epics. In this book, I have discussed how to identify and classify ancient Underworld scenes, specifying the ways that authors have constructed them to function as a form of embedded authorial commentary, both for their frame narratives and society at large. I have argued that Underworld scenes are a medium of communication that ancient authors used to reaffirm shared values, reflect on the place of humanity in the cosmos, criticize the status quo, and promote new ideologies. The earliest Underworld scenes can be categorized as "heroic" because they tell stories of heroes performing *katabaseis* and having necromantic conversations with the souls of the dead to gain something crucial for fulfilling a quest. These heroes, who can survive an encounter with the society of the dead and return to the land of the living to tell about it, gain special status among their peers and in Greek society. Such heroes enjoy special favor from the gods either by birth or because of their deeds and thus are categorized as "blessed" (*olbios*). Their Underworld scenes reinforce the message of their blessedness by portraying them as living separately from other souls in the Underworld, much like they were differentiated from regular people in life. In Homeric Underworlds, heroes appear as a group when Odysseus encounters them in the *Nekuia*, although souls are generally described as lacking self-awareness after death (*Od.* 11.495). Post-Homeric Underworld scenes, on the other hand, begin to emphasize the different treatment of souls in the afterlife, which occurs through

Life / Afterlife. Suzanne Lye, Oxford University Press. © Oxford University Press 2024.
DOI: 10.1093/9780197690239.003.0008

afterlife judgment. Such "Underworlds of judgment," with their visions of a segregated society of the dead, come to dominate over time. These maintain certain aspects of heroic Underworlds, however, particularly the idea that heroes and special mortals, whose *kleos* for great deeds are celebrated in their communities by song or ritual, can be designated as "blessed" (*olbios*) in the afterlife. Such blessed souls then have access to a superlative afterlife in a Golden-Age type of environment similar to the existence enjoyed by the gods, whose nature is also described as blessed (*makar*).

As a narrative tool, Underworld scenes allow authors to activate a network of far-flung texts through references, or *hyperlinks*, to other Underworld scenes. These include tales from myth, religious tradition, and other authors writing in different genres and time periods. Using the Underworld's unique *chronotope*, which operates outside of regular chronological time, authors are able to introduce extra-spatial and extra-temporal information and characters into the audience's view as points of comparison with the story at hand. Thus, Odysseus in the *Nekuia* is able to hear news from his mother's soul about events after he left Ithaca for the Trojan War but before her death as well as about the fate of his former comrade Agamemnon after they parted ways at Troy. Additionally, through Odysseus' Underworld conversation with Heracles, the poet is able to characterize Odysseus more broadly as a hero in relation to other figures both from his own life and from the mythic past. The Underworld encounter in the *Nekuia*, along with a second Underworld scene in Book 24 (*Od.* 24.1–204), frames Odysseus as a peer to famous heroes of the past, thus giving him status among his Phaeacian interlocutors to whom he tells his tale.

In general, Underworld scenes, as embedded scenes, allow authors to open a conversation directly with the audience about the motivations of characters, major themes in the overall narrative, and shared values between the author and audience. Because of their roots in traditional myths and religious beliefs about the hidden realm of the dead, Underworld scenes can claim a certain level of authority as representatives of eschatology and hidden aspects of the cosmos, although the information they present about the Underworld and the experience of souls after death is unverifiable. This leaves much room for authors to speculate, be creative, and partner with their audiences to make conclusions about what matters in life by portraying the long-term effect of such valuations in the afterlife. Although Plato finds the traditional myths of poets misleading and bans them from his ideal city, he nevertheless found mythic Underworld scenes useful tools to think with in supporting his dialectic arguments to make philosophers have the highest status of all mortals.

He underscores his point by portraying philosophers in Underworld scenes as exceeding heroes in blessedness with respect to their afterlife rewards.

Through Underworld scenes, an author has the ability both to halt his story's linear progress and to introduce ideas, characters, and references from a larger archive of information. The new material gives depth and background to the events of the frame narrative in which the scene is embedded. Additionally, an Underworld scene engages the reader in a dialogue about a text's interpretation by operating on a metaliterary level to blur the boundaries between the roles of author and audience. The author calls on the audience to "fill in" the stories evoked by the careful placement of references in the course of the scene. These references then link together hypertextually and allow the author to conjure up multiple narratives simultaneously as *para-narratives* that shape how the audience should view the scene at hand. Such hypertextual poetics demands that audiences take on a quasi-authorial role because it relies on them to pull up different Underworld scenes from memory as points of comparison to the one being presented. An Underworld scene in ancient literature is, therefore, an archive from which an author can introduce new stories into the narrative consciousness of the audience. In this way, Underworld scenes act as conduits between different texts and contexts. In such scenes, authors can be both narrator and interpreter of their own creations by connecting them to other such narratives of the afterlife. In turn, readers interject their own experiences and knowledge to give meaning to the signs and references that the author uses. By allowing this exchange, the Underworld scene proves itself to be a site of embedded authorial commentary that engages in a conversation directly with the audience.

II. *The Afterlife of the Greek Underworld Scene*

Influenced by these early Greek authors, later authors use heroic and judgment-based Underworld configurations to activate networks of Underworld scenes for their audiences, which include many of the examples presented in this book. For example, Vergil, modeling his great Roman epic the *Aeneid* on the *Iliad* and *Odyssey*, devotes an entire book of his work to present an Underworld scene. Aeneas' *katabasis* in Book 6 engages with multiple Underworld scenes. The first reference, which can be identified most easily, is the *Nekuia*. Vergil sets up a heroic Underworld into which his wandering hero Aeneas descends and engages with the souls of his dead father and comrades from the Trojan War. In addition to their resonances with heroic Underworlds, Vergil's detailed descriptions of the Underworld space recall the moral geographies of

Underworlds of judgment, such as those found in Hesiod and Plato, since the location of each soul in the afterlife is presented as a result of its deeds in life.

Like its Greek models, Vergil's Underworld scene in *Aeneid* 6 uses the Underworld image set to contextualize Aeneas' journey and motivation, thus suggesting interpretations of Aeneas' actions and events in the epic's frame narrative. Although writing in Latin for a Roman audience, Vergil and his audience shared a deep interest in and knowledge about Greek literature, particularly Homeric epic. In addition to Vergil, other authors and artists also mediated Greek material for a Roman audience, connecting revered stories from Greece to Roman identity and particularly Augustus' rise. A group of small stone tablets called the *Tabulae Iliacae*, for example, dating from the first century C.E., were produced in the years following Vergil's epic but, like Augustus' other public works, portray Rome as an inheritor of the great cultural products of ancient Greece (Petrain 2014, 2–3).[1] The production of this visual *Iliad*, curated for Roman tastes, speaks to a general, popular, and sustained Roman engagement with Greek literature and mythology, which comfortably situates Vergil's Underworld within this study's discussion of the use of Greek Underworld scenes as embedded commentary, despite the *Aeneid*'s being in Latin and from the Roman context.

Vergil similarly relies on his audiences' interest and proficiency in the stories and themes of Greek mythology, which remained strong enough to allow him to link to Greek material without much concern for references being lost in translation. By creating intentional links in the *Aeneid* to specific Greek literary models, such as the Homeric poems, Vergil demonstrates an understanding of audience collaboration as an important element in the production of his poem's meaning. Recognizing how influential the Homeric epics were to the perceived greatness of Greece and Greek culture overall, Vergil created an epic that adopted this sense of greatness not only to the story of Augustus' divine lineage but also to Roman identity more broadly. Despite the compression into fewer books than his Homeric models—from twenty-four books each in the *Iliad* and *Odyssey* to twelve total in the *Aeneid*, Vergil still devotes all of Book 6 to his Underworld scene to classify his hero Aeneas with the famous Greek katabatic heroes Heracles, Theseus, and Pirithous

---

[1] These tablets portrayed scenes from each book of Homer's *Iliad* and from parts of the epic cycle about the fall of Troy with a central panel scene emphasizing Aeneas' escape. They were meant for public display in Rome and available to wide audiences with a visual shorthand to accompany their inscriptions. For more about these tablets, see Petrain (2014). For more on how *Aeneid* 6 relates to and might have informed audience response to Augustus' building program and propaganda, see Pandey (2014).

Epilogue   255

(*Aen.* 6.392–393). Earlier in the book, Vergil shows his awareness of his Underworld scene's cultural weight by having Aeneas persuade the Sibyl in a very specific way. Aeneas' main argument for visiting his father's soul in the Underworld is genealogical, and he ranks himself as equal to katabatic heroes such as Orpheus, Pollux, Theseus, and Heracles, who each held the favor of the gods and sought to bring back someone from the Underworld:

> si potuit manis accersere coniugis Orpheus
> Threicia fretus cithara fidibusque canoris,
> si fratrem Pollux alterna morte redemit
> itque reditque viam totiens. quid Thesea, magnum
> quid memorem Alciden? et mi genus ab Iove summo. (*Aen.* 6.119–123)

> If Orpheus was able to summon the shade of his wife,
> relying on his Thracian cithara and his melodious lyre-strings,
> if Pollux ransomed his brother with alternating death
> and both went and returned on the path so many times. Why should I
> bring to mind Theseus,
> Why great Heracles? I also belong to the race of Jupiter, most high.

This extension of Aeneas' heroism into a katabatic frame underscores the poet's recognition of the power of Underworld scenes for myth-making.[2] By both length and topic, Vergil signals the Underworld scene's importance to his narrative purpose and his audience, using it to highlight his engagement with revered Greek sources and to relate Aeneas' journey to recent historical events in the Roman world.[3] Through his inclusion of a heroic *katabasis* and an Underworld scene, Vergil explicitly communicates his perspective on Roman self-identity, inherited literary tradition, and historical events from both the legendary and historical past. As a metaliterary space given to this purpose, the Underworld scene also distances the author from the objects of his observations and critiques by allowing him to use the special register of Underworld poetics. In this way, Vergil is able to present his story as authoritative even as he invents wholesale parts of the narrative.

---

[2] The association of Aeneas with a *katabasis* does not appear to have existed before Vergil's *Aeneid*.

[3] See Tatum (1984) for a discussion about Vergil's deliberate engagement with Greek myths and his use of Dido's ghost in the Underworld to interpret her role in Books 1 and 4 of the *Aeneid*.

Vergil adopts famous parts of Underworld episodes associated with many different katabatic heroes to create a heroic aura around Aeneas and "impart to Vergil's readers a sense of familiarity with Underworld topography and personnel, even though Aeneas' journey through the world of ghosts is new" (Clark 2001, 104). Vergil reveals his strategy fairly early in *Aeneid* 6 with three directly traceable references channeling Homer's *Nekuia*: (1) a request for burial upon entry to the Underworld space from a lost comrade (*Aen.* 6.365–366), (2) a failed embrace by the hero of his parent's ghost (*Aen.* 6.700–701), and (3) a conversation with Deiphobus, his ill-fated comrade from the Trojan War (*Aen.* 6.495–534). Each of these moments acts as a hypertext that creates contact points to specific sections of Odysseus' Underworld encounter in Book 11 of the *Odyssey* (11.51–80, 11.206–208, and 11.387–434, respectively), leaving no doubt that Vergil would like his audience to conjure it as a *para-narrative* alongside his own scene.[4] As with his epic predecessor, Vergil uses these characters to expand the audience's knowledge about his hero's motivations and character, showing Aeneas as a conscientious leader, a dutiful family man, and a successful warrior. Unlike in the *Odyssey*'s *Nekuia*, however, the hero is not the narrator of the Underworld scene, and there is no internal audience equivalent to the Phaeacians. The narrator speaks directly to the external audience as a voice of authority and defines how they should characterize his hero Aeneas among the ranks of epic heroes. Besides offering commentary on the hero's values and, by extension, the values of the epic and author, the narrator adds further details about the landscape and its implications from moral and philosophical perspectives. Vergil references Plato's descriptions of the fate of souls and their continual rebirth into history while also underscoring examples relevant to the context of Roman greatness.[5]

By doing this, Vergil presents events from his own recent historical past as a projected, inevitable future within the narrative. The Underworld scene allows him to give his audience a synoptic view that contextualizes the current state of affairs and the greatness of both Rome and Augustus. By incorporating history into myth, Vergil elevates events from his time into a grand narrative of legendary figures while at the same time making them objects of scrutiny and, therefore, open to criticism by suggesting how the story could have gone

---

[4] Clark (2001, 114) documents Vergil's network of Underworld scene *para-narratives* to include Bacchylides 5 in the placement of Hades' house and in the Sibyl's role as guide, saying the latter function was earlier performed by Meleager's ghost or Hermes.

[5] For a discussion about how Vergil incorporates references to genre and geography in *Aeneid* 6, see Feldherr (1999).

Epilogue 257

differently. By being so obvious about his source material and characters, Vergil's Underworld scene acts as a bricolage that shows the mechanics behind creating the seamless narrative of Rome's (and Augustus') greatness. Vergil constructs an Underworld that is temporally congruent with his historical time period (cf. Plato's Underworlds) but does so within the epic genre. In doing this, Vergil is able to make myth lead directly into the history of his own times. Through Aeneas, the son of the goddess Venus and purported ancestor of Augustus, Vergil is able to draw a straight line from the realm of revered myths and the great civilizations of the past to his patron, Rome's leader. In his Underworld scene, Vergil brings into the audience's view a systematic procession through ancient Greek myth and Roman history, starting with the great heroes of the mythic past and ending with the souls of famous Roman figures on their way to reincarnation. By placing historical figures and references to events from recent Roman history into a mythic Underworld, Vergil is able to have a visceral impact on his audience while also presenting contemporary history as worthy of epic *kleos*. Indeed, Augustus' sister was reported by Suetonius in his *Life of Vergil* (33) to have reacted emotionally upon hearing the line *tu Marcellus eris* ("you will be Marcellus," *Aen.* 6.883) about her deceased son, who appears as a soul that Aeneas encounters. Through his Underworld scene, Vergil promotes Roman greatness and Augustus' ascension to power as being part of a larger cosmic plan, thus elevating his history to the status of myth. Through catalog and reference, Vergil reflects with his audiences on the fluidity of relationships between important figures and the various interpretations about Rome's journey to the present moment, using the backdrop of the kingdom of Hades, a fixed, eternal space with gloomy terrain, the segregation of souls, and incorrigible sinners (*Aen.* 6.548–627).

Vergil is not the only author, however, who mines Greek Underworld scenes of the past to bring his world's realities into sharp focus for audiences. Lucian of Samosata, a second-century CE author writing in Greek during the Second Sophistic, similarly adopts the Underworld scenes of his literary predecessors. With multiple scenes across his works, Lucian goes beyond simple commentary and reflection and uses his Underworld scenes as vehicles for pointed attacks against specific classes, groups of people, and ideologies of his times. In his satire, the *True History* (*Ver. hist.*), Lucian uses an Underworld scene to bring his work directly into dialogue with authors and figures of the past. The first three heroes that his protagonist (also named Lucian) encounters when he arrives at the Isle of the Blessed are the famous mythical figures Ajax, Theseus, and Menelaus, who are undergoing judgment before the judge Rhadamanthus (*Ver. hist.* 2.8–9). The next two heroes being judged after them are the historical figures Alexander the Great and Hannibal of Carthage. Lucian describes their ghosts as competing for a seat of honor next to Cyrus the Elder, the Persian king. The anachronistic juxtaposition of these figures in the queue for judgment is meant to be jarring, and their position immediately in front of the protagonist (even though they must have arrived centuries before him) suggests that he is their peer. The author, therefore, builds an Underworld chronotope for his audiences that is expansive and rich for inquiry, suggesting that every famous person from every time period is available to his protagonist's examination. Moreover, by explicitly including the souls of Cyrus the Persian king and other foreigners (*Ver. hist.* 2.17), Lucian creates an inclusive environment in which many more figures of all ranks and classes are accessible to him for literary exploitation than to his predecessors whose Underworlds mostly focused on mythic Greek heroes and famous men. With such a varied host of ghosts to converse with, Lucian the hero is able to make irrefutable claims about different kinds of people in his world by how he portrays their afterlives. At the same time, Lucian can use the Underworld scene to promote himself as a storyteller on par with Homer. In his tale, Lucian the hero portrays himself as a confidant of Homer's ghost, who trusts him to share his latest epic, "The Battle of Dead Heroes," with humanity in the real world:

ἔγραψεν δὲ καὶ ταύτην τὴν μάχην Ὅμηρος καὶ ἀπιόντι μοι ἔδωκεν τὰ βιβλία κομίζειν τοῖς παρ' ἡμῖν ἀνθρώποις· ἀλλ' ὕστερον καὶ ταῦτα μετὰ τῶν ἄλλων ἀπωλέσαμεν. (*Ver. hist.* 2.14)

Homer both wrote an account of this battle, and gave the books to me, when I was leaving, to carry back and preserve for the people in our world; but later, we lost even these along with other things.

This action is presented as a tremendous honor that elevates Lucian from a simple storyteller to the protector of Greek heritage and *the* person to whom the great Homer himself entrusted his final work. After setting up this close relationship between himself and Homer's ghost throughout his Underworld account, however, Lucian immediately informs the audience, almost flippantly, that he lost the epic. The audience, therefore, must rely solely on Lucian's account as a faithful representative of Homer's words. This exchange acts as a metaphor indicating the closeness between Homer and Lucian as authors and storytellers. Lucian, however, draws attention to the actual tenuousness of their connection by how quickly he loses this priceless gift.

Epilogue 259

A similar loss of connection between the past and present occurs in several of Lucian's comic dialogues, including the *Dialogues of the Dead*, and his afterlife-focused plays, such as the *Downward Journey*. These Underworld scenes, like some of the examples from fifth-century BCE Athens, are not technically embedded within a narrative frame story; rather, they present themselves as embedded in civic narratives and local cultural contexts, about which Lucian gives commentary through his parodic Underworld scenes. The humor in these is as biting and aggressive as in Lucian's other satirical works, but they add an extra punch by bringing in afterlife consequences, which make the stakes higher for everyone. Because its chronotope allows access to wider contexts for comparison to revered mythic and historical characters, Lucian's Underworld scenes remind the audience about their own mortality and, like Plato's, work on fear as well as argument to encourage his audience to make choices that are better for society and might lead to a blessed afterlife.

Within his Underworld scenes, Lucian uses the trope of the soul's journey into the Underworld as a mirror to address and criticize his own society's beliefs about themselves and the past. Representations of cosmic judgment, how souls are sorted, and individuals' reactions to their afterlife plights illustrate issues and give distance from the real world for collective contemplation by the audience. By featuring "everyman" figures, these Underworld scenes also remain relevant in pointing out human folly. Lucian's audience members are meant to see themselves in his characters, whether famous or lowly, because he humanizes them with laughter, the pressure valve that takes the sting out of his razor-sharp critiques on specific individuals and classes of people. In the *Downward Journey* (*Catapl.*), for example, Lucian presents a quasi-morality play with stock characters Megapenthes, Micyllus, and Cyniscus as the rich tyrant, poor cobbler, and philosopher, respectively. Megapenthes' antics to try to escape his fate and negotiate a return to his luxurious life elicit laughter as he uses his wily behavior and words to confound the deities Hermes, Clotho, and Charon, who are portrayed as somewhat bumbling characters, similar to Dionysus in the *Frogs*.

The soul of Micyllus, in his own words, is the dead tyrant's opposite, saying his life "is not anyhow similar to those of the rich, for our lives are diametrically opposed, as the saying goes, and the tyrant seemed at any rate to be blessed in life" (ἄλλως τε οὐδ᾽ ὅμοια τἀμὰ τοῖς τῶν πλουσίων ἐκ διαμέτρου γὰρ ἡμῶν οἱ βίοι, φασίν ὁ μὲν γε τύραννος εὐδαίμων εἶναι δοκῶν παρὰ τὸν βίον, *Catapl.* 14). After extemporizing further on the life that Megapenthes led and his difficulties accepting his death, Micyllus speculates on the state of the soul

260   LIFE / AFTERLIFE

and how it clings to life's rich trappings. He then turns the focus on himself, saying he had no security on any level while alive:

ἐγὼ δὲ ἅτε μηδὲν ἔχων ἐνέχυρον ἐν τῷ βίῳ, οὐκ ἀγρόν, οὐ συνοικίαν, οὐ χρυσόν, οὐ σκεῦος, οὐ δόξαν, οὐκ εἰκόνας, εἰκότως εὔζωνος ἦν, κἀπειδὴ μόνον ἡ Ἄτροπος ἔνευσέ μοι. (*Catapl.* 15)

But I did not have an ounce of security in life—no farm, no tenement, no gold, no gear, no reputation, no statues—and was suitably well-equipped when Atropos only gave me the nod.

Micyllus emphasizes his destitution with rhetorical flourish, using asyndeton in an expansive list with repeated, staccato-like "no" (οὐ/οὐκ) before simple, mostly disyllabic words, listing all the aspects by which people define their identities in life. He explains that his status and possessions while alive were not much different than that of his soul in death, which is why he was ready to die when his time came and did not struggle on the journey down to Charon, unlike the unjust Megapenthes. As the tyrant's contemporary who provides the "view from below," Micyllus embodies the human costs of the excesses of rich men such as Megapenthes, which harm not only the people around them but also, ultimately, themselves.

Such social commentary, cloaked in an Underworld scene, personalizes Lucian's criticisms of social inequities during his times. The Underworld becomes the space to explore such issues, and the choice of which ghosts to feature reflects a diachronic shift in interests between Homer and Lucian. Lucian borrows and manipulates his "school classics" (Anderson 1976, 31) to highlight literary themes, societal concerns, and connections to tradition. Furthermore, his Underworld scenes emphasize how the afterlife's eternal "now" can visualize the dynamic interplay between past, present, and future. This allows him not only to summarize past events from a perspective that is seemingly outside of the present reality, but also to guide the audience through a reflection on his innovations and criticisms in light of competing narratives, both past and present.

III. *Conclusions*

There is much more one can say about Underworld scenes in Lucian, Vergil, and other authors through to the present day. The short examples discussed in this epilogue are intended to be illustrative rather than exhaustive of

Underworld scene reception and to demonstrate the persistence and stability of Underworld scenes as a metaliterary device. Because of their temporal and spatial flexibility, Underworld scenes create purposeful inefficiencies in a narrative, which slow down or even halt the plot for an extended period of time. This allows audiences to contemplate the themes and issues relevant to understanding the significance of the story they are attached to and the messages the author wants to convey about the nature of humanity and the cosmos. For authors of the Roman Imperial Period and beyond who received Greek myths from revered authors and traditions of the distant past, Underworld scenes served as a platform for them to balance the external pressure of establishing their work in their canons of literary tradition (i.e., the "anxiety of influence") with the internal pressure for the scene to remain relevant to the frame narrative (i.e., the "anxiety of authorship").

From ancient times to the present, Underworld scenes have been fundamental in shaping human beliefs about life, death, and the choices people have to attain the best outcomes in both life and afterlife. By viewing Underworld scenes as interconnected hypertextual narratives transcending time and genre, this study offers strategies for approaching almost any Underworld scene and for understanding how and why authors use them. For example, Dante could only write his *Inferno* because of Vergil's Underworld, who in turn borrowed it from Homer and Plato among others.[6] By engaging with a vast network of texts and collective myths, Underworld scenes allow authors and audiences to reflect on their societies, challenge their traditions, and create new realities and futures for themselves both in this life and in the afterlife.

---

[6] For more on the post-Vergilian reception of Underworld scenes, see Gladhill and Myers (2020).

Bibliography

Alden, Maureen. 2000. *Homer Beside Himself: Para-Narratives in the Iliad*. Oxford: Oxford University Press.

Alden, Maureen. 2017. *Para-Narratives in the Odyssey: Stories in the Frame*. Oxford: Oxford University Press.

Allison, Richard H. 1983. "Amphibian Ambiguities: Aristophanes and His Frogs." *Greece & Rome* 30 (1): 8–20.

Anderson, Graham. 1976. *Lucian: Theme and Variation in the Second Sophistic*. Lugduni Batavorum: Brill.

Annas, Julia. 1982. "Plato's Myths of Judgement." *Phronesis* 27 (2): 119–143.

Antonaccio, Carla M. 1994. "Contesting the Past: Hero Cult, Tomb Cult, and Epic in Early Greece." *American Journal of Archaeology* 98 (3): 389–410.

Antonaccio, Carla M. 1995. *An Archaeology of Ancestors: Tomb Cult and Hero Cult in Early Greece. Greek Studies*. Lanham, MD: Rowman & Littlefield.

Aparisi, Eduard Urios. 1996. "Old Comedy Pherecrates' Way." *Ítaca: Quaderns catalans de cultura clàssica* 12–13 (1996–1997): 75–86.

Arft, Justin. 2022. *Arete and the Odyssey's Poetics of Interrogation: The Queen and Her Question*. Oxford: Oxford University Press.

Arrington, Nathan T. 2015. *Ashes, Images, and Memories: The Presence of the War Dead in Fifth-Century Athens*. Oxford: Oxford University Press.

Bakhtin, Mikhail M. 1981. *The Dialogic Imagination: Four Essays*. Translated by Michael Holquist and Caryl Emerson. Vol. 1, edited by Michael Holquist. Austin: University of Texas Press.

Bardel, Ruth. 2005. "Spectral Traces: Ghosts in Tragic Fragments." In *Lost Dramas of Classical Athens: Greek Tragic Fragments*, edited by Fiona McHardy, James Robson, and David Harvey, 83–112. Exeter, U.K.: University of Exeter Press.

Bemong, Nele, Pieter Borghart, Michel De Dobbeleer, Kristoffel Demoen, Koen De Temmerman, and Bart Keuen, eds. 2010. *Bakhtin's Theory of the Literary Chronotope: Reflections, Applications, Perspectives*. Gent: Academia Press.

Benzi, Nicolò. 2021. "In Quest for Authority: Parmenides and the Tradition of Katabasis Narratives." In *Aspects of Death and the Afterlife in Greek Literature*, edited by George Gazis and Anthony Hooper, 89–104. Liverpool: Liverpool University Press.

Bibliography

Bernabé Pajares, Alberto. 2013. "Ὁ Πλάτων παρωιδεῖ τὰ Ὀρφέως Plato's Transposition of Orphic Netherworld Imagery." In *Philosophy and Salvation in Greek Religion*, edited by Vishwa Adluri, 117–149. Berlin: De Gruyter.

Bernabé Pajares, Alberto, and Ana Isabel Jiménez San Cristóbal. 2008. *Instructions for the Netherworld: The Orphic Gold Tablets*. Vol. 162. Leiden-Boston: Brill.

Bernabé Pajares, Alberto, and Ana Isabel Jiménez San Cristóbal. 2011. "Are the "Orphic" Gold Leaves Orphic?" In *The "Orphic" Gold Tablets and Greek Religion: Further Along the Path*, edited by Radcliffe G. Edmonds, 68–101. Cambridge: Cambridge University Press.

Bettini, Maurizio. 1991. *Anthropology and Roman Culture: Kinship, Time, Images of the Soul*. Baltimore: Johns Hopkins University Press.

Betz, Hans D. 2011. ""A Child of Earth Am I and of Starry Heaven": Concerning the Anthropology of the Orphic Gold Tablets." In *The "Orphic" Gold Tablets and Greek Religion: Further Along the Path*, edited by Radcliffe G. Edmonds, 102–119. Cambridge: Cambridge University Press.

Blank, David. 1991. "The Fate of the Ignorant in Plato's 'Gorgias.'" *Hermes* 119 (1): 22–36.

Blickman, Daniel R. 1987. "Styx and the Justice of Zeus in Hesiod's 'Theogony.'" *Phoenix* 41 (4): 341–355.

Boehringer, David. 2001. *Heroenkulte in Griechenland von der geometrischen bis zur klassischen Zeit: Attika, Argolis, Messenien. Vol. n F, Bd 3Klio Beihefte*. Berlin: Akademie Verlag.

Bonifazi, Anna. 2008. "Memory and Visualization in Homeric Discourse Markers." In *Orality, Literacy, Memory in the Ancient Greek and Roman World: Orality and Literacy in Ancient Greece*, edited by Anne Mackay, In *Mnemosyne Supplementa* 298, 35–64. Leiden: Brill.

Bosworth, A. B. 2000. "The Historical Context of Thucydides' Funeral Oration." *The Journal of Hellenic Studies* 120: 1–16.

Bowie, A. M. 1993. *Aristophanes: Myth, Ritual, and Comedy*. Cambridge: Cambridge University Press.

Bowra, C. M. 1952. *Heroic Poetry*. London: Macmillan.

Boys-Stones, G. R., and J. H. Haubold, eds. 2010. *Plato and Hesiod*. Oxford: Oxford University Press.

Branham, Robert B., ed. 2002. *Bakhtin and the Classics*. Evanston, IL: Northwestern University Press.

Bremmer, Jan. 1983. *The Early Greek Concept of the Soul*. Princeton, NJ: Princeton University Press.

Bremmer, Jan. 2002. *The Rise and Fall of the Afterlife*. London: Routledge.

Bremmer, Jan. 2006. "The Rise of the Hero Cult and the New Simonides." *Zeitschrift für Papyrologie und Epigraphik* 158: 15–26.

Bremmer, Jan. 2010. "The Rise of the Unitary Soul and its Opposition to the Body from Homer to Socrates." In *Philosophische Anthropologie in der Antike*, edited by L. Jansen and Ch. Jedan, 11–30. Frankfurt: Ontos Verlag.

Bibliography

Bremmer, Jan. 2011. "Initiation into the Eleusinian Mysteries: A 'Thin' Description." In *Mystery and Secrecy in the Nag Hammadi Collection and Other Ancient Literature: Ideas and Practices*, edited by C. H. Bull, Liv Lied, and John Turner, 375–397. Leiden: Brill.

Bremmer, Jan. 2014a. "Initiation into the Eleusinian Mysteries: A 'Thin' Description." In *Initiation Into the Mysteries of the Ancient World*, 1–20. Berlin: De Gruyter. Original edition, 2011.

Bremmer, Jan. 2014b. *Initiation into the Mysteries of the Ancient World*. Munich: De Gruyter.

Bremmer, Jan. 2015. "'Theseus' and Peirithoos' Descent into the Underworld." *Les Etudes classiques* 83: 35–49.

Brown, Christopher G. 1991. "Empousa, Dionysus and the Mysteries: Aristophanes, Frogs 285ff." *The Classical Quarterly* 41 (1): 41–50.

Burgess, Jonathan S. 2004. *The Tradition of the Trojan War in Homer and the Epic Cycle*. Baltimore: Johns Hopkins University Press.

Burgess, Jonathan S. 2009. *The Death and Afterlife of Achilles*. Baltimore: Johns Hopkins University Press.

Burgess, Jonathan S. 2010. "The Hypertext of Astyanax." *Trends in Classics* 2 (2): 209–224. https://doi.org/10.1515/tcs.2010.011.

Burkert, Walter. 1983. *Homo Necans*. Berkeley: University of California Press.

Burkert, Walter. 1985. *Greek Religion*. Cambridge, MA: Harvard University Press. 1977.

Burnett, Anne Pippin. 1985. *The Art of Bacchylides*. Cambridge, MA: Harvard University Press.

Burnyeat, M. F. 2012. *Explorations in Ancient and Modern Philosophy*. Vol. 2. Cambridge: Cambridge University Press.

Bywater, I. 1909. *Aristotle on the Art of Poetry*. Oxford: Oxford University Press.

Calame, Claude. 1990. *Thesée et l'imaginaire athenien: Legende et culte en Grece antique*. Lausanne: Payot.

Calame, Claude. 2009. *Poetic and Performative Memory in Ancient Greece: Heroic Reference and Ritual Gestures in Time and Space*. Vol. 18. *Hellenic Studies*. Washington, DC: Center for Hellenic Studies.

Calder III, William M. 1966. "A Reconstruction of Sophocles' *Polyxena*." *Greek, Roman and Byzantine Studies* 7: 31–56.

Calkins, Renée. 2010. "Making Kleos Mortal: Archaic Attic Funerary Monuments and the Construction of Social Memory." Ph.D. Dissertation, Classics, University of California Los Angeles.

Calvo Martínez, José L. 2000. "The Katabasis of the Hero." In *Héros et héroïnes dans les mythes et les cultes grecs: actes du colloque organisé à l'Université de Valladolid du 26 au 29 mai 1999*, edited by Vinciane Pirenne-Delforge and Emilio Suárez de la Torre, 67–78. Liège: Presses Universitaires de Liège.

Clark, Raymond J. 1979. *Catabasis: Vergil and the Wisdom-Tradition*. Amsterdam: Grüner.

Clark, Raymond J. 2001. "How Vergil Expanded the Underworld in Aeneid 6." *Proceedings of the Cambridge Philological Society* 47: 103–116.

Clay, Jenny S. 1989. *The Politics of Olympus: Form and Meaning in the Major Homeric Hymns*. Princeton, NJ: Princeton University Press.

Clay, Jenny S. 2003. *Hesiod's Cosmos*. Cambridge: Cambridge University Press.

Clinton, Kevin. 1992. *Myth and Cult: The Iconography of the Eleusinian Mysteries*. Stockholm: Swedish Institute in Athens.

Closterman, Wendy E. 2007. "Family Ideology and Family History: The Function of Funerary Markers in Classical Attic Peribolos Tombs." *American Journal of Archaeology* 111 (4): 633–652.

Collins, Derek. 2001. "Homer and Rhapsodic Competition in Performance." *Oral Tradition* 16 (1): 129–167.

Constantakopoulou, Christy. 2007. *The Dance of the Islands: Insularity, Networks, the Athenian Empire, and the Aegean World*. Oxford: Oxford University Press.

Cooper, John M. 2012. *Pursuits of Wisdom: Six Ways of Life in Ancient Philosophy from Socrates to Plotinus*. Princeton, NJ: Princeton University Press.

Corbel-Morana, Cécile. 2012. *Le Bestiaire d'Aristophane. Vol. 144. Collection d'études anciennes. Série grecque, 144*. Paris: Les Belles Lettres.

Cosmopoulos, Michael B. 2015. *Bronze Age Eleusis and the Origins of the Eleusinian Mysteries*. Cambridge: Cambridge University Press.

Currie, Bruno. 2005. *Pindar and the Cult of Heroes*. Oxford-New York: Oxford University Press.

Currie, Bruno. 2011. "Perspectives on Neoanalysis from the Archaic Hymns to Demeter." In *Relative Chronology in Early Greek Epic Poetry*, edited by Oivind Andersen and Dag T. T. Haug, 184–209. Cambridge: Cambridge University Press.

Davies, Glenys. 1985. "The Significance of the Handshake Motif in Classical Funerary Art." *American Journal of Archaeology* 89 (4): 627–640.

de Heer, Cornelis. 1969. *Makar, Eudaimon, Olbios, Eutyches: A Study of the Semantic Field Denoting Happiness in Ancient Greek to the End of the 5th Century B.C.* Amsterdam: A. M. Hakkert.

de Jong, Irene J. F. 2001. *A Narratological Commentary on the Odyssey*. Cambridge: Cambridge University Press.

de Jong, Irene J. F., and Rene Nünlist. 2007. *Time in Ancient Greek Literature*. Vol. v. 2. Leiden: Brill.

Doherty, Lillian E. 1995. *Siren Songs: Gender, Audiences, and Narrators in the Odyssey*. Ann Arbor: University of Michigan Press.

Dova, Stamatia. 2012. *Greek Heroes in and out of Hades*. Lanham, MD: Lexington Books.

Dova, Stamatia. 2020. *The Poetics of Failure*. Milton: Taylor and Francis.

Dover, Kenneth J. 1997. *Aristophanes' Frogs*. Oxford: Oxford University Press.

duBois, Page. 2022. *Democratic Swarms: Ancient Comedy and the Politics of the People*. Chicago: University of Chicago Press.

Bibliography

Dué, Casey, and Mary Ebbott. 2010. *Iliad 10 and the Poetics of Ambush: A Multitext Edition with Essays and Commentary.* Washington, DC: Center for Hellenic Studies.

Dunn, Francis. 2002. "Rethinking Time: From Bakhtin to Antiphon." In *Bakhtin and the Classics*, edited by Robert Bracht Branham, 187–219. Evanston, IL: Northwestern University Press.

Dunn, Francis. 2007. *Present Shock in Late Fifth-Century Greece.* Ann Arbor: The University of Michigan Press.

Edmonds, Radcliffe G. 2004. *Myths of the Underworld Journey Plato, Aristophanes, and the "Orphic" Gold Tablets.* New York: Cambridge University Press.

Edmonds, Radcliffe G. 2011a. "Afterlife." In *The Homer Encyclopedia*, edited by Margalit Finkelberg, 11–14. Wiley-Blackwell.

Edmonds, Radcliffe G. 2011b. "Necromancy." In *The Homer Encyclopedia*, edited by Margalit Finkelberg, 563. Wiley-Blackwell.

Edmonds, Radcliffe G. 2011c. "The "Orphic" Gold Tablets: Texts and Translations, with Critical Apparatus and Tables." In *The "Orphic" Gold Tablets and Greek Religion: Further Along the Path,* edited by Radcliffe G. Edmonds, 15–50. Cambridge: Cambridge University Press.

Edmonds, Radcliffe G. 2011d. "Sacred Scripture or Oracles for the Dead? The Semiotic Situation of the "Orphic" Gold Tablets." In *The "Orphic" Gold Tablets and Greek Religion: Further Along the Path*, edited by Radcliffe G. Edmonds, 257–270. Cambridge: Cambridge University Press.

Edmonds, Radcliffe G. 2012. "Whip Scars on the Naked Soul: Myth and Elenchos in Plato's Gorgias." In *Platonic Myths: Status, Uses, and Functions*, edited by Catherine Collobert, Pierre Destrée, and Francisco Gonzalez, 165–186. Leiden: Brill.

Edmonds, Radcliffe G. 2014. "A Lively Afterlife and Beyond: The Soul in Plato, Homer, and the Orphica." *Études Platoniciennes* 11: Platon et ses prédécesseurs—Psukhê: 1–29. https://doi.org/10.4000/etudesplatoniciennes.517.

Edmonds, Radcliffe G. 2020a. "The Ethics of Afterlife in Classical Greek Thought." In *Early Greek Ethics*, edited by David Conan Wolfsdorf, 545–565. Oxford: Oxford University Press.

Edmonds, Radcliffe G. 2020b. "The Song of the Nightingale: Word Play on the Road to Hades in Plato's Phaedo." *Transactions of the American Philological Association* 150 (1): 65–83.

Edmonds, Radcliffe G. 2021. "A Path Neither Simple Nor Single: The Afterlife as Good to Think With." In *Aspects of Death and the Afterlife in Greek Literature*, edited by George Gazis and Anthony Hooper, 11–32. Liverpool: Liverpool University Press.

Ehnmark, E. 1948. "Some Remarks on the Idea of Immortality in Greek Religion." *Eranos* 46: 1–21.

Eidinow, Esther. 2013. *Oracles, Curses, and Risk Among the Ancient Greeks.* Oxford: Oxford University Press.

Ekroth, Gunnel. 2002. *The Sacrificial Rituals of Greek Hero-Cults in the Archaic to the Early Hellenistic Periods. Vol. 12*. Kernos Supplement. Liege: Centre international d'étude de la religion grecque antique.

Ekroth, Gunnel. 2018. "Hades, Homer and the Hittites: The Cultic-Cultural Context of Odysseus' 'Round Trip' to the Underworld." In *Roundtrip to Hades in the Eastern Mediterranean Tradition: Visits to the Underworld from Antiquity to Byzantium*, edited by Gunnel Ekroth and Ingela Nilsson, 37–56. Leiden: Brill.

Evans, David. 1974. "Dodona, Dodola, and Daedala." In *Myth in Indo-European Antiquity*, edited by Gerald James Larson, C. Scott Littleton, and Jaan Puhvel, 99–130. Berkeley: University of California Press.

Farmer, Matthew. 2017. *Tragedy on the Comic Stage*. New York: Oxford University Press.

Feldherr, Andrew. 1999. "Putting Dido on the Map: Genre and Geography in Vergil's Underworld." *Arethusa* 32 (1): 85–122. https://doi.org/10.1353/are.1999.0002.

Felson, Nancy. 2004. "Introduction: Poetics of Deixis." *Arethusa* 37 (3): 253–266.

Foley, Helene P. 1994. *The Homeric Hymn to Demeter: Translation, Commentary, and Interpretative Essays*. Princeton, NJ: Princeton University Press.

Foley, Helene P. 2003. "Choral Identity in Greek Tragedy." *Classical Philology* 98 (1): 1–30.

Fowler, Don. 2000. *Roman Constructions: Readings in Postmodern Latin*. Oxford: Oxford University Press.

Frangeskou, Vassiliki. 1999. "Tradition and Originality in Some Attic Funeral Orations." *The Classical World* 92 (4): 315–336.

Gager, John G. 1999. *Curse Tablets and Binding Spells from the Ancient World*. Oxford: Oxford University Press.

Gantz, Timothy. 1980. "The Aischylean Tetralogy: Attested and Conjectured Groups." *The American Journal of Philology* 101 (2): 133–164.

Garland, Robert. 1981. "The Causation of Death in the *Iliad*: A Theological and Biological Investigation." *Bulletin of the Institute of Classical Studies* 28 (1): 43–60.

Garland, Robert. 1985. *The Greek Way of Death*. London: Duckworth.

Garland, Robert. 1989. "The Well-Ordered Corpse: An Investigation into the Motives Behind Greek Funerary Legislation." *Bulletin of the Institute of Classical Studies* 36: 1–15.

Gazis, George. 2012. "Odyssey 11: The Power of Sight in the Invisible Realm." *Rosetta* 12: 49–59.

Gazis, George. 2018. *Homer and the Poetics of Hades*. Oxford: Oxford University Press.

Gazis, George. 2021. "What Is Your Lot? Lyric Pessimism and Pindar's Afterlife." In *Aspects of Death and the Afterlife in Greek Literature*, edited by George Gazis and Anthony Hooper, 69–87. Liverpool: Liverpool University Press.

Gee, Emma. 2020. *Mapping the Afterlife: From Homer to Dante*. Oxford: Oxford University Press.

Genette, Gérard. 1997. *Palimpsests*. Translated by Channa Newman and Claude Doubinsky. Lincoln and London: University of Nebraska.

Bibliography

Gennep, Arnold van. 1981. *Les Rites de Passage: Etude Systématique des Rites.* Paris: Éditions A. & J. Picard.

Georgiadou, A., and D. H. J. Larmour. 1998. "Lucian's "Verae Historiae" as Philosophical Parody." *Hermes* 126 (3): 310–325.

Gilbert, Allan H. 1947. "Aristotle's Four Species of Tragedy (Poetics 18) and Their Importance for Dramatic Criticism." *The American Journal of Philology* 68 (4): 363–381.

Gladhill, Bill, and Micah Young Myers. 2020. *Walking through Elysium: Vergil's Underworld and the Poetics of Tradition.* Toronto: University of Toronto Press.

Goins, Scott E. 1989. "Euripides Fr. 863 Nauck." *Rheinisches Museum für Philologie* 132 (3/4): 401–403.

Golden, Leon. 1970–1971. "Euripides' Alcestis: Structure and Theme." *The Classical Journal* 66 (2): 116–125.

Graf, Fritz, and Sarah Iles Johnston. 2007. *Ritual Texts for the Afterlife: Orpheus and the Bacchic Gold Tablets.* London: Routledge.

Green, Peter. 2010. "The Metamorphosis of the Barbarian: Athenian Panhellenism in a Changing World." In *From Ikaria to the Stars*, 104–132. Austin: University of Texas.

Gregory, T. B., J. K. Newman, and T. Meyers. 2012. "Epic." In *The Princeton Encyclopedia of Poetry and Poetics*, edited by Roland Greene, Stephen Cushman, Clare Cavanagh, Jahan Ramazani, Paul F. Rouzer, Harris Feinsod, David Marno, and Alexandra Slessarev. Princeton, NJ: Princeton University Press.

Griffiths, Alan. 1986. " 'What Leaf-Fringed Legend . . .?' A Cup by the Sotades Painter in London." *The Journal of Hellenic Studies* 106: 58–70.

Grossardt, Peter. 2003. "The Title of Aeschylus' 'Ostologoi.'" *Harvard Studies in Classical Philology* 101: 155–158.

Hale, John. 2009. *Lords of the Sea: The Epic Story of the Athenian Navy and the Birth of Democracy.* New York: Viking.

Hall, Edith. 1989. *Inventing the Barbarian: Greek Self-Definition through Tragedy.* Oxford: Clarendon Press.

Hall, Edith. 1996. *Aeschylus: Persians.* Oxford: Aris & Phillips Classical Texts.

Halliwell, Stephen. 2007. "The Life-and-Death Journey of the Soul: Interpreting the Myth of Er." In *The Cambridge Companion to Plato's Republic*, edited by G. R. F. Ferrari, 445–473. Cambridge: Cambridge University Press.

Herington, John. 1986. *Aeschylus.* New Haven, CT: Yale University Press.

Herrero de Jáuregui, Miguel. 2011. "Dialogues of Immortality from the *Iliad* to the Gold Leaves." In *The "Orphic" Gold Tablets and Greek Religion: Further Along the Path*, edited by Radcliffe G. Edmonds, 271–290. Cambridge: Cambridge University Press.

Herrero de Jáuregui, Miguel. 2011. 2021. "Political Imagery in Ancient Greek Eschatology." In *Seelenreise und Katabasis: Einblicke Ins Jenseits in Antiker Philosophischer Literatur*, edited by Irmgard Männlein-Robert, 81–106. Berlin: De Gruyter.

Heubeck, A., and A. Hoekstra. 1990. *A Commentary on Homer's Odyssey. Vol. 2: Books IX–XVI*. Oxford: Clarendon Press.

Hickman, Ruby. 1938. *Ghostly Etiquette on the Classical Stage. Vol. 7*. Iowa Studies in Classical Philology. Cedar Rapids, IA: Torch Press.

Hinds, Stephen. 1997. ""Proemio al Mezzo": Allusion and the Limits of Interpretability." *Materiali e discussioni per l'analisi dei testi classici* 39: 113–122.

Hirschberger, Martina. 2001. "Die Erzählungen der Frauen in der Nekyia der Odyssee." In *Eranos. Proceedings of the 9th International Symposium on the Odyssey (2–7 September 2000)*, edited by Machi Païsi-Apostolopoulou and Kentro Odysseiakōn Spoudōn, 123–151. Ithaca, NY: Kentro Odysseiakōn Spoudōn.

Hoffmann, Herbert. 1989. "Aletheia: The Iconography of Death/Rebirth in Three Cups by the Sotades Painter." *RES: Anthropology and Aesthetics* 17/18 (Spring-Autumn): 68–88.

Hoffmann, Herbert. 1997. *Sotades: Symbols of Immortality on Greek Vases*. Oxford: Oxford University Press.

Humphreys, Sarah C. 1980. "Family Tombs and Tomb Cult in Ancient Athens: Tradition or Traditionalism?" *The Journal of Hellenic Studies* 100: 96–126.

Janko, Richard. 1987. *Aristotle: Poetics*. Translated by Richard Janko. Indianapolis: Hackett.

Janko, Richard. 2016. "Going Beyond Multitexts: The Archetype of the Orphic Gold Leaves." *Classical Quarterly* 66 (2): 100–127. https://doi.org/10.1017/S0009838816000380.

Johnson, David. 1999. "Hesiod's Descriptions of Tartarus (Theogony 721–819)." *Phoenix* 53 (1/2 Spring–Summer): 8–28.

Johnston, Sarah I. 1999. *Restless Dead: Encounters Between the Living and the Dead in Ancient Greece*. Berkeley: University of California Press.

Jones, Christopher P. 2010. *New Heroes in Antiquity: From Achilles to Antinoos*. Cambridge, MA: Harvard University Press.

Jouan, François. 1981. "L'évocation des morts dans la tragédie grecque." *Revue de l'histoire des religions* 198 (4): 403–421.

Kahn, Charles H. 1997. "Greek Religion and Philosophy in the Sisyphus Fragment." *Phronesis* 42 (3): 247–262.

Kannicht, R., and Bruno Snell. 1981. *Tragicorum Graecorum Fragmenta (TrGF). Vol. 2: Fragmenta Adespota*. Gottingen: Vandenhoeck & Ruprecht.

Karanika, Andromache. 2011. "The End of the Nekyia: Odysseus, Heracles, and the Gorgon in the Underworld." *Arethusa* 44: 1–27.

Kosmopoulou, Angeliki. 1998. "A Funerary Base from Kallithea: New Light on Fifth-Century Eschatology." *American Journal of Archaeology* 102 (3): 531–545.

Krappe, Alexander H. 1928. "Teiresias and the Snakes." *The American Journal of Philology* 49 (3): 267–275.

Kristeva, Julia. 1974. *La Révolution du Langage Poétique*. Paris: Seuil.

Bibliography

Kristeva, Julia. 1980a. "The Bounded Text." In *Desire in Language*, 36–63. New York: Columbia University Press. Original edition, 1969.

Kristeva, Julia. 1980b. *Desire in Language: A Semiotic Approach to Literature and Art—European Perspectives*. New York: Columbia University Press.

Kristeva, Julia. 1980c. "Word, Dialogue, and Novel." In *Desire in Language*, edited by Leon S. Roudiez, translated by Thomas Gora, Alice Jardine, and Leon S. Roudiez, 64–91. New York: Columbia University Press. Original edition, 1969.

Lada-Richards, Ismene. 1999. *Initiating Dionysus: Ritual and Theatre in Aristophanes' Frogs*. Oxford: Clarendon Press.

Lane, Nicholas. 2007. "Staging Polydorus' Ghost in the Prologue of Euripides' Hecuba." *The Classical Quarterly* 57 (1): 290–294.

Larson, Jennifer. 1995. *Greek Heroine Cults*. Wisconsin Studies in Classics. Madison: University of Wisconsin Press.

Larson, Jennifer. 2007. *Ancient Greek Cults: A Guide*. New York: Routledge.

Lee, Mireille M. 2004. "'Evil Wealth of Raiment': Deadly ΠέΠλοι in Greek Tragedy." *The Classical Journal* 99 (3): 253–279.

Lefkowitz, Mary R. 1969. "Bacchylides' Ode 5: Imitation and Originality." *Harvard Studies in Classical Philology* 73: 45–96.

Lincoln, Bruce. 1999. *Theorizing Myth: Narrative, Ideology, and Scholarship*. Chicago: University of Chicago Press.

Linforth, Ivan M. 1944. *Soul and Sieve in Plato's Gorgias. Vol. 12., No. 17. University of California Publications in Classical Philology*. Berkeley: University of California.

Lloyd-Jones, Hugh. 1967. "Heracles at Eleusis." *Maia* 19: 206–229.

Lloyd-Jones, Hugh. 1971. *The Justice of Zeus*. Vol. v. 41. Berkeley: University of California Press.

Lloyd-Jones, Hugh. 1990. "Pindar and the Afterlife." In *Greek Epic, Lyric, and Tragedy: The Academic Papers of Sir Hugh Lloyd-Jones*, 80–109. Oxford: Clarendon Press.

Loraux, Nicole. 2006. *The Invention of Athens: The Funeral Oration in the Classical City*. Translated by Alan Sheridan. New York: Zone Books. 1981.

Low, Polly. 2011. "The Power of the Dead in Classical Sparta: The Case of Thermopylae." In *Living Through the Dead: Burial and Commemoration in the Classical World*, edited by Maureen Carroll and Jane Rempel, 1–20. Oxford: Oxbow Books.

Low, Polly. 2012. "The Monuments to the War Dead in Classical Athens: Form, Contexts, Meanings." In *Cultures of Commemoration: War Memorials, Ancient and Modern, Proceedings of the British Academy*, edited by Polly Low, Graham Oliver, and P. J. Rhodes, 12–38. London: Oxford University Press.

Lye, Suzanne. 2009. "The Goddess Styx and the Mapping of World Order in Hesiod's *Theogony*." *Revue de philosophie ancienne* 27 (2): 3–31.

Lyons, Deborah. 1997. *Gender and Immortality: Heroines in Ancient Greek Myth and Cult*. Princeton, NJ: Princeton University Press.

Mackin Roberts, Ellie. 2020. *Underworld Gods in Ancient Greek Religion: Death and Reciprocity*. London: Routledge.

Maehler, H. 2004. *Bacchylides: A Selection*. Cambridge: Cambridge University Press.

Mai, Hans-Peter. 1991. "Bypassing Intertextuality: Hermeneutics, Textual Practice, Hypertext." In *Intertextuality*, edited by Heinrich F. Plett, 30–59. Berlin: De Gruyter.

Marks, Jim. 2010. "Context as Hypertext: Divine Rescue Scenes in the Iliad." *Trends in Classics* 2 (2): 300–322. https://doi.org/10.1515/tcs.2010.016.

Martin, Bridget. 2012. "The Return of the Dead in Greek Tragedy." Ph.D. Dissertation, Classics, University College Dublin.

Martin, Bridget. 2014. "Blood, Honour, and Status in Odyssey 11." *The Classical Quarterly* 64 (1): 1–12.

McCabe, Mary Margaret. 1992. "Myth, Allegory and Argument in Plato." In *The Language of the Cave*, edited by Andrew Barker and Martin Warner, 47–67. Edmonton: Academic Printing & Pub.

McNiven, Timothy J. 1989. "Odysseus on the Niobid Krater." *The Journal of Hellenic Studies* 109: 191–198.

Meisner, Dwayne. 2018. *Orphic Tradition and The Birth of the Gods*. New York: Oxford University Press.

Mikellidou, Katerina. 2016. "Aeschylus Reading Homer: The Case of the Psychagogoi." In *Homeric Receptions Across Generic and Cultural Contexts*, edited by Athanasios Efstathiou and Ioanna Karamanou, 331–342. Berlin: De Gruyter.

Mills, Sophie. 1997. *Theseus, Tragedy and the Athenian Empire*. Oxford: Oxford University Press.

Minchin, Elizabeth. 1995. "The Poet Appeals to His Muse: Homeric Invocations in the Context of Epic Performance." *The Classical Journal* 91 (1): 25–33.

Mirto, Maria S. 2012. *Death in the Greek World: From Homer to the Classical Age*. Translated by A. M. Osborne. Norman: University of Oklahoma Press.

Mitchell, Alexandre. 2009. *Greek Vase Painting and the Origins of Visible Humor*. Cambridge: Cambridge University Press.

Mitchell, Lynette G. 2007. *Panhellenism and the Barbarian in Archaic and Classical Greece*. Swansea: The Classical Press of Wales.

Montiglio, Sylvia. 2005. *Wandering in Ancient Greek Culture*. Chicago: University of Chicago Press.

Moorton, Richard F., Jr. 1989. "Rites of Passage in Aristophanes' 'Frogs.'" *The Classical Journal* 84 (4): 308–324.

Moreno, Miryam L. 2004. "TrGF2 Adesp. fr. 370 K.-Sn.: Aeschylus' Psychagogoi?" *Exemplaria Classica* 8: 7–29.

Morgan, J. R., and Stephen Harrison. 2008. "Intertextuality." In *The Cambridge Companion to the Greek and Roman Novel*, edited by Tim Whitmarsh, 218–236. Cambridge: Cambridge University Press.

Morgan, Kathryn A. 2000. *Myth and Philosophy from the Presocratics to Plato*. Cambridge: Cambridge University Press.

Bibliography

Morgan, Kathryn A. 2015. *Pindar and the Construction of Syracusan Monarchy in the Fifth Century B.C.* Oxford: Oxford Universitiy Press.

Morris, Ian. 1987. *Burial and Ancient Society*. Cambridge: Cambridge University Press.

Morris, Ian. 1992. *Death-Ritual and Social Structure in Classical Antiquity*. Cambridge: Cambridge University Press.

Morris, Sarah P. 1992b. *Daidalos and the Origins of Greek Art*. Princeton, NJ: Princeton University Press.

Morson, Gary S. 1994. *Narrative and Freedom: The Shadows of Time*. New Haven, CT: Yale University Press.

Morson, Gary S., and Caryl Emerson. 1989. *Rethinking Bakhtin: Extensions and Challenges*. Evanston, IL: Northwestern University Press.

Most, Glenn. 1986. "Pindar Olympian 2.83–90." *Classical Quarterly* 36 (2): 304–316.

Most, Glenn. 1989. "The Structure and Function of Odysseus' Apologoi." *Transactions of the American Philological Association* 119: 15–30.

Most, Glenn. 1992. "Il poeta nell' Ade: catabasi epica e teoria dell' epos tra Omero e Virgilio." *Studi Italiani di Filologia Classica* X (I–II): 1014–1026.

Nagy, Gregory. 1981. *The Best of the Achaeans: Concepts of the Hero in Archaic Greek Poetry*. Baltimore: Johns Hopkins University Press.

Nagy, Gregory. 1990. *Pindar's Homer: The Lyric Possession of an Epic Past*. Baltimore and London: Johns Hopkins University Press.

Nagy, Gregory. 1996. *Homeric Questions*. Austin: University of Texas Press.

Nagy, Gregory. 2012. "Signs of Hero Cult in Homeric Poetry." In *Homeric Contexts: Neoanalysis and the Interpretation of Oral Poetry*, edited by Franco Montanari, Antonios Rengakos, and Christos Tsagalis, ix, 698. Berlin: De Gruyter.

Nannini, Simonetta. 2010. *Omero: L'autore Necessario* Naples: Liguori.

Nightingale, Andrea. 2002. "Toward an Ecological Eschatology: Plato and Bakhtin on Other Worlds & Times." In *Bakhtin and the Classics*, edited by Robert Bracht Branham, 220–249. Evanston, IL: Northwestern University Press.

Nisetich, Frank J. 1988. "Immortality in Acragas: Poetry and Religion in Pindar's Second Olympian Ode." *Classical Philology* 83 (1): 1–19.

Nisetich, Frank J. 1989. *Pindar and Homer*. Baltimore: Johns Hopkins University Press.

Norden, Eduard. 1926. *P. Vergilius Maro: Aeneis, Buch VI*. Leipzig: B. G. Teubner.

O'Connor, David K. 2007. "Rewriting the Poets in Plato's Characters." In *The Cambridge Companion to Plato's Republic*, edited by G. R. F. Ferrari, 55–89. Cambridge: Cambridge University Press.

Oakley, John H. 2004. *Picturing Death in Classical Athens: The Evidence of the White Lekythoi*. Cambridge: Cambridge University Press.

Obbink, Dirk. 2011. "Poetry and Performance in the Orphic Gold Leaves." In *The "Orphic" Gold Tablets and Greek Religion: Further Along the Path*, edited by Radcliffe G. Edmonds, 291–309. Cambridge: Cambridge University Press.

Ogden, Daniel. 2001. *Greek and Roman Necromancy*. Princeton, NJ: Princeton University Press.

Ogden, Daniel. 2013. *Drakon: Dragon Myth and Serpent Cult in the Greek and Roman Worlds*. Oxford: Oxford University Press.

Olson, S. Douglas. 2020. "The Fragments of Aristophanes' Gerytades: Methodological Considerations." In *Fragmentation in Ancient Greek Drama*, edited by Anna Lamari, Franco Montanari, and Anna Novokhatko, 129–144. Berlin: De Gruyter.

Pache, Corinne O. 2004. *Baby and Child Heroes in Ancient Greece: Traditions*. Urbana: University of Illinois Press.

Page, Denys L. 1955. *The Homeric Odyssey*. Westport, CT: Greenwood Press.

Pandey, Nandini B. 2014. "Reading Rome from the Farther Shore: *Aeneid* 6 in the Augustan Urban Landscape." *Vergilius* 60: 85–116.

Papadimitropoulos, Loukas. 2008. "Xerxes' 'hubris' and Darius in Aeschylus' 'Persae.'" *Mnemosyne, Fourth Series* Vol. 61 (Fasc. 3): 451–458.

Petrain, David. 2014. *Homer in Stone: The Tabulae Iliacae in their Roman Context*. Cambridge: Cambridge University Press.

Petrovic, Ivana, and Andrej Petrovic. 2018. "Divine Bondage and *Katabaseis* in Hesiod's *Theogony*." In *Roundtrip to Hades in the Eastern Mediterranean Tradition: Visits to the Underworld from Antiquity to Byzantium*, edited by Gunnel Ekroth and Ingela Nilsson, In *Interactions in the Mediterranean*, 2, 57–81. Leiden: Brill.

Pindar. 1975. *Pindari carmina cum fragmentis*, pt. 2, 4th edn. edited by H. Maehler (post B. Snell). Leipzig: Teubner.

Plett, Heinrich F. 1991. *Intertextuality*. Berlin: De Gruyter.

Pucci, Pietro. 1987. *Odysseus Polutropos: Intertextual Readings in the Odyssey and the Iliad*. Vol. 46. Ithaca, NY: Cornell University Press.

Purves, Alex. 2004. "Topographies of Time in Hesiod." In *Time and Temporality in the Ancient World*, edited by Ralph Rosen, 147–168. Philadelphia: University of Pennsylvania Museum Publication.

Purves, Alex. 2006. "Falling into Time in Homer's 'Iliad.'" *Classical Antiquity* 25 (1): 179–209.

Purves, Alex. 2010. *Space and Time in Ancient Greek Narrative*. New York: Cambridge University Press.

Querbach, Carl W. 1985. "Hesiod's Myth of the Four Races." *The Classical Journal* 81 (1): 1–12.

Radt, Stefan L. 1977. *Tragicorum Graecorum Fragmenta (TrGF)*. 4 vols. Vol. 4: Sophocles. Göttingen: Vandenhoeck & Ruprecht.

Radt, Stefan L. 1985. *Tragicorum Graecorum Fragmenta (TrGF)*. 4 vols. Vol. 3: Aeschylus. Göttingen: Vandenhoeck & Ruprecht.

Richardson, N. J. 1974. *The Homeric Hymn to Demeter*. Oxford: Clarendon Press.

Riedweg, Christoph. 2011. "Initiation—death—underworld: Narrative and Ritual in the Gold Leaves." In *The "Orphic" Gold Tablets and Greek Religion: Further Along the Path*, edited by Radcliffe G. Edmonds, 219–256. Cambridge: Cambridge University Press.

Rohde, Erwin. 1925. *Psyche: The Cult of Souls and Belief in Immortality Among the Greeks*. Oxfordshire: Routledge. Reprint, 2001. 1903.

Rose, Gilbert P. 1969. "The Unfriendly Phaeacians." *TAPA* 100: 387–406.

Rusten, Jeffrey, ed. 2011. *The Birth of Comedy: Texts, Documents, and Art from the Athenian Comic Competitions, 486–280*. Baltimore: Johns Hopkins University Press.

Rutherford, Ian. 2000. "Formulas, Voice, and Death in *Ehoie*-Poetry, the Hesiodic *Gunaikon Katalogos*, and the Odysseian *Nekuia*." In *Matrices of Genre: Authors, Canons, and Society*, edited by Mary Depew and Dirk Obbink, 81–96. Cambridge, MA: Harvard University Press.

Sammons, Benjamin. 2010. *The Art and Rhetoric of the Homeric Catalogue*. Oxford: Oxford University Press.

Santamaría, Marco Antonio. 2023. "Las fórmulas de felicitación o macarismos en la literatura griega: de los cultos mistéricos a la iniciación filosófica." In *La felicidad en la historia. Representaciones literarias de la felicidad desde la Antigüedad hasta el presente*, edited by Juan Antonio González Iglesias and Guillermo Aprile, 45–70. Salamanca: Ediciones Universidad de Salamanca.

Seaford, Richard. 1994. *Reciprocity and Ritual: Homer and Tragedy in the Developing City-State*. Oxford: Clarendon Press.

Sedley, David. 2009. "Myth, Punishment and Politics in the *Gorgias*." In *Plato's Myths*, edited by Catalin Partenie, 51–76. Cambridge: Cambridge University Press.

Segal, Charles. 1961. "The Character and Cults of Dionysus and the Unity of the Frogs." *Harvard Studies in Classical Philology* 65: 207–242.

Shea, Tim. 2021. "The Archaic and Classical Cemeteries." In *The Cambridge Companion to Ancient Athens*, edited by Jenifer Neils and Dylan K. Rogers, 140–155. Cambridge: Cambridge University Press.

Shilo, Amit. 2013. "From Oblivion to Judgment: Afterlives, Politics, and Unbeliefs in Greek Tragedy and Plato." *ThéoRèmes, Vol.* 5. https://doi.org/10.4000/theoremes.554.

Shilo, Amit. 2022. *Beyond Death in the Oresteia: Poetics, Ethics, and Politics.* Cambridge: Cambridge University Press.

Sifakis, G. M. 1971. *Parabasis and Animal Choruses*. London: Athlone Press.

Simon, Erika. 1963. "Polygnotan Painting and the Niobid Painter." *American Journal of Archaeology* 67 (1): 43–62.

Solmsen, Friedrich. 1968. "Two Pindaric Passages on the Hereafter." *Hermes* 96 (3): 503–506.

Solmsen, Friedrich. 1982a. "Achilles on the Islands of the Blest: Pindar vs. Homer and Hesiod." *The American Journal of Philology* 103 (1): 19–24.

Solmsen, Friedrich. 1982b. "The Earliest Stages in the History of Hesiod's Text." *Harvard Studies in Classical Philology* 86: 1–31.

Sourvinou-Inwood, Christiane. 1981. "To Die and Enter the House of Hades: Homer, Before and After." In *Mirrors of Mortality: Studies in the Social History of Death*, edited by Joachim Whaley, 15–39. New York: St. Martin's Press.

Sourvinou-Inwood, Christiane. 1983. "A Trauma in Flux: Death in the 8th Century and After." In *The Greek Renaissance of the Eighth Century B.C.: Tradition and Innovation. Proceedings of the Second International Symposium at the Swedish Institute in Athens, 1-5 June, 1981*, edited by Robin Hägg, 33–49. Stockholm: Svenska institutet i Athen.

Sourvinou-Inwood, Christiane. 1995. *"Reading" Greek Death: To the End of the Classical Period*. Oxford-New York: Clarendon Press-Oxford University Press.

Stanford, W. B. 1948. *Homer: Odyssey XIII-XXIV*. London: Bristol Classical Press.

Stansbury-O'Donnell, Mark. 1990. "Polygnotos's Nekyia: A Reconstruction and Analysis." *American Journal of Archaeology* 94 (2): 213–235.

Stansbury-O'Donnell, Mark. 1999. *Pictorial Narrative in Ancient Greek Art. Cambridge studies in classical art and iconography*. Cambridge: Cambridge University Press.

Storey, Ian C. 2003. *Eupolis: Poet of Old Comedy*. Oxford: Oxford University Press.

Storey, Ian C., and Arlene Allan. 2005. *A Guide to Ancient Greek Drama*. Oxford: Blackwell Publishing.

Sutton, Dana F. 1978. "Euripides' 'Theseus.'" *Hermes* 106 (1): 49–53.

Sutton, Dana F. 1980. *The Greek Satyr Play. Vol. 90. Beiträge zur klassischen Philologie*. Meisenheim am Glan: Hain.

Taplin, Oliver. 1995. *Homeric Soundings: The Shaping of the Iliad*. Oxford: Clarendon.

Tatum, James. 1984. "Allusion and Interpretation in *Aeneid* 6.440-7." *The American Journal of Philology* 105 (4): 434–452.

Telò, Mario. 2007. *Eupolidis: Demi*. Firenze: Felice Le Monnier.

Torjussen, Stian S. 2014. "Milk as a Symbol of Immortality in the "Orphic" Gold Tablets from Thurii and Pelinna." *Nordlit* 33: 35–46.

Tsagalis, Christos. 2010. "Preface." *Trends in Classics* 2 (2): V–XIII. https://doi.org/10.1515/tcs.2010.010.

Tsagarakis, Odysseus. 2000. *Studies in Odyssey 11. Vol. 82. Vol. Heft 82 Hermes. Einzelschriften*. Stuttgart: F. Steiner.

Ustinova, Yulia. 2009. *Caves and the Ancient Greek Mind: Descending Underground in the Search for Ultimate Truth*. Oxford: Oxford University Press.

Vermeule, Emily. 1979. *Aspects of Death in Early Greek Art and Poetry*. Vol. v. 46. Berkeley: University of California Press.

Vernant, Jean-Pierre. 1991. "A 'Beautiful Death' and the Disfigured Corpse in Homeric Epic." In *Mortals and Immortals: Collected Essays*, edited by Froma Zeitlin, 50–74. Princeton, NJ: Princeton University Press.

Vernant, Jean-Pierre, and Pierre Vidal-Naquet. 1988. *Myth and Tragedy in Ancient Greece*. Cambridge, MA: Zone Books.

von der Mühll, Peter. 1938. "Zur Erfindung in der Nekyia der Odyssee." *Philologus* 93: 8–11.

von der Mühll, Peter. 1984. *Homeri Odyssea: Bibliotheca scriptorum Graecorum et Romanorum Teubneriana*. Stutgardiae: Teubneri.

Walker, Henry. 1995. *Theseus and Athens*. Oxford: Oxford University Press.

Bibliography

Walton, Francis R. 1952. "Athens, Eleusis, and the Homeric Hymn to Demeter." *The Harvard Theological Review* 45 (2): 105–114.

Walton, Marc S., Marie Svoboda, Apurva Mehta, Sam Webb, and Karen Trentelman. 2010. "Material Evidence for the Use of Attic White-ground Lekythoi Ceramics in Cremation Burials." *Journal of Archaeological Science* 37 (5): 936–940. https://doi.org/10.1016/j.jas.2009.11.026.

Weiss, Naomi. 2023. *Seeing Theater: The Phenomenology of Classical Greek Drama.* Berkeley: University of California Press. https://doi-org.libproxy.lib.unc.edu/10.1525/9780520393097

Whitehorne, John E. G. 1986. "The Dead as Spectacle in Euripides' 'Bacchae' and 'Supplices.'" *Hermes* 114 (1): 59–72.

Willcock, M. M. 1995. *Pindar Victory Odes: Olympians 2, 7 and 11 Nemean 4 Isthmians 3, 4 and 7.* Cambridge: Cambridge University Press.

Woodbury, Leonard. 1966. "Equinox at Acragas: Pindar, Ol. 2.61–62." *Transactions of the American Philological Association* 97: 597–616.

Index Locorum

Aeschylus
  Choephoroi (Cho.)
    124: 190
    124–131: 190
    124a: 190
    124b: 190
    125: 190
    489: 190
    489–490: 190
    497: 190
    497–499: 190
    500–513: 191
  Eumenides (Eum.)
    269–275: 236
  Persians (Pers.)
    215–219: 188
    219–225: 188
    598–680: 185
    658–672: 185
    660: 185
    660–661: 186
    666: 185
    670: 185
    681–842: 185
    683: 186
    685: 186
    688–92: 186, 189
    691: 186–87
    839: 186–87
    907: 187–88
  Psychagogoi
    Fr. 273a: 192, 193
    Fr. 275: 193

    Fr. 277: 193n.28
    Fr. 370: 194
Aristophanes
  Frogs (Ranae, Ran.)
    38–163: 198–99
    112–114: 197–98
    137: 197–98
    137–142: 198n.36
    142–163: 197–98
    172: 198–99
    181–270: 198–99
    190–191: 198–99
    194: 198–99, 199n.38
    269–270: 198n.36
    316–317: 200–1
    340: 199n.40
    351: 199n.40
    405–406: 199n.39
    686–88: 201
  Gerytades
    Fr. 156: 202–3
Aristotle
  Poetics (Poet.)
    1450b15–20: 181–82
    1453b1–11: 181n.19
    1453b1–14: 181–82
    1455b–1456a: 181
    1462a15–17: 181–82

Bacchylides
  Ode 3: 140
  Ode 3.8: 140
  Ode 3.10–14: 140

Index Locorum

Bacchylides (*cont.*)
  Ode 3.22: 140
  Ode 3.83–84: 141–42
  Ode 3.85: 141–42
  Ode 3.92: 140
  Ode 5: 140, 142, 143, 189n.24, 244n.37
  Ode 5.10–11: 142
  Ode 5.50–55: 142–43
  Ode 5.63–67: 143
  Ode 5.71–76: 144
  Ode 5.165–68: 142–43

Demosthenes
  37.58–60: 237n.27
  Epit. 60.34: 178–79

Diodorus Siculus
  11.53.2: 134–35

Gold Tablet
  no. 1 / B10 / *OF* 474: 148–49
  no. 2 / B1 / *OF* 476: 118, 149
  no. 3 / A4 / *OF* 487: 7, 151
  no. 5 / A1 / *OF* 488: 151
  no. 26a / D1 / *OF* 485: 153

Herodotus
  Histories 4.11–12: 57n.19

Hesiod
  Theogony (*Theog.*)
    96–97: 96–97
    119: 95–96
    123: 95–96
    279–731: 95–96
    668–675: 95–96
    669: 95–96
    717–725: 90
    717–815: 88–89
    721–819: 2–3
    722–725: 93
    726–728: 91–92
    731: 90
    740–743: 91–92

    744–757: 92
    758–759: 93
    767–768: 116
    767–769: 93
    772–725: 90
    775–779: 94
    775–806: 89, 125–26
    784–785: 91n.13
    811–816: 94
    969–975: 224–25
  Works & Days (*Op.*)
    59–105: 97–98
    106–107: 226n.22
    109–120: 102
    109–126: 101
    109–201: 97–98, 125–26
    110: 101
    111: 133–34
    112: 230–31
    115: 101
    121: 101
    122: 135n.30
    125: 101, 230–31
    134: 98–100
    134–142: 100
    135: 100
    136: 100
    140: 100
    140–142: 98–99
    141: 99–101, 137
    152–156: 98–99
    156–173: 103
    156–174: 219
    160: 102, 103
    165: 102
    167–168: 100–1, 103
    168–173: 225
    169: 133–34
    170: 103
    170–173: 124–25
    171: 133–34
    172: 103

179: 99
202–212: 97–98
706: 100–1
Homer
 Iliad (Il.)
  1.244: 150
  6.146–49: 144n.43
  7: 15n.1
  8.13–16: 233
  15.187–92: 223
  15.190: 223
  16: 15n.1
  16.666–83: 141–42, 164
  18.497: 53n.14
  20: 47
  21.194: 142n.42
  23: 15n.1, 44–45, 47, 70, 124n.7, 189n.24
  23.3.243–48: 70
  23.12–34: 14
  23.35–37: 14
  23.42: 14
  23.43–53: 14
  23.59–61: 14
  23.60: 14
  23.69: 69
  23.69–74: 46, 68, 195
  23.69–101: 124n.7
  23.69–107: 2–3
  23.70: 68
  23.71: 15–16
  23.72–73: 15–16
  23.75: 15–16
  23.83–84: 69
  23.91–92: 69
  23.94–95: 16
  23.95–96: 71
  23.99–101: 72
  23.103–7: 16
  23.236–48: 70
  24: 15n.1
  24.376–77: 82

Odyssey (Od.)
 1.214–20: 83n.5
 1.258–59: 45n.6
 3.109–11: 53n.14
 4: 9–10, 44, 45–46, 47, 123
 4.561–69: 46, 112, 133–34, 217–18
 4.564: 133–34
 5.203–20: 75n.38
 6.149–61: 83n.5
 6.154–55: 83n.5, 140–41
 6.158–59: 83n.5
 9–12: 48, 240–41
 9.39–75: 53n.14
 9.82–104: 53n.14
 9.105–236: 53n.14
 10: 9–10, 44, 46, 47–48, 49, 91n.12
 10.495: 46
 10.496–98: 56
 10.503: 48
 10.504–7: 49
 10.505–7: 54–55
 10.508: 49
 10.508–20: 50
 10.509: 7, 151
 10.510: 50, 51
 10.515: 50, 51
 10.520: 50, 52
 10.526: 52
 10.526–29: 53, 69n.30
 10.527: 53
 10.566–68: 56
 11: 2–3, 4, 31, 44, 47–48, 54–55, 59–60, 70, 80–81, 85, 91n.12, 98–99, 110n.23, 120n.3, 122n.5, 161f, 186, 189n.24, 191–92, 194n.30, 200n.41, 216–17, 224n.18, 240–41
 11.3–4: 54–55
 11.9–10: 48, 54–55
 11.11–12: 56–57, 90
 11.13–19: 57
 11.14: 57–58

Index Locorum

Homer (*cont.*)

11.15: 57
11.25: 71
11.29: 122
11.51–80: 256
11.57: 57n.18, 58
11.57–78: 46
11.58: 58
11.72–73: 69
11.72–78: 68
11.73: 69
11.75: 68
11.76: 69
11.80: 71
11.84–87: 72
11.90–137: 122
11.93–94: 57n.18, 61
11.99–134: 65
11.152–224: 72
11.155–56: 57n.18, 61
11.206–8: 256
11.223: 61, 64
11.223–24: 242
11.226: 193n.28
11.234–327: 64
11.335–41: 44–45
11.362–76: 44–45
11.387–434: 256
11.476: 122
11.482–83: 83–84
11.483: 110n.23
11.485: 85–86, 150
11.495: 251–52
11.497–98: 58–59
11.509: 51–52, 195
11.511: 51–52
11.512: 51–52, 195
11.513: 51–52
11.513–14: 195
11.516: 51–52
11.567–71: 79
11.568: 217–18

11.568–70: 122–23
11.569: 226
11.576–600: 79, 123n.6
11.617–24: 73
11.620: 73
11.631: 74
11.632: 75–76
12: 72
12.417–19: 72
24: 9–10, 44–46, 47, 59–60,
    62–63, 69, 72n.33, 80–81,
    84, 85, 90n.11, 91n.12, 91n.12,
    110–11, 110n.23, 123–24, 160,
    164, 192–93, 211–12, 216–17,
    252
24.1–4: 59–60
24.1–204: 46, 112, 123–24, 192–94,
    219, 252
24.5: 60
24.5–6: 199–200
24.5–14: 60, 192–93
24.9: 72n.33
24.10: 60
24.11: 198–99, 199n.38
24.36: 110n.23
24.36–37: 85
24.73–84: 70
24.75: 70
24.80: 70
24.80–81: 71
24.103–4: 123–24
24.106–19: 123–24
24.120–90: 123–24
24.192: 85–86

Homeric Hymn
  to Apollo
    315: 100–1
  to Demeter
    302–304: 107
    324–328: 107
    342–343: 105
    344–345: 108

345: 108
366: 105
372–373: 105
375–376: 105
473–479: 218n.12
480: 109
480–489: 109
481–482: 109–10
482: 109–10
485: 109
488–489: 102n.21

to Hermes
460–461: 137–38

Lucian

Downward Journey (Catapl.)
14: 259–60
15: 260

Verae Historia (Ver. hist.)
2.8–9: 257–58
2.14: 258
2.17: 257–58

Pindar

Fr. 133: 134

Nemean (Nem.)
1: 129, 136–37, 138–39
1.8–9: 136–37
1.9: 137
1.40: 138
1.71: 137–38, 139
4: 115–16
4:83–88: 116
4.86–87: 116
8.6–12: 218n.12
9: 129, 136–37
9.3: 139
9.39: 139
9.45: 139

Olympian (Ol.)
1: 142n.40
1.57: 142n.40

2: 7, 125n.8, 129, 129–30n.17,
130, 131–32, 134, 135, 136–37,
148–49, 173, 211–12,
216–17
2.56–80: 130n.19
2.61–67: 131n.20
2.63: 131–32
2.66: 132n.23
2.66–71: 132
2.69: 133
2.70: 133n.26, 148–49
2.70–71: 135
2.75: 133–34, 135
2.75–84: 217–18
2.85: 133–34, 148–49, 216–17
2.56–60: 131–32
2.61–65: 131–32
2.68–70: 131–32

Plato

Apology (Ap.)
28a: 243n.34
38a: 207n.4
40c: 234
40c7–9: 216
40c–41c: 216–17
40e: 216–17
41a: 211–12, 217–18
41a1–5: 218–19
41a3–4: 217–18
41a3–5: 217–18
41a6: 219
41a–c: 7
41b1–4: 219
41c6–7: 206n.2

Gorgias (Grg.)
492e–493a: 220
493a: 221–22, 243
493a1–7: 220
523a: 223, 243, 243n.35
523a1–2: 226–27
523a3–5: 223
523a5: 223

Index Locorum

Plato (*cont.*)

523a5–b2: 225
523a5–b4: 223
523b7–8: 225–26
524a7–b1: 226–27
524c–525a: 227–28
524d: 227–28
525b: 237
525d6: 226
526b–d: 226
526c: 211–12
526d2–3: 227
543b–544a: 224n.19

Laws (*Leg.*)

903c–905b: 213–14, 237–38

Menexenus (*Menex.*)

235a: 178
235b: 178
235c: 177–78

Phaedo (*Phd.*)

85a–b: 238–39
107d: 240
107d2–5: 232
108a–c: 229–30
109a–111c: 232
109d6–7: 230
110b: 243
110b7–c6: 235–36
111: 230
111a6–7: 230–31
111a–c: 230
111b: 230
111b3–c3: 235–36
111c–d: 232
111d5–e1: 235
111d–e: 234–35
112a: 248
112a1–6: 233
113a–c: 233
113b–c: 235
113c8: 233
113d–114c: 236

114a: 213–14, 229–30, 237
114a7–8: 235
114a–b: 237
114b: 237
114b–c: 229–30
114c: 229–30, 234–35, 236
114d1–2: 217n.11
114d2–3: 206n.2

Phaedrus (*Phdr.*)

229d3–4: 221
246a4–6: 217n.11
250b–c: 213–14

Republic (*Resp.*)

2.378c4: 221–22
2.378e3: 221–22
10.614d1–3: 242
10.615a–b: 238n.28
10.616b: 244–45
10.620a–d: 244
10.620c: 213–14
314b: 242–43
327a: 239
330a–331c: 239
330b: 240
330d–331b: 239
330d–e: 239
331b: 239
363c–d: 239
377a: 240–41, 244
386a–387c: 241
386c: 240–41, 241n.32
386c–387a: 239
588c11: 208–10
588c–d: 208–10
588d1: 208–10
607b: 208–10
608c–d: 238n.28
614b2: 240
614b7–8: 245–46
615a–b: 247
618b7–c5: 246
619d–e: 246

Index Locorum

620c: 245–46
621b8–c2: 244
621c: 247
621d: 247
Timaeus
38c6: 55n.17
Poetic Fragment
PMG 893: 172
PMG 893–94: 172
PMG 894: 172–73

Scholiast
Iliad
70bS; 61B: 142
Sophocles
Polyxena
Fr. 523: 195
Fr. 525–26: 195
Suetonius
Life of Vergil 33: 256–57

Thucydides (Thuc.)
2.34.1: 175–77
2.34.1–7: 175–77
2.34.5: 175–77
2.43.3: 174

Vergil
Aeneid (Aen.)
1: 255n.3
4: 255n.3
6: 31, 253–55, 256,
256n.5
6.119–23: 255
6.365–66: 256
6.392–93: 254–55
6.495–534: 256
6.548–627: 256–57
6.700–1: 256
6.883: 256–57
6.893–901: 76n.39

Subject Index

For the benefit of digital users, indexed terms that span two pages (e.g., 52– 53) may, on occasion, appear on only one of those pages

Figures are referred to by "f" following the page numbers. Citations to ancient sources are compiled in a separate Index Locorum.

Acherusian lake, 235, 237
Achilles
  Agamemnon meeting in Underworld, 123–24
  burial urn and tomb orders of, 67, 69, 69n.31, 70
  grief over Patroclus' death, 14–16
  Harmodius compared to, 172
  Hector's body abused by, 31
  heroism of, setting standard for all other heroes, 5, 84n.7, 84, 85–86, 172–73, 174
  Hesiod's Underworld not including, 128n.14
  knowledge of, and reconciling with, his fate, 17, 31
  makar term applied to, 83–84
  Niobid Krater and, 166–67
  Odysseus compared to, 67, 72, 84, 85–86, 110–11
  Odysseus conversing with, 27, 83–84
  olbios term applied to, 85–86, 110–11, 110n.23, 127–28
  Orphic Gold Tablet and, 150
  Pindar analogizing Theron to, 135
  in Sophocles' *Polyxena*, 195–96
  Underworld existence of, 122, 130n.19, 217–18

  war dead connected to, 174, 175–77
  See also Achilles' dream
Achilles' dream (*Iliad* Book 23), 2–3, 14
  description of Underworld in, 17
  earliest extant Underworld scene, 2–3, 17, 80–81
  Patroclus in (*see* Patroclus)
  regaining of purpose from, 16
  soul's consciousness in, 124n.7
Admetus, 159
Aeacus, 217–18, 218n.12
Aeaea, as entry and exit point of *Nekuia*, 67–68
Aeneid (Vergil), 13, 254–56
  Aeneas' character, 256
  Aeneas equated to mythic katabatic heroes, 254–56, 255n.2
  Aeneas' exit from Underworld, 76n.39
  Augustus linked to Homeric heroes, 254–55, 256–57
  Dido in Books 1 and 4, 255n.3
  incorporating current state of affairs, 256–57
  intertextual linking to *Nekuia* (Book 11 of *Odyssey*), 31, 253–54, 256
  narrator of, 256
  para-narrative, use of, 256
  Underworld scenes in, 253–57

288   Subject Index

Aeschylus, 159n.5
   Choephoroi, 179–80, 183n.21, 189–91
   Circe, 191n.26
   Eumenides, 182–83, 183n.21, 197, 236
   Heracles' appearance in plays, 158n.4
   Homeric linkage, 186–87, 194
   Oresteia, 195n.32
   Ostologoi, 191n.26, 193–94
   Penelope, 191n.26, 193n.29
   Persians, 158n.2, 179–80, 182–83,
      183n.21, 185–89
   Psychagogoi, 191–94, 191n.26, 194n.31
   tetralogy by, 191–92, 191n.26
   Underworld scenes, 180, 189, 194
afterlife society
   author's depiction with distinct
      structures, 7, 44, 46
   based on status in lifetime, 97–98, 113
   contrary views asserted in epics, 79–80
   correction of injustices of real world
      in, 218–19
   democratization of (*see*
      democratization of afterlife)
   depiction on vases (*see* white-ground
      lekythoi)
   duration of afterlife vs. lifespan, 237–
      38, 238n.28, 239, 247
   heroes living separately and in
      congenial companionship, 112, 211–
      12, 216–17
   judgment executed in (*see* judgment-
      based Underworlds)
   modeled after Greek society of the
      living, 11, 124, 156–57, 196, 197
   natural laws of world applied to
      (Plato), 212–13
   negative (*see* negative afterlife)
   in *Odyssey* 11, 98n.16
   permeability (*see* breaching life–death
      barrier)
   Plato following earlier model of
      segregated regions in Underworld,
      210, 211–13, 216–17, 219–20

   Plato's new hierarchy for (*see*
      philosophers; Plato)
   positive (*see* positive afterlife)
   positive-plus (*see* positive-plus
      afterlife)
   segregation into different geographic
      regions of Underworld, 10–11,
      27, 37, 87, 104, 111–12, 113, 114–15,
      121–22, 125–26, 129, 156–57, 197–98,
      223, 251–52 (*see also* judgment-based
      Underworld scenes)
   sinners' eternal punishment in, 40,
      74–75, 79, 123n.6, 123, 222, 229, 237
Agamemnon, 14
   Achilles meeting in Underworld,
      123–24
   in Aeschylus' *Choephoroi*, 189–91
   final address to Odysseus and Achilles
      in *Odyssey* 24, 111
   Odysseus conversing with, 27
   olbioi, use of term, 84n.7, 85–86
   Plato's allusion to, 246–47
   recognizing Amphimedon in
      Underworld, 123–24
   in Sophocles' *Polyxena*, 195, 195n.32
agency
   in Plato, 211–12, 213–14, 237, 247
   See also deeds in life connected to
      eternal afterlife
Ajax
   in Lucian's *True History*, 257–58
   "Myth of Er" and, 244, 246–47
   Socrates conversing with in afterlife,
      7, 27
Alcestis (Euripides), 159, 182–83,
   183n.21, 197
Alcinous (king), 44–45, 45n.6
   Odysseus telling *Nekuia* to (tale of
      Alcinous), 240–43, 241n.32, 244
Alcmene, 64
Alexander the Great, 257–58
allegories, Underworld scenes as,
   19, 20–21

Subject Index

allusions, 28–29, 31–32, 31–32n.12
Amphiaraus, 139
Amphimedon, 123–24
Annas, Julia, 206n.1
Anticlea, 44–46, 61, 64, 66–67, 72–73, 242, 252
Apollo, 15n.1, 140–41. *See also Homeric Hymn to Hermes*
Apology (Plato), 12–13, 27, 207–8, 210–12, 214, 216–20, 227–28, 230, 234, 248–49
apple-pickers and apple trees, imagery of, 165n.8
archaeological record, 19–20, 69n.31, 110–11, 127n.12, 146n.45
Archaic epics and poetry, 19–20, 19n.7, 25, 63, 119–20, 143, 155–56. *See also* Homer and Homeric epics; *Homeric Hymn to Demeter*
arete, 9–10, 12–13, 104, 120–21, 207–8, 226
Arete (queen), 44–45, 45n.6
Arginusae, battle of, 198–99, 198n.37, 200
Aristarchus, 18–19, 138n.37
Aristeides, 202–3
Aristomenes: *Dionysus*, 197n.34
Aristophanes
  Babylonians, 197n.34
  Dionysus Shipwrecked, 197n.34
  Frogs (see *Frogs*)
  Frying-Pan Men (*Tagenistai*), 203n.52
  Gerytades, 202–3, 203n.50
  Underworld scenes in, 180
Aristotle
  Poetics, 180–82, 187n.23
Arrington, Nathan T., 179n.18
Atalanta, 244, 244n.37, 246–47
Athenian democracy and identity, 11–12, 200
athletic competitions and victors, 3–4, 116–17, 121–22, 136, 141–42, 142n.40
Atlas (son of Iapetos), 92–93, 93n.14

Atossa (Persian queen), 185–86, 188
audience
  ἀπόλογον and Plato's audience, 242–43
  author's influence by choice of Underworld landmarks and denizens, 6–7, 76, 111–12, 130
  discourse markers for, 52, 94–95
  expectation created by use of framework of Underworld scenes, 25, 39, 60–63, 169–70, 253
  experiencing heroic Underworld scenes, 42
  familiarity and knowledge assumed on part of, 2–3, 26–27, 36–37, 51–52n.12, 57–58, 74–75, 114, 121, 130–31, 142–43, 154, 157, 158n.2, 167–68, 173, 180, 183, 184–85, 186, 193–94, 197, 233, 253
  gap between author's narrative and audience's expectations, 53–54
  hypertextuality and, 5, 32, 261
    (*see also* hypertextuality and hyperlinks)
  as judges of theatrical performances, 180, 181
  learning from Underworld scenes, 6–7, 8, 28, 54–55, 59, 66, 261
  monumental Lesche painting by Polygnotus bringing audience into Underworld, 167, 168f
  Panhellenic, 116–17, 157
  participation, 2–3, 30–32
  in partnership with author, 31–32, 36–37, 48, 63, 113, 157, 253
  Plato leaving audience to draw own conclusions, 12–13, 245–46
  Plato relying on metatextual moments of, 212–13, 233, 245–46, 249
  sense of suspense of, 64–65
  of theatrical performances, 180
Augustus, 254–55, 256–57

Subject Index

author
  hypertextuality and, 32 (*see also* hypertextuality)
  in partnership with audience, 31–32, 36–37, 48, 63, 113, 157, 253
  as reader and interpreter of his own story, 8, 31–32, 39–40
  situating own work against multiple referents by using Underworld scenes, 30
  virtuosity from adapting and relating traditional material, 64–65, 115–16

Babylonians (Aristophanes), 197n.34
Bacchae (Euripides), 197
Bacchylides, 11, 140
  borrowing Underworld poetics from predecessors, 113, 140
  breaching life–death barrier, 115–16, 142–43, 144–45
  compared to Pindar, 140, 142n.40, 143
  Croesus myth in, 140–42
  divine favor in, 140
  Heracles' Underworld myth in, 115–16, 142–43, 144
  heroizing patron, 115–16, 118–19, 144–45, 172
  Homer and, 140–41
  Iliad and, 144n.43
  Isles of the Blessed in *Ode* 5, 142
  judgment-based Underworld scenes and, 11, 142, 144
  kleos in, 140–41
  Meleager in, 142–43, 144, 144n.43, 256n.4
  Nekuia (Book 11 of the *Odyssey*) and, 143
  Ode 3, 140–43
  Ode 5, 140, 142–44, 142n.40, 189n.24
Bakhtin, Mikhail, 6n.4
Bernabé Pajares, Alberto, 148–49, 206n.1
blessedness, 7, 11, 80–81

  Aristophanes' *Frogs* alluding to, 201–2
  breaching life–death barrier, 125
  categories in Homer, 81, 98n.17
  connection to literary tradition, 40
  deeds in life connected to, 97–98, 113, 251–52 (*see also* deeds in life connected to eternal afterlife)
  different forms of, 86–87, 96–97
  elevation of rank of elite in Underworld, 125, 129, 131–32, 131n.20, 153–54
  expanding inclusiveness of, 3–4, 11–12, 121–22, 154
  favor of gods connected to (*see* favoritism of gods)
  genealogy connected to, 79, 96–97, 104, 120–21
  hero cults and, 126n.10
  heroic blessedness crafted through Underworld scenes, 114–54
  in Hesiod, 88–89 (*see also Works and Days*)
  Orphic Gold Tablets and, 152, 210n.6
  patrons as deserving of, 120–21, 128, 219–20
  in Pindar, 129 (*see also* Pindar)
  Plato's new restrictive hierarchy for, 12–13, 204, 206–8, 211, 214, 225–26, 236, 238–39, 247, 248
  post-Homeric Underworld representations and, 80–81, 86, 111–12, 114
  races in Hesiod's *Works and Days* and, 98–102, 99n.18, 99n.19, 125–26, 139
  rise of tripartite Underworld and, 121 (*see also* tripartite Underworld)
  scale of negative, positive, and positive-plus, 120–22 (*see also* negative afterlife; positive afterlife; positive-plus afterlife)
  Socrates' vision of himself in, 218, 219–20

Subject Index

sorting of the dead and, 80–81,
125–26 (*see also* afterlife society *for*
segregation in Underworld)

three configurations of, 120–21 (*see
also* tripartite Underworld)

war dead receiving, 133

ways for mortals to receive *olbios*,
120–21, 125, 153–54, 177 (*see also*
favoritism of gods; *kleos* (glory);
prosperity/privilege during life)

See also olbios; *Homeric Hymn
to Demeter*; *makar*; *Theogony*
(Hesiod): Underworld scenes;
Works and Days (Hesiod):
Underworld scenes

blood offering of Odysseus to call the
dead, 98n.16, 122, 144, 192–93

Bonifazi, Anna, 52, 52n.13

borrowing Underworld poetics from
predecessors, 112, 113, 114, 120–21,
130, 140, 230

successor poets using as shorthand for
themes, 113, 121, 135, 157

See also Bacchylides; Hesiod; Homer
and Homeric epics; Pindar;
Plato

Bowie, A. M., 20–21

breaching life–death barrier
in Aristophanes' *Frogs*, 198–99
in Bacchylides, 115–16, 142–
43, 144–45
blessedness and, 11–12, 125, 251–52
Euripides quoted in Plato's *Gorgias*
on, 220
fifth century BCE Athenians' interest
in, 11–12, 159, 169–70
funerary monuments and, 174–75
kleos and, 114–15, 116
objects with Underworld scenes (*see*
Lesche of the Cnidians; Niobid
Krater; white-ground cups; white-
ground lekythoi)

Orphic Gold Tablets and, 118, 145–53
(*see also* Orphic Gold Tablets)

Pindar and, 115–16, 138, 144–45

Plato and, 211–12, 228, 229, 247

poet's role in, 144–45

snakes' movement and, 138n.36

soul's self-awareness and, 3–4, 118, 125

See also relationship between the living
and the dead

break in narrative, 14–15, 21–24, 26, 62–
63. *See also* Underworld scenes

Bremmer, Jan, 18, 69n.31, 127n.12

burials

Achilles' burial urn and tomb orders,
67, 69, 69n.31, 70

Elpenor's burial directions, 67–68, 69,
69n.30, 71–72

funerary laws, 170–71

orations (*see* funeral orations)

Patroclus' death and burial directions,
14–16, 17, 69, 69n.30, 124n.7, 152

public memorials honoring war dead,
171, 178–79, 179n.18

restrictions and location of tombs,
170–71

unburied and in transition between
life and afterlife, 46, 48–49, 59n.21

Burkert, Walter, 127–28, 191, 201n.45

Calame, Claude, 100–1, 103

Callicles, 226–27, 243n.35

Calypso, 75n.38

calyx-krater by Niobid painter, 166–67,
166n.11

Castor, 64

Catalog of heroines (*Od.* 11 *Nekuia*), 64–
65, 64n.25, 66n.27, 75–76, 246–47

Cephalus, 239–40, 240n.30

Cerberus, 22, 62–63, 138, 142, 142n.41

Charon, 62–63, 158, 158n.4, 162–64, 198–
99, 198nn.35–36, 204, 259, 260

Cheirons (Cratinus), 202n.48

292   *Subject Index*

Choephoroi (Aeschylus), 179–80, 183n.21, 189–91
Chromius of Aetna, 136–37, 138–39
chronotope, 5–6, 252
   author-audience exchange and, 31–32
   derivation of, 6n.4
   in encounter portion of Underworld scene, 27–28
   in entry portion of Underworld scene, 26, 58–59
   funerary monuments and, 174–75
   in Hesiod's *Theogony*, 95
   Lucian's Underworld scenes and, 257–58, 259
   multiple types of time in simultaneous coexistence, 38–39, 252
   in *Nekuia* (Book 11 of the *Odyssey*), 44–45
   new one established in Underworld scene, 22–23, 24–25, 52, 84
   Odyssey's use of chronotopic markers, 47, 54–55, 59–60, 73, 252
   Plato altering, 206–7, 210–11, 228–29, 231, 239, 244–46
   in political narrative to promote civil pride by linking to the past, 177–78
   synchronic and syntopic nature of, 38, 46, 235–36
   synopic nature of, 39, 46
   in theatrical performances, 184–85, 187, 203
   time-space dislocation permitted by, 17–18, 27–28, 37, 46, 58, 59–60, 158–59
   Underworld scenes using, 53, 59–60, 95, 158–59, 252
   Vergil using to incorporate current state of affairs in *Aeneid*, 256–57
   war memorial *stelai* and, 178–79
chronotropic storytelling, 36
Cimmerians, 54–55, 56–58, 57n.19, 191–92

Circe, 18–19, 22–23, 44–45, 47, 48–49, 53–55, 69n.30, 91n.12, 151
Circe (Aeschylus), 191n.26
Circe's island, 18–19, 38–39, 68n.28, 72
   Circe's *nekuia*, 54, 55–56, 62–63
civic messages (*see* politics)
Clark, Raymond, 42, 256n.4
Cleisthenes, 170–71, 175–77
Clotho in Lucian's *Downward Journey*, 259
Clytemnestra, 183n.21
Cnidians, 167–68, 168f
Cocytus, 233, 237
Collins, Derek, 157n.1
comedies, 196
   social commentary offered by, 180, 196
   Underworld scenes in, 179–80, 182–83, 196
   See also theatrical performances
Cosmopoulos, Michael, 110–11, 127n.13
Cratinus
   Cheirons, 202n.48
   Dionysalexandros, 197
   Dionysoi, 197n.34
Critias, 158n.4, 159n.5
Croesus, 140–42
Cronus
   in Hesiod's *Theogony*, 223
   in Hesiod's *Works and Days*, 102, 225
   improper afterlife judgments during reign of, 224n.19
   in Plato's *Gorgias*, 225–26
   presiding over "Isles of the Blessed," 225–26
   tower of, 133–34, 133n.26, 135, 148–49
cross-media portrayal of Underworld, 11–12, 156, 157, 203–4
cults
   hero cults, 126n.10, 136, 136n.32, 164, 219–20
   heroizing mortals to level of famous epic heroes, 118–19

Subject Index

initiation as path to blessed afterlife, 215–16

Plato borrowing imagery and concepts from, 206–7

rituals to honor the dead, 114–15

snake cults, 138n.35

timai (honors) and, 128n.14

tomb cults, 69, 69n.31

See also Eleusinian Mysteries; mystery cults

Currie, Bruno, 128n.14, 130n.19, 136n.32, 137, 145n.44, 179n.18

Cyrus the Elder (Persian king), 257–58

Danaïds myth, 222

Dante: *Inferno*, 33–34, 261

Darius, 183n.21, 185–89

darkness as characteristic of Underworld, 42, 59–60

in Hesiod's Underworld, 98–99, 186–87

in Homeric Underworld, 122, 186–87

in *Nekuia* (Book 11 of the *Odyssey*), 56–58, 57n.18, 61–62

in Sophocles' *Polyxena*, 195

in theatrical performances, 182

Day (Underworld god), 88–89, 92–93

death

audience forced to think about, 5–6

demarcation between life and death (Plato), 228

fifth century BCE Greece's more individualized approach to, 18

likened to dwelling in a foreign land, 136, 216–17

as multistage process, 114

Plato considering as phase in soul's lifecycle, 210–11

Plato on death as change of location for the soul, 216–17

as time for "grand sorting," 78, 98n.16, 109–10, 122–23, 216–17, 232 (*see also* judgment-based Underworlds)

Underworld as something to look forward to, 17

See also afterlife society; breaching life–death barrier; relationship between the living and the dead; Underworld scenes

deeds in life connected to eternal afterlife, 5–6, 11, 79, 96–98, 111, 113, 120–22, 123–24, 127–28, 152, 251–52

in Hesiod, 97–98, 139

in Pindar, 130–32, 228

Plato and, 207–8, 210–12, 213–14, 217–18, 219–20, 229–30, 239, 248

See also timai/time (honors, esteem)

de Heer, Cornelis, 82, 97n.15, 138n.34

Deianeira, 142–43

deictic markers, 50n.11, 51–52, 94–95

Deiphobus, 256

de Jong, Irene J. F., 25

Delphi, Lesche of the Cnidians at, 167–68, 168*f*

Demeter, 106*f*, 107, 110–11, 224–25. *See also Homeric Hymn to Demeter*

democratization of afterlife, 11–12, 156

funeral orations and funerary *stelai*, 173

merger of literature, art, and ritual in portrayal of Underworld, 157

olbios status more widely accessible, 177

Pericles' speech and, 174–77

Plato's challenging and undermining of, 12–13, 204, 210–11, 213, 215–16, 218, 226

rebuilding tombs after Persian sack of Athens, 177, 177n.16

Demosthenes on war dead as mythic heroes, 178–79, 178nn.17–18

deus ex machina, 184

diachronic collapse, 38–39

Dialogues of the Dead (Lucian of Samosata), 13, 259

294 Subject Index

Dido, 255n.3

digital age and web design, hypertext in, 34–35

Diodorus Siculus, 134–35

Diomedes, 172–73

Dionysalexandros (Cratinus), 197

Dionysoi (Cratinus), 197n.34

Dionysus
in Aristophanes' *Frogs*, 196–202
on stage, 197, 197n.34

Dionysus (Aristomenes), 197n.34

Dionysus (Magnes), 197n.34

Dionysus Shipwrecked (Aristophanes), 197n.34

Dioscuri, 138n.35

dirges honoring the dead, 114–15, 129

discourse markers, 52, 52n.13

disorientation, 25, 46, 48, 55–57
of Odysseus' arrival in Underworld, 58–59, 61–62

divine favor. *See* favoritism of gods

divine oath and oath-keeping, 88–89, 91n.13, 125, 133

Doherty, Lillian E, 45n.6

Dova, Stamatia, 83–84, 85n.8

Dover, Kenneth J., 199n.39

Downward Journey (Lucian of Samosata), 13, 259–60

duBois, Page, 200

Dunn, Francis, 155–56

Edmonds, Radcliffe G., 21n.8, 21n.9, 130n.18, 146n.45, 150n.47, 153n.49, 172–73, 206n.1, 227n.23, 235n.25

ekphrasis, 17n.4, 22–23, 53n.14

Ekroth, Gunnel, 51–52n.12

Electra, 189–91

Eleusinian Mysteries, 20–21, 106f
Aristophanes' *Frogs*, initiates as chorus in, 199–201, 201n.45

connection between Athens and Eleusis, 127–28, 127n.12, 200–2, 201n.45
duration of, 127n.12
founding of, 105
inclusive nature of, 127–28, 200–1, 201n.45
influence in late Archaic and early Classical periods, 127–28
makarismos as closing ritual of, 111
olbios used to describe Eleusinian initiates, 110–11
rituals for initiates, 105, 117, 127–28
soteriological element to, 110–11, 127n.13
transition of cult of Demeter at Eleusis to mystery cult, 110–11

Elpenor, 24
acknowledging different chronotopes, 58–59
burial directions of, 67–68, 69, 69n.30, 71–72
compared to Patroclus, 69, 71–72
entry into Underworld, 59–60
Odysseus' encounter with upon entry to Underworld, 44–46, 58–59, 66–67, 73, 160
Odysseus' return to Circe's island to bury, 72
predictive function of, 67–68
Tartarographia compared to tale of, 95
unburied and in transition between life and afterlife, 46, 48–49, 59n.21

Elpenor Vase's Underworld scenes, 160, 161f

Elysian fields, 217–18. *See also* Menelaus

Empedocles of Acragas, 131–32

encounters with supernatural beings, 26
as component of Underworld scenes, 22 (*see also* Underworld scenes)
ghostly (*see nekuia*)
heroic vs. judgment-based, 27, 42n.1

Subject Index

purpose of, 27–28

religious beliefs and, 7

See also Nekuia (Book 11 of the *Odyssey*)

ἔνθα/*entha*-mode of description, 49–50, 50n.11, 52–53, 53n.14, 93, 94–95, 143, 246–47

entry into Underworld, 22, 23, 38–39, 46

Elpenor, 59–60

Odysseus in *Nekuia* (Book 11 of the *Odyssey*), 58–60

Epeius, 244, 244n.36

Er, 22, 242, 245–46, 247. *See also Republic*

Erebus (Underworld god and region), 95–96, 105

eschatology, 106, 114, 131–32, 136–37, 138, 142, 146n.45

Orphic, 206n.1, 221–22

Plato and, 206n.1, 207–8, 210, 213–14, 216–17, 221, 228, 240, 243, 248–49, 248n.38

eternal punishment. *See* afterlife society; judgment-based Underworlds

Eumenides (Aeschylus), 182–83, 183n.21, 197, 236

Eupolis

Demes, 202–3, 202nn.47–49

Taxiarchs, 197

Underworld scenes in, 180

Euripides

Alcestis, 159, 182–83, 183n.21, 197

Bacchae, 197

equation quoted in Plato's *Gorgias*, 220, 247

Hecuba, 182–83, 183n.21, 196

on Sisyphus, 159n.5

Eurystheus, 22

Evagoras (Isocrates), 218n.12

exiting from Underworld, 22, 28

abruptness of, 28, 62–63, 75–76, 76n.39, 76n.40

Er at different point than entry, 247

new knowledge gained by hero, 24–25, 28

Odysseus at same point as entry, 38–39, 62–63, 67–68

The Fall of Miletus (Phrynichus), 184n.22

Farmer, Matthew, 203nn.50–51

favoritism of gods, 48, 79, 82–83, 85–86, 96–97, 104, 109–10, 111–12, 120–22, 125

in Bacchylides, 140

in Pindar, 137, 139

in Plato, 210, 214, 215–16, 218, 229–30

Felson, Nancy, 50n.11

fictional deixis, 50n.11

fifth century BCE Athens, 155–56

afterlife judgment and justice as popular theme in, 218

comedies in, 196

death, approach to, 18, 204

epinician poets (*see* Bacchylides; Pindar; poetry)

goēs (necromancer) role in, 158, 158n.4

new media and methods for depicting Underworld, 160 (*see also* white-ground lekythoi)

piety owed to the dead, 191

present shock experienced by Athens, 155–56

theatrical performances with Underworld scenes, 179 (*see also* comedies; theatrical performances; tragedies)

tombs placed on main thoroughfare, 171

Underworld scenes used across media in, 11–12, 156, 157, 203–4

Foley, Helene P., 108, 181

Fowler, Don, 29, 31–32, 31–32n.12

frame narrative, 17–19

enhanced by Underworld encounters, 23–24, 26–28, 30, 36, 44, 96–97, 253

Subject Index

frame narrative (*cont.*)
  journey motif as signal of break from, 24, 25–26, 29–30
  pause in, 14–15, 21–24, 26, 62–63 (*see also* chronotope)
Frogs (Aristophanes), 5, 7, 11–12, 20–21, 162, 179–80, 182–83, 196–202, 196n.33, 259
  chorus of frogs, 199–201, 199n.39
  chorus of initiates, 199–202, 201n.45
  enfranchisement, advocating for, 200–2
  explanation of why two choruses included, 200–1, 200n.43
  Homeric allusions, 198–200, 200n.42
  katabasis in, 196–99, 201–2
  landmarks of Underworld, 198–99, 198n.37
  Lucian's *Downward Journey* compared to, 259
Frying-Pan Men (*Tagenistai*) (Aristophanes), 203n.52
funeral orations, 3–4, 11–12, 154, 157, 173, 179n.18
funerary rites. *See* Achilles; burials; Elpenor; grave *stelai*; Patroclus; war dead; white-ground lekythoi
future-casting, 2, 7, 24–25, 31, 38
  Nekuia revealing upcoming episodes in main narrative, 73
  Tiresias on Odysseus' future, 44–45, 65

Garland, Robert, 170–71
Gazis, George, 129–30n.17, 130n.19
Gee, Emma, 21n.8, 38n.14
Genette, Gérard, 33
Gennep, Arnold van, 22
Gerytades (Aristophanes), 202–3, 203n.50
ghosts
  rituals summoning, 20

  on stage, 11–12, 182–83, 183n.20, 184, 186, 187, 189, 196
  See also afterlife society; breaching life–death barrier; *Nekuia* (Book 11 of the *Odyssey*); relationship between the living and the dead; Underworld scenes
Glaucon, 241–42, 244, 246
Glaucus, 165*f*, 165–66
gods
  boundary-crossing, 197
  homes of, 94, 95, 105, 125–26, 137–38, 139
  as *makares theoi* (or *makares*), 82–83, 112
  power of Underworld gods, 186–87
  on stage, 184, 197
  ubiquity of minor deities, 159
goēs (necromancer), 158, 158nn.2–3
"Golden Age," 133–34, 136, 222–23, 225, 230
  afterlife, 11–12, 27–28, 124–25, 129, 206–7, 212–13, 215–16
Gold Tablets. *See* Orphic Gold Tablets
Gorgias (Plato), 12–13, 20–21, 207–8, 210–12, 214, 220
  adapting traditional Underworld of predecessors, 222–23, 226, 228, 230
  challenging Underworld formula of predecessors, 226
  compared to *Republic*, 245
  Cronus, evaluation of reign of, 225
  Danaïds myth, 222
  demarcation between life and death, 228
  disclaimers for shortcomings of Underworld scenes, 226–27
  Euripides' equation quoted in, 220, 247
  folktale of water-carrier with leaky jars, 220–21, 222
  Hesiodic allusions, 221, 222–23, 225–26, 227

Subject Index

Homeric allusions, 221–23, 226, 227
Iliad's Olympian divine succession, 223–24
muthoi and, 227, 227n.23, 243, 243n.35, 248–49
myth-telling critiqued, 221–22
new restrictive hierarchy for blessedness, 225–26
Odysseus' cleverness, allusion to, 221–22
Olympians seizing and sharing realm, 223–24
Pluto's name used instead of Hades, 224–25
Pythagoreanism and, 221
segregation into different geographic regions of Underworld, 223
sinners' eternal punishment in afterlife, 222
Socrates' vision of his blessed eternity, 218, 219, 227–28
"special hero" status of Socrates, 228
Underworld meting out true justice, 227–28
values conveyed, 222
Works and Days (Hesiod), allusions to, 225–26
Zeus' myth of judgment, 224n.19
grave *stelai*, 3–4, 11–12, 154, 173, 175–77, 176f
Greek thought, revolutions in, 3, 156. *See also* Plato
grief and individual loss, 14, 19–20, 69n.29, 72

Hades, 8–9, 15–16, 42, 105, 234–35, 238–39, 250. *See also* Underworld scenes
Hades (Underworld god), 62–63, 87–89, 105, 186–87, 193n.28
distinct from but associated with Pluto, 110n.24
kidnapping Persephone as bride of, 104f, 104–5

Hall, Edith, 186
Halliwell, Stephen, 214, 240n.31
handshake gesture, 15–16, 15n.2
Hannibal of Carthage, 257–58
Harmodius, 172–73
Hector, 17, 31, 139
Hecuba (Euripides), 182–83, 183n.21, 196
Heracles, 8–9
Aeneas and, 254–55
Aeschylus' plays on, 158n.4
in Aristophanes' *Frogs*, 196–99
in Bacchylides, 115–16, 142–43, 144
best possible afterlife achieved by, 112
conversation with Odysseus (*Nekuia*), 72, 74–76, 138–39, 252
in Euripides' *Alcestis*, 159
goēs (necromancer) role in appealing to, 158
katabasis myth of, 18, 27, 51–52n.12, 62–63, 75–76, 138, 142–43, 142n.41, 194n.30, 197–98
marriage to Deianeira, 142–43
Nekuia calyx-krater and, 166n.11
Niobid Krater and, 166–67
Odysseus compared to, 42–43, 64, 73–74, 75–76, 75n.38, 76n.40, 120–21
in Pindar, 138
popularity of, 204
retrieving Cerberus from Hades (*see* Cerberus)
snakes associated with, 138n.35
as "special hero," 28
Tiresias' prediction on, 137–38
in tragedies, 158n.4
war dead associated with, 174, 178–79
Hermes, 59–60, 60n.22, 62–63, 91–92
in Aeschylus' *Choephoroi*, 189–91
in Aeschylus' *Psychagogoi*, 192–93
Elpenor Vase and, 160, 161f

Subject Index

Hermes (*cont.*)
  goēs (necromancer) role in appealing
    to, 158
  on lekythoi, 162–64
  in Lucian's *Downward Journey*, 259
  in *Odyssey* Book 24, 160, 164, 199–
    200, 256n.4
  popularity of, 204
  retrieval of Persephone, 105
hero cults, 126n.10, 136, 136n.32,
  164, 219–20
Herodotus, 57n.19, 184n.22
heroes
  ability to access and leave Underworld,
    3, 79
  afterlife of, 24–25, 112, 211–12, 216–
    17, 251–52
  assimilating mortals to, 11, 114–17,
    120–21, 125, 129, 130n.19, 131–32,
    134–35, 136–37, 139, 145n.44
  cults (*see* hero cults)
  famous male heroes forever present in
    Underworld, 75–76
  mortals as new class of, 120–21
  Odysseus counted in pantheon of,
    75–76
  Pindar's use of term, 134–35
  Plato applying metempsychosis to,
    211–12
  Plato demoting below philosophers,
    206–8, 210–11, 214, 215–16,
    249, 252–53
  rebirth of, 20, 24–25
  relationships with dead individuals, 3, 5
  shifting ideas about, 127–28
  trials equated with initiation rites, 117
  war dead equated with mythic heroes,
    174, 178–79
  See also "special hero" status
heroism
  Achilles setting standard for all other
    heroes, 5, 84n.7, 84, 85–86, 172–73, 174

defined by deeds on battlefield, 85
Odysseus and, 6–7, 42–43, 45n.6
Plato countering traditional paradigms
  of, 211, 215–16
shifting ideas about, 127–28
heroizing mortals, 11, 114–15, 118–19, 157
  Bacchylides and, 144–45
  Pindar and, 128, 136–37, 144–45,
    145n.44, 153–54
  Underworld scenes heroizing the
    polity, 172
  for war deeds, 157, 171
  See also laudandus
Herrero de Jáuregui, Miguel, 152
Hesiod, 78–103, 128n.14
  "Ages of Man" (*see Works and Days*)
  dark Underworld depicted by, 98–
    99, 186–87
  "Isles of the Blessed" (*see Works
    and Days*)
  Pindar and, 130, 132, 133
  Plato/Socrates and, 206–8, 211–12, 213,
    214, 215–17, 219, 221, 222–23, 225–
    26, 227, 228, 245–46
  positive afterlife in, 122n.5
  public knowledge of Underworld
    myths of, 157, 173
  Tartarographia (*see Tartarographia*)
  Underworld scenes in, 2–3, 21–
    22, 43, 86
  Vergil and, 253–54
  See also Theogony; Works and Days
Hieron of Syracuse, 137n.33, 140–42, 144
Hipparchus, 172–73
historicism, 20–21
Hoffmann, Herbert, 164–65
Homer and Homeric epics
  Aeschylus' links to, 186–87, 191–93, 194
  afterlife possibilities presented in, 46,
    122–24, 123n.6
  Aristophanes' *Frogs* alluding to, 198–
    200, 200n.42

Subject Index

bleak picture of afterlife created by, 79–80, 144

blessedness categories in, 81, 98n.17

chronology of Underworld scenes in, 33–34

compared to Hesiod's *Theogony*, 87, 88–89, 95

compared to Hesiod's *Works and Days*, 87, 97–99

cosmos layout in, 233–34

favoritism of certain mortals in, 96–97

ghost of Homer in Lucian's *True History*, 257–58

katabaseis not present in, 40n.16

kleos (glory) needed in, 121–22

"little *nekuia*" (Book 24 of the *Odyssey*) (*see Odyssey*)

as main antecedent for Underworld scenes, 4, 5, 25–26, 41–42, 44, 51–52n.12, 111–12, 123, 156–57, 173, 184–85 (*see also* Nekuia (Book 11 of the *Odyssey*))

multiple and interlocking Underworld scenes, 41–42, 43, 44, 45–46, 122n.5*see also* Nekuia (Book 11 of the *Odyssey*))

Orphic Gold Tablets and, 150, 151, 152

Pindar and, 129–31, 132, 133

Plato/Socrates and, 206–8, 211–12, 213, 214, 215–16, 219, 221–23, 226, 227, 228, 240–41, 245–46, 248

proper behavior of mortals in, 111

public knowledge of, 67, 114, 157

Socrates conversing with in afterlife, 7, 27

Socrates critiquing for myth-telling, 221–22

Vergil's *Aeneid* based on, 254–57, 261

See also Iliad; Odyssey

Homeric Hymn to Demeter, 7, 43, 80–81, 86, 102n.21, 104

compared to Hesiod's *Theogony*, 104

Demeter in, 102n.21, 105, 107

Eleusinian Mysteries, founding of, 105

epithets used to describe gods in, 108

favorites of Demeter and Persephone in, 109–10, 117

gods' culture described in, 108

Hades in, 110n.24

makar status referenced in, 107, 108

olbios status referenced in, 107, 109–10

origin myth for marriage of Hades to Persephone in, 105

Persephone in, 102n.21, 108

Pluto in, 110–11, 110n.24

proper behavior of mortals in, 111

relationship between initiation and afterlife status, portrayal of, 105, 109, 110–12

sorting of the dead in, 109–10

Triptolemos in, 218n.12

turn to eschatology and prescriptive blessedness in, 106

Underworld scenes in, 110–11

Zeus' wish for Demeter to return to Olympus, 107–8

See also Eleusinian Mysteries

Homeric Hymn to Hermes: olbios status referenced in, 137–38, 138n.34

honoring war dead, 170–71, 178–79

honors. *See timai/time* (honors, esteem)

hubris, 98–100, 188

hypertextuality and hyperlinks, 5, 32, 33–35, 253

author's responsibility for, 35, 36–37

Elpenor Vase and, 160

fifth century BCE Athens using abbreviated references to earlier Underworld motifs and scenes, 157

Genette coining term of, 33

improving accessibility of the living to Underworld, 160–61

memorial for war dead using names of the deceased as, 171, 174–75

Subject Index

hypertextuality and hyperlinks (*cont.*)
  Nekuia and Circe's forecasting, 54
  Pindar and, 136, 139
  Plato using to redirect from previous
    authors to new paradigm,
    205, 249–50
  temporal and spatial leaps enabled by,
    37
  theatrical use of Underworld scenes,
    196, 202n.49
  Underworld scenes and, 4, 8, 41–42,
    130–31, 261 (*see also* Underworld
    scenes)
  Vergil and, 256
  See also intertext/intertextuality;
    para-narratives
Hypnos, 162–64

Iacchus, 200–1
Iliad
  audience's familiarity with, 67
  Bacchylides and, 144n.43
  earliest extant Underworld scene, 2–3,
    17, 80–81
  heroism defined by deeds on
    battlefield, 85
  Olympian divine succession in,
    223–24
  pause in plot for Achilles' dream,
    14–15 (*see also* Achilles' dream (*Iliad*
    Book 23))
  Pindar and, 130n.19
  Plato's allusions to, 223–24,
    232, 233–34
  "Shield of Achilles" passage, 53n.14
  Underworld scenes in, 41–42, 43, 44–
    45, 79–80, 189n.24
  Vergil modeling *Aeneid* on, 253–54
Iliupersis (Lesche of the Cnidians), 167–
  69, 168f
immortality
  author benefiting as conveyor of, 115–16

  meaning of, 125–26
  in Plato, 228, 230, 231, 232
  in song/poem, 79–80, 121–22, 125,
    128, 128n.14, 179n.18, 214, 215–
    16, 219–20
  of Theron, 134–35
  war dead, implied postdeath status of,
    175–77, 178–79, 179n.18
inclusiveness, expansion of, 3–4, 11–12,
  121–22, 154
  of fifth century BCE Athens, 155–56
  Orphic Gold Tablets and, 11, 153–54
  war dead, treatment of (*see* war dead)
individualism
  acknowledgment of, 127n.13, 152
  of fifth century BCE Athenians, 156–57
  moral values linked to, 96–97, 113
Inferno (Dante), 33–34, 261
initiation to gain favor of Underworld
    gods and gatekeepers, 105, 109, 110–
    12, 117, 121–22, 146–47. *See also* cults
intertext/intertextuality, 32
  chronology, 9–10, 32–33
  definition of, 8, 17–18, 29, 32–33
  distinguished from allusion, 31–32,
    31–32n.12
  horizontal axis of, 32–33
  Kristeva's coining of term
    "intertextuality," 32–33
  Nekuia and Circe's forecasting, 47–
    48, 54
  of post-Homeric authors, 130
  Underworld scenes and, 8, 25, 28–
    29, 38, 44
  usefulness in analysis, 17–18, 28–29
  vertical axis of, 32–33
  See also hypertextuality
intratextual connections (Underworld
    scene with frame narrative), 31
  enhancement of frame narrative by
    Underworld encounters, 23–24,
    26–28, 36, 96–97, 253

Iris (goddess), 91–92, 91n.13, 107
Isle/Isles of the Blessed. *See* Bacchylides;
    Pindar; *Works and Days*
Isocrates: *Evagoras*, 218n.12
Ixion, 62–63

Janko, Richard, 181n.19
Jiménez San Cristóbal, Ana, 148–49
Johnston, Sarah Iles, 125n.8, 134, 158nn.3–
    4, 191n.25
journey to Underworld. *See* breaching
    life–death barrier; *katabasis/*
    katabaseis; *Nekuia* (Book 11 of
    the *Odyssey*); *Republic* (Plato) *for*
    "Myth of Er"
judgment-based Underworlds, 78–
    113, 251–52
    accrual of honors and glory as
        determining factor, 79, 96–97
        (*see also* deeds in life connected
        to eternal afterlife; *kleos* (glory);
        timai/time (honors, esteem))
    afterlife as predictable based on
        examination of person's life, 220
    afterlife status based on moment of
        judgment, 111–12
    Archaic norms reinforced by, 10–11
    Bacchylides and, 11, 142, 144
    change in late Archaic period to favor,
        128–29
    elevation of rank of elite in
        Underworld, 125, 129 (*see also*
        blessedness)
    genealogy as determining factor, 79,
        96–97, 104, 120–21
    Harmodius, praise poem on, 172–73
    hierarchy of, 12–13, 79, 87, 109–
        10, 114–15
    Homer and, 224n.18
    judges involved in, 217–18
    negative, positive, and positive-plus
        rankings of, 111–12, 120–22 (*see also*

negative afterlife; positive afterlife;
        positive-plus afterlife)
    Nekuia and, 98n.17, 122–23, 122n.5
    Pindar and, 11, 129, 133, 144
    Plato and, 12–13, 206–7, 211–13, 217–
        18, 227–28, 229–30, 237
    punishment or reward, 121–22, 124–
        25, 131–32, 156–57, 212–13, 224n.19,
        228–29, 236–38
    relationship to Olympian gods as
        determining factor, 79 (*see also*
        favoritism of gods)
    religious/cult initiates and (*see* cults)
    segregation into different geographic
        regions (*see* afterlife society)
justice system
    afterlife correction of injustices of real
        world, 218–19
    in Plato's *Phaedo*, 229–30
    in Plato's *Republic*, 239, 240
    Plato's Underworld meting out true
        justice, 212–13, 227–28
    same in real world and Underworld,
        210–11
    of Underworld as established by Zeus,
        87–89, 90, 92, 95
    See also judgment-based
        Underworlds
just rulers, 121–22, 217–18

Karanika, Andromache, 76n.40
katabasis/katabaseis (descent to the
        Underworld)
    of Aeneas, 253–56, 255n.2
    in Aristophanes' *Frogs*, 196, 197–99
    association with epic hero, 42, 43,
        251–52, 254–55
    author's choice of, 7
    Bacchylides and, 142
    catalogues of locations and figures in
        Underworld for audience reference,
        29–30

302 Subject Index

katabasis/katabaseis (*cont.*)
  compared to visions or dreams of the
    afterlife, 2n.1
  connection to earlier Underworld
    stories, 39, 40, 42, 62–63, 74–75
  defined, 2, 42
  in Eupolis' *Demes*, 202n.49
  evolution of Greek approach to, 18
  Hesiod and, 90–91
  Homeric epics and, 40n.16
  Iris (goddess) performing, 91n.13
  kleos of katabatic heroes, 127–28
  as major category of Underworld
    scenes, 29–30
  mortals involved in, 128
  necromancy and, 44
  nekuia and, 2, 43–44
  Odysseus and, 64, 74–76, 74n.36,
    129–30n.17*see also Nekuia* (Book 11
    of the *Odyssey*))
  Orpheus' *katabasis* myth, 62–63, 219n.13
  Orphic Gold Tablets and, 152
  patrons compared to katabatic heroes,
    113
  Pindar's analogy of athletic
    competitions to, 136
  Plato's *Republic* and, 239, 240
  reintegration not possible after, 22
  special knowledge gained by, 118
  suitors' descent in *Odyssey*, 44–45, 59–
    60, 72n.33, 90n.11, 193–94, 198–200
  theatrical linkages, 194n.30, 203
The Katabasis of Heracles or *Cerberus*, 142
kleos (glory), 3–4, 44
  author benefiting as conveyor of,
    115–16
  Bacchylides' use of, 140–41
  battle and death as best way to achieve,
    17
  of epinician poetry, 125–26
  happiness of mortals associated with,
    103

  heroizing living person with, 114–15,
    120–21, 135, 144
  Homeric epics promoting need for,
    121–22
  initiation rites and, 125–26
  of katabatic heroes, 127–28
  in late Archaic period focusing on
    earthly deeds of, 128–29
  as motivation for heroes, 5, 79–80, 97–98
  Odysseus as worthy of, 6–7, 75n.37
  Orphic Gold Tablets and, 11, 152
  Pindar's use of, 135, 136, 139, 145n.44
  Plato and, 207–8, 210–11, 246, 248
  shifting ideas about, 127–28
  through song, 5–6 (*see also*
    immortality)
  transcending life–death barrier, 114–
    15, 116, 251–52
  war dead receiving as reward from
    state, 178–79
Kristeva, Julia, 32–34, 38, 38n.15

laudandus, 125, 128, 129, 135, 137, 138, 142,
  144, 157, 174. *See also* heroizing
  mortals
Laws (Plato), 237–38, 248–49
Leda, 64
Lesche of the Cnidians, 167–68, 168*f*
Life of Vergil (Suetonius), 256–57
light lacking in Underworld. *See* darkness
  as characteristic of Underworld
Lincoln, Bruce, 227n.23
Linforth, Ivan, 221
literary tradition, 19–20, 40, 74–75,
  255, 260–61
Nekuia (Book 11 of the *Odyssey*) as
  most famous Underworld scene,
  41–42, 44, 122n.5
Plato using to bolster arguments, 5–6,
  12–13, 205–10, 206n.2, 216–17,
  222–23, 226, 228, 230, 239, 245–46,
  247–49, 252–53

Subject Index

"little nekuia" scene (Book 24). *See Odyssey*

Lucian of Samosata, 257–60
  compared to Plato, 259
  Dialogues of the Dead, 13, 259
  Downward Journey, 13, 259–60
  Homer's appearance in, 257–58
  satire of, 13, 257–58, 259
  social commentary in, 259–60
  True History, 13, 20–21, 257–58
Lysias, 178nn.17–18

Magnes: *Dionysus*, 197n.34
makar, 11, 81–86, 81n.4, 88–89, 100, 102, 103, 109–12, 113, 116, 118–19, 120–21, 125, 133–34, 135n.31, 136, 137–38, 139, 140, 144, 151, 152, 189, 215–16, 219–20, 251–52
makarismos, 85–86, 111, 126–27, 151
Marathon, battle of, 174
Martin, Bridget, 98n.16
Meleager conversing with Heracles in Bacchylides, 142–43, 144, 144n.43, 244n.37, 256n.4
memorial *stelai*, 171, 178–79, 179n.18
memory or self-awareness of souls, 3–4, 18, 148–49, 248–49
Menelaus
  afterlife description in *Odyssey*, 27–28, 44–46, 47, 80–81, 112, 133–34, 217–18, 224n.18
  in Lucian's *True History*, 257–58
  relationship to Zeus bestowing blessed afterlife on, 74n.34, 75n.38, 80–81, 224n.18
Menexenus (Plato), 177–78
metaliterary purpose, 1–2, 5, 13, 21, 26–27, 52, 253, 255, 260–61
metempsychosis (reincarnation)
  mythic heroes not exempt from, 246
  philosophers' souls immune from, 229–30, 236

Pindar and, 131–32, 135, 136
Plato and, 132n.22, 210–12, 213–14, 228–29, 234–35, 237–38, 248–49, 256
Miltiades, 202–3
Miners (Pherecrates), 203n.52
Minos, 8–9, 26–27, 30–31, 37, 62–63, 74–75, 216–17
  as judge of the dead, 79–80, 122–23, 217–18, 222–23
  in *Nekuia*, 224n.18
Minyas (6th century BCE epic), 74n.35, 158n.4, 198n.35
monumental painting, 167, 168f
morality
  in Aeschylus' *Persians*, 188
  in Archaic texts' Underworld, 86–87
  Hesiod infusing into *Theogony*, 96–97
  Homeric Underworld hinting at moral geography, 86–87
  judgment after death, 10–11, 27–28, 44, 212–13
  Lucian's *Downward Journey* as morality play, 259
  in Plato's Underworld, 12–13, 212–13, 235
Moreno, Miryam L., 194n.30, 194n.31
Morgan, Kathryn A., 208–10, 209n.5
Morris, Ian, 170–71
mortals
  assimilating mortals onto mythic/heroic figures, 11, 114–17, 120–21, 125, 129, 130n.19, 131–32, 134–35, 136–37, 139, 145n.44
  Plato's new ways for mortals to receive blessedness (*olbios*), 12–13, 206–8
  pre-Platonic ways for mortals to receive blessedness (*olbios*), 120–21, 125, 153–54
Most, Glenn, 19–20, 64n.25, 134n.28
Musaeus, 219, 219n.13
Muses, 96–97

304 Subject Index

muthoi (Plato/Socrates), 227, 227n.23,
243, 243n.35, 244, 248–49
Mycenae, 127n.12
mystery cults, 11–12, 11n.5, 117, 118, 125–
26, 180
Orphic Gold Tablets and, 11, 11n.5,
146n.45, 146–47, 153–54
See also Eleusinian Mysteries
mythic heroines, 44–46, 45n.6
catalog of, 64–65, 64n.25, 66n.27
Myth of Er. *See Republic*
myth-telling, Socrates critiquing,
221–22, 226–27, 243n.35, 244. *See
also muthoi*

Nagy, Gregory, 130n.19
narratives
building narrative networks through
Underworld, 63
chronotopic break in (*see* chronotope)
embedded, 39–40
heroic vs. judgment-based, 27, 29–30
overlapping, 22–23, 32, 33–34, 37
patterns of Underworld scenes in,
25–26
shadow, 35–36, 39–40, 55–56
as textual database, 35, 95–96
See also para-narratives
narratology, 17–18, 63
Nausicaa, 66–67, 83n.5, 140–41
necromancy, 30, 42–43, 44,
74n.36, 75–76
professionalization of, 158n.3, 170–
71, 191–92
negative afterlife, 98, 109–10, 118, 120–21,
122–23, 122n.5, 124–25, 129–30n.17,
130, 146–47, 148–49, 165n.8
Nekuia (Book 11 of the *Odyssey*), 2n.2,
3–4, 5–6, 41–77
Aeneid's intertextual linking to, 31,
253–54, 256
Aeschylus' *Persians* and, 186, 189n.24

Aeschylus' *Psychagogoi* and, 191–93
Anticlea's presence (*see* Anticlea)
arguments as integral part of *Odyssey*,
21n.9
arguments for omitting, 18–19
authorial commentary in, 63–65, 124n.7
Bacchylides and, 143
blood offering of Odysseus to call the
dead, 98n.16, 122, 144, 192–93
catalogic nature of, 44–45
chronotope in, 44–45, 47–48, 252
compared to heroic *katabaseis*, 42–43
Dante's *Inferno* and, 33–34
darkness as characteristic of, 56–58,
57n.18, 61–62, 195
distance of Odysseus' passage to, 90
Elpenor Vase and, 160, 161*f*
entry and exit at same point, 38–39,
62–63, 67–68
entry into Underworld by Odysseus,
58–60
Eupolis' *Demes* and, 202–3
as evidence of poetic competition,
19–20
exit from Underworld by Odysseus,
62–63, 75–76
expanding Homer's Underworlds
from, 47
frequency in theatrical performances,
194n.30
Heracles' conversation with Odysseus,
72, 74–76, 138–39, 252
heroines' catalog in, 64–65,
64n.25, 66n.27
Hesiod's *Theogony* and, 88–89
hypertextual association with other
Underworld scenes, 4
impetus for, 44–45, 80n.3
interruption ("Intermezzo") in, 65–66,
66n.26, 185, 246–47
judgment-based Underworld scenes
and, 98n.17, 122–23, 122n.5, 224n.18

Subject Index

katabatic heroes in, 62–63

Minos in, 217–18

as most famous Underworld scene, 41–42, 44, 122n.5

"Myth of Er" compared to, 242–47

necromantic rituals in, 120n.3

negative Underworld associated with, 122–23, 122n.5, 251–52

Odysseus' cleverness shown in, 19n.7, 48

Odysseus considered equal to Heracles, 120–21

Odysseus' fear of becoming stuck in Underworld, 58–59, 75–76, 75n.37, 238–39

Odysseus judged by Alcinous, 241–43

Orphic Gold Tablet and, 150–51

Persephone's role in, 7

Phaeacians as audience, 6–7, 19n.7, 44–45, 48–49, 64, 65, 66n.26, 66–67, 73, 240–42 (see also Alcinous (king))

Pindar and, 129, 130n.19, 138–39

Plato's allusions to, 239, 240–43, 241n.32, 245–47, 248–49

Polygnotus' monumental painting of, 167, 168f

public performance of, 189n.24

as quest mandated by the gods, 48

rejection of afterlife depicted in, 11, 129, 156

sinners in, 74–75, 79, 123n.6, 123

sorting of the dead in, 98n.16, 122–23, 216–17

special hero status of Odysseus in, 73 (see also Odysseus)

standard image of Underworld scene, 25

suspense, creation of, 65

tangential encounters in, 44–45

thematic order of ghosts' appearance without intermingling, 63, 216–17

time sequencing in, 57–58

Tiresias in (see Tiresias)

nekuia (conversation with the dead) of Circe, 54

connection to literary tradition, 40

defined, 2, 2n.2

distinguished from *nekuomanteia*, 2n.2

katabaseis and, 43–44

as major category of Underworld scenes, 29–30

nekuomanteia (consultation with oracle of the dead), 2, 2n.2, 7

Nemeans (Pindar), 115–17, 129, 136–39, 218n.12

New Historicists, 20

Nicophon: *Return from Hades*, 202n.48

Nightingale, Andrea, 231

Night (Underworld god), 88–89, 92–93

Niobid Krater, 166–67, 166n.11

Nisetich, Frank, 130n.19, 135

Norden, Eduard, 51–52n.12

nostos (homecoming). *See* Odysseus

oath-keeping. *See* divine oath and oath-keeping

ocular deixis, 50n.11

Odysseus

Aeschylus' *Psychagogoi* and, 191–93

blessedness tradition of afterlife traced to, 7

blood offering to call the dead, 98n.16, 122, 144, 192–93

character of, 66–67, 72, 76

Circe's instructions/directions for (see Circe)

cleverness of, 19n.7, 48, 83–84, 221–22, 241–42

compared to Achilles, 67, 72, 84, 85–86, 110–11

compared to Heracles (see Heracles)

copresence with his peers and suggestions of outcomes for, 39

Subject Index

Odysseus (*cont.*)
  disorientation of, 55–57, 58–59, 61–62
  heroism of, 6–7, 42–43, 45n.6
  immortality offered by Calypso,
    rejection of, 75n.38
  makar term applied to, 83–84, 85–86
  "Myth of Er" and Plato's allusions to,
    244, 245–47
  as narrator, 48–49, 54–55, 65–66,
    91n.12, 241–42
  Niobid Krater and, 166–67
  nostos (homecoming) of, 55, 64–65,
    73, 85–86, 246
  olbios term applied to, 85–86, 110–
    11, 127–28
  Plato's allusions to, 221–22 (*see also
    Republic*)
  rebirth of, 25
  as special hero, 45–46, 48, 57n.19, 73,
    85–86, 129–30n.17, 252
  worthy of immediate immortality
    based on deeds, 123–24
  See also Nekuia (Book 11 of the *Odyssey*)
Odyssey
  Apologos (Books 9–12), 48
  chronotopic markers, 47, 54–55, 59–60
  Circe episode, 7, 18–19, 22–23, 47
  connectivity of multiple Underworld
    scenes in, 45–46, 60–61
  earliest appearance of Underworld
    scene, 2–3
  encounters with the dead, 24, 27
  Hesiod and, 90–91
  "little nekuia" scene (Book 24), 59–60,
    112, 123–24, 160, 164, 192–93, 211–
    12, 216–17, 219, 252
  makar, use of term, 82–83
  Menelaus' afterlife description in, 27–
    28, 44–45, 123
  multiple Underworld scenes in, 43,
    44, 47 (*see also Nekuia* (Book 11 of
    the *Odyssey*))

repeating Achilles' orders for his and
    Patroclus' bones in, 69–72
  suitors in, 44–45, 59–60, 72n.33,
    90n.11, 193–94, 198–200
  Vergil modeling *Aeneid* on, 253–54
Ogden, Daniel, 42–43
olbios, 11, 81–86, 81n.4, 88–89, 100, 102,
    103, 109–12, 113, 116, 118–19, 120–21,
    125, 133–34, 135n.31, 136, 137–38, 139,
    140, 144, 151, 152, 189, 215–16, 219–
    20, 251–52
Olympian gods seizing and sharing
    realm, 223–24
Olympian poems. See Pindar
oral tradition, 19–20, 29
Oresteia (Aeschylus), 195n.32
Orestes, 189–91
Orpheus
  Aeneas and, 254–55
  compared to Odysseus' journey to
    Underworld, 42–43
  katabasis myth of, 62–63, 219n.13
  "Myth of Er" and, 244
  Socrates conversing with in afterlife,
    7, 27, 219
  as "special hero," 28
Orphic Gold Tablets, 5, 7, 11, 20, 21n.8,
    117, 118n.2, 145
  Achilles and, 150
  blessedness and, 152
  breaching life–death barrier, 118, 145–53
  definition of, 11n.5
  description of, 146
  giving instructions for Underworld, 147
  from Hipponion, 147–49
  Homeric connections of, 150, 151, 152
  inclusivity of, 11, 153–54
  katabasis and, 152
  kleos and, 11, 152
  links with tripartite, judgment-based
    afterlife and with Underworld of
    Archaic epics, 153, 210n.6

Subject Index

makar, use of term, 151, 152
modeled on older sources than extant, 126n.11, 134n.28
mystery cults and, 11, 11n.5, 146n.45, 146–47, 153–54
Nekuia and, 150–51
olbioi, use of term, 151, 152
Pindar and, 133–34
Sotades cups compared to, 165–66
special knowledge offered by, 118
Tablet from Greece, 147
Tablet from Petelia, Italy, 117*f*, 117–18, 147, 149–50
Tablet from Thurii, Italy, 126–27, 126n.11, 146*f*, 147, 150–52
Orphism, 146n.45
Ostologoi (Aeschylus), 191n.26, 193–94

Page, Denys, 18–19
Pandora, myth of, 96–97
Panhellenic audience, 116–17, 140
Panhellenic phenomenon of new, expanded Underworld model, 119, 153–54, 156, 173
parallels, 28–29. *See also* intertext/ intertextuality
para-narratives
activating *katabasis* or necromancy, 202n.49
Aeschylus' *Ostologoi* and, 193–94
Aeschylus' *Persians* and, 186
audience's view of hero shaped by, 23
author using to introduce larger archive of information, 3–4, 253
Bacchylides and, 141–42, 256n.4
Circe's *nekuia* as, 54
defined, 4n.3
Elpenor Vase's Underworld scenes and, 160
grave *stelai* and, 174–75
images of Underworld scenes as, 160–61

Odysseus' conversations in Underworld as, 61–62, 64, 66
olbios status accorded to Odysseus and Achilles in (*Odyssey* Book 11 vs. Book 24), 110n.23
Pindar and, 136–37
Plato and, 205, 222, 225–26, 232, 236, 239, 240
Polygnotus' Underworld and, 167–68
role of, 32
Sarpedon story as, 164
Vergil and, 256, 256n.4
Patroclus
Achilles and, 2–3, 5, 14, 31, 44–45, 67, 124n.7
burial in urn with Achilles, 69, 70, 71–72
compared to Elpenor, 69, 71–72
death and burial directions of, 14–16, 17, 69, 69n.30, 124n.7, 152
Sophocles' *Polyxena* and, 195
unburied and in transition between life and afterlife, 15–16, 46
patrons
assimilation to heroes, 11, 113, 115–17, 120–21, 129, 135, 139, 140
Bacchylides' treatment of, 140–42, 144, 172
heroizing in songs, 128 (*see also* immortality)
Hesiod's treatment of, 131–32, 139
kleos attached to, 125–26
makar status attached to, 219–20
olbios status attached to, 128
Pindar's treatment of, 129, 130n.19, 131–32, 134–35, 139, 144, 172
Pausanias' description of Lesche of the Cnidians, 167–68
Peloponnesian War, 3–4, 177
Penelope (Aeschylus), 191n.26, 193n.29
Pericles, 202–3
funeral oration, 174–77

Subject Index

Persephone, 7, 8–9
  in Aeschylus' *Psychagogoi*, 193n.28
  "blessed" state of favorites of, 109–10
  dead sent to Odysseus by, 64, 193n.28
  depiction on Eleusinian relief, 106*f*
  frequent presence in Underworld
    scenes, 62–63
  grove in Underworld as distinct
    marker, 49–50, 151
  Hades kidnapping to be his bride,
    104*f*, 104–5
  Hermes' retrieval of, 105
  in Hesiod's *Theogony*, 88–89
  in *Homeric Hymn to Demeter*, 102n.21,
    108 (*see also Homeric Hymn to
    Demeter*)
  origin myth for marriage to Hades, 105
  Orphic Gold Tablets and, 151
  Pluto and, 110–11
  powers in worlds of the living and of
    the dead, 110–11
  returning souls to world of the
    living after atonement in
    Underworld, 134
  Theseus with Pirithous intending to
    kidnap, 22–23
Persians (Aeschylus), 158n.2, 179–80,
    182–83, 183n.21, 185–89
Persian War, 155–56, 175–77
Petrovic, Ivana, and Andrej, 91nn.12–13
Phaeacians. *See* Alcinous (king); *Nekuia*
    (Book 11 of the *Odyssey*)
Phaedo (Plato), 12–13, 207–8, 210–11,
    212–13, 214, 217n.11, 228
  Acherusian lake, 235, 237
  adapting traditional Underworld of
    predecessors, 228, 230, 239
  audience's familiarity and knowledge
    assumed, 12–13, 233
  blessed environment on earth's upper
    realm for deserving mortals and
    immortals, 230–31, 235–36

change to cosmic layout of Homer,
    234–35
chronotope, change in, 228–29, 231,
    239, 244–45
  compared to "Myth of Er," 244–45
Forms of Hades only known through
    philosophical training, 238–39, 250
Hesiod's *Works and Days* allusions,
    230–31
hollows in Underworld, 232–33, 234–
    36, 248
Homeric allusions, 214, 232, 233–34,
    248
immortality of soul, 228, 230, 231, 232
judgment of souls, 229–30
landmarks of Underworld, 233
metempsychosis and, 228–29, 237–
    38, 248–49
muthoi and, 243, 248–49
new restrictive hierarchy for
    blessedness, 12–13, 231, 236, 238–39
noise of souls waiting for rebirth, 235
philosophers' souls immune from
    cycle of rebirth, 229–30, 236
punishment or reward in afterlife,
    228–29, 236–38
purpose of, 229n.24
real world integrated with geography
    of Underworld, 234–35, 244–45
sinners given path to expiate sins,
    237–38
souls' ability to improve their lot, 236
souls entering Hades, 231–32
souls in upper levels of the earth,
    234–36
Tartarus region and topography taken
    from predecessors, 233, 248
training in philosophy as crucial for
    life and afterlife, 12–13, 237–38
wordplay in, 235n.25
Phaedrus (Plato), 217n.11, 240n.31
Pherecrates: *Miners*, 203n.52

Subject Index

philosophers
  blessed afterlife enjoyed by, 218, 228–29, 238–39
  immune from cycle of rebirth, 229–30, 236
  philosophy on soul's experience, 212–13, 238–39, 246, 247–48, 249–50, 252–53
  Plato according superior status to, 12–13, 205–8, 210–12, 213, 214, 215–16, 228
  training in philosophy as crucial for life and afterlife, 213–14, 237–39, 240
Phrynichus: *The Fall of Miletus*, 184n.22
Pindar, 11, 129
  Achilles in, 130n.19, 135
  afterlives not involving direct interaction with the living, 120n.3
  assimilating mortals to heroes, 129, 135, 136–37
  blessedness in, 114–29
  borrowing Underworld poetics from predecessors, 113, 130
  breaching life–death barrier, 115–16, 138, 143, 144–45
  Chromius of Aetna as patron of, 136–37, 138–39
  compared to Bacchylides, 140, 142n.40, 143
  Cronus' tower in, 133–34, 133n.26, 135
  deeds in life connected to eternal afterlife, 130–32, 228
  dirges honoring the dead, 129
  divine favor in, 137, 139
  elevation of rank of elite in Underworld, 131–32, 131n.20, 153–54
  eschatology and, 131–32, 136–37, 138
  Fragment 133, 134
  gods' homes in, 137–38, 139
  Hector's *kleos* and, 139

  Heracles in, 137–39, 138n.35, 142–43
  heroizing mortals/patrons, 118–19, 128n.14, 136–37, 145n.44, 153–54, 172, 219–20
  Hesiod and, 130, 132, 133
  Homeric epics and, 129–31, 132, 133
  hypertextuality and, 130–31, 136, 139
  Iliad and, 130n.19
  Isle of the Blessed in *Olympian* 2, 130n.19, 131–32, 133, 135, 217–18
  judgment-based Underworld scenes, 11, 129, 133, 144
  The Katabasis of Heracles or *Cerberus*, 142
  kleos in, 135, 136, 139, 145n.44
  local religious beliefs and, 129–30n.17, 130n.19, 131–32
  makar, use of term, 133–34, 135n.31, 136, 219–20
  metempsychosis and, 131–32, 135, 136
  negative view of afterlife, 129–30n.17
  Nemeans, 115–17, 129, 136–39, 218n.12
  oath-keeping in, 133
  odes of, 130n.19
  olbios, use of term, 116, 137–38, 139
  Olympian 1, 142n.40
  Olympian 2, 7, 128, 129–37, 129–30n.17, 130n.19, 145n.44, 148–49, 173, 211–12, 216–18
  Orphic Gold Tablets and, 133–34
  as Panhellenic poet, 153–54, 173
  para-narratives and, 136–37
  patrons of, assimilation to heroes, 129, 130n.19, 131–32, 134–35, 139, 145n.44
  Plato and, 208, 248–49
  positive-plus afterlife created for his patrons, 129, 130–32, 136, 144
  prosperity/privilege during life, connection to good afterlife, 129, 131–32, 134–35, 139, 186–87
  punishment or reward in Underworld, 131–32, 132n.23

Subject Index

Pindar (*cont.*)
  Pythagorean influences, 129, 131–32
  rejecting *Nekuia*'s picture of afterlife, 129
  segregation into different regions of
    Underworld, 129, 216–17
  Sicilian context of, 129–30n.17, 130–
    32, 135–36, 153–54, 172
  Theron as patron (*see* Theron of
    Acragas)
  Tiresias in *Nemeans*, 138–39
  tripartite Underworld in, 129, 129–
    30n.17, 134
  Underworld as foreign land in, 136
  Pirithous, 22–23, 74–75, 74n.35,
    158n.4, 166n.11
  pit ritual, 51–52n.12
Plato, 5, 12–13, 205–50
  afterlife phase outlasting lifespan, 237–
    38, 238n.28, 247
  alluding to and adapting traditional
    Underworld of predecessors, 5–6,
    12–13, 205–10, 206n.2, 216–17,
    222–23, 226, 228, 230, 239, 245–46,
    247–49, 252–53
  Apology, 12–13, 27, 207–8, 210–12, 214,
    216–20, 227–28, 230, 234, 248–49
  audience's knowledge assumed by,
    212–13, 216–17, 233, 245–46, 249
  challenging formula of earlier models,
    12–13, 204, 205, 207–8, 210–11, 213,
    215–16, 218, 226, 247–48
  chronological time used for
    Underworld, 247, 249–50
  chronotope altered by, 206–7, 210–11,
    228–29, 231, 239, 244–46
  compared to Lucian, 259
  confidence expressed by, 248
  contradictory language used by, 221
  cosmos layout and, 233–34, 248
  dialectic arguments, 12–13, 205–6,
    208–10, 209n.5, 212–13, 227n.23,
    228, 236, 249–50, 252–53

  disclaimers for shortcomings of
    Underworld scenes, 208–10, 216–
    17, 226–27
  divine favor in, 210
  on funeral orations, 177–78
  general features of Underworld scenes
    of, 21–22, 208, 215–16
  geographic Underworld mapping of
    morality and justice, 210, 211–13,
    216–17, 234–35
  Gorgias (*see* Gorgias)
  Homer and Hesiod allusions, 206–8,
    211–12, 213, 214, 215–16, 219,
    221–23, 224–25, 226, 227,
    228, 245–46
  influence on later authors, 250
  judgment-based Underworld and, 12–
    13, 206–7, 211–13, 217–18, 225–26,
    227–28, 237
  landmarks of Underworld, 210, 233
  Laws, 237–38, 248–49
  life and death as interchangeable
    states, 206–7, 247
  Menexenus, 177–78
  metempsychosis and, 132n.22, 210–12,
    213–14, 228–29, 234–35, 237–
    38, 248–49
  motivation for Underworld
    depictions, 206n.1, 206–7, 248–49
  multiple conflicting Underworld
    scenes in, 12–13, 205, 214, 248–49
  muthoi and, 227, 227n.23, 243,
    243n.35, 244
  on myths, 208–10, 209n.5
  new social hierarchy of blessedness,
    12–13, 206–8, 210, 215–16, 231,
    236, 238–39, 247, 252–53 (*see also*
    philosophers)
  para-narratives, use of, 205, 222, 225–
    26, 232, 236, 239, 240
  Phaedo (*see* Phaedo)
  Phaedrus, 217n.11, 240n.31

philosophers' and philosophical life's
superiority (*see* philosophers)
promotion of his idiosyncratic vision
of the afterlife, 12–13, 206–7,
206n.1, 247–49
religious beliefs contradicted by, 207–
8, 211, 213, 214, 215–16, 248, 249
Republic (*see Republic*)
restricting accessibility of afterlife's
rewards, 208, 211, 225–26,
247, 249–50
sinners given path to expiate sins,
237–38
soul's movement in Underworld, 211,
212–13, 215, 229, 236, 244–45
Vergil and, 253–54, 256, 261
Pluto (god), 110–11, 110n.24, 189, 224–26
Poetics (Aristotle), 180–82
poetry
Archaic, 19–20, 43–44, 82
in epic genre, 19–20, 42, 111 (*see also*
Homer and Homeric epics)
epinician, 3–4, 11–12, 114–16, 120–21,
125–26, 128–29, 135, 145, 153–54 (*see
also* Bacchylides; Pindar)
Homeric vs. Hesiodic forms of, 19–20,
64n.25, 104
immortality from (*see* immortality)
lyric, 19–20
Underworld scenes viewed as poetic
competition, 19–20
politics
Aristophanes' *Frogs* offering
commentary on, 198–99, 200–2
comedies mocking, 196, 199
enfranchisement, advocating for,
200–2
foreign policy, 159
funeral orations and, 173
intersection with poetic in
Underworld scenes, 173
Lucian's Underworld scenes and, 259

mourning limitations and designation
of private burial places, 170–71
propaganda of incorporating dead into
civic life, 11–12, 157, 170
theatrical performances addressing
present-day Athenian problems,
184, 187–88, 200–2
war dead, treatment of, 11–12, 170–71,
174, 175–77, 178–79
Pollux / Polydeuces, 64, 254–55
Polydorus, 196
Polyeidos, 165*f*, 165–66
Polygnotus as monumental painter, 167, 168*f*
Polyxena, 195
Polyxena (Sophocles), 195–96, 195n.32
Poseidon's earthquake, 47
positive afterlife, 120–26, 122nn.5–6,
128–32, 131n.20, 136, 139, 165n.8,
224n.18, 228
positive-plus afterlife, 120–21, 122, 125–27,
128–29, 131–32, 144, 145, 146–47
Post-Homeric Underworld scenes, 80–
81, 86, 92, 111–12, 118n.2
creating heroes out of everyday
mortals, 118–19
envisioning reward structure based on
blessedness, 80–81, 114
Priam, 31
prosperity/privilege during life,
connection to good afterlife, 111–12,
116, 121–22, 125–26
in Aeschylus' *Persians*, 189
in Bacchylides, 140–41
in Pindar, 129, 131–32, 134–35, 139, 153–
54, 186–87
in Plato, 215–16, 218, 239
Psychagogoi (Aeschylus), 191–94, 191n.26,
194n.31
psychopomp, Hermes as, 59–60, 158,
161*f*, 164
public memorials honoring war dead, 171,
178–79, 179n.18

Pucci, Pietro, 31–32, 71n.32
Purves, Alex, 58n.20
Pyriphlegethon, 237
Pyronides, 202–3
Pythagoreanism, 129, 131–32, 221, 228

real world
   integrated with geography of
     Underworld, 234–35
   Plato folding Underworld chronotope
     into, 210–11
   Underworld as influence on, 159–60,
     201–2 (see also breaching life–death
     barrier)
   Underworld mirroring society of, 11,
     124, 156–57, 196, 197
   Underworld scenes contiguous to, 95
   Underworld scenes in everyday life,
     160, 162
   Underworld scenes removing
     protagonist and audience from, 4,
     5–6, 58–59
   See also breaching life–death barrier;
     relationship between the living and
     the dead
reincarnation. See metempsychosis
relationship between the living and the
   dead, 3, 5, 11–12
   continuous interaction with and
     presence of the dead, 124–25, 173–
     74, 179, 182, 183, 220n.14
   help or advice from the dead, 157, 182,
     191, 196, 198–99, 201–3 (see also
     Nekuia (Book 11 of the Odyssey))
   new media and methods for, 114–15,
     158, 158n.3, 160
   painted vessels maintaining personal
     ties, 161f, 162–67, 163f, 163f, 165f
   reciprocity of, 114, 191
   in theatrical performances, 182, 183,
     189, 203–4
   war dead remaining present, 179

weakening separation, 11–12, 170–71
   See also katabasis; Underworld scenes
religious beliefs and rituals
   encounters with the dead and, 7, 11–12
   in fifth century BCE Athens, 159n.5
   Greeks' changing beliefs about
     the dead and afterlife, 18, 80n.3,
     98n.17, 114–15
   offerings to the dead, 157
   Pindar's inclusion of local and shifting
     beliefs, 129–30n.17, 130n.19, 131–32
   Plato countering, 207–8, 211, 213, 214,
     215–16, 248, 249
   reciprocity owed for sacrifices, 191
   shared by author and audience, 8
   shifts in, 3–4, 5, 129, 130n.19
   theater performances and, 158–59,
     179–80, 189
   tomb cults, 69, 69n.31
   Underworld scenes tied to, 11–12, 19,
     20, 29–30, 113
   widespread influence of Athenian
     beliefs, 166–67
   See also cults; Orphic Gold Tablets
Republic (Plato), 12–13, 207–11, 212–13,
   214, 239
   ἀπόλογον and Plato's audience, 242–43
   agency and, 247
   Alcinous allusion, 240–41, 241n.32
   audience to draw own conclusions,
     12–13, 245–46
   Cephalus describing his wealth,
     239–40
   chronological time used for
     Underworld, 247, 249–50
   chronotope, Plato altering, 244–46
   compared to Gorgias, 245
   duration of afterlife vs. lifespan, 247
   eschatology of Plato, 240, 243
   Homeric allusions, 240–41, 245–46
   justice system in, 239, 240
   katabasis and, 239, 240

kleos insufficient to reach blessed afterlife, 246

metempsychosis and, 229, 248–49

muthoi critique, 243, 243n.35, 244

"Myth of Er," 12–13, 214, 215n.10, 237–38, 238n.28, 240, 240n.31, 241–47

Nekuia (Book 11 of the *Odyssey*) allusions, 239, 240–47, 241n.32

new restrictive hierarchy for blessedness, 247

para-narratives and, 239, 240

philosophy's privileging impact on soul's experience, 239–40, 246, 247

restricting accessibility of afterlife's rewards, 247

Socrates styling himself as Odysseus, 241–42, 241n.33

soul's movement in Underworld, 244–45, 248–49

Return from Hades (Nicophon), 202n.48

Rhadamanthus, 133–34, 135, 217–18, 222–23, 257–58

Rohde, Erwin, 18–19

Roman afterlife of Greek Underworld scenes, 253

   Tabulae Iliacae and, 254, 254n.1

   See also Vergil

Roman identity, 255, 256–57

Roman Imperial Period authors, 260–61

sacrifices, 191

Sammons, Benjamin, 64–65, 66n.27

Sarpedon's death at Troy, 141–42, 164

satire, 13, 257–58, 259

Scheria, 83n.5

Sedley, David, 20–21

segregation of Underworld regions. *See* afterlife society

self-awareness of soul. *See* soul

shadow narratives, 35–36, 39–40, 55–56

shamans and shamanistic rituals, 20, 51–52n.12

Sicilian context of Pindar, 129–30n.17, 130–32, 135–36, 153–54, 172

"side-shadowing," 39

similes, 17n.4, 22–23

sinners. *See* afterlife society

Sisyphus, 26–27, 30–31, 62–63, 74–75, 79, 123n.6, 159–60, 159n.5

slaves, status of, 198–99, 198n.37

sleep, 59–60, 92

snakes, 138, 138nn.35–36, 165*f*, 165–66

social criticism/commentary

   in Aristophanes' *Frogs*, 199

   in comedies, 180, 196

   in Lucian's *Downward Journey*, 259–60

   Underworld scene used for, 39

Socrates

   conversations in afterlife, 7, 27

   encounters with the dead, 27

   equating himself with mythic figures, 217–18, 219n.13

   folktale of water-carrier with leaky jars told by (in *Gorgias*), 220–21, 222

   on funeral orations, 177–78

   myth-telling and, 221–22, 226–27

   philosophical lifestyle of, 206–7, 207n.4, 211–12

   "special hero" status of, 228

   styling himself as Odysseus, 241–42, 241n.33

   vision of blessed eternity granted by Underworld judges, 218, 219–20, 227–28

   See also Plato

Solmsen, Friedrich, 130n.19, 131n.20

Solon, 202–3

Sophocles: *Polyxena*, 195–96, 195n.32

Sotades Painter, 164–66, 165*f*

soteriological elements, 110–11, 127n.13, 152

314   *Subject Index*

soul, 121–25, 154
  in Achilles' dream, 124n.7
  categories as "bad, good, and good-
    plus," 125n.8, 132n.23
  change in late Archaic period, 128–29
  continuity of relationships, 124–25
  correct choices in afterlife (Plato),
    213–14
  Homeric Underworld's souls in
    negative or positive afterlife, 122–
    25, 123n.6
  individualism, acknowledgment of,
    127n.13
  information flowing only from
    living to dead in Homer's positive
    Underworld, 124
  in little *nekuia* of *Odyssey* Book 24,
    123–24, 219
  memory's survival, 3, 18, 148–
    49, 248–49
  movement in Underworld (Plato), 211,
    212–13, 215, 229, 236, 244–45
  negative Underworld's souls lacking
    purpose, 122, 127n.13
  persistence after death, 220n.14
  Pindar and, 133
  Plato and, 206–7, 210–14, 218
  positive-plus afterlife, 124–25, 126–27,
    128–29, 131–32
  positive Underworld's souls having
    consciousness, 122–23, 128–29,
    133
  punishment or reward in afterlife
    (*see* afterlife society; judgment-
    based Underworlds)
  self-awareness, 3–4, 18, 118, 125, 148–
    49, 220n.14, 248–49
  See also afterlife society;
    breaching life–death barrier;
    Underworld scenes
Sourvinou-Inwood, Christiane, 79–80,
    80n.3, 98n.17, 179n.18, 191n.25

space
  Hesiod's *Theogony* indicating distance
    from Underworld to base of heaven,
    93, 93n.14
  Odysseus' passage to Underworld,
    distance of, 90
  See also chronotope
Spartan war, 196, 200
"special hero" status, 28, 74–75
  for contemporary mortal, 115–16, 125
  described as "blessed" (*olbios/makar*),
    118–19 (*see also* blessedness)
  Odysseus and (*see* Odysseus)
  of Orpheus, 28
  of Socrates, 228
  of Theseus, 28, 74–75
special knowledge, acquisition of, 25, 42–
    43, 118, 148–49
spectacle. *See* theatrical performances
Stansbury-O'Donnell, Mark, 168f, 168–69
stelai. See grave *stelai*
Stesichoros, 142n.41
Storey, Ian, 202–3, 202n.47
Storytelling, 65–66. *See also* ἔνϑα*/entha-
    mode of description*; *muthoi*
structuralism, 17–18, 20, 28–29, 31–32n.12
Styx, 29–30, 87–89, 94, 95, 125–26,
    233, 235
  Suetonius: *Life of Vergil*, 256–57

Tabulae Iliacae, 254, 254n.1
Tantalus, 8–9, 26–27, 29–30, 37, 62–63,
    74–75, 79, 123n.6, 142n.40
Tartarographia (in Hesiod's *Theogony*),
    38–39, 89
  chronotope and, 89
  compared to tale of Elpenor, 95
  first-person perspective of Titans in,
    91n.12
  houses of Zeus' allies, 94–95
  landscape description, 90–91, 95–96
  shift in poetic register in, 90–91

Subject Index

Tartarus
both region in Underworld and
manifestation of justice, 86–87,
95–96, 210
in Hesiod's *Theogony*, 2–3, 88–89, 90
Iliad quoted in Plato's *Phaedo*, 233–34
katabaseis using, 29–30
sinners assigned to, 237
as Underworld god, 87–88, 95–96
See also Titans, punishment of
Telemachus, 45n.6, 83n.5
text, 29. *See also* intertext/intertextuality
textual analysis, 28–36. *See also*
hypertextuality; intertext/
intertextuality; intratextual
connections
Thamyris, 244, 244n.36, 246–47
Thanatos (Death), 159, 162–64, 182–83,
183n.21
theatrical performances, 157, 157n.1, 158–
59, 179
addressing present-day Athenian
problems, 184, 187–88, 200–2
Aristotle's use of term "spectacle," 180–
82, 181n.19
audience of, 180, 181–82
chronotope and, 184–85, 187, 203
in Classical period, 179–80
entering public conversation and
knowledge, 180, 203
religious beliefs and, 158–59, 179–80
social commentary offered by, 180
Underworld scenes, use of, 202–3
Theogony (Hesiod), 38–39, 80–81, 87–88
chronotope in, 95
compared to Homer, 87, 88–89, 95
compared to *Homeric Hymn to
Demeter*, 104
compared to *Works and Days*, 96–97, 98
cosmic chronotopes, 88
divisions between mortals and
nonmortals, 88–89, 92

Hades and Persephone as monarchs,
88–89
hierarchy of inhabitants, 87
House of Night in, 92
layout description, 87, 88–89,
90, 91–92
oath-keeping, 88–89, 133
Olympian divine succession in, 95–
96, 223–24
organized society in, 125–26
Pindar invoking, 116
Pluto's first mention in, 224–25
poet as *olbios*, 96–97
Styx as river and overseer of divine
oaths, 88–89
Tartarus as prison of Zeus' enemies,
88–89, 92
war of gods in, 223
Zeus' brand of justice, 88–89
See also Tartarographia
Thermopylae, battle of, 171, 174
Theron of Acragas, 129, 131–32, 132n.21,
134n.28, 134–35, 136, 136n.32,
145n.44
Thersites, 244, 244n.36, 246–47
Theseus
Aeneas and, 254–55
compared to Odysseus' journey to
Underworld, 42–43
goēs (necromancer) role in appealing
to, 158
katabasis myth of, 18, 37, 62–63, 74,
74n.35, 159–60, 194n.30
in Lucian's *True History*, 257–58
Nekuia calyx-krater and, 166n.11
Niobid Krater and, 166–67, 166n.11
with Pirithous to kidnap Persephone,
22–23
rise of myth to central importance, 156
as "special hero," 28, 74–75
in tragedies, 158n.4
war dead associated with, 178–79

Thespis, 194n.30

Thucydides

History of the Peloponnesian War, 174–75

on war dead rites, 175–77

timai/time (honors, esteem), 6–7, 79, 80–81, 87–88, 100n.20, 105, 128, 128n.14, 153–54, 174, 203–4, 214

time

escape from, 5–6

hero's separation from for Underworld journey, 22, 38, 46

in Hesiod's *Theogony*, 88–89

Kristeva's vertical axis of intertextuality and, 33

moral and immortal temporal markers, 58n.20

multiple levels of narrative time in Underworld, 58–59, 58n.20

Odysseus' return to chronological time, 65, 72

Plato borrowing timeline from Hesiod's "Ages of Man," 230

Plato using chronological time for Underworld, 229, 231, 247, 249–50

See also chronotope

Tiresias, 18–19, 22, 38–39, 42–43, 44–45, 61, 65, 67–68, 122, 123, 137–39, 160, 193

Titans

punishment of, 88–89, 90, 91n.12, 92, 94, 95–96, 125–26

war with Olympians, 223

Tityus, 74–75, 79, 123n.6

tomb, heaping of, 71, 71n.32

tomb cults, 69, 69n.31

tombs, location of, 171

tragedies, 184

Aristotle's categorization of, 180–81

Aristotle's view of spectacle in, 180–82, 187n.23

first official performance of, 194n.30

popular characters in, 158n.4

Underworld scenes in, 179–80, 182–83, 183n.21

See also theatrical performances

travelers' tales, 29–30

tripartite Underworld, 11, 114–15, 119

afterlife hierarchy in, 11, 114–15

blessedness and rise of, 121

new class of heroes created from mortals and, 120–21, 125

in Pindar, 129, 129–30n.17, 134

See also negative afterlife; positive afterlife; positive-plus afterlife

Triptolemos, 217–18, 218n.12

depiction of, 106*f*

Trojan War, 15, 17

afterlife for heroes of, 46

analogizing to Persian invasion, 156

leaders from, 44–45, 85–86, 124

Vergil's *Aeneid* and, 256

True History (Lucian of Samosata), 13, 20–21, 257–58

Tsagarakis, Odysseus, 64n.25, 74n.36

type-scenes vs. Underworld scenes, 25

Typhoeus (Gaia's last son), 95–96

Underworld scenes

afterlife of, 253

analyzing as interacting with *Nekuia* (Book 11 of the *Odyssey*), 44–45

break from main narrative or new chronotope established in, 14–15, 18–19, 19n.6, 21–25, 26, 52, 59–60, 62–63, 84, 253

building narrative networks through, 63

catalogic nature of, 6–7, 26–27, 29–30, 49–50, 64–65

classification challenges of, 5, 43

closure offered by, 24–25

component parts of, 22

connection to each other, 2n.1, 2–4, 5–6, 19, 27–28, 29–30, 33–34, 186

definitions and characteristics of,
 1–2, 21
didacticism of, 7, 10–11, 19–20
dominant types of heroic and
 judgment-based, 5–6, 44, 86–87,
 113, 120–21
Elpenor Vase linking to multiple
 scenes, 160
epic (heroic), 3, 21–22, 23, 26, 27, 30,
 41, 111–12, 140, 153–54
in everyday life, 160, 162
exit from, 22, 28 (*see also* exiting from
 Underworld)
first appearance in *Iliad*, 2–3, 4, 41–
 42, 80–81
frame narrative, relationship to (*see*
 frame narrative)
frequency and repetition of, 2–3, 4,
 47, 74–75, 194n.30, 205
generic qualities of, 30–31, 38, 43–
 44, 78, 86
Homeric, 43, 44, 144 (*see also* Homer
 and Homeric epics)
identification of, 21
identifying the Underworld, 2, 21
image elements in, 8–9, 25
implications and influence of, 3, 40,
 44, 78, 203–4, 255
inclusive afterlife society in, 3–4, 11–
 12, 154
interpretive approaches to, 18
landmarks of, 49–50, 52, 59–60, 74–
 75, 111–12, 197–99, 198n.37, 210, 233
layers of, 232
location of, 22
in Lucian, 257–60
names of gods of, 95–96
as place of judgment, 78–113 (*see also*
 judgment-based Underworlds)
Plato challenging formula of earlier
 models, 12–13, 204, 205, 207–8,
 210–11, 213, 215–16, 218, 226

post-Platonic authors, 13
purpose, function, and persistence of,
 19, 28, 40, 66, 76–77, 78, 86, 205–6,
 252–53, 255
recurring features of, 5–6, 7, 78, 205
segregated regions in (*see* afterlife
 society)
as shadow narratives, 35
in theatrical performances, 179 (*see
 also* theatrical performances)
tripartite structure (*see* tripartite
 Underworld)
types of, 8–9
See also afterlife society;
 hypertextuality; judgment-
 based Underworlds; tripartite
 Underworld
utopia, 20–21, 112, 203n.52

values
 of fifth century BCE Athens, 162
 judging individual or community
 values, 76–77, 88–89, 113
 judgment-based Underworld
 reinforcing Archaic norms,
 10–11 (*see also* judgment-based
 Underworlds)
 moral values linked to certain
 individual conduct, 96–97, 113
 Plato's method of conveying, 222
 public funeral orations and, 177
 shared stories and values of author and
 audience, 8, 29–30, 251–52
 of Vergil's *Aeneid*, 256
vases. *See* vessels and vases
Vergil
 Aeneid, 13, 31, 76n.39, 157, 253–56 (*see
 also Aeneid*)
 audience collaboration and
 knowledge, 157, 254
 Augustus linked to Homeric heroes,
 254–55, 256–57

318   *Subject Index*

Vergil (*cont.*)
  Dante and, 261
  Hesiod and, 253–54
  Homeric epics and, 254–57, 261
  hypertextual linkage in, 256
  Plato and, 253–54, 256, 261
Vermeule, Emily, 114
Vernant, Jean-Pierre, 183–84
vessels and vases as everyday artifacts
  theatrical performances depicted on,
    180
  Underworld depicted on, 160–62,
    161*f*, 163*f*, 163*f*, 165*f*, 178–79 (*see also*
    white-ground lekythoi)
von der Mühl, Peter, 51–52n.12

war dead, 11–12, 170–71, 174, 175–77,
    176*f*, 178–79
war orphans, 174
wealth. *See* prosperity/privilege
  during life
well-examined life. *See* philosophers
white-ground cups as grave goods, 164–
    66, 165*f*
white-ground lekythoi for funerary rites,
    154, 162–64, 163*f*, 164n.7, 165–66,
    198nn.35–36
White Rock, 30–31, 60, 198–99, 199n.38
Willcock, M. M., 129–30n.17, 131–32,
    132n.22, 133n.25
Works and Days (Hesiod)
  "Ages of Man" myth, 97–98, 125–26,
    216–17, 219, 225, 226n.22, 230
  blessedness in, 97
  compared to Homer, 87, 97–99
  compared to *Theogony*, 96–97, 98
  Cronus' reign, 102, 133–34, 225
  deeds in life connected to eternal
    afterlife, 97–98, 139
  as didactic poem, 96–97
  geography indicating status of
    individuals in afterlife, 87, 213

Golden race in, 101–2, 135n.30,
    225, 230–31
hierarchy of inhabitants, 87
hubris in, 98–100
humans approaching level of gods in
    eternal lifestyles, 101
Iron race in, 98–99, 99n.18, 100–1
"Isles of the Blessed" in, 98–99, 103,
    111–12, 124–25, 126n.10, 133–34,
    172–73, 211–12, 213, 219, 222–23,
    225–26, 227–28
makar, use of term, 100, 102, 103,
    137
mingling of good and evil in, 99
myth of Pandora and, 97–98
olbios specifically applied to mortals,
    97, 103
Pindar's allusion to, 130, 137
Plato's allusion to, 211–12, 216–17, 219,
    225–26, 230
positive-plus vision of afterlife for his
    patron, 139
races in, 98–100, 99n.18, 99n.19,
    125–26
Silver and Bronze races in, 98–101, 137
as underpinning of afterlife narratives
    in later poetry, 98
Underworld scenes, 7, 27–28, 80–81,
    88

Xanthias, 196, 198–99
Xerxes, 187–88

Zeus
  Demeter's return to Olympus desired
    by, 107
  Heracles as son of, 74
  in Hesiod's *Theogony*, 88–89, 95–96
  in Hesiod's *Works and Days*, 96–97,
    103
  justice system of Underworld and, 87–
    89, 90, 92, 95

Menelaus as son-in-law of, 74
myth of judgment in Plato's *Gorgias*,
  20–21, 224n.19
Odysseus' connection to, 74

Pindar's adoption of Homeric motif
  and, 130n.19, 133–34
rise to power, 38–39, 95–96, 223
Trojan War and, 234